A Pirate's Command

A SECRETS OF THE BAYOUS NOVEL

OTHER BOOKS BY MEG HENNESSY

Dark Secrets, Deep Bayous

A Pirate's Command

A SECRETS OF THE BAYOUS NOVEL

MEG HENNESSY

Entangled Publishing, LLC
2614 South Timberline Road
Suite 109
Fort Collins, CO 80525
Visit our website at www.entangledpublishing.com.

Select Historical is an imprint of Entangled Publishing, LLC.

Edited by Erin Molta
Cover Design by Heidi Stryker
Cover Art by The Killion Group, Inc.

ISBN 978-1-943336-88-3

Manufactured in the United States of America

First Edition July 2015

For my mother, whose wit and grit has helped her reach ninety years still full of life, love, and vitality.

Chapter One

The night's winter chill dug into his resolve. A cold, clawing mist weighed heavily inside his lungs as he stood at the helm. The ship silently plowed through the waves; frothy fingers grabbed at her gunwales. He held their course steady, seeing only the faint coastline of America dead ahead.

A most precious cargo had been taken from him, and he was coming to take it back. As a man who rode the open sea, he always reclaimed what was rightfully his. He blinked to clear the misty air from his eyes. His gaze never wavered from the shores of Louisiana, where the prize awaited.

His son.

Risking life—or worse, capture—as a wanted pirate of the gulf waters, Donato de la Roche would be in New Orleans before dawn. He had no choice. Colette had left him when her brother arrived on the island to take her home, but with her, she had taken Donato's son. He would now take him back before Colette awoke and knew anything was amiss.

He adjusted his course, seeing the mouth of the river ahead, trying not to think about her, fighting the memories. The pain of her betrayal had curled deep inside his gut so many times, it had adhered to his body, like thick tar cured in place, though a gaping wound still bled.

No, he'd not think about her. Not tonight.

He'd not think about the tawny color of her hair and how it would flutter in the wind when she'd stand on the shore of his island. Or how she'd complain about the natural curl frizzing in the humidity. Nor would he remember her oval eyes, which would turn from green to hazel in the wisp of a second, the silky feel of her skin beneath his sea-roughened fingers.

Those memories were buried beneath the weight of one. One that surfaced from deep within his gut every time he remembered the day she had left him and with her, had taken their son.

"Land ho…" came a soft warning from aloft on the shrouds.

"Mark your head."

"Two on the starboard bow, *Capitán*."

"Quarter left."

"Going quarter left."

In spite of the cold, the wind had been subtle and gentle for most of their journey, but she resisted the change in direction and fluttered with a snap above deck, shivering the lines.

"Brace with the wind," Donato ordered. As they slowly trimmed sail, he dropped his speed to three knots to ease his way into the Mississippi. To her.

That's when the other ship appeared.

"Sail up!" came another warning from the crow's nest, but Donato needed no warning, having already seen the dark silhouette of a United States gunboat.

Donato glanced up at the gaff sails. He didn't have enough wind to outmaneuver them.

"Steer full and by," he responded. Trying to avoid the navy was pointless. They would give chase. Since its second victory over Britain, the U.S. Navy flexed its muscles at the slightest provocation. He hoped to get beyond them and into New Orleans, but they were at least three miles to his starboard bow, closing in quickly.

His men lowered their black flag with the white letters *Nunca más víctima*, meaning a victim never again, and replaced it with the flag of Spain, transforming his ship to *La María*, named after his mother.

The gunboat fired a warning shot.

His crew looked to him for an order to clear for action, for they were seasoned men of battle, fighting men, who had defended their honor more than once. The American gunboat would not be a formidable foe, for what they exceeded in guns, they lacked in experience.

Donato refused to fight his way into New Orleans. He glanced toward the shore, knowing he was but a few miles from her, then shifted his attention to the U.S. Navy.

"Trim the yards." He motioned for his men to slow his ship, knowing he'd face a boarding party if he didn't change the navy's way of thinking. He had to prevent a boarding. The condition of his ship, the cannons, the weaponry, would tell a story of piracy and high seas robbery. A boarding would be fatal to his mission, and he had sworn before setting sail that nothing would get in his way tonight.

The U.S. ship came in closer, allowing leeway to their larboard bow. A ploy, Donato recognized, to keep him from either firing on them or making a run for it. He'd not run. Tonight, he was a Spanish merchant en route between Cuba and Mexico, having detoured to the American coast for medical supplies.

The ships bobbed in the water only two hundred feet from each other, closing the gap.

"Ahoy!" an American officer shouted, no doubt noting the Spanish flag fluttering above the ship. "You are in United States waters. Where are you bound?"

Donato picked up a speaking trumpet.

"*Honorables caballeros,* we port in New Orleans."

"Prepare for boarding." The demand was followed by a scurry of men working to lower the tender. Donato's men lifted their sidearms from beneath the gunwale. He motioned for them to stay calm. He couldn't get into a squabble out here, ten miles from the coast, ten miles from her. "As you board, kind senors, bring your physician. We fight a storm and lose much of our water supply and medicines. Several of the men are with fever. We must dock in New Orleans for quinine and fresh water."

The activity on the other ship ceased. The officer who had communicated with him turned and spoke with another officer who stood in the shadows of the main mast. Donato couldn't see him, but felt the man's penetrating eyes.

The first officer came back to speak. "We will not board. Do not de-board any men with fever on the mainland."

"*Muchas gracias.*" Donato motioned for the sails to be dropped and returned to the helm.

Silently they floated past the U.S. gunboat. The officer in the shadows followed along the gunwale as the ships passed each other, watching. Donato debated, dare he place himself between the U.S. shore and a U.S. gunboat, but unless he was willing to take that risk, he'd not get his son back. But he was wanted for piracy in the gulf waters. If the Americans knew who he was, he'd be under fire. Tonight, under the guise of a merchant, he'd sail directly into New Orleans.

The water sloshed around the hull that skimmed the surface, calming into a silent wake as the ship sailed into the Mississippi River. The wavering lights from shore glowed through the shroud of fog hovering like a veil of night.

Ships were six deep near the port, forcing him to anchor several hundred feet from shore. He hated to be that far in case he needed a quick escape. But with barely a breeze in port, he'd need the winds to make headway once he had his son, Enio.

"Half touch left," he called out.

"Half touch left, *Capitán*."

The flying jib steered between two tall ships.

With the yards trimmed, his ship skimmed atop the water and slowed to nearly a stop.

"Drop anchor."

Men ran the capstan blocks lowering the anchor. The heavy iron chain hardly made a ripple in the silent night. Riggings of the surrounding anchored ships whined and groaned with the rise and fall of churned waves, stretching their tethered bows.

Donato glanced around, noting there were some men on ships while lying to, and several small tenders and clippers lined the docks.

The air smelled of salt, dead fish, and seasoned cooking. The mist brought the smell to his lips, and he tasted the mixed flavors of Spanish and French foods. Music drifted down the canal. From his ship, he heard the boisterous noise of the Hôtel de la Marine on Levee. A refuge for pirates, outlaws, and rebels of all causes.

Donato knew the city well, even before Colette had brought their son here. He had visited often in the early years when he was attempting to find legal help against the constant harassment of the pirates in the gulf. After many failed attempts, he decided to take back from those scoundrels what they had stolen from him. But after the war, these same scoundrels walked free in New Orleans and he, labeled a pirate, was still a wanted man.

Colette had been en route to New Orleans when her ship was taken. Donato had rescued her from the pirate ship and from the fiends who thought to sell her as a slave. From the looks of this city, he had saved her from this, as well. But all the time she was with him on the island, supposedly content in their marriage, she had longed to remember her past, to go home. By the time Donato had figured out her identity, it was too late. Her brother arrived, and she left. She might be happy with her brother and his family, and... their son, but Donato was not. He would leave Colette to her decision, but he wanted his son back.

A round of laughter rose over the levee from La Veau Qui Tête, a small restaurant in the hotel. The doors were wide open in spite of the chill in the air. Knowing their clientele, it was a safe house in the case he needed to disappear within the city, though that was not his plan. In two hours he'd be back on the ship with his son in his arms.

That thought brought his heart to a standstill. He hadn't held his son in well over a year, and the waiting had been painful. Donato glanced down at his shaking hands; he could hardly think for want of holding his boy.

Within minutes the crew had the polly ready to board. Donato slipped over the side, slid down the wet cargo net, then dropped into the small boat. Quietly, they rowed to the dock, gliding over the rolling waves with precision, not a ripple in their wake. Donato glanced around, knowing most of the ships in port. At least, the ones that had entered from the gulf.

Except one.

He assessed it as they rowed past. A large frigate with a Spanish flag, not only Spanish, but royalty. He turned, watching the heavily armed frigate ride the soft rises of water to then sink into the swallows. Any arrival from Spain was a concern, especially for him. Without Spain he wouldn't have his island, but with that contract from the king came obligations for the good Spanish citizen, which he had chosen not to be. But tonight, he had to keep his focus on what he wanted more than anything life could offer.

His son.

One of the men, his most loyal, Ramónez de Cadiz, grabbed a rope as they bumped lightly against the water-soaked pier, pulling Donato into the moment.

"I return soon. Be at the ready."

"I wish to come, *Capitán.*"

"No, he is my son. I do this alone."

Donato noted that the U.S. gunboat had rounded about and now entered the breakwaters of port, compromising his escape route. His story had not fooled them. His ship was being watched.

He looped the rope of the polly over the port stump and pulled her parallel to the gutted shore.

A sense of frustration bled into his mind, tangling his thoughts the moment the gunboat emerged over the horizon. He tried to shake free from the feelings, but they clung to his every hope of seeing his son, changing his thoughts from anticipation to despair.

Like a body on the rack, he physically winced, feeling the pain more intensely since his French wife, Colette, had left him. To hell with her. She was no longer a part of his life.

His heart ached with missing the child, wondering what Enio was doing now; would he know his father once they were reunited? That thought alone had kept him awake for nights on end, weeks, months, until his plan had come together. A child needed his mother. It was for that reason alone, Donato had waited before taking Enio back, but now the boy was older and would adjust to the proper care Donato could give him.

Collette's brother, Jordan, had thought to be clever and had disappeared with the family, including Donato's wife, for a few months after the war, but he had returned to buy a home in Faubourg Sainte Marie, on the exclusive American side of the canal. Easy to find. Easy to enter. Donato knew the streets, the back alleys, the movement of the night clock men, the police, every pedestrian who walked the streets— he knew their pattern.

His plan had allowed him two hours to retrieve his son and sail out of New Orleans—until that damned U.S. gunboat had shown up. Not wanting to risk his men or ship, he leaned down and spoke in a low tone.

"Ramón, take the ship out of port. Come back in two days. I will have my son by then."

"This is too dangerous, *Capitán*," Ramón whispered.

"*Si*, but it is my danger. Be back in two days."

• • •

Toma, hermosa. Te hará bien.

Colette gasped, waking with a jerk. She sat up, dragging in air, breathless. With a hand to her chest, she glanced around her dark bedroom, having heard a voice as clear as if it were standing over her. "Donato?"

A chill of awareness rode up her spine, forcing her to throw back the bedclothes, needing to see her son.

She pulled on a morning frock, careful not to lose her balance on her bad leg, which had been aching more than usual these past few days. Limping across the floor to her son's connecting room, Colette opened the door.

Enio, her and Donato's son, was sound asleep. So was the nurse who slept in the adjoining room. Colette ran her fingers across the boy's forehead, pushing aside his silky black hair, his skin soft to the touch. His face was nothing more than innocence. The window to his room was locked, but unsatisfied and unable to quell that uneasy feeling that sucked the life out of her sleep, she lifted her lantern and took the stairs to the first parlor.

Shadows fluttered about the room from her candle, adding to the deception of the night. She checked all the locks. The house seemed secure, but she couldn't shake the feeling nor the dream. Donato was Spanish, but she couldn't remember him having said that particular sentence. But night after night, the Spanish words would work through her sleep until she'd awaken and feel on the verge of remembering... something.

"Colette?"

She jolted with a hand to her heart before realizing it was her brother standing on the last step. "I'm sorry, you startled me, n'est-ce pas?"

"You must stop this wandering at night."

She looked away, knowing she had been doing just that, every night after her return home, as dreams and images had invaded her sleep. But tonight felt different. "I woke up... with the same dream. I hear his voice but no memory with it. I don't remember so much, Jordan."

"I know, Colette. Perhaps it will never come. You now remember us, your family. The important things. It might be time to put this in the past. You left Donato to start anew."

She had not left Donato to start anew, but to return to her real life, to learn who she really was. His life was dangerous as a pirate, and she had sometimes feared for herself and her son. When her memory had returned of her family, with it came the obligations she had, the pledges she had made more than nineteen years ago when her parents had been taken by the Tribunal during the Revolution of 1798 in France. The things she must do.

Colette turned to face her brother, a comrade, a victim of the same crime that had separated them on their journey to America from France. The fear from that night bubbled to the surface uninvited, yet popped like painful slaps of a whip against her body. She swayed and grabbed the nearest settee to keep her balance.

As always when she was in need, he was there. Jordan

walked toward her with his arms outstretched to nurture her weakened body.

"I'm all right, Jordan. I've learned to walk despite the injury."

He nodded and hesitated in his step, but Colette knew it was a struggle for him. Jordan had been her sworn protector from the time she was five years old when the Tribunal had arrested their parents. He was her rock in the stormy seas, but she had leaned on him far too heavily since her return from Donato's island. Her rescue back to her own life, or so it was meant to be, had made her unusually dependent. Jordan's life was now settled. He no longer dealt with the same demons that visited her nightly.

"Jordan, how much do you remember from the night the *Loirie* was attacked and we were taken?"

He attempted to shrug off her inquiry, but she could see that the casual response was merely a decoy to the true feelings that tightened his brow and pursed his lips. "I remember the attack, seeing the flag of the *Lady Tempest*, and being boarded. Sometimes, I think there was a third ship, but nothing comes to mind. I remember trying to get to you, but I was knocked out and found myself in the water. I heard the American voice that we know was the consulate, who was on the *Lady Tempest*. Other than that, not much."

"There was a third ship. I remember the cannons, the fire, men shouting, shooting, then someone grabbing me and pulling me over the gunwale into the other ship. I'll never forget hearing you hit the water when you were thrown overboard. I fell into a dark place." She sighed, frustrated with her lack of memory. "A dark, dark place. I remember so little."

"I no longer care, for I know that the men responsible have met justice."

"Except Donato. You blame him."

"Do you not?"

An odd feeling of loneliness rose through the ashes of her memory, flashes of Donato's island, his voice, his touch, candlelight dinners on the terrace, and the lulling sound of Spanish guitars serenading them at night. A life filled with luxuries and riches. Only snippets dared surface before they were immediately wiped clean by the memory of her brother walking through the door of her son's room to take her home, away from Donato and his island.

"I do not blame him."

Her brother shook his head in disagreement but let her comment pass. "Colette, we are safe now. I no longer search for clarity. I want the same for you, sister. Don't search for answers that have no relevance."

"The answers seem to seek me out. I have no choice." She set the lamp on the table and lowered herself to the settee, needing this moment of truth, having never really spoken about their experience together. "I have dreams and I don't know from what memory they come."

"Maybe they are just dreams, Colette, nothing more, nothing less."

"*Toma, hermosa. Te hará bien,*" she repeated for his benefit.

"Spanish."

"*Oui,* I only know a little Spanish that I learned from Donato. It means something about being beautiful and getting well. I hear it, Jordan, over and over in my sleep."

"Did Donato ever say that to you?"

"I don't know. I think not so. But he spoke mostly Spanish when I was first with him. Why would it be important?" She could see Jordan preparing to dismiss the topic. "Understand, Jordan, it is the final stitch to a tapestry. I need all the threads in place to tie off the ends."

"Then eventually it will come." He ambled over and kissed the top of her head and wrapped her face within his large hands. "For tonight, let's go back to sleep. Tomorrow, you have much work to do with your charities. They count on you."

Her charities, a selfless giving for others. It was a duty she had assigned herself after nearly losing her parents. Her servitude was a promise to God, should her parents survive and return, which they had. Thus began her charity work.

She accepted Jordan's kind show of affection with a squeeze to his arm, unable to make him understand how muddled her memory was before and since her return from the island.

"Do you think he will come?" Colette asked before realizing she had once again asked a question that had become a part of her daily ritual. *Is today the day?*

"He's had the opportunity. It's been several months, and we moved. I don't think so. He's wanted for piracy. It could be dangerous for him to appear here, especially with the American navy anticipating trouble with Spain, since Britain has been defeated. You're safe as long as we stay within the city."

She had heard those words before, even caught the same sigh Jordan released before giving her the same answer to the same question she had asked for the past several months. But she had done the unthinkable: taken a man's son away. Not just any man; a very powerful man. She had heard numerous stories about his escapades; Donato de la Roche, the father of her son, was the most infamous pirate of the gulf waters.

Jordan waited for her, motioning for her to go back to bed. "Come, I'll escort you upstairs. Try to sleep."

But she was not ready to surrender to the feelings that would toss her about her bed all night. She had to exorcise them in some way. "I wish to stay up. I cannot sleep. The servants will keep the fire going. Please, Jordan, you have a long day of travel tomorrow. Go to bed."

He started to shake his head, but she knew he wanted to retire. His head shake turned into a sigh, then he nodded. "If you need anything…"

The flames of the fire reflected off the walls and played over Jordan's face. For a moment they watched each other, and she knew he worried that she might never return as the same sister he had known all his life. But after Donato, after living with a pirate on an island, *was* she the same reserved woman, with the piousness and devoutness that had kept her anchored through the years of her life? "I'm not in need, thank you. Good night, Jordan."

She remained watching the fire; the flames wrapped around the logs and whispered into the night, into her mind, her heart, trying to unite with that one little flame burning deep inside her heart, the one she had failed to extinguish.

Besides the shadows cast by the fire, the house was dark, silent, and every churn of the wind brought out a new crop of goose bumps.

She heard a bump, a slight thump outside the house. Her spine stiffened, and she leaned her head to the side to hear it again. When there was nothing, she pushed out of the settee and walked to the window. Pulling back the curtain, she strained her eyes to see through the gloomy mist, but fog had settled over the city, making the night exceptionally dark. A sweep of wind pushed a branch of the magnolia tree up against the house, creating a knocking sound. Relieved to know what had made the noise, she dropped the curtain.

"Colette?"

She turned to see that Jordan had returned to the stairs. She braced herself for a lecture.

"I think you should leave with us tomorrow."

Jordan and his young family were going to Boston for business and to show off his new son to relatives, but Colette wouldn't step foot on a ship and had refused to go, citing her work at the hospital as far too valuable to travel again.

"Jordan…" she protested, but knew her words fell on deaf ears.

"I know you want to do your charity work—"

"It is important," she interrupted, but wanted to ask him, how should she reconcile a promise to God when her heart yearned for something more, something that bordered on sinful—Donato?

"I know it is important to you, but it is not the right time to be here alone. We leave in the morning."

• • •

Donato watched the curtain close over the window of Jordan's house. Colette was still there and most likely, so was his son. Unfortunately, so were her brothers. Through the raised curtain, he had caught sight of Jordan.

Not that it mattered; Donato would still take his son. His ship would be back in two days, giving him about thirty-six hours to make his move. He watched the light of a lantern move to the upstairs window, casting a shadow against the window lace.

A woman's shadow.

He leaned against the black iron fencing, debating the decision of separating mother and son, but he had already waited out the past year until the child was old enough. Donato had given thought to taking Colette as well. Not to reunite them as a family, for he'd never give her that much power again, but because she had fled his island as an escaping captive. How easy it would be to remind her of the passion she now denied and leave her craving more, all for the taste of sweet revenge. Captive?

But that was not his mission. He'd take only Enio and start anew, as had Colette.

Colette moved across the window, as if pacing. Her lithe shadow floated about the room, with an occasional shake of her long wavy hair. He remembered combing his hands through her honey-colored tresses as if spinning his own gold, and he had felt rich beyond any number of coins. He ran a tongue through the seam of his lips, trying to wash away the memory of her mouth to his, the moist tantalizing heat, the taste of her, the feel of her pressed against his chest.

He put his feet into motion, pulling his mind back into his body and on his mission. He had become a master of revenge; why should Colette be any different? She had betrayed him in the worst way. She had taken his son. Now it was his turn. He had thirty-six hours to take Enio, board his ship, and go out to sea without being discovered.

He hadn't attempted a disguise while walking along the docks, but had employed caution. Dressed plainly in dark breeches, half boots, and a blue cotton shirt, he was sure not to draw attention to himself. His hair had been tied in a queue and covered with a black felt hat that shadowed his face.

Hearing only the hourly calls from the town crier, he crossed the canal and turned down the Rue de la Levée toward the Hôtel de la Marine, knowing he'd get a room there with no questions asked. Already his plan had hit more obstacles than he had anticipated. That gunboat nagged at him, their immediate capitulation, the officer in the shadows, and the silent pursuit into the harbor. He halted, realizing the fool he had been. All of it had been by design; they had known who he was from the first time they'd stopped him.

The men on that U.S. gunboat had recognized him.

He hadn't outsmarted them by claiming to have ill men. They had outmaneuvered him by allowing *La María* to pass right into the hands of the authorities. He rounded the corner of Saint Ann's. In the opaque night he could barely see the outline of the Spanish royal ship silently riding the rolling water. Near that large frigate, he had anchored. He crawled along the port spears until he could see the U.S. gunboat. His ship was still in port, lying to, barely visible in the faint moonlight. Why were they still here?

He continued toward the landing. Muffled voices lingered over the water, American voices. He caught a flash or two of a rapier. He watched, his eyes slowly adjusting to the darkness, to see U.S. Navy soldiers standing on the stern of *La María*. He swallowed hard, recognizing his miscalculation.

His ship had been seized.

Donato heard the sound of running feet, and within seconds he was surrounded by men with pistols aimed. To their center stood the officer who had been on that U.S. ship.

"Donato de la Roche?"

Donato nodded, knowing he had been bettered. With the elegance of a seasoned fighter and gentleman, he allowed the naval officer his victory. *"Si."*

Chapter Two

"I'll be fine, Jordan." Relieved to have convinced her older brother to let her stay in New Orleans and to have her half-brother Loul stay with her, Colette handed Jordan his hat and walking stick, more than anxious for him to depart. "What more protection would I need but a brother, n'est-ce pas?"

"Two brothers. You need two brothers against a man like Donato."

She loved her brothers, but they must allow her to rebuild her life, and the idea of being against Donato, against her son's father, brought a slight halt to her heart.

Before he could change his mind, Colette ushered him toward the door. "You go, s'il vous plaît."

Jordan looked at his wife, Aurélie, who nodded toward the door. In some way, validating his decision. "All right, Colette, you be careful, and I appreciate your charity work, but you work too hard at times. Please don't find any more lonely souls to save."

"It is all I have, Jordan. I made a promise."

"To?"

"Just a promise. Besides, my work keeps me busy." And her mind off the life she had left behind, the life she had had no right to in the first place. Donato was never a part of her pledge, her promise on that fateful night when her parents were taken away. Even her first marriage in France had not been out of love, but to care for an aging man who needed her help.

Jordan had no idea how much she needed to keep her mind busy, not to think and rethink her decision to come home with him, to be with her family, leaving her life with Donato behind. Perhaps the years of not seeing them had made her decision for her, for when Jordan had arrived to "rescue" her from Donato's well-fortified island, she had not hesitated to return to her world. A safe world away from pirates and thieves. Surely Donato understood that. Or did he? After so long without an attempt to contact her, had he dismissed her and his son from his life? Had he forgotten the passion— She halted her thoughts and glanced up at her waiting brother and repeated, "Just a promise."

After kisses and well-wishing hugs, Jordan and his wife and children were finally on their way. Jordan's daughter, little Maisie, was still waving out the window when the landau turned the corner toward the canal.

Colette strolled back inside and drew a deep breath, enjoying the silence, the quietude her mind and heart so needed in order to truly mend. Her half-brother, Loul, would return later. He lived on Rampart Street in a house Jordan had originally bought for Aurélie before they married.

Colette ambled upstairs to get her son, Enio. The nurse who cared for him would have him bathed and ready to start his day. There he was, smiling the moment she walked into his room.

"How's my *petit garçon*?"

His nurse passed him into Colette's waiting arms. "I will return in the morning, Miss Colette. Tonight is Carnival."

All of Jordan's servants were taking the night off. "Of course. Enjoy the celebration."

Colette adjusted the small boy on her hip and headed for the outdoor courtyard. With the servants gone for Carnival, she settled in to relax, spending nearly three hours in complete repose as Enio played. The winter sun warmed the chill from her body, and the scent of ocean air brought back hazy memories of a beautiful island, a paradise between land and sea, between a man and a woman.

She shook her head, refusing to allow those memories of Donato forward, or remember his thick raven hair, wavy and disheveled, brushed back on the sides and parted slightly over his shoulders. Or acknowledge the matching dark eyes that always held a tone of intrigue and danger. Donato had stood tall, broad-shouldered, aristocratic, and his deep resonant voice matched his swarthy looks.

Colette's breathing deepened, and she placed a hand over her chest to ease the sudden pain in her heart, unable to sort through so much at once. Images of her abduction at sea invaded her mind. She glanced down at her leg, trying to remember how or when she was injured. She had nearly forgotten everything about the night she was taken captive until flashes of an auction block doused her mind. She remembered being in pain, her leg burning and her ankle swollen. Why did she feel so tortured about that night? Why could she not move on as Jordan had?

"Colette!" Loul shouted through the iron fence of the courtyard, before opening the gate and coming inside. Breathing hard, his face was drenched in sweat.

"What is it?" Colette pulled Enio onto her lap.

Loul knelt down next to her and took her hand. "Colette, don't be alarmed, because we'll get out of here, but they seized Donato's ship last night."

The sudden rush of memories would have washed her off the chair had it not been for holding Enio in her arms. Amazingly, unable to breathe, she still formed a word. "Where?"

"In port."

"His ship seized?" Colette's breath locked down deep inside her stomach. Her voice barely a whisper. Loul leaned in to hear. "And...Donato?"

"Captured, but he broke free."

Her breath escaped through tight lips. She glanced around the patio, expecting him to step out of the nearby shadows. Hearing he had escaped brought on a sense of relief. They could not hold a man like Donato. They simply could not. "He has left New Orleans, *non*?"

"How could he? He has no ship."

"They don't know where he is?"

Loul rose to his feet and slid into the chair across from her. "They're looking. This is the plan, Colette. We'll go up to my mother's until this is over. I'll get a pirogue ready for the backwaters."

"No! Not water."

Loul halted. Reading the expression on her face, he added, "We don't know where Donato is. The bayou is the safest place to put you. Agreed?"

She couldn't stop her heart from hammering so loud in her ears. She couldn't think. Her mind raced with images of ships, and even a small pirogue was more than she could bear. No, she couldn't step foot onto anything on water. "I know it is to be foolish—"

"It's all right, Colette, we'll go by land, but then we must leave before Carnival starts. I don't think Donato knows where you are, or he would have been here already. Jordan boarded his horses and carriage near the river. I'll get them rigged. Then we leave. Agreed?"

Though her mind was whirling with possibilities of seeing Donato, she reacted as she had when Jordan had arrived on Donato's island to return her to her family—as the obedient sister. "Agreed."

• • •

Colette folded the last of Enio's flannel longs for the damp trip through the backwaters to Yellow Sun, as well as an extra shawl. Though her hands were shaking, she managed to pack them neatly in his small trunk, stacked atop his lawn shirts and cambric gowns.

She then started the task of packing her own items, filling another small trunk with two muslin walking dresses, two wool gowns, a light *douillette,* a pair of tan gloves, winter half boots, and a walking *pelisse.* Assuming she'd not be gone long, she packed privy items and undergarments for two days and tossed her great wool coat trimmed in fur on the bed to be worn for travel.

How long would she be in exile? How long before Donato

would stop looking for her? Is that why he was here?

Returning to pack another pair of stockings, she watched the crystal ornament rock back and forth atop her armoire when she closed the drawer. Jordan had hidden the crystal inside a crate of flour in hopes it would reach her, bringing a message of hope that her brother searched for her. She sat on the bed holding the crystal in her hand, trying to remember the events that had led to that rescue. For some reason the crystal spoke, not of her family and her past, but of Donato and his kindness for having given it to her. She set it back on her armoire, refusing to reminisce about a life that had never really existed. A life she should never have had, for she had made a promise to carry on charity work and leave passionate love affairs to women like her brother's wife, Aurélie, who sparkled with life and draped her body in silks and satins.

Having locked her trunk as well, Colette returned to the parlor to wait, and still no Loul. She checked the clock. He should have been here by now, and if not soon, they'd have to wade through a night of Carnival merrymakers to leave the city. Giving up, she finally put Enio to bed and collapsed on the settee to wait for Loul to return.

The sounds of Carnival started early. Fireworks and jesters of all colors bounded about the street. Colette changed into a muslin negligee, over which she had wrapped a shawl. After sipping a warmed drink, she fell into a restless sleep, her mind rolling between ocean waves, sun rays, and rum that heated her insides and made her feel safe. It was Donato's concoction that he'd heat by the fire, sometimes igniting the liquor. But it was good, and it had felt wonderful on nights like tonight when her body felt tight as if braided into pigtails.

She stood up and poked the fire, not wanting to think

about the past. After a stir of burning logs, she heard a frantic knock on the door. Finally, Loul had arrived.

"Loul?" Colette rushed to the door and unlocked it. But before she could see who stood to the outside, it was pushed open with the power of many. Suddenly, she was surrounded by costumed men. Weird masks closed in around her.

"Who are you? Go away, go away!"

But no one listened. A musician who accompanied them serenaded with loud, strumming music on a guitar, as if to intentionally drown out her voice, her screams.

"What is this? Who are you? Get out of my house."

One grabbed her, twisting her arms behind her back. Pain radiated through her shoulders.

"*¡A por el niño!*"

"For the child? No, no!" Colette screamed, as two of the men raced up the stairs toward her son's nursery. She heard doors slamming and Enio cry out for her. She kicked at her captors and wrestled to break free, but the strength of their hold was akin to the chains she had worn as a slave. Her efforts were of no use; she fluttered within their arms like a dying swan with a broken wing. "*Non, non, ne le prenez pas!*"

Her head started to spin; memories poured through her mind like an open sieve, the ship, men, the auction block. She screamed, fighting to free herself until a hand came up over her mouth, squeezing so tight she could hardly breathe.

"Do not come looking for the boy," he rasped in her ear with a thick Spanish accent. "He is ours."

With that she was tossed to the floor with such force, she hit her head on the settee. Blood rushed her eyes, and she fought a faint as the men raced from the house carrying her frightened son. The moment Enio saw her, he screamed for her, arms outstretched. She fought to get to her feet, but her head felt dizzy and her ankle gave out.

The door slammed behind them, sucking the life out of the room.

Colette fought tears and gasping breaths as she pulled herself from the floor. She knew then, Loul was not coming. Donato knew who Loul was; he had seen him on Jordan's ship. It would make sense to eliminate Loul, the only protector she had. She should have known this would happen the moment Loul told her Donato was in New Orleans.

Standing now, her body shook and her legs felt like wilting weeds in the heat of the day. She held on to the back of the chair for her balance, waiting for the pain in her leg to ease enough to walk. She looked around, not believing what had happened.

Her stomach clenched into a painful roil. The men who took Enio were dressed in costume. How would she ever find him?

But she'd never forget that musician, the wicked mask he wore, and the screeching music on his guitar.

She climbed the stairs to Jordan's room and opened his wardrobe. After changing into his clothes, she pulled out a flintlock pistol and a knife. Loading her own muff pistol to wear concealed, she tied the knife to her side and loaded Jordan's flintlock, as well.

It was then she heard something.

She opened the door to Jordan's room and listened, hearing soft footfalls of someone in the downstairs parlor. It wasn't Loul.

She palmed the flintlock and slipped onto the landing. A shadowy form stepped lightly through the lower parlor and glanced up toward the stairs. She pulled back and slid into her room.

There she waited.

The stairs creaked as the intruder took them step by step, hesitating as if wanting to ensure he didn't awaken someone. Colette moved to the back of the room, pistol in hand. The intruder stepped onto the upper stair landing, paused, then took the hallway entrance to Enio's room. Finger on the trigger, she waited, inching closer to the door, listening.

He returned to the hallway.

She could hardly breathe. The pistol growing heavier with every second she waited.

He was outside her room. The light carried his distorted shadow beneath the door. She sucked in air, praying for strength as the doorknob slowly turned.

She held her breath.

The door swung open.

A man stepped inside.

In the dark she couldn't make out his face, but knew that profile, knew the breadth of his shoulders, the swagger to his walk, regardless of the silent steps he thought to take. Her blood boiled; her heart peppered her ribs with an out-of-sync staccato.

He turned to face her. His expression void of anything but determination. The moment he saw her, he raised a flintlock and aimed directly at her.

She raised her pistol and they faced each other.

"Where is he?" he said at the exact same moment as she.

Donato lowered his flintlock but only slightly. It was still at the ready. "Where is he, Colette?"

Her fingers nervously traced over the trigger of her firearm.

"As if you don't know. You had him taken from me tonight. Did you come back to finish what one of your men didn't? Me?"

"If I had wanted to do that, I would not hesitate now."

"I will shoot." Her voice shook more than her hand.

"As will I."

"Then I'm never to see him again?"

"Was I?" He started to pace in the other direction, taking a wide berth around her. She turned with him, keeping her pistol in her hand, wary of his next move.

In all the time she had lived with Donato on his island, she had never been at odds with him. She always knew who he was and what he did, but she had never challenged him. Now, here, it was different, and being in opposition to Donato made her damned uncomfortable.

She ran a tongue over her dry lips. "I didn't want him raised in your world."

"Perhaps I don't want him raised in yours. Where is he?" Without his glorious ostentatious style of fashion, she expected that he'd seem diminished. But that wasn't the case. Dressed in plain clothes, he still had a regal presence about him. His hair, longish and black, had broken free of a queue, barely gracing his shoulders. Dark eyes, deep and probing, were nestled well within the strong framework of his face.

"You wish to torture me with this game of yours. If that was your goal, you have succeeded. Where is he, Donato? He was taken tonight. Only you would know where."

"You heard I was here and chose to hide him." Donato motioned to the open trunk.

"No, I mean…" She could hardly lie when standing next to the child's trunk packed for travel. "I was planning to travel to the bayous because of Carnival. My brother, Loul, he was to bring Jordan's landau but he never came back. I waited for him, then these men broke into the house and took Enio. They were Spanish, Donato. Your men."

Donato hardened his gaze on her; she felt the brush of fire along her shoulders, but held herself steady in spite of the pain eating at her leg from standing so long.

"Believe what you like, Colette, but until I find my son, you will not leave my sight."

She allowed her lips to pull tight, returning his deadly gaze with fire of her own. "We agree, Donato. Until I find Enio, you will not leave mine."

Chapter Three

"They are gone only an hour at the most. We leave, d'accord?" Colette stuffed the long pistol into her oversize breeches.

"In New Orleans, on festival night, that is a lifetime." Donato was not so convinced of her innocence, suspicious that she knew where Enio was and was playing her part well. If Loul were standing here, testifying to the truth of her statements, Donato might believe her, but he was not. How convenient to have her brother suddenly disappear at the same time as did Enio. If he were a gambling man, the money was on Loul. Find Loul, and he'd find Enio. Donato watched her tighten up her rope belt. "Why are you dressed like a man?"

"To hide my pistol better."

"Wear something that will blend with Carnival. Do you have anything fancier?"

"No…"

Of course she didn't. Having checked on her several times

over the past few months, he had noticed Colette dressed more the nun than the beautiful woman that she was. She seemed to catch the judgment in his eyes.

"But I'm sure I could find something in Aurélie's things. Are we not going after them? There was a musician—"

"Change your clothes. Where is your brother, the infamous captain of *Le Vengeur*? I'm in need of a costume as well. I'm sure he has a pirate one about."

The color bled from her face as if shocked that he'd dared to say that aloud, looking around as if someone would hear the truth that would endanger Jordan's precious war hero reputation.

"The house is empty," he reminded her.

He hadn't forgotten about the secrecy of Jordan's outlaw past, but it was still a thorn stuck in his foot. It mattered little if Jordan's true identity were known; the man would have been pardoned along with the rest of those river rat pirates just because he was French. Donato had sunk more British ships to Lafitte's battlefield, but Spain was a worry for the young country, and its fear of Spain had escalated after the war. In spite of the pardon for all sea rogues, only the French had benefited. Donato, being Spanish, was still a wanted man, while the French corsairs, like Jordan, walked the streets of New Orleans as free men. But Jordan had pulled it off, lived off the seas for three years, while searching for Colette, to safely return to his previous life as if nothing had ever happened.

"He left for Boston today."

"Of course he did. Without Enio?"

"Without."

A likely story, but he had nothing more to go on. "Where

are his things? I need to create a disguise. They are looking for me."

"To the end of the hall."

He lit a lamp, then headed toward the door when she stopped him.

"Donato? How did you know which room was mine? When you came into the house you came directly to this room, then turned into the baby's room."

He wanted to tell her how many times he had stood outside at night and watched her tuck in his son and herself. Standing through wind, rain, and moonless nights, he had waited, hoping for just a glimpse of his little boy. Endless days, he'd sneaked a peek while the child played in the courtyard. But Colette hadn't earned the right to know that, any more than she had earned the right to take his son away. He dismissed her question with the turn of his shoulders and walked down the hall to her brother's room.

Jordan's room held no surprises. Donato casually walked around the tester bed and ran his hand along the armoire that held Jordan's clothes. Wouldn't Colette's brother be surprised to find the one man he considered his adversary, if not rival, standing in his private bedroom? A hollow victory, but a victory all the same.

He opened the first wardrobe. Women's gowns. He motioned toward them as Colette followed in behind him. "I assume Aurélie's?"

Donato continued to the next wardrobe opposite of Aurélie's and opened it. Shirts, breeches, and overcoats. He pulled out a pair of black breeches, white shirt, ruffled cuffs, and a gray overcoat.

Rushing to change, Colette had stepped out of her

brother's attire.

Donato looked away, not wanting to see anything before him except the woman who had betrayed him. He ignored the milky sheen to her soft skin in the fluttering light of the lamp, and the shapely mature curves that spoke of a woman who needed a man for satisfaction. But she had had one and tossed him away.

He dressed quickly, hiding the wound in his arm garnered from his flight from the law, then leaned against the doorjamb watching her body move within the silhouette of the night. Her fingers, long, slender, moved to lace her corset. She had turned her back on him, but he could see every curve reflecting off the mirror. Her honey-gold hair brushed across her lower back and hugged her hips.

He turned away from her, feeling the rejection all over again, feelings he had managed to tame, not conquer, but keep to a bearable level, until he was standing here with her.

"I'll be downstairs." He picked up another black cotton shirt and turned to leave.

"Oh no you don't." She advanced toward him, but halted. "Until we find Enio, I'm closer to you than your own shadow."

He smiled wickedly, meant to send a shiver through her spine. "If you insist on standing in such a state of undress, it is your shadow that will have to get out of my way."

She whirled around and picked up her pistol, raising it level with her chest. "I don't think so."

Donato resisted taking the weapon away from her, knowing he could with the sweep of his hand. He had no fear she'd pull the trigger, at least on purpose, but had caught one lead ball too many tonight. She was on edge, but he'd show no mercy. Instead of compassion, he'd push her until she was over the ledge and admit to where Enio was, and this charade would be over.

"Be careful, Colette, I might decide to take that plaything away."

But she didn't wilt as he had hoped. "Be careful, my pirate, there is a bounty on your head. I might decide to pull the trigger and live a wealthy life."

"Warning noted. Now might I wait for you in the parlor?"

She nodded. "Leave the door open."

• • •

Colette waited until Donato had left the room before putting her pistol down. Yes, he could have taken it from her if he had wanted, but not without a damned fight, because right about now she could easily scratch his eyes out, knowing he had Enio but persisted in this tortuous game of cat-and-mouse.

Her shadow move out of his way? Why must he say anything that referred to their past? The mere mention of their nights together brought a rebellious skip to her heart. *Damn him.*

Was his point to punish her? If so, he had succeeded in his little mission, because that's who Donato was, a man of vengeance. How long would this persist? Dress in costume, for what? Were they really going after someone, or was she a pawn in a rendezvous with the very men who had taken her son? Either way, she released a deep, tired breath. She'd play along; she'd do what he asked. She had no other option.

Aurélie had a lot of gowns, and her style of dress was very different from Colette's. Aurélie loved colors, silks, and had jewelry of bedazzling sparkles to match, including masquerade masks and fluffy plumes.

Colette pulled a red silk dress over her head.

The bells that hung from the shoulders tinkled with her movement. But the silk felt wonderful against her skin, reminding her of a time when she had worn dresses of silk all the time. Donato's choice, not hers, but the material hugged her body with a feathery touch, reminding her of the warm evenings when she'd dress for dinner and fall into his dark eyes over the fluttering light of a candle.

She drew a deep breath, erasing the titillating sensations that flooded through her body, and pulled herself back to the present. She packed her muff pistol inside her boot and picked up a shawl. If Donato had Enio, then where was Loul? It was that disturbing thought that made her pick up Jordan's pistol and carry it with her as she went down the stairs.

Donato was there, as she expected, knowing that the form of torture he had chosen was far from over.

He turned as she took the stairs, watching her every step. Feeling his gaze from head to toe, she drew in one deep breath after another, exhaling her reaction to him, not holding on to any sensory feeling that might start her thinking, wondering, *God...yearning*. Her heart burned with each breath. She swallowed hard, unable to stifle her response to his mere presence. Not again, never again would she allow her heart to fall into his pirate hands.

When she was standing on the parlor floor, he approached her, handing her a mask he had cut out of Jordan's shirt.

"Not the best, but it'll do for tonight." He leaned back, taking her in, then flashed a satisfied smile. "I'll be the pirate and you…you're my captive."

"Again." The moment the word slipped out, she regretted making such a comparison, for she had never felt the captive while living with him, though her brothers had thought she was.

"Si." His response was harsh and curt.

His unveiled anger brought her blood to a boil. Barely keeping herself in check, she said, "You have won, Donato, I am at your mercy. Now give my son back to me."

"If I have won, why have you not given him to me?"

She flew at him, flinging her balled fists hard against his chest, steely and lean, just like she remembered. His arms came up around her and held her firm. She could hear his heart beat and feel the pulsating power of his arms around her. Just like before —

She gasped, remembering too much.

His embrace, his kiss, his love — She broke free of his arms. Wiping at her eyes, she tried for even breathing, but her mind suddenly felt jumbled as anger faded and something not foreign, but certainly not welcome, flooded her body — desire.

For a moment they stared at each other. She nearly swayed from the impact, resisting each shred of memory trying to coalesce in her mind, trying to rekindle what hovered just below the surface of her faulty guard. She swallowed the knot in her throat and felt it sink to her stomach. But one recollection had slipped through…the feel of his arms around her, and oh, how she needed them right now to console her. But that was not to be.

She dried her eyes and pulled in a deep breath, taking another protective step away from him. He noted her retreat with a glance to the floor as she backed away, then to her face, but in that glance she caught a grimace and noticed blood trickling down his hand.

"You're hurt."

"It had stopped bleeding until now." He nodded, pulling off the overcoat and vest, then shirt to expose a raw hole in his left shoulder. He had tied it off with a strip from Jordan's shirt, but it wasn't holding well, and her attack must have restarted the bleeding. "Caught a ball when I escaped. I tied a bandage around it."

She noted the sweat across his forehead and running down the length of his temples. This wound was not as casual as he pretended.

"And the ball?"

"Clean through."

"Then you did not catch it. I'll get something to make bandages."

With make-do bandages in one hand, she placed a bowl of water on the table. The fluttering light from the fire played over his chest, wove with abandonment across the muscles of his broad shoulders, and curled around his thick arms.

"Sit, and I will fix."

After cleaning the wound, Colette wrapped bandaging over and under his shoulder and around his chest. His skin felt moist from the night and hot from the fire. Her fingers found the ends of his hair that brushed the tops of his shoulders. She couldn't help the slight shift of her hand to glide over the side of his face until he looked up at her.

She pulled back, but he caught her with his other arm. Wrapping his hand in her hair, he forced her knees to bend and brought her closer to him, so close his lips nearly brushed across hers. But he didn't kiss her. Instead, his hold on her hair tightened, pulling her into him. He closed his eyes and inhaled the scent of her hair as she was held motionless, unable to move a finger. Helpless.

"Colette, I don't wish to harm you," he whispered, his breath hot against her face. "So I beg you for the truth. Where is Enio?"

His hold on her hurt, but she didn't resist, knowing he was a man of reason. "I do not know."

"You understand, I am a threat to you if you lie."

"I do." Her voice as faint as she felt, unable to breathe.

"This story you tell me is true?"

She prayed he was no longer playing with her, having taken mercy. "I swear upon my heart, upon my son's life."

His grip on her slowly ebbed, and she could see he was thinking about her answer, giving her the courage to ask, "Donato, do you know where he is? Tell me you have him and only wish to punish me for taking him and that is what you do tonight."

His hold on her dissolved, and she pulled back enough to see him more clearly.

"I beg, Donato." She crumpled before him. "Do you have him?"

"You are not weak. Do not be so." He pulled her off her knees and into his arms, wrapping her within the strength she had always appreciated. "No, Colette, I do not have him."

. . .

Donato pulled the hair back from her face and caught her profile in the firelight. Moisture filled her eyes, reflecting the light of the flickering flames, and for the first time since he arrived, he believed she might be telling the truth. A weight fell to the pit of his stomach heavier than a cannonball from an eighteen-pound gun. He had so wanted her to have Enio somewhere.

He released her and pulled away, the intimacy of the moment too intense for him. Colette was the reason they were in this situation. He wouldn't be searching for his son had she never left.

She looked up at him as he stood, quickly wiping her eyes as if to hide her emotions.

"What do we do now?"

"How many men were here tonight?"

She shook her head, her hair radiating sparks of gold off the fire. "I guess, six to eight."

"All in costume?"

She nodded. "They had a musician with them that played loud music, Spanish music, on a guitar that hurt my ears."

"Both of your brothers are gone. That makes me suspicious."

"I know you hate my brothers, but they had nothing to do with this. They would not hurt me like this."

"Unless you are part of it, and your part is to distract me."

"I am not, Donato."

Grasping for some idea as to who and why six or eight men would barge into Jordan's home for the purpose of stealing a small boy left Donato's nerves raw and dangling. At this point, he had no choice but to believe her. If Loul was supposed to be here tonight and they were trying to escape with the baby, where was he? As protective and tenacious as her brothers were, unless they were a part of the plot to take him, they'd be here.

He looked at Colette, who had risen to her feet.

"They were Spanish, Donato." Her hands were shaking, and she reached out for him from time to time as she spoke, like she had after he had rescued her from the auction block. But this time, he couldn't offer any reassurance because he had no idea who or why someone had taken his son.

"Are you ready? Put on your mask."

"To go where?"

"Loul's. We start with your brother."

"He lives—"

"I know where he lives." He ignored the surprised expression on her face, wanting to tell her he knew just about every detail about her and her outlaw brothers, but it was of no importance and would only throw kerosene on his burning need for revenge.

Carnival had the city in complete turmoil. The noise made his ears ache for the soft strum of a Spanish guitar. The fumes of lighted torches burned his eyes.

He wove through merrymakers with Colette behind him and turned down Toulouse Street toward the promenade on the ramparts. Musicians and dancers bobbed back and forth ahead of them. Finally able to break through, he approached the small two-story whitewashed home with black shutters. He stopped under the abat-vent with Colette close to his side. The house was dark. He knocked, but no one answered. He tried the door, it was locked.

Colette searched around the doorjamb. "There is a key…"

Donato smashed the glass of the door window and

flipped the lock to open it. "I don't need a key."

Donato stepped into the porte cochere of Loul's home and followed the gray flagstone path until passing under an archway into the courtyard. No sound. No lights.

He pulled Colette up close to him. "Any servants?"

She shook her head. "Not on Carnival night."

"Good night for a crime." Donato glanced around the courtyard, noting the tall white statue in the center that nearly glowed in the dark night. Redbrick walls surrounded where they stood, and on the second story, a balcony.

"Which room is his?"

"To the front of the house." She pointed above them. "Donato, this is wrong. Something is wrong."

He glanced up to the windows: no lights and draped with batten blinds. He couldn't deny he had the same feeling. The house had a ghostly feel to it. Shadows created by the activity on the street bounced off everything, giving life to inanimate objects that would look harmless in the light of day.

"You can wait here. I'll go up."

"No." She reached out and took hold of his coat. "We go together."

Donato lit the lamp near the base of the staircase and climbed upward with Colette close behind. Once on the balcony, he neared the room as directed by Colette.

Slowly, he pushed the door open.

Colette reached out and grabbed Donato's arm. He felt her fingers pull tight as the door swung to the inside. Nothing but darkness awaited them.

Donato walked into the room with lantern held high.

"Look." Colette walked over the bed. "He was packed to leave. Oh my God, something has happened to him."

Donato couldn't deny the obvious intent of Loul. The satchel was on the bed, and inside he had packed clothing and privy items. He searched around the room but found nothing amiss.

"Where did he go to retrieve Jordan's landau?"

"I don't know. There are several stables, but only Loul knew which one." Her voice wavered, clearly shaken over this discovery. She looked at him, her gaze following along his shoulder lines; he knew she wanted to feel his support, but that was not for the giving. He turned away from her, refusing to see.

"I'm going to search the house. You can wait or come."

"I come." She rushed to his side.

Donato glanced down at Colette.

Her hair was loose, freely landing over her shoulders and falling the length of her back. He remembered her complaints that her hair frizzed in the torrid heat of the island. To him, the long tresses had always been beautiful and seemed to offset her flawless skin and almond-shaped face that highlighted her cheekbones, usually tinted with a hint of color. He remembered running his fingers over her face, her skin like glass.

But that was his Colette, not this stranger who had chosen to return to an old life that held no meaning, over a life filled with passion and a man who knew how to touch her, love her, and the handsome little boy they had created. She had shunned the life he had given her. Would her brothers have left her as bait? Would she have allowed herself to be used as bait? At this moment, he wondered if he really knew Colette at all.

But she had sworn, crossing her heart in the eyes of

God, that she was not lying about the men who had taken Enio. Colette was a devout Catholic, as was he, and wouldn't take an oath like that lightly. He had to take that into consideration, but he couldn't help but feel like the pawn in somebody's game.

Colette sank to the edge of her brother's bed, massaging her leg, raising the hem of the dress to just below her knee. Donato knew how to relieve her pain, but she was no longer his concern and she didn't ask for his help.

He watched as she ran her hand over her ankle, kneading the muscles. His fingers curled inside his palms, fighting the need—no, the desire—to run his healing touch over her silky skin and erase the pain that had come from the night of her abduction.

She glanced up at him. Her hand resting on her ankle. She said nothing. Neither did he, but knew they both thought about those moments when he'd done just that. He forced his mind away from the image of touching her, reminding himself of who she was not. His loving wife. "Colette. Do you know any of your brother's acquaintances? A place he'd go in case of trouble?"

"He'd go to Jordan." She answered barely above a whisper, tired and looking more disheartened than she should if this were a plot in which she played a part. The usual green of her pupils had darkened, blending into the shadows around her teardrop eyes. He almost wished he could trust her, making this situation easier, but as it stood, he couldn't.

"But Jordan's not here—" He stopped, hearing something from the courtyard. "Did you hear that?"

"From inside," she again whispered. "Could be a cat or something, *non*?"

"You stay here." He headed toward Loul's door, when he hesitated and faced her. "Colette, I know you have the pistol under your shawl."

She nodded.

"You know how to use it. I taught you. In the case…"

"I know how to use it," she whispered, but an underlying hint of surprise at his concern changed the tone of her words slightly. "You taught me well."

Yes, he had, but he didn't appreciate the betrayal of his own words in making her think he cared in the least.

"Wait here." Donato entered the upper balcony and treaded lightly on his feet, working his way to one of the corner stairways to the courtyard. He didn't know the layout of the house, and in the darkness found it difficult to navigate. Once there, he saw nothing but convoluted shadows until someone moved behind the tall white statue in the center of the courtyard. "I see you, *camarada*, you come out and we talk."

Donato kept walking toward the water fountain, but to his disappointment, no one was there. He didn't know when or how, but the culprit had escaped. He glanced up the stairs and allowed his concern for Colette to find his voice.

"Colette, lock the door!"

He shouted the warning only a second before something came down on his head. He heard the *crack* and felt his skin give way. Colette's scream penetrated his throbbing brain. Blood poured over his eyes. He sank to the cold flagstone of the courtyard. Carnival raged outside those walls, but the voices faded as Donato fell into a cavern of blue and black shadows.

Someone slapped his cheek, but he couldn't respond.

He heard scuffling sounds, and then water hit his face. He jolted. Coming to life, he wiped his face and looked up at his assailant.

Loul.

Donato pulled himself to an upright position, rubbing the back of his head, which hurt like an iron ball had gone through it. "What did you hit me with?"

"This." Loul held up a brick and smiled.

"Why?"

"I've heard enough Spanish tonight to knock every one of them to the ground. I would have finished you off with a lead ball to that thick Spanish head of yours if Colette hadn't stopped me."

"And this is your brother?" Donato rubbed his head. Damn, it hurt.

"He is, but can you get up? I help you upstairs, you must lie down."

"He's already done that," Loul snipped before offering a hand. "I'd just as soon leave you flat out on the ground, you bastard."

Donato said nothing, not wanting to further inflame the situation until he could handle his own feet. Colette had delicately wrapped his arm around her shoulders, but the brother, he grabbed Donato's other arm and started to drag him.

"What the hell is he doing here? Come back for more?" Loul acted as if Donato was a sack of dead meat, keeping his conversation directed toward Colette.

"We were looking for you, Loul. What happened?"

"It's been a long night, thanks to this bastard."

Donato couldn't keep up; his feet staggered under

him, and every thought that tried to make headway fell underneath his own confusion.

"Forgive him, Donato. He did not know who you were, n'est-ce pas?"

"Sounds like he knew exactly who I was," Donato said.

"I knew you were Spanish, and for tonight, that's all I needed." Loul followed them into a bedroom, where Donato flopped on the bed in a seemingly drunken state. His mind whirled with no brakes, and he couldn't sort out Loul's words fast enough.

"Here, we wash that." Colette, who had returned with a bowl of water and cloth, started to wash the injury toward the back of his head. Her touch was more soothing than he'd like to admit, reminding him of only a moment ago when he had denied her his tender ministrations.

"Don't make a habit of this, Colette."

She smiled, the first one he had seen all evening. He had always liked her smile. Her lips, full and sweet, formed a perfect square, and when she'd smile, that little square would stretch across her face and brighten all her features. But that was yesterday. This was today.

"I'll be in the parlor, sister, when you are done pampering him."

"Go, Loul, build a fire. There is a chill in the air."

Donato wanted to complain about all of it, but he couldn't keep his eyes open.

"I'll build a damn fire. You tell that pirate to wake up if he wants to know where his son is, because I know."

Chapter Four

Colette nibbled on the breakfast Loul had thrown together for them, waiting for Donato to wake up. Loul's story made sense. She only hoped sharing it with Donato would give them more insight. She glanced up at the clock, and it was after dawn, and the streets of New Orleans had started to quiet once again. Carnival was over for another year.

Loul finished off a cup of coffee. "Need another?"

"No." Colette didn't have an appetite but knew she had to eat something to keep up her strength. Right about now, Enio might be stirring to wake, if he had been allowed to sleep. What would he think not to have his mother at his side?

The thought brought on such a painful squeeze to the middle of her chest she didn't think she'd ever breathe again. She wouldn't survive this, if Enio were gone. She simply could not go on, not knowing what had happened to him, what he was doing at that moment. She put down her plate, unable to finish, when Donato walked into the parlor.

She rose to her feet, reaching for a plate she had fixed for him of eggs and warmed-over ham. "Loul made us something to eat."

Donato didn't hesitate, but accepted the plate as he walked by before taking a seat in front of the fire. He noted Loul sitting across from him. "I'll eat, then we talk."

Loul took a long drink of coffee, then lowered his cup. "I didn't nap through the meal. I talk while you eat."

Donato was shoveling his food in quickly. "Then speak."

"I found out about your ship being seized this morning. A couple of hours after Jordan left for Boston."

Donato watched Loul from those dark, sometimes unfathomable, eyes. His ebony hair had been brushed back on the sides, but splayed out in waves that trimmed his neck. Colette watched his mouth as he ate, remembering it was cup-shaped and how his smile would thin out the upper lip, but not the bottom. The flames from the firelight blended well with the olive tint of his skin and settled into the hollows of his cheeks.

In spite of his lifestyle and weathered, rough exterior, he was a handsome man, with an aristocratic look, contrary to that of a pirate. She remembered thinking that the first night she had seen him, but couldn't remember when that had been.

Donato reached over and picked up a cup put out by Loul, washing his food down as her brother explained his efforts to leave New Orleans. But in doing so he had seen a band of men carrying Enio, and he had followed them. With Donato's continued silence, Loul elaborated on his story.

"One must have doubled back behind me. I was knocked

on the head in very much the same way you were tonight, except you woke up here. I woke up on a ship."

Donato finished off his plate, rose from his chair, and brushed his hands off over the fire. "You have wine?"

"Over there." Loul pointed, looking frustrated. He glanced at Colette, but she had nothing to offer. She knew Donato wasn't believing a word of it.

"Please continue with your fascinating story, young Loul. I'm—what is the American word?—riveted."

Loul drew a sharp breath. "Sounds like a waste of time."

Colette rose to her feet, but losing her balance on her sore leg, she sank back down. "Donato, you must listen, d'accord? For it is dangerous not to."

"I am listening, Colette, but have heard nothing that tells me where my son is."

Colette motioned for Loul to continue.

Loul, looking as angry as Donato, cleared his throat. "I woke up in the cargo hold. Now I know ships—"

"Quite well. Did you silently disembark like you did on my island?"

Colette started to rise, sensing an altercation, but remained seated when Donato motioned for her to relax.

"Mis disculpas." He apologized. *"Continuad, por favor."*

Loul had poured his own wine and downed the last of it before dropping his attention on Donato. "I thought I had been pressed into the Spanish service until I heard voices. Men were talking, mostly Spanish, I couldn't understand much of it."

Donato looked to offer another remark, but pressed his lips together as if barely holding the comment in check. "Can you repeat any of the, ah…Spanish words you heard?"

"*Niño*."

"Boy. But were they talking about my boy? There are many who work ships."

Loul leaned forward, putting his elbows on his knees. "I don't understand."

Donato was about to answer until Colette interrupted. "Loul, he doesn't believe any of this. He believes we have hidden Enio and this is an elaborate scheme to throw him off track."

Surprise lifted Loul's brows into a twisted arch above his eyes. He leaned in real close to Donato. "I have an easier way to throw you off track. I could shoot you dead in my parlor and be hailed a hero for doin' it."

Donato's expression remained impassive, but Colette could see him thinking. After a long moment of silence that thickened with each tick of the clock, he motioned for Loul to continue. "What other words did you hear?"

"*Heredero.*"

"Heir," Donato interpreted.

"*Nobleza.*"

"Nobility," Donato whispered, as if something was fitting into place.

"I heard a woman's voice. She spoke Spanish, but I heard nothing that I can remember except what I think might be her name."

Loul glanced up as he tried to recall it. "Renee? Rita? Something like that."

"Rayna." Donato visibly paled. "Was it Rayna?"

"Yeah, that's what it was. Rayna."

Donato silently stood, putting down his glass of wine. He gathered his things, hooked his flintlock onto his braces, and pulled on an overcoat, compliments of Jordan. "Let's go, Loul."

Loul jumped into action, grabbing his own pistol. "If you think Enio is on that ship, you and I aren't enough to take him off."

"But who is she? Why would she have Enio?" Colette stood as well, ignoring the burning pain in her leg that nagged continuously. "Donato?"

"I can tell you the who, not the why." He turned just as he reached the door leading to the courtyard. "She is Rayna de la Roche. My sister."

. . .

Donato checked the street before stepping free of the abat-vent. It was approaching seven in the morning, and some of the shops were beginning to reopen. Horse-drawn carriages slogged through the street as New Orleans finally returned to normal.

Loul stepped out after Donato, followed by Colette.

Donato motioned for her to stay. "This is not a place for a woman."

"But a day for a mother. I go with you."

Knowing the futility of arguing with her and not wanting to delay, he acquiesced.

"Stay close to me."

That same look of surprise usurped her beautiful features, as when he had tried to keep her safe earlier. He wanted to tell her that his concern was only because she was the mother of his son, but that might be a lie, and he'd had enough deception for one night.

A light fog rolled off the gulf and tainted the buildings and roads in a gray light. The smell of sewage and old seawater saturated the air. He hated this town. He hated America, for he had fought as much for her freedom as Colette's swamp-rat brothers, yet Jordan and Loul were free, hailed as heroes for it, while Donato remained a wanted man.

"The ship you were on. It flew a Spanish flag?"

"I couldn't see, too dark."

"Trust me, it did." Donato started walking down Rampart with his small entourage behind him. A swamp rat and a woman. It sounded like Rayna had an army with her, and Loul was right, they were no match.

Between Donato and Loul, they were able to shave off some time by cutting through alleys and courtyards, but would it be enough? By the soft breeze that spun out over the gulf, the weather gauge was perfect for gaining headway out of the river and into the ocean. The morning was crisp with winter, but ships would come and go in such favorable weather.

Rayna.

His thoughts kept floating back to his sister, remembering all too well her expression when she had learned he intended to leave Spain. They had always been a unit, supporting each other through the difficult years of their youth, but she had wanted no part of leaving Spain and had tried desperately to discourage him.

He hadn't heard anything from her in five years. A message had arrived a year ago, before Colette had left him. Rayna had talked of his obligation to their father and his need to return home. But Donato saw that relationship differently and would do nothing for the need of his father.

They were not only miles apart in their location, but miles apart in their political beliefs. He didn't welcome that connection to home and had never responded. Apparently, that was a mistake. Whatever she was trying to communicate to him was serious enough to sail the ocean and steal his son.

How had she known about Enio?

His marriage to Colette had been kept relatively secret. And what purpose would Enio serve? An heir? Not possible. Enio was not Spain-born and only half Spanish.

The trio cut through another alley to emerge on the corner of Saint Pierre and Chartres Streets, then halted. The morning sun had burned off the early fog, and the Place d'Armes had several constables standing about, conversing with one another.

Donato motioned to back out of the square until one of the constables turned and saw all three of them. Donato had worn a hat in hopes of disguising himself somewhat, but the constable took an extra interest in them.

"Get out of here. Go." Loul stepped to the forefront, motioning for Donato to keep going. "Go. I will stall them."

To deflect their attention, Donato stumbled and swung Colette around in his arms and kissed her while swaying as if he had indulged in spirits. Loul picked up on the charade and wove his unsteady gait toward the police.

The moment Donato's lips touched Colette's, he lost the stumble to his gait and held himself steady, needing all his strength to keep the kiss as nothing more than a pretense. Out of the corner of his eye, he saw that Loul had distracted the police. He could have let go, but he allowed himself to feel her lips beneath his, flooding his body with a need so intense, an undeniable yearning that he could not deny.

He pushed away from her, sucking in enough air to clear his head, at least enough to stay steady on his feet. A slight rose color shaded her lips swollen from his kiss, and he didn't miss the slight mist in her eyes. He turned away from her, unable to contemplate her response to their intimate touch.

Having evaded the interest of the police, they turned and crossed behind the square, turning down Saint Ann's toward the market where vendors were beginning to open up their stalls for a day of selling. Continuing beyond the market, he and Colette walked along the levee toward the port. He started to rush his step, knowing his sister's ship might not be there. The weather was so favorable, he'd set sail if he were in port. Colette was struggling to keep up, her limp more pronounced, but he kept going, needing to ensure his sister's ship was still in harbor.

When he reached the jagged shoreline, the Spanish frigate with a flag of royalty had just pulled anchor. Her sails captured the wind and her hull plowed the waters. Colette started to run down the levee but her bad leg hampered her, and she fell. She fought to get to her feet. "No!"

Donato wrapped her in his arms and started to pull her back.

"No!" She fought. "Don't let them leave! Don't let them get away!"

But Donato continued to pull her away from the water and onto solid ground. She struggled, kicking him in the shins, swinging her fists, but he held on.

"You let them take our son!"

"We can't stop them."

"But Enio, he does not understand this. He needs me."

"Not today, Colette, not today."

A woman appeared on the starboard side as they floated free of the port. He recognized her long black hair fluttering in the wind, her petite frame leaning against the gunwale, and the royal tilt to her chin.

Rayna.

"Oh, *mi adorado hermano*, how nice to see you," she shouted through a speaking trumpet in her usual condescending way. Some things never changed.

The regal ship, with embellished bulwarks of carved woodwork and golden trim, floated along the river with a royal flag fluttering overhead. His father was rich, but not that rich to fund such an expedition. Flashes of their childhood, him and Rayna, niggled beneath his thoughts. He dismissed them, swallowing hard, not letting the memories forward because if he did, he'd remember it all.

"He is of no use to you, Rayna," Donato called as her ship sailed toward the sea. "He is not Spain-born; he is not all Spanish."

"Oh but *sí*, he will be of great use. Such a *dulce niño*. I knew the moment her brother escaped us, he'd find you. I hate to take and run, but you know, I must," she responded in her thick Spanish accent, offering a throaty laugh before disappearing below deck as the bow broke into open waters.

"No!" Colette screamed. "No, oh God, no!"

Her body crumbled in Donato's arms, shaking, sobbing.

Holding her back flush against his chest, he wrapped his arms around her, cocooning her within. She curled over his arms in agony, lifting her feet from the ground. He knew her pain; he had felt it the day she had taken their son and left the island, but that didn't make him as immune to her anguish as he would have liked. Her cries pierced his pride.

His wife and son were in trouble, and he was helpless to stop it. Colette was fragile and in need of him. He fought the squeeze her cries brought to his heart, reminding himself this wouldn't have happened had she not taken Enio off the island into her world with her brothers.

Donato glanced around, not wanting to attract attention. "Colette, be quiet."

"You let them take our son!"

"For the moment." He made sure she was steady on her feet before he released her, but he realized his mistake the moment she jabbed the end of her pistol into his throat.

"That ship flies a royal flag." She pulled back the hammer. Her voice as lethal as the muzzle pressed into his neck. "Who—are—you?"

• • •

Loul came running up behind them, immediately putting a restraining hand on Colette's arm. "This isn't the place. You're attracting attention. I have an idea."

Loul's words neither distracted her nor discouraged her desire to release her weapon. Her finger on the trigger wanted nothing more than to pull. She knew she shouldn't—couldn't, wouldn't—but that didn't stop the determination her body seemed to have. Through tight lips and without a breath in between, she answered her brother, "He let that ship leave with my son."

"*Our* son," Donato corrected, despite the dangerous position of not only her pistol, but her finger on the trigger.

"There was no way to stop it, Colette." Loul worked his hand up along her arm until he was able to block the trigger.

"Let go."

Her body started to shake uncontrollably. Her teeth rattled, and a shudder raced across her shoulders, yet she wasn't cold. She was angry, devastated, and defeated. Her only hope to get her son back was the very man who stood within her crosshairs. The very man whose chest she wanted to pummel, eyes she wanted to scratch out, glorious hair she'd willingly pull out, strand by strand. Only God knew how much she wanted to pull that trigger.

Donato made no attempt to stop her. He made no attempt to free himself. Instead, he watched her with those dark eyes, trimmed with long thick lashes and topped with thick black eyebrows that were angled slightly. But his expression, like before with Loul, had remained impassive, and she knew by that stonewall look, he blamed her as much as she blamed him.

"He could not stop it." Loul peeled the gun from her hands. "I was on that ship, Colette."

She stepped away from Donato, waiting for an explanation, but he said nothing. "Why do you not defend yourself?"

Donato glanced around them before he spoke. "Because I do not care what you think. But that is the last time you will aim a pistol at me."

"You did not answer my question. Who are you?"

"A man who's trying to get *our* son back." Donato dismissed her with the turn of his head toward Loul. "What is your idea?"

Loul nodded over his shoulder, indicating the constables. "Had a little discussion with them. They are looking for you. They seized your ship and your men. They are in the Calaboose, near the courtyard, where prisoners of war are held. To go after Enio, we'll need a ship and a crew."

For the first time, Colette noted a change in Donato's expression. Impressed with Loul, he responded, "We have to break them out and steal a ship."

"What?" Colette could hardly swallow. But seemingly undaunted by the task ahead, Loul jumped right in.

He wet his lips, then looked around to ensure no one was within hearing distance. "Jordan has a ship. It's not equipped like *Le Vengeur* was, but it's all we got. Your ship would be too difficult to steal. They are manning it with U.S. sailors. I think Jordan's is seaworthy."

"I can sail anything." He slid a glance at Loul. "Even a polly boat in thirty-foot swells."

Colette braced herself for a defensive rebuttal from her brother, having seen the small boat he and Jordan had forced Donato into when they had cast him upon the gulf waves after her rescue.

"So you did." Loul gave him a casual nod followed with a slight smile.

Donato drew a deep breath, most likely to calm himself. Colette could see the muscles twitch near his mouth and the slight squint to his eyes. "I have other ships that are equipped right. We only need to get as far as the island. But I won't leave my men locked up. We must have a crew to sail any ship."

Colette looked between them, not believing the situation they so casually discussed. The Calaboose was the infamous prison located on the corner of Saint Pierre and Royale, behind the Cabildo, government buildings. "We are not talking about breaking pirates out of jail, are we?"

Loul shrugged. "Unless you have a better idea. That is our only option. I could try to round up some of our old sailors, but they were pirates as well—"

"And not as trustworthy as my men. They are as loyal to me as I am to them. I will not leave them." Donato met Colette's eyes. "I surrounded you with gentlemen. You left to be surrounded by thieving swamp rats."

"My brothers are not—" She didn't bother to finish, because as quickly as he shifted his thoughts to her, he shifted them away.

Loul dismissed Donato's comment with a wave of his hand. "We are brethren in this cause."

"So we are." Donato glanced between the two of them, as if sizing up the measly entourage. Colette didn't miss the tightness of his jaw, the slight pull on his mouth. He stood a good head above Loul, and Loul was taller than Jordan. Among the three of them, Donato was the man who could make something happen. She and Loul knew it. So did Donato. He narrowed his gaze on Loul. "Where is the ship?"

"In the bayous, Yellow Sun." Loul gave Donato a suspicious look. "You must be familiar with it."

"*Si.*" Donato thought a moment. "I have heard there is a water route through the swamps from New Orleans, do you know it? To travel by land would take too long."

Loul nodded, stealing a glance at Colette, as if expecting she would protest going by water. But, how could she? As they stood debating their next move, her sweet little boy was sailing to the open sea. With her silence, Loul continued, "I can have a pirogue ready at a moment's notice. That is the only way to travel those backwaters. There are many routes."

"We need only one route, but three to four of these… ah…pirogues."

His request surprised Colette. "And who is going with us?"

Again he dismissed her, concentrating on Loul. "Can you get them?"

Loul nodded with confidence, even breaking his face with a slight smile. "I can do that."

"All right," Donato conceded, and without warning he scooped Colette up into his arms. "You can't make the walk back."

He tried to say it with indifference, as if the overture were simply in their best interest. But beneath his constructed facade, she caught the gentle tone he used to reserve only for her.

She placed a hand to his chest for balance, not wanting to feel the movement of his muscles beneath her fingers, nor the solid wall of strength he presented. He carried her with little effort, and he was right, she could not have made the walk back. But the close proximity to his body, being in his arms, brought on a rush of feelings more crippling than her leg.

She tamped them down with a deep breath and a hard swallow, refusing, simply refusing to feel anything as the heat of his body soaked through to hers. She closed her eyes, begging her body to stop feeling what her mind refused to remember.

As if hearing her thoughts, Donato looked down at her huddled against his chest.

"Get your rest, Colette. You'll need it."

"For?"

"You're going into the Calaboose."

• • •

Colette approached the Calaboose with Loul at her side.

He played the servant; she, an Ursuline sister. There was something sinful in pretending to represent the Lord. Colette prayed Sainte Ursula would understand as she walked through the gates into the long courtyard, but thoughts of Enio made her capable of just about anything.

She had borrowed a change of habit from the Ursuline Sisters as well as a basket of tapers made by the orphans to raise money for their hospital. The long flowing black gown, covered by another black tunic, weighted down her steps. With a throat dry from nerves and a tight-fitting wimple, she could barely swallow. Her veil hung straight down her back, and she had tied the rosary to the cincture. She tried to walk with ease as if she wore this clothing on a daily basis, but it was heavy, warm, and cumbersome.

The plan was for her and Loul to gain entrance to the police prison by offering the tapers to sell to the civil guards and to offer spiritual nourishment to the prisoners.

Loul kept step beside her, holding the basket of tapers. Donato had laid out everything she was to learn as she walked through the courtyard, but the closer she came to the city guard's office, the more muddled her mind became.

The Calaboose had a reputation that spanned the foreign seas. Anyone and everyone knew of the Calaboose, and most pirates were in fear of ending up there. Standing behind the Cabildo, the building was long, black, with grated windows.

The courtyard was the only entrance and exit, and many of the prisoners could see those gateways from their cells. To the rear of the yard were cells that housed prisoners from the war and some British sympathizers who found themselves on the losing side after the War in 1812. Loul had learned that Donato's men, because there was a fear that Spain would become their next enemy, were considered political prisoners, meaning they would be accessible from the courtyard.

She approached the city guard's office with care, adjusting her wimple and veil to not only cover her hair but offer a certain amount of anonymity. Not well known in the city, she still didn't want the city guards to get a good look at her. Loul wore a hat that hung down over his forehead and obscured some of his dark face. She admired Loul's countenance— steady, unwavering, committed to finding her son.

There were two city guards in the office when she entered. Both were overly respectful of the Ursuline Sisters, granting nearly every wish, but not before asking for a personal blessing of their own. They knelt before her, and she placed a hand to each man's head and whispered a prayer in Latin asking for God's blessing. The entire time, Loul kept glancing over at her as if he couldn't believe her level of masquerading.

Though the officers tried to discourage her from seeing the prisoners, finally, in hopes of giving them redemption in their darkest hour, they obliged, starting with the far side of the prison, where the political prisoners were held.

After wading through British sympathizers and British soldiers, she moved to the last cell in that row, the farthest from the gate, but on the ground level. There were four men in one cell. It was large, with a bench along each wall and a view of the courtyard. She recognized most of the men as Donato's, but motioned with her hand for them not to give her away.

"The sister is here to give you a blessing," the city guard announced as he had in the previous cells.

"Ah… S'il vous plaît…I will speak with them, d'accord?" Colette motioned for the guard to leave her.

The guard knew he had been dismissed and seemed to give that a second thought before he nodded and pointed toward the office. "I will be very close if you need me, Sister."

"*Merci.*" Colette bowed her head slightly as the officer left her standing to the outside of the cells. The moment he was out of hearing range, she turned to the prisoners.

"La senora." Ramón came to the grated window. "How is it that you are here?"

"Donato sent me."

"He is free then?"

"*Oui,* and this is my brother, Loul."

"Where are the others?" Loul immediately started the questions. "There are only four of you here. What cells are they in?"

But Donato's men were not so quick to trust her or her brother. She could see the excitement of seeing a face they knew fade the moment Loul started to interrogate them.

"Ramón, Donato sent me to find out information about all of you. Our son, Enio, has been taken." Saying those words aloud brought on a rush of fear so crippling she nearly lost sight of where she was and why. Fighting to take a breath, she reinforced her needs. "Enio has been taken by Rayna. We—Donato, my brother, and I—are not sure why, but must give chase. Donato needs his crew to sail, even if he must break them out of here. But where are the others?"

"Rayna?" Ramón glanced back at the other men, as if to validate her story.

"You must help us get you out." She could hear the fear in her voice. A plea that left her cold to think she desperately needed these men to help her. The same men she had left behind and the same men who had fought gallantly against her brother's ship and lost. Men she had betrayed, like Donato, and that thought drained her remaining strength.

Loul seemed to sense she was folding under the pressure and again pushed for information. "We need to plan how to get you out of here, so where are they? We have seen all the cells on the ground level. Were they taken somewhere else?"

"No, senor, they are not here. It is only the four of us who were captured."

Colette felt the blood leave her face as quickly as she saw the pale hue of Loul's against his dark skin. "Then... where are they?"

"Gone. They took the tender and polly and scattered, left port before the U.S. soldiers were able to board. There is no crew to sail a ship. They're gone."

• • •

"They had to have gone upriver." Donato paced back and forth; the heels of his half boots struck the wood flooring with every turn. The entire notion of nearly forty men crowding into two small boats and heading to the open sea was preposterous.

He couldn't decide if Ramón was telling the truth or feeding Colette information that would throw her off track. Perhaps he thought Colette was working with the law to capture the rest. In the eyes of Ramón and most of his men, Colette was not to be trusted.

"They would not have gone into open waters in a tender," Donato reiterated.

"The Calaboose strikes fear in every criminal." Colette tried to add reason to the conjecture. "Maybe they believed they could do it. Like you said, Donato. You sailed a tender across the gulf."

"I did, but no one sails like me."

"Except Jordan." Loul raised his hands in surrender the moment Donato whirled on him.

Donato flexed his fist, using all of his strength not to swing it. Colette's little brother had begun to wear on him; he had seen him on the forecastle of *Le Vengeur* when *El Diablo* and Jordan's ship had crashed bowsprits. Had it not been for Jordan and Loul, Enio would not be on his way to Spain.

"We are brethren in this cause," Loul asserted, as if reading Donato's thoughts.

"Then don't try my patience with the likes of Jordan Kincaid."

Donato glanced over to Colette, having heard a slight intake of air.

She was sitting by the fire, still dressed in her sisterhood robes. From where he stood, he could see the mist in her eyes, the slight tremble to her lip, and how she forced her spine straight with every breath. Her pain so visible, he could reach out and touch it and damned if he didn't want to. He wanted to pull her into his arms and promise to make this all right again. He had every right to. She was still his wife, he, her husband, but soothing Colette's broken heart was for a man with an open heart who loved her. She had made her choice, and so must he.

He was not that man.

He pulled in a deep breath, sorting through their

options. He had a missing crew and a questionable ship. He glanced at Loul. If Jordan had walked away from the life of piracy, why did he have a ship hidden in the bayous? Donato shook his head, staying on task. The only thing that mattered was the fact that Colette's older brother did. Without a ship, Donato would never get Enio back.

"How many guards?"

"Two," Loul answered. "The gate is unlocked. There is one locked door between the men we saw and Chartres Street"

"The guards were armed, Loul." Colette added, "With flintlocks, I think."

Loul confirmed. "They were."

"Not as armed as I will be. This is the plan."

Colette turned and watched. Loul slid to the edge of his chair and listened.

"You said you could get pirogues to go out the back way of New Orleans to get to Liberty Oak, ah…Yellow Sun?"

Loul nodded that he could.

"Good, draw me a map of where to meet you. Have a few ready to go by five this afternoon."

Colette slowly stood as he continued to speak. Her body turned with his pacing, and she listened to his every word and watched his every step.

"You and Colette meet me there. Garner as much supplies as you are able. Do you need money?"

Loul shook his head that he did not. "There are supplies at Yellow Sun. And you?"

"Me?" Donato stopped pacing and looked at the two of them. "I'll be at the Calaboose."

Loul's eyes widened. "That's the plan?"

"No!" Colette came to life. She reached out to him, but when Donato's attention swung toward her, she hesitated, pulling back her hand. He hated himself for having wanted to feel the light touch of her concern, but only a fool would think more of it. He was her only hope of getting Enio back, and that alone drove her to worry about him. "It is too dangerous."

He dismissed her comment and faced Loul. "Meet me by five."

With that said, Donato left Loul's house, unable to shake that moment of concern Colette had and wondering, perhaps savoring, the underlying reason. His reaction to her sudden caring nearly blindsided him, and before he made a fool of himself, he left the house to focus on how to get his men out of the infamous Calaboose.

He headed over to the Café de Réfugiés, next to the Hôtel de la Marine, for a heavy rum and time to think, to distract his mind long enough to pack up those meandering emotions about Colette and stick them back into the dirty little box from which they had escaped. Colette care? *Why do I care?*

He stepped inside the small café. In spite of the hovering smoke, he found a table facing the only door and pulled back a rugged wooden chair that made tracks in the dirt floor and sat down, measuring up the room's patrons with a glance. He wasn't exactly in disguise, but neither was he dressed as most had seen in the past.

When a waiter approached, he took Donato's order without giving him a second glance. Donato ordered food but mostly spirits, needing a wash down of anything stronger than Loul's wine to settle further memories of Colette that still managed to stay afloat, in spite of his protest. He refocused his mind on his son, why his sister might have taken him, and how the hell he would get him back.

No sooner had his food arrived when a shadow covered his table. He looked up at the clandestine figure looming over him. He felt no need to pull his weapon or attempt an escape. Instead he awaited the man's next move.

"Donato de la Roche," came a hoarse, whispered voice with an American accent. "The most wanted pirate in New Orleans?"

"Si." Intrigued, Donato motioned for the man to sit down. *"Tomad asiento a mi lado."*

The man slid into a chair opposite and leaned his elbows on the table. Blond hair stuck out from under his hood and his eyes appeared blue in the darkened room. He looked straight at Donato.

"I know your situation," the American whispered, then looked around at the other patrons before continuing. "As does most of New Orleans."

With wall-to-wall sea rogues and smugglers, secrecy was always best. Donato leaned in to be heard. "Tell me why you seek me out. As no else in New Orleans would have such courage to approach me."

The American smiled as he spoke. "I have a proposition that will benefit you…and me."

• • •

Colette waited near the river's edge, setting her small valise on the shoreline, inhaling thick, damp air that filled her lungs with worry. Taking care to stay out of the tall marsh grass, she paced under a large cypress tree whose shadow had killed off most of the foliage beneath the spread of its branches. A chilly wind brushed off the waters and rushed in beneath her sister's habit, freezing her bones and making her body shake nearly as much as when she had foolishly marched into the Calaboose. But now, Donato had made that same march and had yet to return.

"Why isn't he here? He said five."

Loul had lined up three pirogues with their pilots and tied them at a wharf just off the inlet, little traveled, except by smugglers. As Loul explained, since the war, the smuggling business hadn't been as good and many a pilot needed work. The men Loul had rented the pirogues from had often been used by him and Jordan during their smuggling days. But reassuring her that they were trustworthy and dependable and wouldn't discuss their movements, even if they learned Donato de la Roche would be on board, did little to ease her nerves.

She again paced, wishing this were done, wishing Enio were home and safe, wishing Donato— She halted her thinking. What did she want Donato to do?

She had almost betrayed herself when she reached out to him, revealing her concern for him. That kiss in the street, though meant to ward off the police, had nearly melted her body into his. When he had pulled away from her, the cool morning air had chilled her to the bone, leaving her craving a kiss for which she had no right.

Her pacing added to the pain in her leg. She started to limp, but couldn't stop her repetitive movement. On the water's edge, they were surrounded by large cypress trees and underlying palmettos and brush. The bayou, which smelled swampy and thick, was shallow with rippling black waves of water. The pirogues had been pushed through the thick mud to the shoreline and now waited, hidden by the tall marsh grass and falling sun.

As day retreated into dusk, rayless shadows replaced sun-filled spaces, and the water around them turned inky. Colette hated the idea of getting on anything that floated over water, especially something as precarious as these boats looked. Unable to go back to Jordan's home, she had little to pack. With the day nearing its end, the habit had some warmth, but she sorely missed the fur-lined coat she'd left at Jordan's.

"Loul, something has happened." Her impatience had overpowered her nerves, making her body feel the bite of a hundred mosquitoes when none had yet to find her skin. "It is well past five and getting dark."

Loul nodded in agreement, but she knew he refused to buy into her fear. "He will come. We have no other option but to wait."

"But with only four men, we cannot sail a ship that needs fifty."

"We take this step by step, Colette. He must have a plan. We did our part. He'll do his."

"What if it is a trick and he is now sailing off with Enio?"

"It is not a trick and you know that."

"If that is true, it might be worse, *non*? What if he's in danger? What if they recognized him and he's now in the same cell as the men he thought to rescue? Don't answer me, I can't bear to think of anything happening—" Colette sucked in her words before they spilled out for the world to hear, but it was too late. Loul glanced over at her.

"Who are we talking about, Colette? Enio or Donato?"

Colette drew a sharp breath, stunned her feelings had become that obvious. If Loul could read her soul, what did Donato know? "We are talking about my son."

"Someone comes," alerted one of the pilots.

Loul pulled Colette down next to him, hiding in the high marsh reeds until they were sure as to who approached. Soon she heard Donato's voice.

The relief turned her knees to mush and lifted her heart to her throat. Before betraying herself, Colette tried to dismiss her response as having a simple need of him. She needed him desperately to rescue her son, but the denial lasted only seconds until other feelings bled through her defiance.

Loul stood. "Here he comes, and not with four men. He's got many more."

"From?" That should have been welcome news, but Colette hadn't liked Jordan's crew of pirates any more than she did the pilots waiting to leave shore. They reminded her of the awful men who had stolen her off the ship she had been on from France, who had nearly killed her brother and had sold her at auction. With what kind of men would she once again be immersed?

Colette gathered her strength and rose to stand next to Loul as the men and Donato approached.

"Oh my Lord, Loul." Relief washed the strength from her legs; she fought to remain standing. "Those are his men, the ones who sail his ship!"

Donato halted at the water's edge, surrounded by at least forty men. He grinned, something she hadn't seen in a long time, and she realized how much she had missed seeing him like that.

"We found each other. They weren't captured."

"And the ones in the Calaboose?"

"Got them, too."

"And what of those young guards?" Colette asked, envisioning their inexperience against a man like Donato.

"They were no trouble."

Colette hesitated and wrapped her hand around the large cross hanging over her habit, saying a silent prayer for the guards who had met their fate. A motion Donato seemed to catch.

He waited as his men started to board the other pirogues before addressing her.

"No need for prayers. They're already in heaven, Colette. I told you I'd be heavily armed." He pulled a bag of coins from his pocket and jiggled it so the coins made noise. "Amazing what a few Napoleons will buy."

"You bribed them?"

He looked surprised at her conclusion. "What else would I have done in the middle of the city, in the middle of a prison that they'd like to put me in?"

A lighthearted chuckle escaped her lips. "I don't know."

"Pray if you like, but I suspect they're at the grog shop." For just a split second, his eyes met hers before he whispered in his thick Spanish accent for only her to hear. "*Tal vez*, I am not this bad man one thinks."

"Perhaps," she conceded, unable to form another word. The heat of his breath touched her cheek lightly before it was gone, more a mirage than real, a tease, nothing more. She fought to maintain her posture when all she wanted was to fall into him. "Perhaps."

Once loaded, the pirogues were listing at least three to four inches below the water line. The encroaching water nearly paralyzed her. She thought to complain, but noted that the water around their ankles caused no concern for either Loul or Donato.

"You know how to go?" Donato asked, looking a little unsure of their traveling arrangements.

"I do." Loul nodded, but gave Donato a suspicious glance. "Would you rather steal a ship in port?"

"I prefer not to be chased. There's a gunboat in port."

"Then we do it this way. No fear, these are my men."

"I have no fear." Donato winked at Loul. "The forty-plus aboard are *my* men."

The pilots pushed off and they were slowly gliding down the bayou, each turning to follow the previous. Colette's feet were cold from the water, and lines of green slime started to collect on the bottom of her robe.

Dark, dense green foliage lined the banks. They pushed beyond tussocks and cypress trees, and the night grew darker, colder, and more forbidding. The men were silent; the only noise was that of a small indiscernible wake as they passed over the still water.

Colette started to shiver. A cool winter breeze pushed against the pirogues. Relieved to still have on her habit, she pulled the wimple and veil in closer around her head and neck. Then a coat was draped over her shoulders. She half turned to see Donato standing next to her. She wanted to turn completely and sink into his warm arms, but she would not be welcome.

"*Merci*" was her only acknowledgement.

Donato whispered to Loul, who stood to the other side of her. "There is something ahead in the water."

She inhaled, a deep, wet breath of air. "What is it?"

"A pirogue like us," said the pilot over his shoulder. "But smugglers."

"And how is that different?" Donato asked, the sarcasm heavy in his voice. "Will they let us pass?"

"I don't know," Loul answered.

"They are thieves." A man from the back of the first pirogue spoke. He sounded American. Confused, having never heard an American around Donato, Colette glanced over at him, but he was focused on the immediate situation.

"*Si*, I believe. Tell them we are armed but wish to pass in peace," Donato instructed.

"That will not work." Again the American spoke up. Colette leaned back to see who the man was, but he wore a knit cap over his head that shadowed his eyes and a shawl bunched up around his shoulders.

"It is worth a try or I must destroy them," Donato answered, without looking back.

The pilot did as instructed, but there was no answer from the pirogue as it disappeared into the shadows. Their poles continued to dip into the water as the pilot warned they were armed but only wanted to pass.

"Are they going away?" Donato asked.

"It is an ambush," the American spoke.

The pilot nodded and whispered to Donato. "Be ready."

"Draw arms," Donato ordered in a hushed voice. It was passed quietly through the ranks of men. Flintlocks were pulled and at the ready.

"There." Loul motioned toward the shore. "They lie in wait."

Colette couldn't stop the gasp that stole her breath and

left her nearly faint. She'd been here before. On the water, attacked, and only God knows what had happened after that because she couldn't remember! She tried to tuck her memories to the back of her mind, but they were tenacious and clung to her conscious brain, and though they weren't at sea, the back bayous of Louisiana were just as lawless.

Slowly they floated forward, toward the waiting trap.

"Colette," Donato whispered in her ear. "Come here."

Colette stepped closer to him. He pushed her behind him, shielding her body with his. As they approached the trap, Donato motioned for his men to get down. She crouched next to him, kneeling in the water but hanging on to his powerful shoulders with her hands. Her breathing rasped in and out of her lungs with the feel of the same grit and dirt that covered the pirogues.

One shot was fired from the shore, sending off a puff of light before the sound could be heard. Loul shifted position, coming to his knees next to Colette.

"Loul?" He fell against her shoulder. "Loul?"

"A warning shot," the pilot whispered.

Donato glanced toward Loul.

"Warning shot, *diantre*." He raised his pistol. "*¡Fuego!*"

A shower of balls hit the shoreline. Two men fell through the grass and hit the water, the bayou scum rippling around their bodies. The pirogues rocked in the water. Movement started behind the shore trees, followed by the parting of tall marsh grass before all fell silent.

"My warning shot." Donato nodded to the pilot's surprised expression to see such a massive response. "Loul, are you wounded?"

Colette pivoted on her knees toward her bother. "Loul?

We got through, Loul."

He didn't move.

"Loul?

Loul tried to stand but clutched his side as blood seeped through his fingers. He swayed with the rocking planked raft.

"Loul!" Colette shouted seconds before he fell into the black water.

Chapter Five

Within seconds, Donato was in the water, pushing Loul onto the pirogue. Loul's eyes were closed, and he flinched in pain with every movement, but he remained insistent that it was only he who could lead them through the swamp, and they had to bandage him quickly and get him to his feet.

"Do you have a knife?" Colette asked Donato, lifting a portion of her scapular to be cut for a dressing.

"To be this terrifying pirate, I must have a knife."

She had never referred to him in such terms, and it bothered her that he'd think she believed that, but for now she held her tongue and focused on the issue at hand. Donato cut a large square from the scapular of the sister's habit. Colette threw up a quick prayer, entrusting God to understand why she had stolen the habit and now why it would not be returned.

She folded the square over twice and pressed it against her brother's wound, her heart nearly in a free fall. When her ministries had worked and the bleeding stopped, Donato helped Loul to his feet. She hated to see Loul push himself, but appreciated the gentle care Donato gave him. Only Donato was strong enough and caring enough to see her brother through.

The night had turned dark, and the swamp odors of waterlogged vegetation mingled with the cold. Colette tried to keep herself warm in spite of the icy feel of both air and water, even with Donato's coat over her shoulders; her focus never left her brother.

Donato brought one of Loul's arms around his shoulders and leaned his broken body against his. Colette could hear Loul's weakened voice giving directions and the slow, quiet turns of the pirogue. Behind them followed three more pirogues more weighted than they, all working through the dark, silent waters like a huge snake in search of prey.

"I'll try to take you to the ship," Loul barely managed a whisper.

Donato shook his head. "For tonight, *camarada*, you take us to Yellow Sun. I would not take such a ship out on dark waters strange to me."

Loul winced with pain, then whispered after a slight smile, "Jordan would."

"Of course he would." Donato responded drily, but Colette hadn't missed the slight pull of his lips. He seemed to like Loul, and the idle conversation was for distraction. "It is my life's dream to sail like Jordan."

Now it was Loul who laughed, guarding his side from the pain, but Colette was not fooled by his brave mask. The wound was serious. Donato was doing all he could to keep Loul's spirits up and his condition from worsening before reaching Yellow Sun.

Several hours later, they made the final turn. Colette

suspected the ship was hidden where *Le Vengeur* had been moored, but in this darkness, every direction looked the same. Yet Loul knew the waters as easily as giving directions in New Orleans with named streets and lighted lamps, and the pilot followed his instructions to the letter.

Finally, the large hipped roof of Yellow Sun became visible. Though a commanding white mansion in the light of day, it appeared, dark, large, looming, nearly lifeless. The lightless air, the suffocating night, and the silence of the back bayou waters dulled the approaching outline of the great house. The men rode in silence, including the intriguing American, as they glided toward Jordan's docks.

Loul was barely conscious. The last hour or so, Donato had held him against his own body so he wouldn't have to lie in the water, but his color had paled and his breathing had become almost indiscernible.

Slowly the pirogue glided into the wharf, bumping lightly against the wooden deck. The last time Colette had arrived at Yellow Sun like this had been after her rescue. Oddly enough, the man she had been rescued from was with her, and she didn't want to imagine what this trip would have been like without him.

One of Donato's men hopped out onto the pier and reached back to offer her a hand. She accepted and stepped clear of the pirogue. Donato was next. With gentle hands, he shifted Loul in his arms. Once on shore himself, Donato started toward the house.

Colette kept pace ahead of them, but hesitated nearing the door. Jordan had always kept a key hidden outside somewhere, but with all that had happened, she could not recollect where. Donato came up behind her.

"I told you before." He walked past her and kicked in the door. "I don't need a key."

Colette followed through the broken door, across the lower loggia, and up the stairs to the butler pantry. Before she could get ahead of him, Donato kicked in the second door and entered. There he waited until Colette caught up.

"Where do you want him?"

Loul was unconscious.

"He usually sleeps in the *garçonnières*."

Donato shook his head. "Not going there. Where's Jordan's room? The ball is still inside him."

"No, lay him on the table." Colette cleared the table off, making room. "We take the ball out first."

Donato did as she asked, then waited for instruction. She swallowed hard, hoping she could do this. With all of her hospital experience, she had seen many pistol wounds, but with the large group of men that now surrounded her, she had an audience. The men filled the lower loggia, and some had taken the stairs to the kitchen.

"I'll need fresh water from the well."

She heard someone yell that they'd get it.

"All right, I'll need some bandages. Donato, in the dining room, find a tablecloth and cut it into squares with a few long strips to tie it off."

She searched the garde-manger for anything to be used as a surgical tool, finding a sharp knife, forceps, and a small spoon. Her hands trembled slightly when she picked up the knife.

Donato had returned to stand beside her. Seeing her shaking, he reached over and covered her hand with his, the heat of which soothed her nerves. He leaned toward her and whispered, "You can do this, senora. You can save your brother's life."

Loul was lucky. Colette didn't have to do a lot of exploring to find the ball, and its removal was done. She bellied the wound with a flaxseed poultice, reinforced it with cloth bandages, and secured the dressing with the strips Donato had cut from the tablecloth.

Loul never woke up as Donato and another man he called Silvano carried him to Jordan's old room. After placing Loul gently on the bed, Silvano turned to leave, allowing a short bow to Donato.

"Silvano, see to whatever the men need. They can sleep anywhere they find in the house." Donato shifted his attention back to Colette. "Acceptable?"

"*Oui*," she whispered, knowing they needed these men to sail after Enio. But with Loul unconscious, she felt adrift, lost, aching for a sense of teamwork.

With the other man gone and Loul sound asleep, Colette stood alone, facing Donato.

"*Merci*," she started. "For the care you gave my brother."

"*No las merezco*." He responded that she was welcome. "I need your brother."

"I need you." She said it without thinking. It flew out of her mouth without any censorship, without filtering it against the world she had escaped or the world in which she now lived. She corrected. "To—to find Enio."

"Does your brother have any whiskey?" Donato either purposely ignored the remark or hadn't heard. Her color must have flushed, considering the heat that seared her cheeks. Either way, she was relieved to move on.

"*Oui*, in the adjoining parlor." She led the way into the

parlor that was situated between Jordan's and Aurélie's rooms. She shivered when she saw the cold, empty fireplace. How nice a fire would feel right now. "There are several decanters on the wine table."

Donato followed behind her. The room was not that big and for some reason felt incredibly small and...intimate. She faced him, running a tongue over her lips, garnering courage to be alone with him but drained of all strength.

He poured himself a drink of whiskey and downed it in one gulp. She had never known Donato to drink whiskey. It was usually wine they had enjoyed together, but tonight, he did so with purpose.

"What do you think Enio is doing now? Without me—"

"It is late, Colette. He is asleep."

"He must know his mother is not with him."

"He does, but he is a good little boy—at least I assume, and will win the hearts of those who take care of him."

"You believe he is not mistreated?"

"He is not." He poured another glass of whiskey and handed it to her. "*Te hará bien.*"

She started to shake her head. "I do not drink whiskey."

"Tonight, you drink." He motioned for her to swallow it. "It will stop the shivers."

She took the glass from his hand, her fingers gliding over his. She closed her eyes for a second, not wanting to remember the feeling of his hands on her, touching her, stroking her body. Memories that seeped through the facade she wore, despite the sister's habit. But her dress of the sister's reminded her of her charitable pledge, and the two could not coincide. The prosperity of Donato's island negated any need for charity. Once, when the British had attacked his island, she had performed the duties of a nurse. Her memories coalesced into soothing images. Life with Donato had been beautiful. Why, after all she had endured, could she not embrace it?

Needing to pull her mind free of him, she threw back the drink in the same way he had. The liquor burned her throat and went clear down to her belly. She hadn't realized how cold she was until the whiskey washed the chill away. She put the empty glass down, facing Donato.

Though his dress was nothing like his usual attire, he still looked the handsome rogue, gentlemen, and insatiable lover. His raven hair, longer than usual, hung around his face in messy waves. He had a broad face, with wide-set eyes framed in dark lashes and brows. His nose had a downward bend from the high cheekbones of his face. A light beard shadowed his face. He looked hard-bitten, rugged, and weathered. In spite of his altered dress, he looked much like the Donato with whom she had spent nearly three years in seclusion.

He said nothing, perusing her in the same way she did him. What did he think? Was she the same woman? Probably not, because she wasn't. Even she knew that.

"Donato, will we get Enio back?"

"*Si.*" He nodded. "I will."

She dared approach him in this dimly lit room, where the sound of their breathing filled the air and they were too close for idle talk. She started to reach out to him, wanting to press her palms against his chest, wanting to feel the wall of power beneath her fingers—but she never engaged his body, held back by some invisible force. She desperately needed him, and that reality was not as displeasing to her as she would have thought.

But Donato was a man of mystery. What kind of woman was Rayna de la Roche, and why would she travel thousands of miles over the ocean waters to simply steal her brother's son? Donato knew Enio would be well treated because he knew his sister. Colette was not so convinced, and she couldn't stop the worries from turning her heart inside out.

"Will you tell me now?" She dared to place her hands square on his shoulders. "Who you are?"

"Not tonight, Colette." He sounded tired. She let it go for now, knowing his answer was final. He opened the door on the other side of the parlor. "Whose room is this?"

"Aurélie's."

Donato motioned for her to enter the room. "You sleep in there tonight. I'll stay in here for Loul."

"I will watch my brother. It is you who must stay strong and well rested."

"For our son?" He asked but didn't wait for an answer. Instead, he nodded that he understood. "*Buenas noches.*"

"When?"

He stood with his hand on the door, his back to her, but his shoulders tensed and his fingers gripped the edge of the door. "When what?"

He knew in spite of his question. "When will you tell me what this is about?"

"I do not know, Colette. I do not know." He opened the door and disappeared into Aurélie's room.

• • •

Donato stepped into the room of Jordan's wife and closed the door behind him, leaving Colette in the adjoining parlor to watch over her brother. Whether Colette was concerned for Donato's health or not, he wouldn't stay in here. He couldn't sleep in a bed that Jordan had. He looked around the woman's room, very feminine, very Creole.

He didn't know the woman personally, but had seen her from a distance when he'd watched Enio play in the patio. But from the looks of this room, he understood the dress Colette had put on for Carnival.

Aurélie was a woman with fire and expressed herself through her style of dress. He had seen Colette in dresses like that, when she had lived with him, and she had worn them with perfect ease, the satins and silks fitting her beautiful body like a royal glove.

Now, back in this life she had so desired, Colette had folded up like a cheap fan, retreating into a woman he hardly recognized. But maybe he had never known her at all. Maybe the life she'd led with him had been the real lie.

Donato walked through the upper hall, then down the back stairs and into the butler pantry. Most of the men were sleeping, some were sitting about talking, and some were not there. He didn't care as long as they were ready in the morning, knowing none wanted to be left behind.

He glanced up the stairs, wondering if Loul would lead them to the ship in the morning. The young brother had been unconscious since they arrived. Donato could catch his sister's ship, but if her lead stretched much longer, it would be difficult. As it stood, twenty hours had been lost, he was already exhausted, and it was another four hours before daylight. Having no knowledge of these backwaters, he needed Loul alert and ready, but with a gunshot wound, that seemed highly improbable.

Jordan might have some maps of the bayous in the house. Donato left the small kitchen and crossed the hall to what appeared to be a library. There was an entire wall of shelving, books, wall-hanging portraits, and statues. A prayer chair stood in the corner with a family Bible atop.

When they had come to take Colette home and away from the island, someone had told Jordan where to find Donato's gold. It was only fitting to return the favor and find any hidden stash in Jordan's home. Donato opened every door, cabinet, and drawer he could find, looking for secret locks. Jordan had a ship hidden in the bayou. Why, if he was a retired swamp rat?

Donato had nearly given up when the last peg he pushed opened a hidden drawer. Inside was a small piece of paper, folded. He pulled out the paper and flattened it across a wooden shelf. Looked like a map of France, but he couldn't quite tell what it was about. Had to be important if stored under such conditions.

He opened a fresh bottle of whiskey, ignoring the decanters, and poured himself another glass that tasted far better than the stuff in the parlor. He might like a man who hid his good whiskey, but it would take a hell of a lot more to make him like Jordan.

As much as he hated to admit it, he had started to like Colette's younger brother, Loul. Young, gutsy, a man of action who showed no fear. Donato liked that in him. But he sure as hell never would, could, or should forgive Jordan.

Donato pulled a chair up to Jordan's desk, liking the feel of it, of being in the house of the man who had invaded his. He studied the small map in his hand until he noticed what appeared to be a larger copy of the same map under some papers on Jordan's desk. Maybe the maps had something to do with the fact that the family was from France. Other than that, he saw no significance.

He dismissed the maps, looking around Jordan's library. He wanted something to mark his presence, like Jordan had done in his home. To stake a claim of some sort. He was enjoying his idea of revenge until he heard movement from behind the door. Slowly it opened, and to his surprise, Colette stepped inside.

"Donato, can you not sleep?"

He shook his head. "Wanted to find where your brother kept the better whiskey."

He held up a glass half filled with the amber fluid as a salute to her.

"It is better, *non*?"

"Considerably." He smiled. "Have one, Colette."

"I know I did upstairs, but I don't indulge in whiskey."

"Shall I pour you a wine?"

"No." She walked into the room, her steps slow, hesitant. Stopping at the prayer chair, she made the sign of the cross.

"Of course you won't," he said under his breath, remembering her love of wine while on his island. He watched her pious movement as she lightly fingered the Bible before turning to face him.

She was still dressed in the habit of the Ursuline Sisters, but that wouldn't have mattered. She wore her hair coiled and off her face, removing all the pretty waves that would frame her expression and accent her natural beauty.

"I figured Jordan owed me a shot of good whiskey, considering he robbed me when he took you off my island. Who told them where to find my gold?"

He saw Colette swallow hard after an attempt at a deep breath. But before she answered, he waved the question away, because he knew the answer and hearing her admit it would be more painful than thinking it. "It does not matter."

"Pirates need to be paid."

"Especially swamp rats."

"You misunderstand my brother." Colette continued to pace around the room with slow, even steps. Her hands were folded, and she repeatedly threaded and unthreaded her fingers. She was thinking, and the dead silence nagged at him until he had to find something to say.

"Could you not sleep?"

"I came down for fresh water. Loul is in fever."

"Do you have quinine water?"

"I do. One of your men has offered to bring it to the upstairs."

"But a fever, that is not good news. What does tomorrow bring us?"

Colette shrugged. "Having worked at the hospital, I have seen many pistol wounds, but predict, I cannot."

"Then we will leave it in God's hands."

His comment seemed to surprise her, though he didn't know why. He was a religious man, and she knew that.

"*Oui*, it is in his hands."

She faced him in the room lit only by a flickering lamp and the moon-washed floors. The iridescent glow glided over her face and body, highlighting her delicate features, her nose that turned up slightly. Her dark green eyes with lashes that formed little fans, shadowed her face.

And her lips…he allowed his gaze to linger on them, knowing their taste, their sweetness that he'd never again partake. As if hearing his thoughts, her lips pulled inward and her eyebrows tilted up slightly. A question was forming in her mind. He waited, chasing away the thoughts he had of her lips, her mouth, her heated responses to the swipe of his tongue along their moist seam.

"Do you know the why? Why he was taken?"

He knew that the moment she had walked into the library and risked being alone with him that she was in search of information. She wanted to know why their son had been taken. A question he could not answer. She loved Enio. He couldn't fault her for that. So did he.

He shook his head. "I do not."

She turned slightly to dab at her nose. He could do nothing to make this easier. Nothing.

"I came in here looking for maps of the bayous. But instead found maps of France. What are these maps all over Jordan's desk?" Knowing they were not of the bayou, he succeeded in drawing her attention away from Enio, at least for the moment.

She turned and looked at them, then shrugged. "My brothers are working on a mystery. Jordan and I had been given medallions from our father. We both thought they were nothing more than our coat of arms, but learned that might not be the case."

Donato remembered having received an offer from a man to buy Colette for the price of a jewel-encrusted medallion. He hadn't known it was her father who had made the offer until he had been killed. Donato had refused the sale. He had had something far more valuable, Colette. How soon he had learned her level of treachery. But he was intrigued. "What are they, if not a coat of arms?"

"Well, Jordan figured out that if you put the two medallions together they form a map. Those on his desk are a reproduction of the original, which he has in safekeeping."

The original in safekeeping was now in Donato's hands. "A map to what?"

"Treasure." She smiled with her statement. "It's just nonsense."

"And he's trying to figure out where that treasure might be?" Captivated, Donato pushed the other papers to the side and analyzed the maps. He could see several notations made here and there, indicating some thought was going into the project. "So that is why your brother harbors a ship in the bayous. He thinks to go after treasure?"

"He doesn't tell me his every thought—"

"But you do know he keeps a ship for that purpose."

"Possibly."

"Whose treasure is it?"

"Well, that is the question. We think it is somehow related to our mother's family. If there is a treasure at all, it would be because of the revolution in France. We left France in the middle of the night, escaped to America. My father was American."

Donato finished off the whiskey, allowing it to soothe his nerves. He thought about Rayna and her motivation to come to America. Who manned that massive ship? Who had funded an expedition like that?

Trying to silence the thoughts that kept wrapping his mind in memories of Spain, home, and the night he had left his country, he poured another drink. Colette had been talking, but he wasn't really hearing her words. He wasn't a man to drink, nor to indulge, but tonight it was the only thing that would keep the voices inside his head quiet.

He glanced up at Colette, watching her move around the room, talking about the pictures that were on the wall, ancestors, people of importance to her father and the American Revolution. He didn't give a damn about the old portraits or about Jordan Kincaid. In fact, he was dammed tired of hearing about him.

But Colette continued to move around the room, so much so he began to think he was spinning. Was the room turning or was it really her effect on him? The habit she wore dragged the floor as she strolled, but it did not disguise her limp. At least she had removed the veil and wimple that hid her hair. It was such a shame to hide hair as beautiful as hers.

He glanced away, not wanting to think about it, but his attention floated back to her faster than he would have liked. She was still his wife, in spite of the distance she had put between them. She was still his wife, and he had every right to take her down on the floor and make love to her.

"Colette," he said, startling her. She turned to face him. "Sit down, *os lo ruego*. You make me dizzy with your walking."

She angled over and attempted to slide into the chair across from him, but her leg gave out and she started to fall. Donato pushed from his chair and caught her nearly on the floor, managing to soften the impact. Her arms wrapped around his shoulders for balance. The heat of her breath fluttered against his neck and rolled down over his heart and lower.

He felt the blood rush his face and pound through his long muscles, pooling near his groin. His skin burned where her breath skimmed across his body, and a large void filled with want of her opened inside him. He bled within; pain radiated outward to heat his face.

He tried to dismiss every carnal thought that raced through his mind. The emerald color of her eyes deepened, her gaze falling to his lips. He pushed to his feet, breaking the intensity of the moment, the hot, sizzling moment when passion and lust drove out all rational thought and left him with a wanting that only Colette could satisfy.

He pulled her to her feet and placed her in the chair.

She winced, reaching for her ankle. The ankle that had been broken the night her ship was taken. But she didn't remember that. Was it guilt that made him want to knead her muscles into submission, feeling responsible for her injury? She had no memory of that night, but the sight of her struggling to relieve the pain reminded him of the beautiful woman, battered and injured, who had been pulled from the wreckage. His fingers itched to touch her, make the pain go away, make his memories go away.

"Here." He pushed her hand away, reaching under the long robe to pull her foot from underneath. "You work this leg too hard."

"Donato…" She started to protest his touch, but stopped, leaning back in the chair and closing her eyes. "I have to keep up with a strong man who has two working legs, or I fear he will leave me behind."

He said nothing to reassure her, for the thought had crossed his mind. He had thought to leave her here when they left in the morning. He now knew who had his son and no longer needed to watch her. The last thing he wanted was to find himself on a journey with Colette at his side. The only woman he had ever loved…and lost.

He massaged the muscles of her foot, her ankle, her calf, enjoying the feel of her soft, near-satiny skin beneath his roughened fingers. She felt like a glass statue, smooth, fragile, and beautiful. He remembered the many times he had massaged not only that leg, but her entire body, erasing the pain of her injuries before making love to her.

She had a room in Jordan's home with a vacant bed, and right now, he wanted her in it. But she made no motion to leave, instead sitting in a calm stillness. The fireplace dead, the room was silent except for the ticking clock on the mantel. She remained, sitting, looking deep in thought, twirling a strand of hair between her thumb and forefinger, a habit he had noted long ago, when she was his and they had lived on the island as a family, with their son.

He felt a pull to his emotional wall and knew a rock in his steadfast foundation had shifted ever so slightly. Whether resentment or love, something shifted, moved, and seeing her in the flesh, after so many nights of missing her, a lump grew in his chest and migrated upward until he thought he'd never breathe again.

He'd not allow her to torture him anymore. He'd leave her behind in the morning.

"You should check on your brother."

"*Oui*, I should." She was quick to answer. A pretense. She knew it and so did he, but within seconds she was on her feet and on her way out the door before she hesitated, keeping her back to him.

"I know you think to leave me behind." She turned to face him with eyes darker than an angry sea. "That will not happen. *Bonne nuit*, Donato."

Donato nodded an acknowledgment of her warning, having made his decision the moment he touched her body and felt his weakening resolve, but to dispute her statement now would only open old wounds, something both wanted to avoid. "*Buenas noches*, Colette."

After hearing the door close behind her, Donato set the empty glass on Jordan's desk and again focused on the mysterious maps spread atop. Donato took the smaller version he had found in the secret drawer and held it up to compare. Through the lamplight behind it, he could see the mystery. The sketch of each medallion when transferred over the top of the other formed a map.

Donato scoured the small study, checked every possibility for hidden clues, and assembled all that he collected, everything related to a mysterious treasure. He had no real interest in Jordan's treasure, but could see the meticulous work the man had put into solving the puzzle.

Donato smiled, admiring Jordan's hard work. But all would be lost.

He had found the prize he'd steal from Jordan's house.

His treasure maps.

Chapter Six

Colette readied herself, not only for the journey through the swamp to find the ship, but to convince Donato to let her go at all. After he had made no claims to the contrary, she knew he planned to leave her here, waiting, dying slowly with each passing day.

She would not let that happen.

Her plan was simple. Loul's fever had broken, but he was too weak to travel, and though he was willing to try, Colette would not let him risk his life any more than he had already. Donato had no idea where to find the ship, so that left her. Loul had given her the directions.

She was Donato's only hope. Dressed in Jordan's clothes for comfort and armed with a pistol and dagger tied to her braces, she was the only one who could lead them to the ship.

From a distance, she heard Donato shouting out orders in Spanish. As she approached, she could see him more clearly in the morning light. He stood tall against the rising sun, broad-shouldered and lean. The men had made a morning meal from Jordan's supplies and were loading up what remained of the demijohns. She'd not protested taking anything of Jordan's; her brother had robbed Donato when on the island—it was a vendetta she'd not refuse.

Her gaze fell to his hands as he helped load the pirogue. The pain in her leg had disappeared under those gentle hands. He had a magic healing touch when it came to her body, and last night the feel of his caressing hands against her bare skin had shredded her defenses. She wanted him to glide his hands up her body like he had done in the past and kiss her passionately, in a way she'd never been kissed by anyone except him, so very long ago.

But that was not to be between her and Donato. She had left him because of the man he was, and he would never forgive her because of the woman she was. They were from different worlds, and the merging of the two would never happen…again.

He turned, noticed her standing near the front gate, and took a purposeful stride her way. She knew he'd be angry to learn she was his scout and that Loul's journey ended here. A fact he'd have to accept. Her other worry, Loul. She refused to leave Yellow Sun until she had the assurance that someone was taking care of him, but finding his mother's family would burn valuable daylight, an obstacle Donato would not find palatable.

"How is Loul?" he said when within hearing range.

"He cannot lead us."

"This is not true." His skin paled with a glance to the upper windows. "I appreciate his condition but he is the only—"

"Not the only."

"There is someone else who can lead us?"

She swallowed hard, keeping her nerves steady. "There is."

"Then who? Tell me. I will bring him about."

"Not a him, a her."

He caught her meaning immediately. Though his eyes were dark, she could see the smoldering fire simmering beneath the gentleman's facade. His lips tightened when he stepped back, as if seeing her for the first time.

"You are a woman. You think to dress like a man makes you my equal?"

"You think because I am a woman, I am not?"

He whirled on his foot and headed toward the house with Colette close on his heels. Within seconds they were standing next to the bed that held her dear younger brother, weak and wounded.

"Young Loul, tell me how to find that ship."

"I can't, Donato, it is too difficult, but Colette has seen it, she knows." Loul forced an exhausted smile. "Move with haste, Colette, I am anxious to see Enio back home."

In spite of Donato's fuming stance, Colette christened Loul's brow with a light kiss, then faced Donato. He leaned against the wall, defeated, his eyes on Loul.

"Then get yourself well, young Loul, for you will have to travel to Jardines de la Reina to see Enio. That is where his home is and always will be. But rest assured, I will return Colette." He pushed away from the wall and motioned to her to follow. "Come, scout, we have to leave."

By the time she caught up with Donato, she was seething with indignation. She yanked on his arm. "You will not separate me from my son."

He spun on her. "You separated him from me."

"To keep him safe."

"Excellent accomplishment, and now we must rescue him. Let us leave."

"No!"

"No?"

"I must ensure Loul's family is here to care for him."

"There are servants about. Instruct them and we leave."

He again turned down the hall. She caught up. "No, I must find his family."

"We must find our son."

"I love my son." Her voice cracked slightly at his thought that she did not. "But I also love my brother."

Donato's expression changed slightly, and his shoulders dropped with a hint of defeat. "How long will this take?"

"Two miles down the road. I will make it quickly."

"*Si,* you will, because I'm coming with you."

A glaze of frost covered the winter-darkened oak leaves, and the sparse grass, faded and brittle, crackled beneath the weight of the horse. Appreciating the unrestrictive clothing of her brother's breeches, Colette pulled her good leg up and folded it over the saddle, giving her some stability. The wind created by their galloping horse opened the collar of her shirt like cold prying hands and brought on a shiver. Her hair broke the confines of a loosely knit braid and fluttered around her head as they rode. She had never really enjoyed riding—until this very moment.

The horse was tall, well-muscled, and sound, feeling more like an extension of her body. Unlike the trot, the animal's smooth gallop made her feel as if she were flying, and the sense of freedom that came with it made her almost regret having not exposed herself to horses more often.

"Turn here."

Donato made the turn and slowed the horse down to a fast trot, then transitioned into a walk. "Which one? These are slave cabins."

"Were. My father owned no slaves, and Jordan owns no slaves. There, the third one."

Donato reined up and dismounted before reaching up and helping Colette dismount, his arms feeling incredibly good. "I will be only a moment."

"Hurry. Once that sun hits mid sky, we have lost our advantage. This isn't just to get Enio, Colette. My men are in danger because they tried to help me."

"I know you blame me—"

"I do not blame you. I blame us." That admission hurt him to say; she could see his jaw tighten, accentuating his high cheekbones. But to know he had not laid the burden of the situation at her feet gave her hope, reminding her of his kindness.

"I will hurry."

Colette took the stairs to the house and knocked on the door. After a big welcome hug and short explanation, Loul's aunt stated she'd be there within the hour.

When Colette walked back to meet Donato, he nodded to indicate the woman she had just spoken to. "That explains the difference between you and your brother."

"His mother's Haitian. We share a father, and though our skins are different colors, we are brother and sister."

"He is close with his brother, Jordan. As soon as he is

able, he will get Jordan back from Boston and into this fray of ours."

Colette knew that to be true and hoped it would be soon. For her, having Jordan involved was a good thing, but to Donato it was not. She held her silence, not wanting to deepen the rift between him and her brothers. Right now, she needed them on the same side.

"Are you satisfied that Loul will get help? Can we depart?"

"Donato, it was important. I appreciate so much your helping me do this."

He flinched, turning away from her as if her gratitude affected him in a painful way. She could not withdraw her words, for they were spoken from her heart and meant for a man who had done kind things for her many times over.

With the reins locked in his hands, he swung up on the horse.

"We have lost time." He pulled her up and situated her body close to his lap. "Steady?"

She nodded, and a second later they were flying across the landscape atop the pounding hooves of muscle and power. Her hair flew wild around her, the moist air forcing the length to frizz and curl. She closed her eyes, enjoying the feeling, never realizing that riding a horse could be so intoxicating. For a moment, she lost herself in the feeling and lifted her arms into the wind and smiled.

"Careful, *pajarito mío*, I do not want to lose you to the wind."

Her smile grew with hearing his voice calling her a little bird, caring words spoken softly in her ear. His arm around her waist tightened, and he pulled her close against his chest. The heat of his body washed the chill from the wind, and his secure hold gave flight to her sense of adventure.

But that was always the case when with Donato. He was a powerful man whose virility protected his body like the armor of a knight, paving the way for the predictable to be as intoxicating as the unpredictable. Her sudden awareness of her past life bled through her heart and mind with a dying need for more, to quench an undeniable thirst that had remained dormant, unknown, until this very moment.

That had been life with Donato, and she had left him.

. . .

A blistering wind struck the moment the first pirogue was launched. After the fifth raft left shore, a long, winding snake of mounted planking had been formed. Four carried men; the fifth carried supplies taken from Jordan's warehouse. Every earthenware straw-encased demijohn from the porte cochere had been loaded. Slowly, the line began to weave through the still waters with Colette in the lead.

Donato stood next to her, repeatedly checking their direction against the rising sun, adding to her overly taxed nervous state. Could she do this? Having made the journey once and in the opposite direction, even Loul's descriptions did not make it any clearer.

Donato was nervous as well, tapping his fingers along the railing of the pirogue. She wanted to reassure him, but couldn't. Only the grace of God would get them there.

The pirogues floated through the long, marshy grass, around tussocks, and silently grazed over the murky waters floored with quicksand. The cypress trees were close together and filled with palmetto brush, adding to the eerie shadows that played along the water. The wind had turned cold and ripped at her clothes, leaving a chill in its wake.

Donato took in a deep breath, drawing her attention.

"We're to go due east until we come to what might appear to be a delta," she attempted to reassure him.

"Might appear? Do you not know? That sounds like directions, not your memory." Donato looked at her, then leaned in and whispered, "Does any of this look familiar to you?"

Colette reluctantly shook her head that it did not. "I have only seen it once, when Jordan brought me back from…"

"*La Isla de la Luna Llena*. My island," he finished for her.

"*Oui*." She could only muster a nod.

"And you agreed to lead my men into a swamp that could very well be their death?"

"And mine." She returned her focus on the muddy waters in front of her. "And mine, Donato."

"Foolish courage, but we must find that ship."

A soft reprimand, for he knew as well as she, their options were limited.

They rode in silence, pushing through the liquid land. As Loul had predicted, the farther east they went, the darker it became.

They cleared a small lake and glided through a long narrow inlet where gum trees and heavy willows entangled overhead to form a dark tunnel, forcing them to duck as they floated through.

"Water's getting shallow," the assigned pilot whispered to Donato. "Water's changing to dark green."

"Keep going," Donato responded without consulting

with her.

Tussocks started to appear. Some they floated over, some they had to go around. Marsh grass of tall reeds began to appear looking more like a swale.

Their pirogue halted in the water.

The pilot turned to face Donato. "We've hit a shoal."

"A sandbank." Donato jumped off as well as the other men. Colette held on to the railing. "Pull it over."

This didn't look right. They were in some creek, way off the canal, and at this point she could not see going farther. Ahead, there was nothing but tree-shrouded banks with moss-draped branches. The hiss of the barred owls had stripped her nerves raw. Beneath her pirogue, she could sense the unpredictable tides of the bayous shifting.

With a jerk, the pirogue was over the small reef, and the well-soaked men climbed aboard. Word was sent back through the flotilla to avoid the ridge.

"How much farther, Colette?"

"I didn't think it was this far," she confessed.

Donato looked at her, and she could read his every thought. He looked ahead of them and to the back of them.

"I saw nothing to be called a delta," he validated for her.

"Neither did I." She appreciated him saying that, feeling the weight shift slightly from her shoulders to his.

"Then we keep going."

Their forward movement lasted only minutes.

"Hitting sand."

"Keep going." The men followed Donato into the water.

As the men pushed, Colette focused on what was before them until she heard a trickling of water, like a flowing creek. "Listen."

The men stopped.

"Running water." Donato glanced up at Colette before giving his order. "Forward."

She had to duck when they pushed through the pitch pine. Branches sweeping over the raft nearly knocked her off, but the tinkling sound of moving water grew as they approached. Finally, they popped free of the blinding foliage to see acres and acres of an open bog. Her heart skipped a beat.

Donato climbed back aboard; his water-soaked half shoes squeaked as he shifted his weight. The rest of the men stayed in the water pushing the raft over the rolling sandbars.

"Any of this familiar?"

Colette thought to lie, but didn't. "No, but I hear water ahead. Could it be—?"

"The delta? Could be. Look at the embankment. It's rising for deeper water."

Another fifteen feet and the rest of the men climbed aboard and the poling began again to glide them over the top of the water. They entered another shaded area, made darker by the falling sun. Then she saw it.

The delta. It wasn't as large as she had expected, but it had to be the place. The water ran perpendicular to the open marsh, depositing mounds of silt and mud to spread out over the embankment. Only a river would move the soil like that, and she had vague memories of having seen this before.

"There, we turn."

The pilot pushed the poles and made the pirogue change direction. Going directly north from their eastern route. She held her breath, analyzing every tree, every bush along the embankment, watching for that large oak tree that Loul had described for her.

Soon a magnificent, sprawling tree with lithely curved trunks and branches graced with moss loomed over the edge of the water like a statue of Rome, tall and majestic.

A tingle of excitement rose from her feet to wiggle across the top of her head. Colette smiled. "There it is. We pull up here."

Donato looked around them. "How can you be sure?"

"Check that tree. It should have a carving of an eagle on its trunk."

Donato jumped off the pirogue onto the land. He bounced on the boggy floor, but it held his weight. He plowed through the tall grass surrounding the tree until he hesitated and bent down to get a closer look. "This is it. If you want to call that an eagle."

Colette's relief nearly washed her off the raft. She had to hang on or fall in the water, from the unending stress of the swamp journey.

All the pirogues had pulled over to the embankment and were in the process of de-boarding when Donato came back for her. He stepped onto the pirogue, scooped her up, and stepped to the cushiony ground before placing her on her feet.

"Where now?"

"East again, a quarter of a mile."

"And is the ship there?"

"*Oui,* in brackish water."

"Salt marsh. So that's the way out of here." He picked ten men to come with them while the others waited with the supplies. "We find it first, then unload."

Without consulting her, Donato swept Colette up into

his arms and started tramping through the long grass due east.

"I can walk this."

"No, you can't, Colette, and as much as I appreciate your willingness to try, you will only slow us down, even in your male breeches."

She rode along in his arms, not protesting, knowing the walk would have been a challenge for her leg. Besides, the comfort of riding against his chest and feeling his arms around her, gave her, without doubt, the best seat in the house. "Loul said there is a tidal pool, to be careful. The ship is behind it."

"Probably where the salt water comes in."

They waded through the long grass. There was no sun, with the thick overhead trees knit above. They stirred up a whitetail deer that ran across their path, stealing her breath away. But Donato pressed on until suddenly he stopped, his gaze traveling upward.

She turned to look.

The ship.

Donato lowered her to her feet. Men sent up a cheer and eagerly raced toward the ship. Donato's warnings of tidal pools faded in her ears. Her legs would not hold her, and she started to collapse. Her mouth had gone dry, and her stomach turned into an icy knot that clawed at her insides.

Falling into Donato's arms, he lifted her from the damp marsh grass, but the warmth of his body couldn't stop the images that robbed her of the present. Ships colliding, men shouting, smoke, fire, cannons, until someone grabbed her and pulled her over the gunwale and onto another ship, much like Donato held her now. The pain in her leg intensified. A cold shiver with serrated teeth cut through her body, chasing away the heat offered by Donato.

She fought to keep the words of panic from escaping her mouth, betraying her strength, making her sound weak, weak enough for Donato to leave her behind. After a deep breath, she tried to reassure herself. She could do this; she could once again board a tall ship. She had to, for Enio.

"Are you all right, Colette?" Donato leaned his head down to hear her.

"I am fine, just lost my footing." She peeled his hand away from her arm as she steadied herself on her own feet. But the images that attacked her mind were cruel and vivid. She swayed from the impact, feeling like she was being dragged deep into the forest by a wild animal—pain—the awful pain.

"Colette." Donato took her into his arms. "Listen to me."

But she couldn't. She was miles away, somewhere in hell.

She twisted her fingers into his clothing, frantic for solid ground. Tears ran down her cheeks as she buried her head against his chest, whispering, "Help me."

"I have you. Nothing will happen to you." He wrapped her deeply within his massive arms and held her tight against his chest. She could hear his heart beating, strong, rhythmic...soothing.

The haunting images dissipated like fog under a hot sun, retreating to the dark recesses of her mind. But they'd be back. She drew a deep breath. Her mind slowly cleared, and sounds of the mourning doves filled her ears. Pushing her hands against his chest, she broke free of his hold and distanced herself from him.

"I..." She stopped, not knowing how to explain herself. "The ship reminded me of the past."

"I know, but you will be safe with me."

Like he had kept her safe once before. The night of the auction, when she was to be sold, he had rescued her, but that was all she could remember of before or after, only that night.

He had kept her safe from the pirates who had taken her ship, but now, who would keep her safe from him? Failing on all fronts, she fought for composure. She looked at him, feeling a mist rush her eyes. In his, she caught a glimmer, a tiny hint, of the love he had shown her before all of this happened, when she had lived with him on the island, unaware of her real life. "Why do you care, Donato? I know how betrayed you feel. How easy it would be to toss me aside and leave."

"Because I am a man of honor, regardless of what you think, and you're the mother of my son. For that, I will always care for you."

She held her disappointment in his answer, kept her distance from him, resisting the need, the want, the desire, to fall into his arms. She drew a deep breath to wash away all those imprecise thoughts and fortify her strength for the present. "And where do we go from here?"

"I need a better ship. We head to *La Isla de la Luna Llena*."

"Your island?" Images of the island—the warm evenings, the soft music, the sultry dances beneath the candlelight chandeliers—filled her mind. Her breath left her heart and raced deep inside her belly, where she had thought recollections of his embraces, his kisses, his bed, had been safely disarmed. They had not and begged for release. "You're taking me to your island?"

Chapter Seven

The ship was a schooner, nicely equipped, but not heavily gunned, nor modified for sea roving. Maybe Jordan had left the life; Donato really didn't care. If he was saving this for his treasure map, he'd be sorely disappointed. Donato had left nothing behind that would give the slightest hint to a treasure.

Donato had expected to find an old ship, remnants of the war or the privateer days. Instead, Jordan had landed himself a new schooner. It had two masts, one gundeck, and a berth for living quarters. At best it had eight guns and four swivel guns, but it looked as if more were being added. They checked the hull and found rammers, sponges, powder horns, powder cartridges, and balls. If necessary, he had firepower.

From Jordan's warehouse, they had taken vinegar, molasses, coffee, rum, candles, and several demijohns filled with fresh water. But they needed much more to retrieve his stolen child, and that he had on the island.

Donato left Colette in the captain's cabin below the quarter deck. She agreed to rest while he and his men readied the ship. He knew her memory of the night of her abduction was muddled, but something had flooded her mind today when she saw the ship. The man who had taken their ship was dead. Killed by her brothers, Jordan and Loul. But what if she remembered everything that happened that night? What would she do when she learned the truth about him? That it was he who had orchestrated the taking of the *Loirie*. He had done it for political reasons, but he doubted she'd consider that in his defense.

The rest of the men arrived, and stocking the ship with much needed supplies began. Sails were unfurled. The depth of the water was shallow enough to question launching a ship, and the unpredictable nature of the waning tides of the bayous only added to their peril, but if Jordan could do it, so could Donato.

While the ship was readied, Donato took the polly boat and looked for the route out to the sea. Then he analyzed the ship, how it was moored, the path it had to have taken to get to this point, the position of the helm. Surrounded by uninhabited wild land, he knew Jordan's knowledge of the bayous allowed him to use the surging and retreating tides to maneuver in and out of the swamps. A luxury Donato did not have. There had to be a way to pick up the wind and move this ship over the liquid land and into the gulf.

He climbed aboard and ordered the gaff sails unfurled and dropped all sails aft. But if he picked up the wind, where the hell would he sail it?

"Colette."

Resting on the only bed in the captain's quarters, she had

one arm across her eyes and was breathing slowly, shallowly, and evenly. Her hair, loose and free from the horseback ride, hung wild around her face, framing her beauty in the way he remembered. Her long dark lashes from closed eyes cast a thin shadow over her cheeks. She was a slightly built woman, five foot two, if that.

His gaze slipped downward along the narrow turn of her throat to the soft pulsating point in the middle where he had so often kissed her, running his tongue over her life's beat. The collar of her man's shirt had shifted, exposing well-defined cleavage between her breasts.

He walked over to the window, refusing to allow his mind to go where he knew she'd forbid him. But she was still his wife, and he had every right to take her as his.

Colette stirred slightly in her sleep. He glanced over at her, remembering the day she had left him with so much clarity it had grown fangs and bit into his flesh every time he allowed the thoughts to the surface. She had left him. The instant her brother showed up, she had tossed her life with Donato aside and had taken their son and left him.

Here Donato stood on Jordan's new ship. Revenge was so sweet when so exact, but Donato knew, as soon as Loul was able, Jordan would be notified of the situation, and knowing Jordan, he'd catch a wind and go after Colette. He had done it before.

She claimed she had to return to a life she had so yearned for, missed with every waking breath, a safe, calm life with Jordan. Donato's life was too dangerous to raise a child, to keep her safe; she wanted nothing of his pirate world, yet had run into the arms of her pirate brother.

Donato turned and watched her sleep.

Yes, she had left him, and as hard as he tried, he was never sold on the reason why.

"Colette." He sat down on the side of the bed. "I need to speak with you."

She stirred again, stretching her beautiful body with arms and legs going in all directions. Her eyes fluttered open and she looked around, a little confused at first, until she realized she was on the ship and turned her head to see Donato. "How long did I sleep?"

"Not long. Colette, do you remember any landmarks when your brother sailed *Le Vengeur* into these backwaters?"

"I was on deck." She rested her hand on his arm, casually put there as if that were a natural thing to do, a connection between them, until she noticed. She pulled her hand back, rolling her fingers into a ball as if burned by their touch. She pushed to the other side of the bed. Rising to her feet, she brushed her wheat-colored hair off her face and behind her shoulders. "Jordan had gone to Barataria first."

"Why?"

"To sell your ship. The one he had taken from you."

"And did he?"

"No, Barataria had been destroyed by the American navy. He left your ship there and we sailed in open water for a while." Her eyebrows slanted downward as she was trying to remember. He watched her knead her upper lip. Those full, kissable lips that formed a perfect square. "There was a rocky shore that had a large boulder; he turned to the east of it."

Donato circled around the bed, pleased with what she was remembering. "Was the water deep? Did the men pull it? Did he sail directly in here?"

"Directly in on *Le Vengeur*. I do not know about this ship."

That was true. The circumstances of this ship could be different, the deadrise, the tide, the foliage. "You returned in December. The tide could have been higher at the time."

"Can we not get out?"

"As shallow as it is right now, it would be very easy to run aground. Once that happens…we are trapped."

"And your sister gets away."

Donato wasn't willing to go that far. She was on a square-rigged frigate, seaworthy but making no more than three to four knots. Not a match for his schooner that awaited him on the island. That ship had superior speed and maneuverability at fourteen knots. He would catch Rayna if he could just get to the island.

There was a knock on the door.

"*Adelante.*"

Ramón stepped inside. "*Capitán*, the reading is a quarter less than three."

Donato turned and glanced out the stern window.

Maldita sea.

It was half less than four when they had boarded. The water level had dropped. Donato didn't know the bayous like Jordan did, but he did understand the fickle waxing and waning of water level and tides. They had to be on a bayou fed by a river—fed by the gulf—fed by the tide. Brackish water. And that's how Jordan did it. He knew when and where to bring that ship into the bayous. Now wasn't the time; the tide was going out.

• • •

"Oh my God, we'll be aground." Colette covered her mouth as if to stifle her panicked response.

Ramón nodded. "It is true, senora, that the tide ebbs, but a shallow draft we have here."

"Well, that answered one of my questions," Donato said more to himself than anyone in the cabin. "Jordan knew when to sail in and when to sail out. And by that rigging, Jordan used his sails to maneuver the ship leeway."

"*Si, Capitán*, so it appears."

"We have to get out of here." Donato climbed the stairs to the gundeck with Colette close behind him. The men were waiting for orders, standing around the deck, knowing the water level was dropping.

"Ramón." Donato started speaking more in Spanish than English. "Dump the supplies, everything except the demijohns of water and smoked jerky. Silvano, dump the cannons over the side. Move the swivel guns to the tender. Adan, take some men, find anything you can use, axes, spikes, whatever you can find in the hold. Flush the ship."

Colette had followed Donato to the gundeck, standing beside him when he issued the orders. "What does that mean? Flush the ship?"

"Clear the decks, make it lighter, take anything off that can be spared."

Men raced about. Jordan's cannons were released and pushed off the deck, one after another, creating dangerous holes in the bulwarks. The supplies that had journeyed through the swamps were again brought up on deck and minus the demijohns of water and candles, the entire supply of vinegar, molasses, coffee, and rum was moved to the tender.

Below deck, walls came down, cargo holds were opened

up. Boards and planking were thrown over the side. Furniture from the captain's cabin was dumped. Soon men started ripping up the planking above the quarter deck.

"Donato." Colette pulled on his sleeve. "The more they work, the less seaworthy the ship looks."

"The less seaworthy she is."

"But…" She dropped her questions and remained near the helm. A good choice, with all the activity; that was the most stable place for her to stand.

Soon only a faint orange swipe of sun across the horizon was left. But the men worked feverishly, lightening the load and transforming the ship. When most of the work was done, Donato took the helm, where Colette stood. He hated the idea that she was going to be on this dangerous trip. Odds on whether or not they'd make it on a flushed ship weren't very good.

"Colette." He started but didn't know what to say. Yes, the trip would be dangerous, but what else could she do? She couldn't return to Yellow Sun by herself, and he couldn't send any men with her. "This will be dangerous."

"I am going with you."

He admired her spunk, even if foolish. "Very dangerous."

"I am going with you. I made you a promise that until I have my son back I will not let you out of my sight. You told my brother that you will not bring Enio back."

"*Si*, I did say that." He dropped that subject faster than a cannon tossed over the side. "You need a lifeline."

He tied a rope around her waist, trying to ignore the soft feel of her warm body, the slight rise and fall of her breasts as she stood before him. He handed her the end of the rope to hold. "After they haul anchor, hold on to the capstan, and the other end will be tied to a cleat. Once we are on the gulf, the deck will be wet the entire time and waves will easily swamp us."

He hesitated. "Still want to go?"

"I'm going."

"Pull anchor, unfurl the yards, fore and aft! Man the shrouds. Hold her tight to the wind!"

The men in the tender started to row, and with a slight breeze caught in the top sails, the ship started to move, ever so slowly, until she pulled free of the foliage. Donato steered her to the very middle of the narrow channel and hoped to hell he would not run her aground.

Men leaned over the larboard side on the only railing left, after the flush, watching the water, listening intently to the man dropping the lead line and calling out the depth in fathoms.

The ship slowly plowed through the foliage, parting a wake of pond scum behind them. Sometimes it looked as if they were atop ground and not water, but the weights would sink and he'd get another reading.

"Rig a square sail."

The big square sail pulled in more wind and started the ship moving faster, but the water level dropped equally fast. If he hit less than two fathoms, they would run aground.

And they did.

The ship jolted, dragging the bottom, but her lightened load kept her afloat. The man-propelled tender tugged on her bowline. If he could only take the wind.

"Square the yards!" He'd risk a turn if he could pick up speed. The ship slowly rounded two points to starboard, but it was getting late, and darkness folded over them like a broken umbrella. He squinted trying to see ahead. "Level?"

"By the mark ten!"

A cheer went up among the men. Donato sighed with relief and saw Colette glance his direction. "Are we all right?"

"*Si*, we are free, but the gulf is a challenge of its own."

She started to untie the rope around her waist that held her to the cleat.

He placed a gentle hand over hers, feeling the soft warm flesh of her skin beneath his coarsened fingers wanting to explore. "Not yet, Colette, there is much still to face."

With the tender safely tethered, the swivel guns were mounted in place, and other supplies that had been moved to the small boat were hoisted over and packed below deck.

"Set sail!"

The ship picked up speed and broke free into open water.

He dared to unfurl the squares and pick up as much speed as he could to keep them afloat. Racing across the open gulf, water sloshed over the flushed ship. Men held on to railings, shrouds, riggings, and masts. If he wasn't seen by the navy and could make at least six knots, they'd be on the island in about nine to ten hours.

Colette was holding on, but he knew she could not stand much longer with her impaired leg. He knew her limitations, and this voyage would test them.

He looked through the binoculars Jordan had kept in the captain's cabin. The water was quiet, smoother than he had expected, a serene quiet before the storm. The smell of rain hung in the air, and clouds started to churn around them. He caught a flash of lightning in the distance.

It would be a long night.

Colette shivered and readjusted her position. Donato

pulled off his coat and wrapped it around her. "Put your arms through, it will be warmer."

She did as he asked, returning her hands quickly to the capstan to hold on. "I had packed leather gloves in my trunk along with my fur coat, but Loul refused to return to Jordan's house for fear of your sister's men."

"You have things on the island. Perhaps not a fur coat, but dry clothes." He didn't know why he bothered to reassure her, or admit that nothing had changed since she'd left him. Maybe her hands turning white and looking as frigid as he felt brought out the compassion in him.

With only two masts, he had no crow's nest and felt blind at sea. He glanced around, sensing that the men were as tense as he. He could see concern in their eyes, the tight lips, the hardened stare toward the sea. They were here because of him, because Colette had left with his son, because Rayna had stolen him. They were here as men of honor to support him, and now their very lives were at risk. He held the helm steady navigating toward home, a tropical cay in the Jardines de la Reina, south of Cuba.

"*Capitán.*" Ramón approached him and whispered, "Sail, two points larboard."

"Man the swivel guns, lock and load."

Colette turned to hear what he said. "You expect trouble?"

"They see a sail. With a flushed ship, we are pirates from a distance. Ramón, take Colette to the hull in the case they fire."

"No," she refused. "I will stay above deck."

"All right." Donato took the helm. "Let's get out of range."

The wind picked up a little, giving him what he needed to outmaneuver the clumsy navy ship, which couldn't follow his tacking. Donato increased speed, filling more sails, until they were pushing close to nine knots.

The wind churned and the clouds thickened and the sea waters started to roil. Lightning flashed across the sky in zigzag shapes, illuminating the dark thunderous clouds of the gulf as a billowy black curtain fell over his ship.

Donato squinted to see through the squalling black wind. Thunder rumbled across the sky, shredding the clouds. The gulf began to swell. The U.S. Navy turned back to port. He said a silent prayer of thanks, then pressed for home.

The swells started to build, tossing the ship from side to side, threatening a roll. Waves nearly ten to fifteen feet high would sweep the deck. Donato kept his focus straight ahead. Two men manned the tiller that fought his every order, surrendering to the force of the waves. Soon a third man joined them.

Twenty-foot swells careered across the deck.

Colette screamed and was swept off her feet.

Donato started for her when another wave crashed into the deck with the force of a cannon gone wild. Jerked off his own feet, he was dragged across the decking and nearly out to sea when he grabbed the bulwark. He pulled himself back onto the deck and to Colette.

He wrapped her in his arms, then locked his fingers around the capstan blocks when a wave hit. He hardly caught his breath when another wave hit him. He could hear Colette sputtering, gasping for air, still tethered to a block.

"Dig your feet into the pawls around the capstan."

She did as instructed. The pale skin of her face matched the stretched white skin of her hands.

"Hang on tight, Colette. In this kind of storm, a man

overboard is gone. We cannot come about in winds like this."

The storm was astern, billowing the sails and taking the wind. The ship picked up speed and buried the bow into the large waves. But the jib broke free and rode high above the thirty-foot swells. They sailed over the top of the water, nearly airborne at times. Their speed was deadly, and the threat of rolling over was as real as the wet decking.

Donato ordered the sails shortened, some poles bare. But the storm pushed them onward like a cork in bad whiskey. The groans of the wood matched that of the shivering timbers.

Waves were so frequent, he couldn't tell where the sea ended and the sky began, nor see his hand in front of his face. Sprays nearly thirty feet flew up and over the bow with each strike of the swell. Rain pelted their bodies like nails raked against soft skin until he thought he'd be bloody.

Wave after wave skimmed over the deck. The ship rolled from one side to the other. The force pulled free planks of wood in the only deck they had left. Donato ordered bare poles, and still they were thrown over the waves.

Finally, there it was, like a mirage of a beautiful sunset in spite of the churning ocean and driving rain. There was his island, emanating a beacon of light. They had only a few miles to go.

"Land ho!" he shouted just before a massive wave took him off his feet.

The main yard mast broke and crashed into the capstan. The bars broke, and the rope holding Colette unraveled. She screamed just before the water dragged her through a cannon port and out to sea.

Chapter Eight

"Colette! Speak to me."

Her eyes fluttered until her mind was able to focus. She looked above her and glanced around. She was in a bed with Donato sitting next to her. She was dry, in a bedroom, in a home—on the island. "Oh my Lord. I live?"

Donato chuckled with a broad, pleased smile. She missed that laugh of his. "I believe that to be true."

"I thought I would not."

"As did I."

"I remember flying out over the water and dangling off the ship. The rope, it held?"

"I caught it. It had started to fray and with the storm it was difficult to pull you aboard, but we did. You were not conscious and badly bruised. It might be a while before you are able to move about."

"I think not. I'm giddy to be alive at all. Move about, I will."

Colette glanced at her arms, they were indeed bruised. She was in a soft cotton nightdress, and even her hair was neatly tied to the back. She didn't ask who dressed her. The nightdress felt so comforting to her body, she didn't care who was responsible.

"I thought I would die, that I would never see Enio again," she whispered, painfully remembering the million thoughts that had raced through her mind before she passed out. "I thought once I fell, that I was lost forever."

"I would have come about. No storm would have stopped me."

She glanced up at him. His words said so casually, so easily, she knew they were from his heart, and his compassion toward her after what she had done to him surprised her. When he caught her revelation, he looked uncomfortable, as if he hadn't meant to say that so convincingly.

"I have food coming for you."

"Donato, I will see Enio again, won't I? We have lost valuable time."

"In this storm, they most likely found port."

The rain and wind were still scratching at the bedroom windows, still raging outside, a temper yet to be diffused.

"And my valise, did it survive?"

"*Si*, it did, but you have all you need here."

A woman came in with a tray of hot soup and warmed whiskey. "La senora, you look good now."

Colette smiled, recognizing the woman who had been her personal lady's maid when she had lived here on the island. "I am breathing, Clarita."

"Place the tray here," Donato instructed. "And leave us."

"As you wish, *su excel—*"

"Clarita, put the tray down," Donato interrupted her.

Clarita clamped her lips tight and placed the tray down. She bowed her way out the door and closed it.

"What did she say to offend you?"

"She did nothing."

The room fell silent, and suddenly Colette was aware how intimate that closed door made her feel. She was in the bed where Donato had made love to her many times.

She waited for him to speak, to say anything to relieve the tension she suddenly felt. How easy it would be to lift the bedclothes and invite him under. So many times, he had come at her bidding. Would he now? And why would she think about it? He had made his feelings very clear. He had promised Loul that he'd return her to Louisiana like a long-lost package.

Donato arranged the soup bowl, as if nothing were different about her once again being in her bedroom—his home. He raised a spoon to her lips. *"Tomad, hermosa. Os hará bien."*

Colette closed her eyes briefly, recognizing the words of her dream, though they varied slightly. Was the dream a premonition instead of a lost memory? But here she was wounded and hurt, and he was taking care of her and calling her beautiful and telling her the soup would be good for her.

She opened her eyes, then her mouth, to accept his nourishment, putting those thoughts aside for the moment. "The ship is much damaged?"

He nodded, but she didn't miss the pleased look on his face.

"You do not care, because it was my brother's ship."

"Makes it all that much sweeter."

"You blame my brother and call him a swamp rat, when you are the same, *en fait.*"

He leaned forward, capturing her attention with his dark eyes, wide-set to show his power, high cheekbones to show his integrity, and a square chin to show his strength. "Did I look like a swamp rat in that pond of your brother's?"

He did not, *en fait.*

"You are both men of vengeance." She pulled free of his gaze, which made her hunger for more. She wanted the conversation to lead to anything that would validate her leaving him; instead, every breath she took screamed otherwise. Admittedly, he'd never look the swamp rat in any garb.

"Perhaps we are both men of vengeance, Colette. That will make our meeting in the future that much more interesting. I scuppered his ship with a shot below the waterline. But he should not take the issue too seriously; I left most of the ship behind in his swamp."

"I don't think Jordan will see it quite like that." Colette couldn't stop the chuckle that left her lips without permission. His laugh matched hers, and for a moment after the levity, her gaze hung with his for what seemed an eternity. Her body rushed with a blazing heat, and her heart pounded against her sore chest. Her scalp tingled, and her face was on fire.

"Colette, when you were swept off that ship…" He allowed the words to drift away, brushing her hair to the sides of her face and fanning her curls out on the pillow. "For just this moment, I wish to pretend you never left me."

· · ·

Donato watched as Colette ran a nervous tongue over her lips. Her gaze never disengaged from his. He wanted her at that very moment, in his bed, in his life, with their son. He wanted her, but she had made a choice, and he was not it. But for this one moment of pretense—

"Donato," she started.

He regretted suggesting the charade. How foolish a man could be when in the presence of a beautiful woman who still held his heart in her hands. He needed to keep his head about him, remind himself her presence was nothing more than the logistics of getting their son back. With her refusal coming, he pushed off the bed and winked at her. "Only wanted to see if you have fully recovered."

"I have, I mean, Donato..."

He motioned to the tray. "Let Clarita know if you need anything more."

Before she could respond, he stepped through the door and closed it behind him. Needing his distance, he took the hallway to the stairs, crossed through the courtyard and entered his office.

"How goes your *esposa*?" Ramón asked.

"She will be fine, needs rest."

"Is she glad to be back home?"

"She will be fine." Donato sent Ramón a look meant to silence further discussion about Colette, though his mind was on nothing but. He couldn't shake the images of her hair draped across the pillow, her soft nightgown that opened at her throat. He had watched that small point of pulsation, wanting to touch it lightly with his lips, run his tongue over it and savor the life's breath of her. No, he wouldn't discuss Colette, the mother of his son. He wouldn't discuss the memories of seeing her with his child, holding him, loving him, caring for him, the times they had enjoyed him together. He wouldn't discuss the nurturing, passionate woman she was, beautiful inside and out and how her so-called true life had drawn her spirit dry. Not tonight, not tomorrow, not ever. She had left him.

He marched to his bookcase and pulled free a large map, spreading it out on the desk. "We must map our next voyage."

"To?"

"Spain. That is where Rayna is taking Enio."

Other men joined them in the office, each with a cigar in his mouth and whiskey in his hand. They were good men. Men who, like himself, had been wronged by their own government, the Absolutists, the French corsairs, and the Americans, forced into a shadowy life of crime and hidden agendas until the time was right. The men would go because they were loyal to Donato and because they knew that Donato would take off across the ocean in search of his son, whether they went or not.

As they discussed the map, questions surfaced. Returning to Spain was a great risk for all of them, including Donato. Could they avoid that? Could they catch Rayna de la Roche, and if so, how? And what then? It would be impossible to pack provisions for a return journey without a port.

Most of them had sailed from Spain to Cuba only once, but after much discussion, a navigational route was mapped and the supply list developed. They would take the schooner, *La Revolución,* for it was the most seaworthy of Donato's fleet and would provide the best accommodations for provisions, guns, and…a woman.

Preparations had to wait out the storm. Donato hoped, if his sister faced the same storm, that she had found safe harbor, for the sake of his son. If anchored, she wouldn't build the miles on him. He could catch her, he was certain.

He had a ship, a schooner, that would provide all he needed for a journey across the ocean.

The planned departure would be the moment the storm lifted, but he had one detail to yet attend. Colette. If he couldn't catch Rayna and she reached Spain, that would be thousands of miles to travel, months at sea. He had to make her understand it was too dangerous. But he wasn't sure for who? He shook his head, refusing to accept what his heart already knew. The danger was not what the ship would encounter, but close quarters with Colette.

All his men departed for the night, having families and homes on the island, as well, except Ramón. He had been on his own since his wife died several years ago.

"I will have dinner served, *Capitán*."

Donato nodded, thinking through the impending journey, wondering how long this had been planned by Rayna and who had financed her? He looked up to find Ramón still waiting for affirmation. A comrade of many years, he and Ramón had fought side by side through the endless Peninsular War. He trusted no one more than Ramón, and over the years, they had become friends and family.

"*Gracias*. Please inform *mi esposa* she may have dinner served in her room if she'd like, for she is not well, as of yet. If not, I will await her in the *comedor*."

Donato returned to his room to change his attire for dinner. Colette was in the adjacent room with only a connecting door between them. On the other side of her room was Enio's room. The room where he had entrusted her with his son.

Here she was, back in his house, but not as a rescued captive with a lost memory, nor as his wife. She was here as his adversary. Or so he had thought, but when she'd gone over the side of the ship, he had felt his heart rip from his chest. He did not want to give her such power. Having thought the past had been sealed, he had learned otherwise; the moment she had disappeared through the bulwark, his heart had opened up and bled.

After he washed, he pulled on a white ruffled shirt, a doeskin waistcoat, matching breeches, and a pair of recently polished shoes with silver buckles and white stockings. After tying his hair back into a queue, he pulled on his coat of black velvet. Though anticipating dining alone, it was only proper to dress appropriately when eating off china, with silver utensils in one's hand. A long-standing tradition of his upbringing.

After dressing, he waited in the *comedor* as he had done many times when he and Colette had lived here as man and wife. He extended an invitation as a matter of politeness, but with her injuries would not be surprised if she had opted to dine in her room. But to his amazement, she sent word that she'd attend.

Her attending would give him the opportunity to discourage her from making the journey with him. He would provide transportation back to the mainland, thereby eliminating Jordan Kincaid's need to interfere, knowing he'd pursue Colette the moment he returned to New Orleans.

Tipping his hand to Loul by stating he'd return Colette but not Enio had been a mistake. He had let a moment of frustration come out in words that might haunt him. That admission only emboldened Colette, making her all the more determined, as she said, to keep him in her sight.

He poured himself a small glass of wine when the double doors slid open and Colette stepped inside.

His breath slid into his stomach, and for a moment he couldn't speak.

She was wearing one of the green silk dresses he had had a seamstress make for her when she lived with him. A Spanish style, the dress hugged her curves and accentuated every beautiful attribute the woman had. She was gorgeous as she sashayed around the room, the hem of her skirt swaying with her movement. Her hair had been rolled and tied up on the sides and adorned with sparkling jewels of glass. A lace shawl draped her arms, covering the bruises that remained from when she had been swept overboard. She wore a small *peineta*, and a black lace mantilla draped down along the small of her back. Exquisite. Exotic. Sexy. That was the Colette he knew, not the plain-dressed, inhibited woman who needed rescuing by her brothers.

He rose to his feet and bowed, pulling out a chair opposite him.

"I am pleased mi senora joins me."

She smiled, that square smile that made her face look so impeccably balanced, as if finely chiseled by a loving artist pleased with his work. Yet her smile was measured, polite, lacking passion, making him suspicious she had an agenda, for the spark of her rescue had faded.

"*Merci.*" She moved into the chair.

"I didn't expect you to recover so quickly, or to see you at my table awaiting dinner."

"I am much better and needed to feel active again."

The first course was set with a glass of wine. He wondered what she was thinking, sitting in this room where they had once shared many candlelight dinners. His inference in his statement as having returned home had gone unchallenged.

She sipped the wine poured for her enjoyment. "I want to thank you."

"For?"

"Saving me, pulling me aboard. At least this time I remember all of it, every second. I remember so little about the other ship, the one taken by pirates."

He swallowed the deception, hating every moment she would try to remember, because one day…she would. One day she would remember that he was a revolutionist, and because of his war with the king of Spain, he had taken her ship, that he had been the one responsible for her terror at sea and the loss of her memory and family. "What do you remember?"

She took another swallow as if thinking about her answer.

He downed a large swig of wine, not waiting to enjoy the taste, but keeping his mind busy, or he'd dwell too long on the past and what she might remember someday.

"Not a lot." She placed the glass down next to her plate. "You rescued me from those awful men who took me, but I don't remember the robbery or the immediate after. But I will remember. Each day, tiny bits come forward, little flashes of things. You'll see. I'll remember."

Donato watched her over the flickering light. Taking a sip of wine to silence the angst that filled his chest. Someday her mind would flood with memories of that night and the truth about him. What would she do then? Would she poison Enio against him?

• • •

Colette hadn't missed the glances from Donato over the candelabra. His dark eyes and slight perspiration across his forehead reflected the flames. He had combed his hair back in a queue and off his face. He wore a striking black velvet overcoat with a tawny vest, had rings on nearly every finger, and one gold earring. For a man who protested the swamp rats, he did indeed look the pirate.

The wine was good, lingering in the back of her throat with a woody, fruity taste before warming the pool of her stomach. Maybe it wasn't the wine, but the handsome man who sat across from her. A man whose touch she had never stopped craving, whose kisses had lingered on her lips long after she had left the island, leaving her weak and wanting.

For a while, they ate in silence with only an occasional stilted conversation about the food, the storm, anything to avoid the obvious that they were here, together again. After the dishes were cleared, Donato refilled her wineglass. She braced herself, knowing he'd try not to take her on this voyage, and she had prepared herself a defense.

"Colette," Donato said, and she tensed. "About Enio… about the journey. I will not take you with me. The mishap aboard the last ship convinced me of this."

Colette didn't react, having expected as much. Keeping her face impassive, her body cool, her shoulders relaxed, she calmly sipped her glass empty before raising her eyes to meet his. "I do not need your permission."

He glanced around them as if she wasn't aware of where she was, then smiled in a checkmate type smile. "*Si*, mi senora, you do."

She pushed her chair back, bringing Donato to his feet. He was always the gentlemen. She had not intended to disturb his meal.

"Sit, finish your wine, s'il vous plaît."

"A gentleman does not sit as a woman stands." He remained on his feet.

She ambled over to the dining room window that overlooked the water. Tonight the waves slammed against the island, water in turmoil, like her and her husband, but he was right— he was in the position of power.

She faced him, forcing a tight smile. "You gave your permission when you said you would stay with me until Enio was in our hands. Are you not a man of your word?"

"I said that when I didn't know who had Enio. I now do and no longer need you, as you are no longer a suspect."

Though his point was valid, Colette waved her hand in the air, hoping to dismiss it. With a slight shake of her head, she narrowed her eyes at him. "But I need you to get him back. As I said, I will stick so close to you; your own shadow will be behind me. And you are still a suspect."

"Ah, Colette, that is very close. Shall I show you how close that is?" He stepped around the table toward her. Expecting his reaction, she had come prepared. From beneath her shawl, she pulled out her small flintlock.

"I go."

He stepped closer. "You do not."

She aimed her small shooter at his chest. "I do."

He stepped closer, so close she could smell the minty oil he had used to bathe. She drew a deep breath, remembering that scent. Her knees caved slightly under the weight of the memory. She forced her feet apart for better balance.

"What did I say about you pointing a pistol at me?"

He reached behind her and pushed the dining room door. As the heavy mahogany fell into the frame, the small *click* of the latch echoed throughout the room. Her breath caught deep in her throat; standing so close to him, she could hear each breath he took. "I believe I was not listening."

He leaned in to her; the heat of his skin radiated off her cheek.

"Are you listening now?" he whispered, his breath hot against her cheek, melting her body clear through to the floor. His lips roamed along her throat until he nuzzled her ear, taking a slight nibble on her lobe that made her nearly sway into him. He started to run his hand down her arm and she knew he was angling to take her pistol away. She tilted her face upward to place her lips to the lobe of his jeweled ear. With pistol in hand, she cocked the hammer in his other ear.

She felt him smile, stepping back from her. A tiny spark lit each of his dark eyes and matched the slight turn of his lips. "*Si*, senora. Perhaps you will go, but only if you are aware when I leave."

Her heart sank. *He wouldn't.*

He would.

She bit her lip thinking through her next step. He had her in check, but she had a few rooks and knights in her arsenal. "If I am left, I will engage my brothers and give chase, to Spain, if necessary."

He chuckled, his white teeth in contrast to the honey tint of his skin. "Your threat has no meaning, for they will follow, regardless."

"Perhaps."

He stepped away from her. His posture stiff and unyielding, he had grown tired of the game. "I will remind la senora, she is still my wife."

He noted her silence with the nod of his head. He refilled his glass of wine, offering to refill hers, but she declined. "This journey might be a long time at sea."

"You will catch them soon?"

"Could be, three, four months if we are forced to follow them all the way to Spain."

"We will not."

"Then I give you this challenge." He turned those dark dreamy eyes on her, her skin grew warm all over, and an odd little current traveled down her spine. "Thirty-five days."

"Thirty-five days?"

"If we are still at sea in thirty-five days, I will bed you as my wife."

"Thirty-five days? Why that number?"

"Disappointed? Shall we discuss no days, say, zero days and I bed you?" He waited for a response then added, "Tonight."

Her mind screamed yes, but her lips held tight. The time frame intrigued her, nearly as much as the idea of having him again.

"Thirty-five days?"

"*Si*, those are the only circumstances under which you will board my ship."

That little current changed direction and dived deep inside her belly.

"I agree." Not wanting to discuss her future intimacy with her husband, she left the dining room and headed back up the stairs, the route so familiar she didn't need to think about where she was going. Yet her teeth chattered slightly, and her heart hammered, radiating up the sides of her neck to her temples. She rubbed tiny circles around them with her fingers to little relief. He had bested her. She had thought to joust and lost. But she'd accepted his challenge. He had to catch that ship. Neither wanted to sail to Spain.

But thirty-five days…why such an odd number?

Could he catch his sister's ship in thirty-five days?

She pushed the door open to her bedroom and stormed through, noting that the adjoining door to Donato's room stood open.

He better catch his sister in less than thirty-five days.

"Unfasten quickly, then leave. *Merci*," she instructed Clarita, who had shown up to help with the undressing, but Colette wanted to think without distraction. When the door closed behind her servant, Colette dropped her gown.

The soft, luxuriant silk puddled around her feet. She stepped free and picked up the dress, a beautiful green gown heavily trimmed with satin ribbons that set off the low-cut neckline.

Unlike fashions she'd worn since her return home, this dress had been made to speak of Spain, with a tight bodice and sleeves adorned with ruffles. The lower third of the gown had more layers of lace ruffles, highlighted with gold embroidering. Donato had had the dress made for her, supposedly to honor her spirit of fire.

Where did he see that? Colette never saw herself as anything but plain and uninteresting. Spirit of fire…it nearly made her laugh if it weren't for wishing it to be true. As her memory had slowly returned after seeing the crystal, she felt out of step with the island, with Donato. Dressed in silks and satins, draped with jewels, she had remembered a covenant she made with God. And this life was not a part of it.

She pulled off the lacy mantilla, dappled with diamonds, and unrolled her hair, letting the long tresses fall around her shoulders. She shook her head, loosening the curls and combing through them with her fingers.

She opened the wardrobe and hung her dress on a hook, running her hand across the fabric of another dress; the smooth satin felt like warmed silk. With the candelabra in hand, she allowed herself to fall back in time and opened the door wider to see what had once been her wardrobe. They were gowns of such beauty, bright beautiful colors, that she had taken for granted until now. She fingered their hems, remembering their caressing feel against her skin. Everything in the room had been left as is, as if she had never left.

When recovering from her injury after her abduction, Donato had brought in a seamstress to make a wardrobe for her, for she'd had no gowns with her. She remembered him saying he wanted her in colors to celebrate her beauty and her return to the living. Colette smiled, remembering the joy of wearing such dresses, things that would never have found their way into her wardrobe in America or France, for Spain had her own style of dress.

She fingered the fine jewelry still neatly organized in the top drawer of her cedar chest. Pulling free a pair of long diamond earrings, she slipped them into her ears and felt them dangle against her neck. She glanced into the mirror. Beautiful, all of it.

To the bottom of the wardrobe sat a row of delicately hand-stitched slippers, one pair for every dress. She slipped on a pair, lacing them up, remembering the feel of such quality leather against her feet. What a luxury they were, then and now. She hooked a matching diamond necklace around her neck and placed it to rest within the cleavage of her breasts.

There she stood before the mirror, watching the candlelight play amid the diamonds, dressed in nothing more than a thin cotton chemise, with short sleeves and a low-cut neckline. It had been a long time since she had worn her hair loose and free around her face, and the sudden infusion of freedom brought a painful twist inside her chest as her heart squeezed out one beat after another.

Who was she really? Why, after learning her real identity and being reunited with her family, did she still feel so lost? Because she had forfeited the only life she had ever made for herself, Donato, and her son? If sitting in that chair now, in Enio's room, would she again so easily leave? Thinking over that decision, she instinctively knew she'd not make the same one again. She had earned the right to choose something else rather than service, whether Donato or not. She had more than paid her dues for the lives of her parents.

She heard Donato enter his room from the patio. She went to close the adjoining door, not wanting him to see her, but Donato reached it first. He looked her over, taking in the jewelry and chemise. "If you remain in a state of undress, my shadow will have to get out of my way."

"Your shadow will have to wait for thirty-five days. Not my rule, yours." She took pleasure in spouting off what he had thought was a check point. He had thought that would deter her from sailing with him. But nothing would; nothing would stop her from boarding his ship.

So far, she had avoided going into Enio's bedchamber for fear the loneliness and worry would be unbearable, but at this moment the memories of her little baby boy were so strong, she could almost hear her son's cooing. She spun on her heel, needing to dismiss the want in Donato's eyes that mirrored her own need for him, and walked into Enio's room.

There stood the rocker she had been sitting in the day Jordan arrived to take her home. Some of Enio's clothes still hung over the crib, the ones she had tossed aside in her rush to pack. They would no longer fit the growing boy.

Her life had changed the second Jordan walked through the door, just like it had three years before when pirates had captured her ship. Looking around her son's room was like a memory come to life with no Enio. Her heart sank; mist filled her eyes.

How could this have happened? And why?

Sensing Donato standing in the doorway, she didn't turn around, but asked him, "You will catch your sister?"

"*Si.*"

"Why does she have him?"

"I know only the who, not the why."

She no longer believed him. His calm aplomb ate at her nerves, making her all the more suspect that he and his sister were a part of some greater plan, and perhaps Colette was a victim once again.

"You must have an idea; you let them take our son." She turned and faced him.

"I could not stop them."

But the denials, the questions, the suspicions had twisted themselves in her mind and settled with a heavy weight in her stomach. "Of all the men who ride the sea, you are the most feared man of the gulf, yet someone had the courage to take your son? I do not believe you!"

She rushed toward him, halting a few inches from his body, trying to quiet the angst, the fear, the suspicion that this was a plan. Her heart raced, pounding at her temples, not with anger, but with her desperate need of him.

"It is the only truth, Colette."

Feeling helpless and missing her son more than she could imagine, she brought up her hand and slapped him.

He said nothing but looked down at her, though she could see the marks of her fury against his skin. "I cannot change what has happened to Enio or...to us."

The finality of his statement, as if he were through with her, made her anger soar to the surface faster than the storm wailed outside. She raised her hand again, but he caught her wrist and reeled her into his arms.

"I cannot change this, Colette."

"But you are the most powerful man I've ever known. If you can't, who can?"

"It will take time."

Water filled her eyes, and damn it, tears rolled down her cheeks, making her look weak. The emotions she had kept in check for days now boiled into a dark roux that started to burn under the heat of his touch.

"Let me go," she whispered, feeling weakened by his strength.

He didn't move, nor did he release her. They stood with bodies locked together simmering in a heat only they could generate. As it used to be. She sank into his arms, her face flush with his chest, finding solace in the warm beat of his heart. He gently stroked the side of her face and whispered, "I will get Enio back."

Whether he meant it or not, his caring love bled through that simple touch, a touch she craved, yet could not accept. The damage between them had been done.

She pushed free of his embrace, looking away from him. "Only you can."

Chapter Nine

Donato stepped back from Colette, pulling free of the spell in which he found himself, but his withdrawal was too late. He had held Colette in his arms, an embrace for no other reason but to embrace, something that he had thought would never happen again. Not like he had on the dock when she had fought to reach his sister's ship, or when he had lifted her to negotiate the high marsh grass. This was different.

It was a moment of vulnerability for him and her. A moment of love they felt for their son, a moment of grief, loss, and betrayal. A moment when his emotions drained through his facade and he could pretend no longer.

That step back gave him the second he needed to rein in unfettered feelings and collect himself. It was Colette who spoke first in the uneasy silence that followed their embrace.

"You've changed nothing since I…I left." She indicated their son's room with a sweep of her arm. "Have you not been in here?"

"My son was no longer here. For what purpose would I come in?" He almost thanked her for the reminder of how he had felt that day, the day her brother had arrived and taken Donato's world away. The day Colette had betrayed him and left a gaping wound that would never heal.

She thought to leave him, leave his life, to protect their son. But that wasn't the real reason. She had wanted to retreat into that safe little world her brother offered. The one she had lived in since the French Revolution. Instead of growing from it, she had withdrawn.

He hadn't known her true identity when he'd bought her off the auction block. By the time he learned that her brother searched for her, he didn't want her found. She was his world, the mother of his child, and the only woman he had ever given his heart.

So much pain between them and here she stood, dabbing at eyes that continued to tear, against her efforts. The light of the lamp wove delicate sparkles into her long golden-brown hair that splayed across her shoulders and down her back. Her eyes, oblong, dark green, and trimmed in sweeping lashes, were soiled from teardrops and glistened nearly as much as the diamond earrings she had donned.

Her body stiff, she nibbled on those lips that normally formed a four-cornered square when closed, but now, they had elongated, wanting to turn down and barely holding back the emotional dam that was about to break.

He could see her breasts rise and fall beneath the low-cut chemise as she breathed heavily. They pressed the fabric to experience life then retreat, a lot like Colette. The lamplight ebbed on and off her body with each breath, highlighting the juncture of her breasts, the hollow of her throat he so wanted to taste. He ran a tongue over his own lips, savoring the taste he knew to be there.

As she stood, dressed in a chemise with diamonds hanging from dainty earlobes that once had felt his kisses, wearing a necklace that trimmed the contours of her throat, supple, soft, and so inviting, wearing satin slippers, she looked more the expensive courtesan than a wife gone rogue.

But his compassion was gone, vented, like a winded sail suddenly pierced. He reached out and laced his fingers in the wild and free locks of her hair and wound them tightly in his hand.

Slowly he reeled her into him, pressing her body close to his with her face upward. He ran his other hand up along the terrain of her throat as would a sculptor admiring his work. She inhaled deeply and ran a tongue over her lips.

He held her there, immobile, vacillating between cursing himself for wanting her and cursing her for having left him. He tilted her head slightly, allowing his hand full access to her throat, cupping her neck with his thumb and forefinger. Straddling her larynx, he applied light pressure because he could, and she couldn't stop him.

"Where is this little pistol of yours?"

"I do not have it." She didn't try to resist; instead she closed her eyes. He wondered if she thought he would end her life here, for she resisted not. His thumb stroked the flawless skin beneath her chin, reminiscing about the feel, having never touched a woman like her.

She opened her eyes and met his. The sea-green color reflected the mist she had thought to dab away. A tear rolled down her cheek and over the tips of his fingers.

"You wish to harm me?" she whispered. "It will not

make this go away."

He kept his focus on her face, her eyes, for in them he would always find his truth.

"Do you think I wish to?" His voice as low as the rumbling thunder that rattled the window panes. "Or that I would?"

She drew another long, deep breath. Her breasts pressed against his chest; he felt the air come and go and a slight muffled sob that escaped. She was powerless and she knew it. "No, I do not think that."

Her voice was just a whisper, but had a hungry sound to it that made him wonder who he was speaking to, his wife or Jordan's sister?

"No, harm you, I will not, but take you at my leisure, I will." He brushed her lips with his. Her mouth opened slightly for him. She tasted sweet and salty, tears mixed with beauty. He dropped his hand from her throat and wrapped it around her body.

At more than six feet, Donato towered over Colette. He nearly lifted her from her feet. But he didn't care; he had wanted this kiss since he'd seen her in New Orleans, when she had fought him on the dock, when she had kept a rigid spine and led them through the swamp, and when she had fallen overboard and dangled above a furious sea. He had almost asked her permission before, only to be rebuked, but not this time. This kiss was his, and damned if he wasn't going to take it.

He unwound his fingers from her hair and pulled her flush against his chest. He wanted to feel her every response, knew her breasts would pump with each labored breath, her nipples tighten and rise. He knew her hand would touch his arm, then journey upward until she reached his shoulders.

He knew how Colette would react, even if she didn't.

With her lips parted slightly, he maneuvered his tongue between her teeth and slid it into her mouth. He savored the taste of her, allowing the hotly stirred mixture of her mouth to marinate him in her natural scent of saccharine and danger. Feeling the hot pulsation of her mouth against his, he drew his only breath before her hand slowly migrated upward; not in protest, her fingers walked along his lower arm.

She tried for a breath but he held her firm, reminding her of his strength and that no other man would love her as much as he had. But that was then, not now. She had betrayed him.

Her hand moved up his shoulder, pulling him deeper into the kiss that he had thought to demand from her. Damn her, he wanted her to resist, insist he release her, be forced to accept his power over her, but that wasn't happening.

Instead her power oozed over him like molasses on a hot day, robbing him of the strength he needed to resist.

Her fingers continued across the breadth of his shoulders and played with the hair at the back of his neck, like she had done so many times before. He liked it now as he had then. His body nearly curled in response, heat turned inward, upward, so quickly it was now he who needed that breath of fresh air or he'd topple her over and submit to the most beautiful woman he'd ever known. But she was more than that; she was the woman who had betrayed him.

He pushed her away, dismissing her from his arms—his heart—his life.

He noted she swallowed hard and forced a straightness to her back, like he had seen on the pirogue. She wet her lips, tasting the remains of their kiss, never taking her eyes off of him. "Disappointed I did not resist?"

There they were standing in their child's room, his son's room, where he had entrusted his son to Colette and she had taken him to America. The sense of betrayal so real, he needed to breathe it out before it suffocated him.

"Perhaps." He had to admit, a little struggle of resistance might have relieved the cork inside him that was about to blow.

She straightened her shoulders in an attempt to look stronger, but she had melted under his touch, a fact they had both witnessed. He had found her vulnerability, her weak spot, the way to render her helpless. He didn't want Colette back in his life, for he no longer trusted her, but in thirty-five days, she'd be begging him for mercy.

"But I enjoy much more the fact that you could not resist. *Buenas noches.*"

• • •

Toma, hermosa. Te hará bien.

Colette tried to wake up, but the dreams kept her paralyzed in the bed. A shadow appeared over her and she heard the voice again saying, *Toma, hermosa. Te hará bien.* Her body felt weak, and suddenly her ankle started to throb. She bolted upright in bed.

She was covered in sweat. Her heart hammered, and she gasped for air. The pain in her leg blazed a streak of fire from foot to hip. She threw the covers off and hoped the air would chill her to an awakened state.

Glancing around the room, she felt disoriented at first,

until she remembered Donato, the house, Enio's room, the island. Her eyes moistened, tears fell down the sides of her face, each drop filled with the burning anguish over her missing son.

She crushed the pillow to her face and for the first time since his abduction, she allowed herself one and only one deep-seated cry.

Finally recovered from the dream, Colette noted that the pain in her leg had vanished. She pushed free of the bed, trying to walk off the odd feeling that had swept over her tonight.

Donato's kiss had surprised her, especially when he had run his hand over her throat. She knew what he was thinking. They were standing in the very last place he'd seen his son, thanks to her. As a man of vengeance, the temptation to exact revenge on her was clearly in his mind. But fear him, she did not. She had learned who he really was long ago, when he had surrendered to her brother's ship, risking death and Jordan's fury to keep her and Enio safe.

In spite of his attempts to pretend otherwise, the loving touch had been there. Whether he wanted her to feel it or not, the stroke of his hand was gentle even when he had applied pressure to her throat. How easily he could have crushed her. He had thought to force the kiss, but try as she might, she could not resist. The hot touch of his lips over hers had turned her knees to mush, leading her back in time, when she had been here, with him.

Unable to quell the pain of separation from her son, she retraced her steps into Enio's room and sat down in the leather rocking chair, the same chair she had been rocking Enio in when Jordan had arrived to take her home.

Enio would be safe now had it not been for her leaving, for Donato always had the island well-fortified, and no doubt the security had increased since she left. Without hesitation, she had packed up her son that night and had led Jordan's men to Donato's gold. Once on the American mainland and back with her family whom she had missed for so long, she had lived her proper life in fulfilling her long-ago vow through her works of charity. She had never allowed herself to think about her decision to leave Donato, because it had been expected that she return home. Now... back here...back on the island...his home...his arms, her mind felt muddled and incapable of sorting anything out rationally.

Her heart started to sputter against the wall of her chest, and taking a breath made her dizzy. She ran her fingers over her temples, refusing to allow herself to remember this.

She turned out of Enio's room and back into their adjoining rooms. It was too late to rethink all of this. When Jordan had appeared, it had been like a dream. She hadn't known who she was for so long, and when her memory had started to work, she'd only remembered bits that had been lost, and she'd thought she wanted to return to her life.

She walked over to the window and watched the angry wind. *Then whose life was this? Who had stood at this window many times? Whose dresses filled the wardrobe? Whose son once slept here? Whose husband—* She stopped the tumbling thoughts.

The storm had abated, and though it wasn't howling, the wind still blew across the island, creating a menagerie of whitecaps spilling over the banks of the cay.

She turned to her room and opened her armoire packed

with beautiful dresses of red, gold, green, sheer, and sparkling, all from Donato. She pulled on a robe, high-necked and long-sleeved, then threw a woolen mantilla over her head and shoulders.

Walking through her bedroom and Donato's, she hesitated, seeing the fluttering light from his office across from the indoor patio. A sense of guilt niggled. Jordan's men had robbed Donato. She had told them of the hand-painted vase with a key to the hidden drawer of gold.

Unlike Donato, Jordan's men had been pure pirate and loyal only for coin. Though they had proven otherwise when the British had attacked New Orleans, Jordan knew he had to pay his men. It had been the only way to guarantee her passage.

Donato had always claimed his men were loyal to him, *sus camaradas*, he'd call them, but who and why, she never knew.

The fountain in the center of the patio continued to spill water over the basins, powered by the large cistern on the hills behind the hacienda. The soft pinging sounded rhythmic and soothing. The lanterns along the indoor patio created shadows in the long corridors leading to the kitchen and dining room. For only a second or two between gusts of wind, she heard the soft melodious sound of guitarists, reminding her of the beautiful dances held in the ballroom.

She walked across the inner patio to Donato's study. The door was open, and when she slowly walked in, he was there, poring over the maps, planning their journey.

He had shed the black velvet coat and waistcoat. He wore only a shirt, opened at the collar and rolled up over each forearm, exposing luscious thick muscles she ached to touch with her fingers.

He looked up, surprise raising his dark eyebrows, accentuating his rakish look, but the usual soothing color of his eyes darkened. Slowly, he came to his feet and gave her a slight bow, acknowledging a woman entering the room.

"Colette." His voice low, hesitant, as if waiting for battle.

Colette lost her nerve, suddenly feeling stripped of strength, for she had no reasonable ground to stand on for having taken his son from him. She froze, cleared her throat. "I must speak with you about…about what happened in our child's room."

"I have much on my mind and no longer wish to spar with you." He dropped his stylus and came around the desk. "I don't deny the temptation, for I miss my son, but I do not blame you nor do I wish to harm you, Colette."

"I know that." Colette tried to stroll naturally around the room, running her fingers along the desk as she passed it by, but Donato looked tired and impatient.

"Then what is it you must speak about tonight? If the storms abates, we have a long journey starting tomorrow. That is, if you still insist on coming?"

"I do." Her glance around the intimate shadows of the study made the stolen kiss in Enio's room resurface in her mind, along with the feelings of craving more, wanting more from him. She swallowed hard, packing desires away and trying to put her mission back on track.

"I am here…" She inhaled, regrouping her thoughts. "Donato, I am sorry that I took your son from you in the way that I did."

She waited, hoping he wouldn't ask for an explanation, for at the moment, she didn't have one. But instead he looked away from her, and that brought a slight chill to her heart. Had he become so hardened toward her that he would not, or could not, accept her apology?

"I apologize for the kiss," he responded.

Was that a reciprocal response? Did he accept her apology if she accepted his?

"But..." he continued before she had time to respond, "I will remind you, tomorrow will be here soon. Get some sleep."

"I know." Defeated in her attempt, she tried to explain, anyway. "There was so much I do not remember, but seeing my brother that day when he arrived, I felt...I had to go home."

"But your home was not America."

"No, but my family..." Her attempt to mend a wrong failed. He continued to watch her as if waiting for more, but more she could not offer, not now, not until she remembered. "I cannot say more, or explain, for I do not remember much of that night when I was taken."

"That was nearly four years ago. Perhaps you should not try to rekindle the past."

"I wish that to be true, but my mind nags me to remember. My apology was for the sake of civility. We will be together for a time. I know I hurt you, Donato, so terribly. I am deeply sorry." Wrapping the mantilla around her throat, she headed for the door but halted when he softly spoke her name. She kept her back to him.

"I know how hard it was to say this apology to me. *Gracias*. Does that mean you regret having left this life here?"

Keeping her back to him, Colette closed her eyes, striving to keep herself calm, unbroken. If she collapsed her facade, even for a second, and allowed her feelings free rein over her actions, she would turn around and put her arms around his neck and kiss him like he'd never been kissed. But that was not possible, for she was who she was and nothing would change that reality. "No, Donato, I left to return to my own life."

"And you are happy, with this life that is yours?"

Her body physically swayed from his question as if hit broadside. The burn dived down into her belly as the words fell away, leaving only a raw passion for life bubbling to the surface without permission.

Her apology was necessary, for she had hurt him tremendously. Having Enio taken from her, she now understood the great pain she must have caused Donato, but she could not dismiss his life filled with vengeance any more than she could deny her chosen life.

She turned to face him, needing to take the focus of the conversation off her. "You will get Enio back?"

"*Si.*" He allowed her to change the subject.

"Will you then take him from me, as you told my brother?"

"No, I did not." He shook his head. "I meant…my son will always be with me."

Colette caught the meaning, even if he didn't say it. He just let the statement float around them. He didn't invite her to return to him, nor did he say she couldn't. It was simply a fact: he'd never allow Enio to be taken from him again. If she wanted Enio, she'd have to be with Donato.

"Why did you not come sooner?"

He looked surprised by her question. "Were you disappointed?"

"I…" She couldn't admit that buried deep inside her heart there had been a desire to see him from the moment she left. She swallowed hard and pulled in a labored breath. "I was puzzled."

"When a mere baby, Enio needed his mother. Now, at eighteen months, there is a role a father has to play as well. It is time for the boy to return home."

"*Capitán!*" Ramón's voice came from the inner patio. He sounded breathless as footfalls pounded through the inner patio.

"What is it?"

"The storm has abated."

Donato nodded. "I know, tomorrow we prepare—"

"No, *Capitán*, you must come, all the ships are damaged from the storm. We have no ship worthy of sail."

Chapter Ten

Donato heard Colette's intake of air. She walked over to stand next to him and placed a light touch to his arm. He wanted to shrug off his reaction to the feel of her fingertips, of her deferring to him for support, the tenderness, the feeling of being in this together. He glanced down at her hand, then up at her. Just as quickly as she had put her hand on his arm, she removed it.

"The fleet?" Donato returned his attention to Ramón.

"Gone."

"Gone? How?"

"The waves pounded the docks."

"No ship is seaworthy?"

"None."

Donato pushed through the study door with an entourage behind him consisting of Ramón and Colette. Some of the men, who lived in the *portales* perpendicular to the house, had lined the outdoor gardens.

The storm had abated, leaving everything sea-washed and cold. It was a chilly night, and though the rumbling clouds had moved on, the angry sea continued to roil with frothy waves that hammered the coast.

Any hope of catching up with Rayna ended with Ramón's message.

That meant he'd have to go to Spain. If he had to, could he get Enio back and escape? Would he be arrested? How much did his father know of Donato's treasonous acts?

Colette was behind him as they ran to the dock. From his corner vision, he could see her limping; the faster they went the more pronounced her limp. He slowed down for her, taking her arm to assist. Together they surveyed the damage.

Hulls crushed, poles down, sails ripped into shreds. He checked his schooner first, having planned to take that ship across the Atlantic. The hull had been smashed against the wall of boulders he had thought guarded his island. But now they had destroyed his ships. The ships would have been moved to the other side of the island for protection, but the men who did that had been on the water with him.

"All of them damaged, *Capitán*." Ramón continued to describe the obvious to Donato.

He had to think. His heart pounded against his chest; fear of not being able to give pursuit paralyzed his mind. He felt numb. Defeated.

"Can we repair the sloop?" He visually evaluated a different ship, but feared the worse.

"Perhaps, but it would take a few days. We don't have all that is needed on the island."

"*Maldita sea*," Donato swore under his breath, knowing the isolation of the island did not lend itself to this type of emergency, and if he had no ship, getting anything would be difficult. But that reminded him of the supply ship. "Where's the clipper? Wasn't it on the other side of the island?"

He had bought a small clipper during the war, had used it for supply runs between the Jardines de la Reina islands and Cuba. It was a small ship and not heavily armed to survive the open waters, but if intact, he had no choice.

The island was twenty miles long and thirty miles wide, which made the cay more than six hundred square miles. On the eastern side of the island were several coves surrounded by boulders. Though much farther from the hacienda, the clipper was usually moored there for easier access to Cuba.

Donato retraced his steps back up the hill and toward the stables. Colette tried to keep up with him, but fell on the cobblestones of the large walkway. She didn't cry out for help, but struggled to get to her feet. Her robe was soaked from the dampness, and her hair stuck to her face.

Donato raced back and scooped her up before she could resist his help. He changed direction and headed for the inner patio.

"No, I go with you," she protested.

"No, this time you do as I say."

"But I can ride now."

"One ride does not make you a rider. You slow me down. Wait here."

He pushed through the outside gate and ran the length of the gardens to enter the inner gate, taking an immediate left into his room, then hers. He put her on the bed and turned to leave when he caught her grimace of pain as her body shivered from the wet robe.

He unbuttoned her wet robe and peeled it off her body,

then covered her with a warm quilt. She pulled it up to her chin, her teeth chattering. "*Merci.*"

From under the coverlet, he pulled off her boot and started to massage her ankle, because it was habit, because he cared, because it was what he had always done when she was in pain and it had always worked.

She groaned, rolling her head from side to side, her breathing labored. A slight film of perspiration shone across her forehead.

"Relax, *cariño.*" As everything else he was doing by habit, so was his sobriquet for her. He dismissed his mistake and ran his hands over and over her ankle, working the muscles to release under his expert fingers. He felt them give, and Colette moaned. "Better?"

She kept her eyes closed, but her thrashing had ended and her breathing had calmed back to normal. "It is better. Only you have such a touch, Donato."

He looked down at his hands on her sore ankle. Her skin glowed like porcelain in the fire-washed room, smooth as silk beneath his coarse fingers, fragile and delicate. He felt her female energy rush through his body with unrepentant heat. He allowed his hand to travel upward along her leg, kneading her calf with the palm of his hand. How easy it would be to slide along her body, dipping into every contour, emerging in more need of her. He heard a slight intake of air as he pushed his hand up behind her knee.

"It is better?" He massaged her knee, wanting to move his hand upward along the inside of her thigh.

"I hurt no more. I appreciate."

He withdrew his hand before tucking her leg in under the quilt. Without thought, he leaned down to kiss her on the forehead. The moment his lips touched her warm skin, he knew he had fallen into the habit of what he had always done in the past. But she wasn't his anymore, and that little touch of affection should not have happened. He straightened up, feeling her gaze on him.

"Are you all right? I need to check the ship," he said as dispassionately as he could.

"Ever so."

He turned to leave, but hesitated at the sound of her voice.

"I beg you to find a way for us to leave. We must get Enio back."

"That's a promise." Donato closed her door behind him and met Ramón coming in through the inner patio.

Within seconds, they had tacked horses and pounded across the island at breaking speed.

The air was damp and smelled of rain when he reached the clipper. Waves slapped the hull, rocking her back and forth. The ropes groaned and creaked with every swell.

Donato had wanted to use a fast ship that would cut through the waves and give him an advantage with the wind. He had a reputation for getting speed where others would fail. Ships ate out of his hands. A good captain knew when to stretch those sails and when to have them soft and slack. But could he push this small clipper into service and meet the challenge of an ocean voyage?

The clipper had two masts. The foremast with two shrouds and the mainmast with one. It was 123 feet in length with a breadth of twenty-four feet, three thousand square feet of main deck. Its rake of stern was so excessive it could not stow more than two months of provisions nor bear the weight of bow guns, creating a disadvantage if not able to outrun a man of war. But it had a bowsprit designed for ramming, a slight plus.

The first hatch going fore opened into a stateroom and captain's quarters. The companionway hatch opened into the main hold where there was a galley, and a fireplace opened aft. The crew of sixty men would swing their hammocks in the wardroom.

The problem with this particular ship was her stability, but she'd offer speed. Her sloping V-shaped hull would cut through the waves rather than ride above them, forcing a nearly constant water spray over the main deck.

"Can we provision in twenty-four hours?" he asked Ramón.

Ramón nodded, animated with a new plan in place. "*Si, Capitán.*"

"Good. I have listed our supplies." He pulled from his pocket a list of what provisions they'd need. The list included water, salted beef and pork, hardtack, bread, flour, pickled hog, oatmeal, rum, coffee, vinegar, molasses, potatoes, cheese, butter, brown sugar, and a few hundred candles. "But for this ship, considering her size, cut everything on that list in half, except water and candles."

Donato took the stairs down to the stateroom and entered his cabin. It was a small room of decorative panels with carved badges of leaves and scrolls over the arched stern windows. Mounted against the larboard side was a small bed with a small built-in wardrobe next to it. To the stern stood a small table and two chairs.

Close quarters for a long journey.

Close quarters for him and Colette.

He returned to the stateroom where Ramón waited and pulled out a set of nautical maps he kept stored in every vessel.

He drew an imaginary line across the drawing of the Atlantic Ocean. "Here is where I hope Rayna stopped through the storm, unless she made enough speed to put the storm behind her."

"If that is the case, you won't be able to catch her."

"No." Donato looked up at his trusted friend. "We'll end up in Spain. I would understand if you do not wish to make this journey."

Ramón blinked in surprise, then his face grew tight. "I would think to do no other."

"Do the men know this journey might land us back in Spain? In harm's way? We are traitors to the crown."

"*Si*, Your Excellency, like in New Orleans, we are with you."

"Ramón, the title." Donato motioned with a clip to his throat. "Don't use that."

"I sometimes forget, Your Ex—*Capitán*, I forget."

After Ramón left to start the laborious task of rerigging her sails and provisioning the ship, Donato continued to review his nautical maps, hearing the constant activity above on the main deck.

Nearly five thousand miles. That's how far Spain was, and right now his sister had built quite a lead. The idea of returning to Spain brought on a tight painful turn in his stomach. He had no choice but to return to where it had all started, where the saga must end.

He pulled out his dagger and jammed the sharp point into the table marking their destination.

Spain.

• • •

It was an unusually pretty day, considering the ravaging

storm of just hours before. Colette had been up, bathed, and dressed for hours, but no Donato. She tried to inquire as to his whereabouts, but the servants politely pretended not to understand her broken Spanish, and she knew why. She had taken the much-loved Enio away.

She continued through the inner patio, walking by beautiful fountains of stone basins and poetic statues. Citrus and palm trees lined the corridors and bathed the walkways in dappled shade. She continued through the outer gardens and patios, noting the sprinkled color of the oleanders just starting to bloom. Above the kitchen chimney rose a hazy smoke that smelled delicious, and she knew the evening meal was in preparation.

Standing on the cobblestoned road, she could see the fields where the hacienda grew sisal, henequen, and sugar. All exported. The grounds had a granary and a henequen factory. There was a network of rails and tracks to move fiber to the factory, then to the docks.

A small town was to the south end of the island. She had often heard ringing bells and had visited the small adobe church. There were several merchants and private homes off the main street. The island was bustling with economic activity, six hundred square miles of robust commotion, making her curious as to the revenue of the island and the relationship with other islands. Why would Donato be involved in piracy, for it appeared he was a man of means?

Afraid of being left behind, she demanded a horse be tacked up for her to ride, then headed toward the other side of the island. Keeping her mount at a slow walk, she followed the road that crisscrossed the island. The sun migrated upward into the sky, telling her it was noon before she found the dock.

She reined in, halting the horse.

Floating atop the undulating water rode the clipper. He hadn't left without her. Still docked, the ship bobbed freely in the waves that ricocheted off the large boulders as the men readied her for sail.

They had a ship!

Colette slid off her horse and ran along the gangplank, dodging between men laden with crates and demijohns. She found herself on the main deck, but it was a different ship than she'd ever been on and had no idea how to find Donato's cabin.

She hesitated, pulling together her little knowledge of Spanish. "Ah, *¿dónde es el capitán?*"

One of Donato's men motioned for her to follow and opened a hatch to the back of the boat, exposing a short staircase.

"*Muchas gracias.*" She climbed into the hatch and down the stairs, her leg giving out twice. Once on the quarterdeck, she turned into a small room where Donato stood working over some maps.

"We have a ship?" She was so excited she couldn't stop herself from throwing her arms around his neck. "You are provisioning?"

In her excitement, she temporarily missed how tired Donato looked, his drawn expression, and that those broad shoulders that her arms had embraced were tense and burdened with worry. She knew without asking, he had not slept at all. It had been hours since he had slept; he must be exhausted.

"You must need sleep," she whispered in his ear. She felt his arms come up around her, but it was nothing more than a polite embrace before he stepped back from her.

"There is much I need, but little time."

"You must sleep, to keep yourself strong. But this is good news, to have a ship?"

"She'll have to do." He looked around as if wondering who had accompanied her. "How did you get here?"

"I rode a horse." She couldn't suppress an eager smile over that accomplishment.

"Alone?"

"Why, of course I did, but that is not important. This is." She opened her arms and twirled through the map room.

"But we are still married, Colette. This is not a proper way for my wife to board my ship."

She halted her spin. A slight tingle raced up her spine when he said they were still married in his low, heavily accented voice. She swallowed hard, pushing her reaction deep inside. "*Pardonne-moi*, I don't wish to disturb, but we sail when? And before you try to convince me not to go, remember I have sailed the ocean three times."

"Not on a ship like this. She's a small clipper."

"Being small, she flies over the water."

He watched her for a second or two before responding, making her feel the fool. "It drives through the water, not atop it."

Her heart moved a notch up into her throat, painfully remembering her near flight off the deck of Jordan's ship. "Like my brother's flushed ship."

He seemed impressed with her conclusion, raising one dark eyebrow over his left eye. He nodded. "Not as perilous as that, but she dives into the water, too much wind and she buries her and us under the sea, or capsizes."

"I will go."

"Thought so."

"We sail today?" Colette had gotten a little ahead of the conversation, but Donato made no note of it.

"There is much to do to secure the island and bring in material for repairs on the other ships. Not to mention the westerlies." He shook his head. "I will have you escorted back to the hacienda. Tomorrow before dawn, we sail."

"We?"

"We." He nodded. "You and me. It's time we get our son back."

• • •

"You didn't tell her." Ramón had been standing at the base of the companionway when Colette left the map room. "You didn't tell her the danger that awaits you in Spain."

"What am I to tell her? Who I really am and that my piracy is a cover-up? That I am a revolutionist and believe that Spain can govern herself, as does America? That I have turned my back on my birthright, my nobility, and have taken action against my king? It matters not, for we no longer share our lives."

But her apology had run through his mind several times during the night. She hadn't apologized for leaving, but for doing it in the way she had. Again, he didn't believe the why, and maybe that was the discussion they should have had.

Colette rode across the island today. The same woman who knew nothing about horses just days ago. But Colette and the island brought life to each other, unlike the stuffy Kincaid residence that seemed to subdue her spirit rather than let it fly. He doubted she'd understand that, though. Having lived her prescribed life for so many years, she had immediately fallen into the mold upon her return.

Donato had double-checked the list of needed supplies and preparations for the trip to Spain. He had sailed enough in the open sea to know the many moods of the water and how often the weather might turn without notice. He knew storms and wind droughts awaited them, not to mention pirates in the form of French naval ships, British, or worse, Spanish. There was no flag in particular that would ensure safe passage, so several would be on hand and at the ready.

He'd never catch Rayna, but he'd arrive not long afterward. She'd most likely port in Cádiz, the closest to their father's estate. She knew Enio was not Spain-born, and why that didn't matter puzzled him, but the answer was ahead, and forward he must go.

To Donato's appreciation, Ramón dropped the subject of Colette and returned to the journey ahead. "This is dangerous travel with this ship."

"*Si*," Donato reluctantly answered. Though many like it had crossed the Atlantic, it had a low freeboard combined with a deep deadrise, not much different than the schooner of Jordan's he had flushed before leaving Louisiana.

This ship would ride through the waves, creating a lot of spray, and be less stable. But with flushed wide decks and high bulwarks, the men would be able to work the sails and guns should the occasion arise. "We will find ourselves back in Spain."

"We all expect as much and are with you as always, but your *esposa*? It is dangerous."

"She must come. She is Enio's mother. She understands the stakes at hand. She risked her life in the bayous without hesitation. She risked her life on the sail here without complaint.

She has earned the right to follow her son." Donato pulled out a flask of whiskey and poured a cup for him and Ramón. After a sip, he ambled over and closed the door to the stateroom. "Ramón, how much gold was in the ship that foundered?"

"At least twenty thousand that is lost. We might get some back, but the shoreline is too deep, I fear."

"We have supported the revolution well, but will not ship this month."

"No, Your Excellency. Until we are paid, we are low on gold."

Donato again sipped on the whiskey. "Ramón, did you ever hear a legend about medallions and gold?"

Ramón nodded. "*Si*, a story, I thought, told in the establishments along Saint Ann's. When combined they made a map, but the medallions were lost at sea. Just a story."

"Not a story. The medallions belonged to Colette and her brother." Donato pulled out a leather wallet, having stashed it in the clipper this morning with important papers. In there, he had Jordan's notes and handwritten maps. "Copies of the maps, compliments of Jordan Kincaid."

He smoothed the maps out on the table over his nautical charts.

"The senora's brother." Ramón leaned in with interest. "Appears to be a map of France."

"By the notations, Jordan believes this to be France. He is from France but…his father, who had the medallions made, was an American. I am certain Jordan is looking under the wrong rock."

"And you know where the gold is, Your Excellency?"

"I have an idea. But there are other markings that are strange. Two notations, death before dishonor and crooked cross. What could that mean?"

"One is a common saying. The crooked cross, I do not know."

"If the story is true, this hidden treasure is worth close to a quarter of a million in gold."

"That would go a long ways to fight our cause."

"It would, indeed." Donato smiled. "I'm sure Colette's American father would approve. He was a revolutionist."

"Do you think to find this treasure?"

"I do, and when I do, I will take it right out from under Jordan's nose."

Chapter Eleven

Colette dropped the cotton gown around her ankles and stepped out of the dust-covered clothes. Her bath had been drawn and awaited her aching muscles. She might have conquered her fear of horses and ridden on her own today, but her body ached with the slightest movement. She had spent the rest of the afternoon riffling through her clothes for what to pack for the journey. It appeared, from what she saw, that storage space was at a premium.

She had seen a lot today on the back of a horse. She had traveled not only to the ship but to the town, and had visited the church where she and Donato had been married in the eyes of God.

The memories of that day hung around her head like the white mantilla and beautiful dress she had worn on her wedding day, the excitement of the townsfolk, the street lined with well-wishers as they had ridden back to the hacienda. She had been happy that day…really happy.

What had changed?

Donato?

Jordan?

When she returned to the house, she retreated to Enio's room, sitting in the rocker, remembering the nights and days she had held Enio in her arms for hours, holding the most beautiful baby she had ever seen. Remembering when she had sung to him, rocked him to sleep...

She had not had children with her husband in France, though she had so much wanted children. When he had died of lung disease she thought she'd never have another chance to conceive. Then Donato had come into her life, rescuing her from the men who had taken her ship, and had given her the greatest gift a man could give a woman—love and through that love, a child.

But she had taken Enio away.

There was a slight knock on the door, jerking her from her thoughts. "Enter."

Clarita came into the room and bowed before she spoke. "I am to inform you that dinner will be served in the *comedor* at seven this evening. El Senor de la Roche would like for la senora to attend."

Colette nodded without hesitation. *"Merci—gracias."*

Knowing Donato always dressed for dinner, she opened her armoire and fingered the beautiful dresses draped on every hook.

She pulled out the blue satin dress trimmed in yellow sparkling lace ruffles that hung around the hem. Opposite of what she might do at home, tonight she allowed her hair to hang the length of her back and topped her head with a sapphire-endowed *peineta*, and hung from it a white mantilla with diamonds sewn throughout the lace.

Donato had never spared expense when buying her things. It was a Spanish-style dress, but those were the clothes Donato had provided for her, and she could not deny their beauty. He had said it was to celebrate her ability to find life again after her abduction, her fiery spirit. She stepped back from the mirror.

Oh, how wrong he had been about her. She could barely muster a spark. But tonight she'd wear a gown he'd bought for her, because unless they found common ground and reciprocated respect, they were doomed before the voyage began.

She opened the door to her room and walked into the *Sala de Recepcion* where Donato waited. He stood near the arched window overlooking the indoor patio, swirling a drink in his hand.

"Colette." He turned, offering a slight bow. "How beautiful you are tonight."

She loved hearing him say that, and wished she could hear it over and over, and that she could be that beautiful woman who deserved such a man.

"Would you like a cordial before dinner?" He broke the silence.

She nodded that she would, though right about now, she wanted a much stronger brew. A servant made her a cordial. She accepted and noted the nod from Donato for the servant to leave the room. The door closed behind him, leaving them alone.

The reception room, where she remembered many a gala, had been furnished with numerous leather-studded chairs, ottomans, and conversation tables set strategically around the walls, all marble-topped. But there was no gaiety tonight. The entire hacienda seemed to be in a grieving state for Donato; the only sign of life was the sad, melodious sounds of a charango from the inside patio. Music floated through the open window of the salon.

She sat at one of the tables, knowing they would be summoned when the dinner was served, as had always occurred when she'd lived here. She placed her glass on the marble top, then closed her eyes, feeling the sadness that seemed to have drained all happiness from Donato's home. Sadness she had brought on by taking Enio away, and now he was in danger.

The *charanguista* continued his harmonic beat of music, striking low chords and high chords all mixed beautifully together to create a blend of intoxicating music. There was nothing as beautiful as a Spanish charango, and the rhythmic strumming soothed her body.

She started to sway with the music, bending from the waist in one direction, then the other until she felt like a lily pad atop gently moving water. The notes moved through her mind with images and memories of her life here on the island.

She glanced up to find that Donato had approached the small table and watched her from behind the fluttering flame of the colorful centerpiece.

"I like the music," she whispered, feeling intoxicated though she had drunk little of the cordial.

He extended his hand across the table. "Honor me, Colette."

Her breath caught in her throat as if she were a maiden and this was her first social. His hand extended, he waited for her to take it. Well-manicured nails, sparkling rings on four of the fingers. As expected, Donato was dressed for dinner in his red velvet long tails, white waistcoat, white breeches, and highly polished Hessians that folded over the muscular calves of his legs. His raven hair had been neatly combed back into a queue, but a strand or two had found freedom and floated around his temples, adding to his sultry look.

With hesitation that made her movements exceedingly slow, she lifted her hand to his. His fingers were warm and firm as they curled around hers. She rose, nearly floating upward until her slippers were on the ballroom floor.

Donato raised his voice and asked the musician to play a favorite of his and hers.

"*Si, Capitán.*" The music shifted, the staccato faster, yet tamed by the slow strumming.

Donato pulled her to the center of the floor and stepped away from her. She started slowly at first, pairing Donato's movement, the sway of his arms, the ever-moving positioning of one hand over the other. With each gentle rotary movement of his wrists, he'd snap his fingers, take a quick step closer to her. Her gaze fixed to his, his eyes remained on her as they both circled the floor and each other.

Her body came to life, and a flush heated her cheeks as she mirrored his movements, so rhythmic, so intoxicating. He came within a breath of her, then stepped back in time with the music. She inhaled the mint scent of him. With the click of his heel, he again stood with his lips a mere breath from hers. The heat of his body swelled around her. She inhaled deeply, savoring the musk of such a handsome yet dangerous man.

He joined their right hands, palm to palm, and across their bodies, he joined their left hands. With each strum of the charango, he pulled her into him and pushed away. Back and forth he moved their bodies, touching ever so slightly, then apart once again. His dark eyes, trimmed in those heavy midnight lashes, remained fixed on her.

She tried to swallow, but her mouth had gone dry. Her heart raced ahead of the rhythm, beating its own cadence far beyond the *charanguista* on the patio. The overhead chandeliers created wavering shadows within his face and shone slightly on the perspiration along each temple.

He swayed them together again. This time his heat lingered around her, caressing her, then leaving her chilled and wanting each time he stepped away. The music worked toward a crescendo, building the tempo to match that of her beating heart.

Donato raised their right hands and swung her underneath until her back was flush against his chest. With their hands joined and arms out to each side of them, in unison they dipped in one direction, then the other.

His heart hammered against her body. Her rounded backside slid back and forth against his hips. The flutter of his warm breath spread across the base of her neck, spiraling down her spine to settle somewhere deep inside her belly, stirring to life feelings she thought she had left behind, but they were here on this island, and every spin of the dance awakened yet another.

He turned with their hands still clasped at her waist and her left arm drawn across his chest. They floated around the center of the ballroom. She inhaled, allowing her head to fall against the strength of his shoulder and permit the breeze created by their dancing to waft through her hair.

The diamond mantilla sparkled in the candlelight as it fluttered about her face with each turn they took. Her skin, like the air before a storm, ready to ignite. She trembled, allowing the feelings to surface, choosing surrender over resistance.

He turned her again; the music from the charango echoed through her mind, over and over. She felt the beat work through her feet, her legs, her body, moving, excited and terrified all at the same time.

Does he know the effect he is having on me? Is he purposely making me feel what I have so wanted to forget? And Donato, what is he feeling?

He twirled her under his arm again and pulled her close to his body. Face-to-face, he wrapped the other arm around her torso, crushing her breasts to his chest. She felt the air move in and out of his lungs, her heart beating in rhythm to his. She smiled, consenting to have the freedom to react to the music, to feel its every breath, every movement, every strum that rang through her mind.

She suddenly felt free, twirling about the room in a beautiful gown of silk, sparkling under the candlelight of the chandelier. Feeling light-headed, she feared she might take flight and leave his arms, until she realized the magic she was feeling was not the music, nor the beautiful candlelight, but was contained solely within the arms of her husband.

Gazing into his dark eyes, she sank into their alluring velvety texture. Sweat trickled down his temple, and she couldn't resist reaching up and tracing the same line with her fingers. He seemed to react to her touch by swirling her off her feet and into his arms, releasing her slowly along the length of his body until she thought she'd never breathe again.

He pivoted with their joined left hands at her waist and dipped to their knees. Using his body as leverage, he gently held her to hover above the floor. They slid to a stop the same instant the music ceased and the magic came to an end.

Donato lifted her from the floor to regain her footing. He twirled her through his arms to face him, then stepped away.

"*Gracias*." He made a formal bow, then snapped the heels of his boots together. She stood with him, face-to-face, breathing hard. Sweat shone over his face, and the wild little strands of hair that had escaped the queue were curled and framed his dark eyes.

He wrapped his arm around her waist. Holding her flush against his chest, he looked down at her, first her eyes…then her lips.

Colette knew he wanted to kiss her. Any and all words bottled up in her throat as she waited. Her emotions wrestled while her mind waited for answers. Sorting through any feelings rationally would be hopeless with his arm around her waist, the heat soaking clear through her body. Her breasts were crushed to his chest. Her hands migrated up along his arms until the tips of her fingers rested atop his shoulders.

He said nothing.

Neither did she.

She raised her chin to align herself with his face, his lips that hovered so close, yet so far from her. She ran a tongue across her lips, anticipating his touch.

He wrapped his other hand in her hair and gently wound it within his fingers.

"We have nothing to say to each other," he whispered in a low, controlled voice.

"I do not," she whispered in response.

"Then I won't hear the word 'no.'"

Her eyes watered up. She shook her head ever so slightly that she would not resist, as he held her so tight against him she thought never to breathe again.

"Do I disappoint you again?"

"No, Colette, you do not."

Using his hold on her hair, he tilted her head back and slowly lowered his lips to hers.

. . .

She melted into his arms. Colette was exactly where he wanted her, but victory did not have the sweet taste he expected. Instead it was her lips that gave him the elixir to which he had become so addicted. Her lips were warm and receiving, opening slightly as he slid his tongue to the inside of her mouth. She inhaled, her breasts pressed against his chest. She was small, petite, frail. A woman he had wanted to protect, for life had not been kind to Colette.

Her fingers migrated upward to play with the hair at the base of his neck. A slight groan escaped her throat as she reciprocated the kiss. He wrapped both arms around her and pulled her closer, putting her between him and his shadow. It felt good to hold her like this again, to feel this woman glazed to his body, wanting him.

He ran his hand from her waist up and around her breast until he held the soft mound within his hand, kneading her, hearing her purr. He leaned down and kissed her throat, then hovered slightly over that shallow basin, nibbling on that sensitive spot before moving along her exposed collarbone, following the curvature of her delicate body with his tongue.

She inhaled again and whispered something. He thought he might have heard his name, but didn't hear no. If only he had waited and marinated this victory in revenge and vengeance, but it wasn't. He wanted her as much as she wanted him. And that was not in his plan. He refused to surrender that power to Colette ever again, for she had nearly destroyed him in the past and would only finish him off completely if given another chance.

He summoned every vengeful thought he'd had of her since she'd left him. The sense of loss and the deeper remembrance of her betrayal whittled into his conscious brain. Once it surfaced, he regretted entangling this moment with anything. But the error had been made, and though he tried to push it back, deny the importance of it, deny past hurts, they charged to the surface and exploded.

He broke off the kiss.

Colette stumbled, looking shocked, but caught her balance quickly. In a second, she had her sea legs and marched past him toward the door, as if to leave.

"Will you not stay for dinner?"

She stopped at the door but did not turn to face him. He wanted to tell her what that kiss meant, what that dance meant, but couldn't. He'd never admit that, for it would make her too powerful. Having already experienced her unforgiving power over him, why would he give it to her again?

Her head moved slightly as if to say no. He knew she felt rejected. That should have given him some satisfaction, having felt it himself from her, but it didn't. Instead his heart reached out to her and again he wanted to protect her... from him.

With a gentle hand to her arm, he escorted her into the dining room.

"You...we must take care of ourselves to be strong for

the journey." He attempted to bring a rational mind to the conversation. "Enio needs us to be strong, Colette."

Her shoulders rounded, and he knew she fought tears with each step she took. Damn, victory didn't taste good at all. "*Os lo ruego,* senora."

She drew a deep breath and straightened her shoulders before turning to face him. When she did, he motioned toward the table and pulled out a chair. She slid into the chair without a glance in his direction.

"*Gracias.*" Donato opened the door to the *cocina* and ordered that dinner be served.

There was no conversation, only the clicking of utensils against dishes as she ate in silence, as did he. The meal consisted of five courses, all delicious and heavily spiced. To his surprise, Colette ate every bite put on her plate. She was hungry, and he was grateful she had stayed to dine.

He downed a swig of wine after the plates were cleared from the table and they were again alone. "Colette, I have heard much about your need to return to your life, but why would you take my son from me?"

"I explained, my brother—"

"You explained the idea of returning home, but in that decision, you thought to make me an unfit father. Which I am not."

She looked down at the table as if thinking of her response. Donato was patient; he wanted an answer, to understand how and why he had come to represent everything bad in her life, when in essence he was not.

"Do you remember…" she started, but her voice faded off.

Donato sat up, interested in what she had to say. Was it

possible that she remembered too much of the night of her abduction?

"Do I remember what?" he asked with concern for what she was referencing.

"The night that British ship attacked the island?"

He sat back in his chair, relieved to hear an entirely different subject surface. "I do."

"I hid." She glanced up to catch his expression, but he held it firm, unsure of where this would lead them. "I took Enio and hid in the wardrobe of my room. You didn't know that because you were fighting the British to keep the island safe."

"Sì."

She was beginning to fight tears as her eyes reflected the candlelight. "I couldn't do that again."

"You were in no danger, Colette. No danger."

She shook her head, barely keeping the tears under wraps. "You do not understand."

"I try."

She glanced around the room as if the answer hung out of her reach, then again she focused on him. "When I was five, my parents were arrested by the Tribunal in France."

"I did not know that." He knew they had fled the French Revolution, but was surprised to hear another portion of the story, for she had never mentioned it before.

"I know you did not." Her hand swung over and picked up his glass of wine and downed it, for hers was empty. He picked up the wine bottle and refilled both glasses. "I was so young. I cried so hard and was so scared. If not for Jordan, I would have cried myself to death. He hid with me and held me all night, until family could come and help us."

He knew the parallel she was making, but for him it

didn't apply. "The British attacked the island to steal, nothing more, nothing less."

She covered her face with her hands as the tears escaped. "You do not understand."

Donato swallowed hard, not sure what she was saying. "I try again."

"I wanted to be where I felt safe, and that…had always been with my brother."

That statement nearly knocked him off his chair. He couldn't react fast enough, as the hurt from her words nailed to his ribs and pierced his heart without a trumpet blast, without warning, just a deep stabbing pain that made each breath feel like a sword slicing clear through his body. "You did not believe that I would keep you safe, my wife and son?"

He couldn't bear to hear the answer. Anger pushed him off his chair and made him pace the room. Colette glanced up at him but dropped her gaze the moment he looked back at her.

"I was alone when the British attacked."

"But you were safe, Colette. You were safe."

"It so reminded me of that moment in France. It brought much of my memories back. Revolutionaries. I hate revolutionaries. They did nothing to better our country, only take and destroy good people."

"But your father was an American."

"It did not matter to them. He had money, therefore deserved to be punished. My mother was wealthy. That is how revolutionists think, Donato, that is how they think. They think only to self-serve, not for a greater cause, a better future, it is to serve themselves wealth and power. It is to take what is not theirs."

Donato refused to take in her words against revolutionaries, for he had been one for years, fighting what he believed was an oppressive government, the Spanish monarchy. But Colette wouldn't understand that. He opted not to draw a parallel with her father being a revolutionary. "Is that how your mother died?"

"No, when they were taken, I prayed and prayed for their return. I even promised God, I'd do his work if they were returned to me. We escaped through Bordeaux and went to Boston. But my father owned land in Louisiana."

"Your mother?"

"She died a few years later in America."

"Did you take care of her as you had promised God?"

"I did."

"And Loul's mother took care of her, as well?"

"Yes, until she died. Hattie was good to both of them and a great solace to my father. They fell in love after my mother died. My father cared little for protocol. He openly loved her. She gave us Loul, whom we all love very much."

That he knew, having seen the interaction among the two brothers and their sister. He wasn't as thrilled to hear of Jordan fulfilling the role of protector when it was he, her husband, Colette should have turned to for such. But this discussion did not give him the information he wanted. Through her family's saga, he had lost his son.

"Why did you leave me, Colette?"

She motioned she was done talking, but Donato was not. He leaned forward and took her hand across the table. "I deserve an answer. Why did you leave me and take my son?"

"I was afraid of how you lived. A pirate. A man of the seas.

A man feared by many and by that many have you enemies. I never wanted Enio to live through what I had, and wanted him safe. Jordan's piracy was a ruse to find me; he wasn't a pirate before we had been attacked. And when he arrived…" She waved her hand to indicate she had explained. "Please, Donato, do not hate me for this. I had much work to do as well."

"I do not hate you, Colette. It would be so much easier if I did. As far as your promise to God, I think He releases you of that obligation, Colette. You have well served Him."

Chapter Twelve

By the light of dawn, Colette waited by the outside patio for Donato to take her to the ship. Though he didn't sleep in his room last night, he had left orders that he would escort her shortly after six. The sun had lifted, casting a golden hue over the water that rippled in the warmth. The sky was blue and clear and smelled of ocean waters.

The sounds of hooves beating the cobblestones caught her attention. She stood to see the oncoming carriage Donato had sent for her. A large park drag with a team of six beautiful black horses turned into the drive, stopping in front of her. There were two men in front and a footman standing to the rear. As it rolled to a stop, the footman dropped off and opened the door for her. The last time she'd seen a similar carriage was in France, never in New Orleans.

She picked up the only bag she had. In it, she had packed her two cotton dresses, slippers, undergarments, a nightgown, a gauze morning dress, two shawls, privy items, and her brother's clothing from the night in New Orleans. It might be handy to appear as a man at times, only God knew, but she packed it just the same. On her feet, she wore leather lace-ups with matching leather gloves. Her hands would not freeze again.

This morning, she wore a light gold dress of satin and lace ruffles trimmed with silver thread that lined the hem. Her hair drawn back and up, was topped off with a plain *peineta* of white and a matching plain mantilla of woven silk that hung around her shoulders in the form of a shawl. She had seen Donato's clothes laid out for him, and had noted the style of dress and the gold sash. Her attire would match and she suspected, as his wife, she was being conveyed to the ship, and was to dress for the occasion. One thing she had learned about Donato in all the time she had lived with him was that he was a man of formal tradition. Besides, it allowed her to bring one beautiful dress with her.

"*Buenos días*," the man offered, along with his hand for an assist up.

Colette stepped inside. She held her breath as they pulled away from the hacienda.

She chewed a little on her lower lip, thinking about the dance last night. Did she want the thirty-five days to remain in effect? He had kissed her with the passion she thought to forget, but the moment his lips had touched hers, she knew that would never be possible. But what had stopped him? Did he want resistance from her? Would that be his goal and therefore she had disappointed him? He said she had not, but something had made him pull away from her when it was he who had instigated the entire rendezvous, music, dance, and dinner, a reminder of the many galas and fabulous evenings they had had in that same room with numerous guests from the island.

She ran her fingers over her lips, still tasting the man, still inhaling his scent. She closed her eyes, reliving that moment when he had slowly lowered his head to kiss her, remembering how anticipation had sped up her heart and had nearly stolen her breath away.

If he had wanted to remind her of the island and their passion, he had succeeded, but why did he dismiss her before that kiss had turned into more?

"We are here."

She peered through the window, allowing her gaze to travel up along the tall poles to see the small triangle sails, unfurled and picking up wind. The larger square sails were still brailed. It was a clear day, and though she had little understanding of sailing, she knew the wind would be at their back.

The gangway was still busy with preparations. The moment she stepped clear of the park drag, a call went out among the men that Senora de la Roche would board. The men dropped everything they were doing and formed a line along the main deck. Her one bag was carried as she followed along the plank and stepped on board.

The line of men awaited her entrance, each bowing with respect as she walked by. Her knees started to give way at the idea of once again being on a ship, but seeing her reception, she forced her legs to move. She had survived the last journey across the gulf in a storm, but in spite of her bravado, her teeth chattered and her knees knocked so soundly they hurt.

She continued down the lane created by the men. This

is what Donato meant when he had scolded her boarding yesterday. His wife would not board in such a fashion, and today, he proved just that.

To the end of the line of sailors was a short set of stairs that led above the helm and over the stern. Donato stood atop those stairs. Cleanly shaven, his ebony hair had been allowed the freedom of a queue. Brushed back loosely from his face, it hung about his shoulders in long waves. Tied across his forehead was a red scarf. A striking color against the olive tint of his skin and coal-black hair.

Those dark eyes, framed in long black lashes, that had seduced her throughout the dance watched her as she walked the deck toward him. He acknowledged her entrance with a slight bow of his head, then took the stairs down to meet her midway.

Whether dressed in cotton shirts and trousers of the back-water pirates or in his finest, Donato had a regal, if not royal, look about him. He wore a white ruffled shirt beneath a short waist jacket of embroidered green velvet. His breeches were black, anchored by the high leather boots. Linking the two, he wore a broad gold satin sash that held both sword and pistol.

"A beautiful woman, again today." He held out his hand to escort her. "This is how my lady boards my ship."

"I don't seem to remember such fanfare in the bayous, aboard a stolen ship."

"Ah." He grimaced as if remembering something unpleasant. "I believe that was when we played at being swamp rats."

Colette allowed the comment to float away on the early morning breeze. "*Merci.*"

"For?"

"Taking me. I know you do not want to do so."

He lifted one side of his mouth in a half smile. "A point on which we both agree."

He guided her toward the hatch that stood open. "It is a small ship. I will show you where you will stay."

He disappeared into the hatch with Colette following behind. She took the stairs downward into the bowels of the ship and felt his hands about her waist guiding her to the deck. She saw her travel bag sitting opposite the map room, in the doorway of what she assumed was the captain's cabin. "I will stay in there?"

He nodded.

"And you?"

"Close by. This is a very small ship."

"How many men have you?"

"Sixty-five total. They will hang hammocks about the stateroom, wardroom, and above deck." He meant there would be no privacy for him or her.

"I see." She forced a swallow through her tight throat. "When do we sail?"

"Now." Donato raised his hand to draw her attention to the calls above to unfurl the sails and lift anchor. The helmsman shouted out his course. Before she realized it, the ship started to move, leeward at first but soon making headway, and true to her analysis, the wind was at their back.

"If you need anything, I'll be on deck."

Colette nodded her appreciation, then walked through the stateroom and into the cabin. From the stern window, she watched the last shreds of the island disappear over the horizon. Images of Loul, Jordan, and Hattie, wondering what had happened, where she was, was she again in danger, floated through her mind. For Jordan had sacrificed so much to find her the first time. Would he set sail, in fear she was in danger? Once again, but this time through her own choice, she had separated from all who loved her. Her stomach tightened as a knot slowly turned inside it, remembering the painful isolation of the past.

She was entering into Donato's world, and she was truly on her own.

• • •

The sails picked up the wind, and the small clipper plowed through the small waves. It was a clear day, with no clouds in sight. Donato stood above the helm, watching the sails. They had changed some of the square rigging to triangle sails to allow for more maneuverability, but those were smaller and forced the wind.

The ship had been renamed last night by the men. The small clipper would be known as *El Rescate,* for it had become a rescue ship on a mission of mercy to bring back a little boy who had been swooped up into a political fight of which he had no understanding.

Only the king of Spain could have financed his sister's ship. Meaning the monarch must know something of Donato's activities, but he had no choice but to continue. As the boy's father, he'd get Enio back, at any cost.

The ship handled the waves nicely, plowing through but not too deep, but still spraying water over the main deck with each swell. The crew was prepared for a wet journey. Besides being donned in oil slicks, they had taken precautions to ensure that what needed to be kept dry had been strategically stored. Gunpowder, matchsticks, wicks, and flintlocks were all kept below. In open waters, they would have the time to retrieve them, if necessary.

Colette had appeared this morning in a yellow gown that highlighted the golden color of her hair when the sun filtered through her wavy tresses. She had looked the angel when she boarded, with white slippers and a white mantilla draped around her shoulders.

Her skin picked up the color of the rising sun, making her face appear well-scrubbed and transparent. He noted the veins that traced down her temples that seemed to darken every time she spoke. A ruby tint flushed her cheeks when he told her they would both occupy the same room. The same tint he saw last night the moment before he kissed her. A kiss that had convinced him he wasn't over Colette.

What would she think when she learned the truth about him?

"Donato?"

He turned. Colette had ventured out onto the main deck. She had changed into one of her own dresses from Liberty Oak, and had covered her shoulders with a large shawl that protected her from the ocean spray. "Be careful on the main deck, Colette, a wave could wash over."

"The sea looks calm today. I don't think I am in danger."

So she saw through his attempt to dismiss her.

No, the skies were clear and a nice tailwind kept them going. He drew a deep breath trying to clear his head for sailing. He liked being at the helm of a ship. There was something so freeing and humbling about it. For the sea was a beautiful creature, abundant with riches beyond what mortal man could imagine, but she was equally brutal and could turn on a tiny ship in her waters faster than the sands of an hourglass. But he loved her, for she offered man the way to move about the world.

Spain had done that, developed colonies in Cuba, Mexico, and America. But Spain gave no quarter to those residents. If not Spain-born, they were not a citizen. With no voice in government, they still had to live under the laws of the monarch. Days of absolute power for any authority were numbered; the American Revolution had proven that.

It was a belief in man governing himself that had made Donato take up the cause, for no man should live under another man's rule, simply due to the fate of birth. The Americans had rejected royalty. Men in Spain, as well as the colonies, were attempting to do the same. They just needed the money to keep on fighting. And that's where he came in—as a pirate who stole from the French corsairs, he had sent money back to Spain, to the revolutionaries who risked their lives for the cause.

Donato glanced over at Colette, who stood near the helm, with her hands wound around the bulwark. Her golden hair sparkled in the sun as it fluttered in the wind. With the sun overhead, he could almost see through the dress she wore, and could see her brace her legs for support. A light spray showered the deck, and Colette laughed as the water soaked her hair.

She turned to face him with a smile as bright as he'd ever seen. "I think you might be right, Donato, I do indeed get wet."

"But a pleasant wet. The water is refreshing in the heat of the sun."

"Ah, so it is." She laughed again. "I see you don't wear velvet coats on deck."

She motioned to his changed attire of a sailor's shirt worn under a waterproofed tunic and pantaloons. Around his head and forehead he wore the bandanna, and over that a low-crowned leather bicorn. All more suitable for sailing.

"I see golden dresses with sparkle disappeared as well."

"Too beautiful to get wet." She smiled and glanced over at him, as if acknowledging the dress had been a gift from him, long ago. It had…been given with much love.

Though she seemed to be unaware of it, she was nothing like the unfalteringly quiet, reserved woman of the Faubourg Sainte Marie and Jordan's home that Donato had observed from afar, while he had waited to take Enio back.

In that year, he had never seen Colette smile or laugh as she did just now, or as when she had ridden the horse in Louisiana and raised her arms to take flight. He could see it as plain as the nose on her beautiful face, but she seemed so unaware of her own transformation.

"I never think to like a ship again, but this, Donato, I like…I think."

He had to laugh at her uncertainty, knowing at some point she would hate this ship. "I think it is the sleeping arrangements that have you enamored."

She stepped closer to him, looking around before she spoke under her breath. "It is not I that will be disappointed, Donato, for she sails with might and we will catch your sister in less than thirty-five days."

He couldn't hold back a smile. "If not, my dear wife, you will hold up your end of the bargain?"

She met his gaze straight on, and he noted that her color darkened slightly. She was about to deny her interest, but that little tint of color that flooded her cheeks told a different story. "I am a woman of my word."

"As am I a man of mine."

"Then we have an understanding." She held his attention with her expression unyielding, but her cheeks had turned a cherry red. Her breathing became labored, and she ran a tongue over those sweet kissable lips. He suspected that like his, her mind had traveled beyond the sea and back into the ballroom of last night. He should have swept her up in his arms and taken her then. He had every right to her as his wife, and at that moment she had been more than willing — she'd been panting.

But that was not his intention. He'd wait out the thirty-five days. It was important he do this in that way.

"Come steer a ship you like." He motioned for her to join him on the tiller and took the stairs down to the helm. The other sailor stepped aside to allow her to stand next to Donato.

Her expression shifted to surprise, but he could see her immediate interest. She stepped closer and cautiously lifted her hands to wrap around the handle.

"You hold here and here." He directed and she followed.

He let go and stepped back, giving her full rein.

The tiller shifted. "Oh, this is hard!"

"Can be impossible in storms, but must be done." Donato laughed at her small body trying to wield such a large tiller. He reached over her shoulders and brought the tiller in line, wrapping his hands around hers. Her hair, fluttering in the wind, brushed his face and smelled of roses. Her fingers felt warm to his cold wind-blown hands. "Takes practice."

"I will learn."

Jordan's Colette would have said no, but his Colette tried. He didn't realize until this moment when she made him laugh, showed off that childlike excitement, and when he ran his hands over hers, how much he had missed her, how deep his longing for her had become.

"Then I will teach you, on days like this when the seas are calm." Donato motioned for his men to take over the tiller. He turned to climb the stairs over the helm.

"Donato?"

He hesitated as she stepped closer to him. "You have yet to tell me who you are. Why your sister—"

"Sail up! Sail up!" the crow's nest shouted. "Two points, starboard!"

Donato rushed the stairs to see over the bulwarks, picked up a pair of binoculars, and scanned the horizon. A large British warship was heading straight for them.

"Hoist the flag of Spain. For the moment, they are allies."

He glanced at Colette. "Go below, in the case it is dangerous."

"I will never sit below again, I told you that before."

"And you were nearly washed out to the sea."

Her lips pulled tight at the reminder as she squinted to see the oncoming ship. "I cannot go below."

"Then stay close." Donato motioned to the men. "Fire off a cannon, just one, to acknowledge our great English friends."

One fourteen-pounder belched out a ball, falling starboard side of *El Rescate* to show the shot was for no other reason but a salute. The British ship changed direction, fired off a response, then pulled sails and picked up speed. Within minutes, the British warship disappeared over the horizon.

Colette glanced about the ship. "You don't have the same flag as your sister's ship. Why?"

Donato braced for a discussion he did not want to have. "It represented her province."

"You tease me, I think."

"No."

"Then why was her flag different?"

"Perhaps you tease me. It was a royal flag." He stole a glance at her. "I know you know that."

"And I have asked before." She watched him as he scanned the horizon. "Donato. Who are you?"

"Ah, senora." He gave her a sly look. "You don't have your pistol at my throat, so I think not to answer."

Chapter Thirteen

The ship lurched, throwing Colette across the cabin for the millionth time in the past few hours. For three days, *El Rescate* had battled strong winds and twenty-foot swells. After being thrown about on deck, Colette decided it would be best to stay in the cabin, despite her aversion to staying below. She watched the storm from the stern window rather than struggling to stay afoot in biting gusts of wind and punishing sprays of water.

After several days of calm, peaceful sailing, the sky had turned nearly black in midday and a storm had churned the surface of the sea. As Donato had said, the ship plowed the water, which already sent a spray over the deck. Add twenty-foot swells to that and the ship felt nearly underwater, and the danger of sinking became more a reality.

Colette pulled herself to the anchored chair and tried to remain in it. Motion sickness had tangled up her insides to the point she thought she might heave.

Above, she heard orders being shouted, recognizing

Donato's voice and the stampede of running feet across the main deck. Her enchantment with the ship had vanished. She wanted nothing more than to feel solid ground beneath her feet. *Would land never come?*

They had passed another English ship, and it ended the same. Though Donato was Spanish and Spain and Britain were allies, he seemed to hold them in contempt, and her inquiries as to who he really was had been left in as much of a lurch as she was right now.

Donato had never spoken of his family in all the time she had been with him on the island, which added to her curiosity. When she had lived there, nothing seemed wrong or questionable, but now, having returned and seen the island through a different set of eyes, much was suspicious, and his life as a pirate was the most suspicious of all.

Water covered the window, then retreated to the sea. The air was damp, cold, and salty. Every breath dragged in more moisture until she thought she'd drown. She wanted to go above to see how Donato was doing, but knew her presence would be a hindrance, since a sailor, she was not.

She continued her vigil at the window, wishing the storm would abate and the horizon would clear enough to see his sister's ship directly in front of them. Her heart ached for Enio, and today the loneliness spread throughout her body and made every movement hard and stiff. She rubbed her arms to ease the pain, but it did little to help. Until she saw Enio again, that pain would never subside.

Sitting here was tedious, and she needed to get her mind off the storm. She pulled out of the chair and managed to get herself through the door and into the stateroom just as the hatch opened.

"Colette?" Donato called out as he came down the stairs two at a time.

"I am here."

"Are you all right?"

"Tossed a bit, but all right."

"We're plowing water deep — " He stopped as if no further explanation were necessary.

"We might sink."

He hesitated as if not sure to confirm her concern or dispute it. "I'm trying to slow us down. We're traveling with the storm. We need it to pass us."

She knew from the expression on his face that he had decided not to dispute her concern, because there was more. "Go on."

"I want you on deck."

"All right, but why?"

"If I can slow her down, the danger is not that we will plow too deep and bury the bow, but roll, capsize. I don't want you inside the ship."

"I'd not survive it either way." She knew swimming was not an option, as her leg would not work to support her.

"We are provisioning the longboat." He motioned to the cabin. "Dress warm and put on one of my oil slicks. I'll wait here."

Colette spun on her heels with haste. He wouldn't have asked this of her if it weren't the absolute only way. After donning her brother's clothes and borrowing an oil slick tunic from Donato's things, she returned to the stateroom where he waited.

"Donato…are you frightened?"

He winked at her. "We will get through this, but when at

sea, always prepare for the worst."

She emerged from the hatch before Donato.

There was a flurry of activity on the ship. The wind howled, and the waves clamored to get aboard. Water, sometimes knee deep, ran over the main deck, forcing the men to stop what they were doing and anchor themselves or be swept away.

The overhead sails billowed and strained against the swirling clouds, the rigging about to pop. What the men called the flying jib would disappear under the water before reappearing and throwing more water over the deck. The sea boiled into huge swells that seemed to mock their very presence, rolling up to touch the sky, then sinking back into the frothy waters.

Donato directed her toward the longboat. Men were loading it with supplies, and she wondered how many it would carry. Donato was the captain; would he go down with the ship or survive to find Enio?

He stood her near the longboat station as it was being made ready for launch. Others were posted along the rigging.

"Colette, wait here. If all goes well, we'll have no need for that." He pointed at the longboat, then turned away from her, focusing on the ship and the deadly storm that had seized *El Rescate* by the teeth and threatened to shake her by the timbers until she broke and sank into the ocean.

Donato shouted orders. The men responded, scurrying along the rigging like monkeys on a tree. In the wind, she could hear words like "heave to" and "close to the wind," "tacking" and orders to the helm. She watched what appeared to be a well-orchestrated play, with all the moving parts working as one.

Most of the sails came down, but two large square sails were left to manage the wind. The poles were close to bare, to slow the ship down.

Colette watched the agitation of the seawater. She glanced up, seeing some of the sails billowing in opposite directions. As Donato intended, the large square sails fought each other for control of the ship, which made it slow down, in spite of the driving storm.

No longer did the bowsprit dive under water. Now it rode through the waves at a steady pace. But with the slower speed, the ship started to turn with the combative sails above. Waves came over her edge, broadsiding the ship, rushing over the bulwarks. Colette grabbed the longboat and lifted her feet long enough for the water to pass, but the sudden movement burned her leg from ankle to hip.

"Ship is broached," someone shouted.

"Haul in spanker!" Donato suddenly appeared at her side. Within seconds, he lifted her over the longboat and dropped her inside. Four other men were in the boat.

"Hold on, she's going to roll. Longboat!"

Colette glanced up to see the main masts leaning to the larboard side; the longboat shifted and she rocked toward the sea.

"Fore topsail, four points starboard. Main topsail, four points larboard!" Donato shouted orders and several men, barefoot and wet, bravely climbed the riggings to reach what she knew were yardarms.

As the sails were slowly changed in the fighting wind, the ship started to right itself.

"Reef those sails! Mark the helm!"

"Broad on the starboard beam, *Capitán!*"

"Shift the helm!" Donato raced over to join the two men who were already struggling with the helm. The men pressed themselves to the tiller and pushed. Soon a fourth man joined, and slowly the tiller started to shift.

The ship suddenly lurched in the other direction and as if being lifted by some force, water poured over the other side. For the first time since she had come to the upper deck, Colette felt the ship stabilize. A sense of calm fell over the men as they gauged their work and the results.

Donato turned and looked at her, and for a moment, he seemed not to see anyone but her. She smiled back with a nod, congratulating him on a job well done, feeling not only pride for him, but relief as well. The longboat didn't look that big when compared to the vast ocean that surrounded them.

"We hold for a while." Donato walked over and lifted her from the longboat. "Till the storm passes by."

His eyes canvassed the ocean, the ship, his men, and turned to her. He reached up and stroked the side of her face. "I hope you were not too frightened."

"Not a thought about it." She shrugged, pretending it was nothing, but her expression said it all. She had been terrified.

He wound his hand in her hair and brought her face to his, then sniffed her breath. "Wondering what you were drinking, because I was most scared."

She reached up and took his hand that had traced along her face, his skin cold, wet, and pale. His fingers were bloody, broken, and cut. Expecting him to notice his pain, she looked up at him. The pallor of his face near dead white, his lips clamped so tight they were of the same color.

He was a man facing exhaustion. While others had slept, he had planned their navigation. While others had slept, he had planned their provisions. He had forfeited his sleep for their son's rescue. He had pushed himself beyond a mortal man and then had battled a sea storm for nearly thirty-six hours.

He was beat up and exhausted. For his son. For her.

His hat was gone, and the hair hanging beneath the bandanna was plastered to his face. Deep lines had formed around his eyes, aging him beyond his years of thirty-two. He was eight years older than she, but he looked drawn, haggard, a fighting man after a battle. His chest rose and fell with deep breaths and the color of his eyes darkened as he squinted upward, gauging the bare poles and the position of the ship.

Could not someone else watch for a while?

But Donato was a man of his own destiny. He would watch the ship for the night. It would be he alone who would ensure their safety, like that of their son whom he struggled to rescue. She had never considered him an unfit father, and it broke her heart to think that is what he thought she believed.

After several more hours of waiting out the storm, it finally passed, and calmer waters smoothed the horizon.

Colette was fatigued from the long hours of standing on the deck. She could only imagine Donato's exhaustion, yet he continued to sail. With the sea calm and the air quiet and peaceful, she sought him out.

"*El Rescate* is safe. Come, husband, you are in need of care." She draped his arm around her shoulders with hopes he would come back to the cabin, to the bed they had yet to share.

He resisted, glancing about the deck as if there were

much to do but she could feel his unsteady gait and braced her body.

"No, Colette, I cannot leave—" His words failed as his legs folded beneath him.

. . .

Colette pulled back the bedclothes of the small bed in the cabin next to the stateroom. The men carried Donato down the stairs, through the stateroom, and into the captain's cabin. Gently, they placed him atop the bed. He was unconscious and pale, and a thin film of water covered his face.

"*Merci*." Colette waved the men out of the way. Ramón waited as the room was cleared.

"What does la senora need?"

"Help get him out of these wet clothes." She felt his forehead. "He is burning up with fever. Have clean water and cloths for bandaging brought in. He's hurt."

Ramón ordered the basin, then pulled off Donato's boots.

Donato didn't react to it. His eyes remained closed, and his face turned from pale to a feverish red. Within minutes, Ramón had relieved Donato of his clothes, and Colette had him tucked beneath the bedclothes. He started to shiver as she tucked the corners of the bedding around him.

A man appeared at the door with a basin of water and cloth.

"Set it there." Colette turned to face Ramón. "You sail this ship. Leave a man in the stateroom if I need help."

"*Si,* senora." Ramón bowed and left the room, followed by the other personnel who had followed their captain. "I will leave Jose. He will await your command."

"That is good." Colette pushed them out the door and closed it behind them.

She had spent many years working as a volunteer in hospitals and orphanages. She knew the signs of exhaustion and fever. She sat down on the bed, took a cloth, dipped it in the water basin, and wiped his face. Then she folded it over his forehead. He made no attempt to open his eyes as she smoothed his hair back. Shadows from the lantern framed his face. For the first time since she had known Donato, he looked vulnerable, in a weakened state.

She pulled back one edge of the blankets and began to wash him down, cooling him with each stroke. Her cloth traveled along the length of his arm, over the well-defined muscles that had been pushed beyond their capacity. She wiped each deeply cut and bruised finger clean, relieved to feel that his bones were intact. Fighting the wind had been a painful process. She wrapped each gently cleansed finger with bandages, securing them with a tie.

Pulling back the blankets, she ran a cool cloth across the expanse of his chest, dipping into each shadow within his collarbones, relieved to find them intact. She brought the cloth over his shoulders and back across the apex of his chest, noting a battle scar here and there.

His muscles moved with a slight twinge under her care. Her cloth migrated back and forth, lower and lower over his chest until she felt the edge of his rib cage and the firm muscles of his abdomen. With each inch she covered, she imagined the feel of his arms around her, of being pressed to his chest, and the sheer male power of his body.

He stirred, trying to open his eyes, but failed, then

whispered, "Colette."

"*Sshh*." She quieted him. "You must get well. The men need you."

"I need you," he said before he drifted asleep.

Her eyes filled with tears, and she brushed them away, feeling her nose stuff up and a choke fill her throat.

"And I you," she whispered, though she knew he did not hear her.

She rewrapped the wound he had from New Orleans. It had been healing, but had started to bleed again with the strain his working muscles put on the thin scar.

Upper body done, she focused on his legs. His feet were cold and wet in spite of the fever that ravaged his body. She wiped them clean and found a warm pair of stockings in his valise. She pulled them onto his legs. She worked her way upward, her cloth removing the soil and fever. His legs were thick with muscle. Her hands moved along his calves, solid and firm, and over his knees, remembering the feel of his weight atop her.

A light breeze touched on the windows, and the floor beneath her was flat and straight, the ship on an even keel. He had saved them from this storm, again, like he had in the gulf. Perhaps, she smiled to herself, he *was* a better sailor than her brother.

The bedclothes were draped across his thighs. She stood and peeked out the window, noting that the waves were less roiled, and the dark sky had started to clear. She had no idea what time of the day it was, but guessed it to be close to evening. How grateful she felt not to be out in those vast waters in a longboat filled with men.

He stirred again with a deep sigh, pulling her attention

back to him and the course of action she had yet to finish. She had given many bed baths over the years on ailing men and woman in hospitals, but Donato was different.

His muscles seemed to respond to her touch, moving slightly beneath her massaging fingers as she cooled his burning skin. She slowly savored her time to explore his body, falling into the memories of his love for her and how only he could make her feel.

He stirred again, making her pull back and cover his body with the blanket.

She opened the door to the cabin. "Clean water in the basin and drinking water."

Jose took the basin with a bow and left the stateroom.

Donato had fallen back to sleep. A touch to his forehead confirmed the fever. Having tucked the bedclothes in around his body, she awaited the chills.

The clean water had been delivered, and now her only recourse was to wait it out. She pulled off her wet clothing and laid it about the room to dry. While standing in her chemise, fighting chills herself, Donato stirred again.

"Donato?" She migrated back to the bed and gently lowered her weight to the mattress. She felt his forehead, hot to the touch. His eyes fluttered open and he looked at her.

"What happened?" he whispered, glancing around, confused.

"You are exhausted, Donato. Allow yourself to rest." She smoothed back the hair from his forehead, running her fingers along the stubble of his overgrown beard. "The storm has passed. We are again smooth sailing."

He caught her hand in his and looked up at her. She wanted to fall into those dark eyes that slowly roved over her appearance. Her hair was down and dressed in a chemise, her neck, bosom, and arms were exposed to his visual exploration. In his eyes, she saw what she had been feeling moments ago… desire.

"A beautiful nurse, I have." He started to reach for her when he realized his fingers were bandaged. He wiggled the fingers of both hands. "Whom I cannot touch. Is that by design, Colette?"

"If only I were that clever, but no. Why did you not wear your gauntlets?"

He dropped his arms to his side. "Too wet and heavy. I had much to do."

"Rest now, please, you must, for all of us." She ran her fingers along his collarbone and hesitated near a scar on his shoulder. "I have seen these scars before, but never knew from where they came."

"Frenchmen."

"And the one over here?" She swept her fingers across his chest to settle just between his first two ribs.

"Frenchmen."

"And over here." Her fingers slid to the opposite side of his chest.

"Frenchmen."

"I see. I would ask about more, but I think I would get the same answer, *non?*"

He reached up and grasped her hand between his bundled fingers, placing it palm side down across his heart. "You do not ask about this wound?"

Colette inhaled a deep breath, unable to let it go. A wave rushed her head, making her feel underwater and woozy. She wet her lips, trying to assimilate what he had said. For if he were to look very deeply at her, he might see the very same wound.

"Donato, there is no wound there." She tried to deflect the pain his statement brought her.

"*Si*, look deep. A Frenchwoman, whom I loved very much, wounded my heart."

"A foolish Frenchwoman, I fear." She fought her own pain, her own distrust, her own desire to little avail. "Perhaps, if allowed, she would heal you again."

"Perhaps." He again dropped his arms to his sides and closed his eyes. "Perhaps."

"Donato—" Her voice fell on deaf ears, for as quickly as he had awakened, he fell back asleep. She pushed off the bed and pulled on a nightdress. The dark sea had merged with the dark sky, and the slow rocking motion of the ship made her sleepy.

She settled next to him on the bed with her arm across his chest. She felt the beating of his heart, each breath he took, and the burn of fever that threatened his health. A lone tear escaped her eye, irritating her, feeling weak, when after such a journey, she knew she was not. No longer able to fight the soothing rock of the ship and his even breathing, she closed her eyes and allowed sleep to take her away.

• • •

Before the sun rose over the waters, Donato woke up. He opened his eyes slowly, trying to focus in the early dawn light that reflected off the ocean waters and shimmered on the ceiling of the small cabin. He looked around, orientating himself to where he was and how he'd gotten here.

Memories of the previous night were few, and what he could remember was confusing. He felt on fire, hot, sweaty, and drew in each breath with much effort. He glanced at his hands; the morning light made the white of his bandaged fingers glow. The dressing on the wound in his arm had been refreshed.

The journey, the long voyage to find his son, filled his mind, and he was overwhelmed with panic. He remembered the storm, the longboat, and trying to save—Colette. Where was Colette? What had happened? "Colette!"

"*Shhh*." She rose up from next to him in the bed. "What is it? What do you need?"

He dropped back on the bed, relieved the moment he heard her voice. "*Lo siento, lo siento*. I dream bad. Go back to sleep."

But she didn't; instead she pushed off the side of the bed and lit a lantern. She ran her hand over his forehead. "You are burning up."

He watched as she brought a basin of water over and set it next to the bed. She then poured him a drink of water and sat down on the edge. "Here, you must drink. You have a fever. You need this."

He did feel thirsty, his mouth parched. He accepted the glass as she tilted it to his lips. The cool liquid eased the tightness in his throat. He placed his hand over hers to steady the mug. Through his thick bandages, he felt her respond. The touch so innocent, yet so intimate.

In the flickering light of the lamp, he noted she was wearing a nightdress, her golden hair swept over one shoulder and loosely braided. The neckline of her chemise dipped low enough to expose the rounded edges of her breasts. Her cleavage vacillated with the soft intake and release of her breath. Her narrow face, widened by prominent cheekbones, was accentuated by her large green eyes. Even in the dark, he could see their color. Heavily lashed, they were mysteriously caressed in the soft, iridescent light. Everything he had seen the first time he saw her.

The night her ship had been taken.

She captivated him now as she had then.

Waves sloshed against the hull with a soothing rhythm. The ship creaked with each slight turn and dip in the calm waters. The salty air felt heavy on his face, and moist within his lungs. "What happened?"

"You haven't slept in days, and now you must." She spoke in such a low whisper, he had to struggle to hear her. But it was sultry with a hunger that only Colette would understand. And right about now, he wanted to know if the beautiful woman who sat before him in a magnificent state of undress was his Colette or…the dutiful sister of Jordan.

He slid the palm of his hand up along her arm. A slight gasp escaped her lips, but she held steady. His hand traveled along her shoulder until, in spite of the bandages, he was able to cup the base of her neck within the palm of his hand. Her gaze fell to his lips. As he slowly pulled her toward him, she licked her mouth once, then twice, in anticipation.

He pulled her into his web, wrapping both arms around her body. Her lips touched his the instant he had her completely within his grasp. They were soft, sweet, and inviting.

He kissed the corner of her mouth, then the other, before running his tongue along their seam. A soft moan escaped her throat as she moved her weight over him. He pulled off one cap sleeve of her gown and then the other, running kisses along her collarbones.

A fine mist of ocean air gave her body a light sheen; her skin tasted salty. He drew aside her long hair to expose her throat, and this time he wanted nothing more than to savor the flawless pearl luster of her skin.

He drew her over his body to the side of him. With her next to him, he pulled the nightdress down to expose her breasts. He hesitated, taking in the beauty of her sculpted body, feeling a strong charge through his own as if still in a storm of thunder and lightning. The torrid heat of his body that might have been a fever turned on him and plunged low inside to start a throbbing need for her.

With clumsy, bandaged fingers, he captured her breast in the palm of his hand, bringing the round full nipple to his mouth. He sucked each one with patience, rolling his tongue around their nubs, lightly taking them between his teeth until he felt her arch toward him and place her hands on his shoulders, clawing at his back.

"Donato." She whispered his name, not attempting to disguise her want.

The bedclothes were between then, her on top, him underneath, and perhaps that was the best scenario, for he wanted nothing more than to roll over on top of her, spread her legs, and sink inside her. He suspected by Colette's response, she'd not resist that idea, but that was not what he wanted, how he wanted this to happen.

It was a thirty-five day wait, for her as well, for she had made no attempt to change the timeline whether by lengthening it or shortening it. But fifteen days had passed. Thirty-five days of waiting had dwindled to twenty.

He unwound his hold on her and fell back on the bed.

The fever burned through any resolve he might have had. Whether thirty-five days or twenty days, it did not matter, for he was a victim of fever and exhaustion, which allowed for rest only.

She positioned herself beside him in the dark, not asking why he had disengaged. But instead she reached up with her hand and traced it along the side of his face. "You will be strong again."

Her comment made him curious. "How do you know that, Colette?"

"God is with us on this journey. He will keep you strong for the sake of your son."

Donato was a religious man and believed God could, and sometimes would, intervene. Perhaps their survival of the storm made that a reality. But where had he been during all the years fighting in war, the endless days of killing and blood for the ruling class of Spain?

He glanced to the side of him. Colette had her eyes closed and breathed easy. She had pulled the gown up and had the cap sleeves in place. He needed to distract himself before he risked his health and broke his own rule.

"Colette," he whispered. "How did Jordan find you when you were on the island with me? How did he know the precise place to breach the island?"

"Aurélie," she answered, sounding half asleep. "Jordan's wife, she has the power of sight and was able to lead him to me."

"Then why did she not lead him to the mysterious treasure?"

"She had read France from my medallion, but nothing else from the hand-drawn maps."

"One of the medallions was yours?" Though he knew

the answer, he liked her talking about it.

"My father had them made." She stirred, then shifted her position as if he were disturbing her sleep.

"Jordan believes this mysterious treasure is in France?"

"That is what Aurélie read." Colette yawned and readjusted herself. "Jordan did not share with me his thoughts."

"Do you believe the legend? That there is a treasure?"

She turned and faced him, running her gaze over him as if to see his motive. No motive, at least not yet, but soon. "There is something, I think."

. . .

Colette sighed, watching the waves that stretched out behind the stern. The days ran into more days. Donato had given himself less than twenty-four hours to recover and though in her mind, he was not completely well, he was again at the helm. She longed for his company and felt her heart to be as much adrift as the widening wake behind them.

She had chosen to spend more of her time in the cabin, for she felt underfoot when on the main deck, especially when her leg would ache and slow her movement, but the crew was always kind and overly respectful, which made her wonder about them.

Jordan had immersed himself in the world of piracy to find her. When they had sailed back to Louisiana, he had warned her about his crew. They were in it for prize, he'd said. If no bounty under his leadership, they'd find a different crew to join, or worse, take his ship. He had warned that to be a captain of pirates was no guarantee of obedience or loyalty.

Donato's crew was different. She had noticed it earlier, but confirmed it when Donato was ill. She noted the solemn mood of the ship, the constant inquiries to his health. When Donato walked about the ship, the men would stop their duties and give a slight bow of their heads in respect.

Why? If they were pirates?

Adding that observation to the fact that they were chasing a ship sailing under a Spanish royal flag moved her from curiosity to suspicion as to the real identity of Donato de la Roche.

Donato had a reputation as a terror of the gulf waters. He was wanted for piracy, and as Jordan had confided, even Jean Lafitte had feared him. But Donato, like Jordan, robbed only French corsairs…for the same reasons.

Then…where were the pirates?

She leaned on her elbows, watching through the stern window, day turning to night. The fire red of sunset played off the rolling waves that lingered in the wake of their ship, cutting through the water. Her mind fell into the rhythm of the moving waters, remembering the night she and Donato had slept together when he was ill.

Twenty-eight days at sea.

Twenty-eight days with no sign of the Spanish royal.

Seven days left of the thirty-five.

And why thirty-five, exactly?

She rose from her chair and changed her attire for bed, pulling a nightdress over her head. Donato rarely appeared in the cabin; with hammocks swinging from every crossbeam, he must sleep elsewhere. By day, the wardroom and stateroom were clear and clean. At night it looked like a hundred bats hung from the ceiling.

The bed felt cold and damp as she crawled beneath the

blankets and coverlet. She appreciated that Donato had brought silk and wool coverlets from the hacienda for the bed, along with feather pillows and satin bedclothes—a special touch for a female passenger.

Donato had asked about the treasure, and she wondered why the interest. On her return to France to see her grandmother, the older woman had talked about hidden treasures and the foiled revolutionists and how victory had been theirs, though no one would ever know. She had instructed Colette to never part with the medallion, one made for her and one made for Jordan.

Colette watched out the stern window as she rested on the bed, seeing the moon rise over the soft, undulating waters in rhythm with the silent rock of the ship. Having said her prayers, she hoped God heard her pleas to have her son restored to her and they could all return home safely to the island.

That thought choked up in her throat. Her broken marriage, her lost son—how would she put the pieces of her life back together, and would Donato want to try again? When he had said he had a wounded heart, the pain of knowing what she had done to him had pierced her own.

Having lived for so long with no memory of who she was or where she had come from, the moment she had heard Jordan's voice, she had remembered her family. She had felt obligated to go home, for Jordan had always been her safe haven. So much so that she had willingly destroyed the life she had made for herself with the man who rescued her from pirates. Without Donato, what might her life have been? What might she have suffered?

When she had danced with Donato at the hacienda and he'd kissed her, she had nearly died from wanting more, but he had withdrawn from her. The night he had fallen from exhaustion, his kiss was as passionate, as ardent, as core-stirring as were all his kisses, yet again, he had withdrawn from her.

She had pretended not to notice, but had stayed awake afterward, burning with an unfulfilled need that nothing would relieve accept Donato's kisses, his arms around her, him inside her.

She now knew that, understood that, but unfortunately, she suspected, so did Donato.

She drew a deep breath, already feeling deprived of something only he could give her. Hadn't he tortured her enough by now? Why day thirty-five? What was the significance?

She heard men enter the stateroom, talking in low voices as if not wanting to be heard.

She swung her legs over the side of the bed and pushed to stand. Gaining her sea legs, she silently crossed the room and pressed her ear to the door.

"We could launch the longboat when we reach Spain. Make contact and deliver." A man's voice could be heard.

"Too dangerous." Donato spoke. "It would be better to do this on land."

"Now who has the dangerous idea?" another asked. "If caught, we are revolutionists, and would be tried for treason and all lose our heads."

"If caught," Donato agreed. "But that is a risk we have taken."

"Too risky, *Su Excelencia*. You do not know what King Ferdinand knows or why he would lead you into such a trap by taking your son."

Colette sucked in her breath and flattened herself against the door, her mind spinning faster than her heartbeat.

Donato was the one who had placed their son in danger, not her.

. . .

Exhaustion had started to assault Donato's ability to think. As revolutionists, the idea of sailing into Spain had them all on edge. The discussion had barely begun when the door to the cabin opened. The men shifted their attention when Colette stepped out with that damned little pistol of hers.

"*You* have put our son in danger, not me. It is *you* who made him a pawn in a political game. It is you, not I! You are a revolutionist against your own country."

Obviously, she had been listening at the door.

The salty ocean suddenly turned acidic and as silent as death. The only sound was the lapping waves against the hull of the ship. The men slowly stood and faced Colette. Her hair hung wild and free over her shoulders. Dressed in a chemise, every deep breath reflected the cleavage between her breasts. Her round full hips were accentuated in the moonlit room. As foolish as her move was to point a pistol at a man of his rank, Donato had to admire her raw guts to do so.

"*Podéis retiraros*." Donato asked the other men to leave, but they weren't quick to respond.

"*No, Su Excelencia, debemos protegeros,*" Ramón answered quietly.

"Mi senora knows enough Spanish to know what we are saying. I do not need your protection. Leave us, *por favor*."

The men filtered out the door and up the stairs, though Donato knew one or two would linger in the companionway.

Colette hadn't taken her eyes off of him from the moment she entered the stateroom.

Donato walked around the table so that nothing stood between them. "I warned you about that pistol."

"Since it is I and not you who has the pistol, a warning from you seems rather foolish."

"What is it you wish to do with it, shoot me?"

"The idea has more merit than perhaps you'd like to think."

So she had heard the discussion, knew their fears of Spain, and now knew why.

"All right, Colette, you have me at your mercy, do with me as you wish."

"It is what you will do for me."

"Anything for the lady with a pistol."

"Answer my questions. Why did you lie to me?"

"About?"

"Who you are. You have a title. These men aren't pirates. In what political scheme have you involved our son?"

Donato took a step closer to her.

She retreated the same. "Do not."

"You will run out of room if you continue to retreat from me."

"I do not retreat."

"Then I guess you will not use that pistol on me."

"I hate revolutionists."

He had heard the story about how revolutionists had taken her parents and how the great Jordan had been there to save her. But that had been nearly twenty years ago, and the plight of Spain was now, today, urgent. He was as sure of his cause as he was of her undeniable passion.

"I know one revolutionist you don't hate." Donato approached her, but halted with her pistol held flush against his chest.

"You play a dangerous game, Donato."

"Ah, but you like danger, *cariño*," he whispered in her ear before he wrapped his hand around her wrist and forced her to drop the pistol. A slight whimper came from her throat as he pulled her into his chest, his lips a fraction from hers. "You try to deny, but you like everything about me."

"No, no, you are wrong," she whispered, but the force of her voice had been usurped by her desire for him. He could feel her heart beating against his chest, pulsating like a leaf in the wind. "I hate you, a revolutionist."

He wrapped his hand in her hair and forced her face to his. "Tell me again, Colette, I did not hear."

"I hate revolutionists, and that's what you are," she again whispered, though barely audible.

She kept stepping back. He kept pace until he had her against the wall between the stateroom and the cabin. He held her flush against the wooden panels, kissed her temples, her forehead, and ran his tongue along the seam of her mouth.

"You don't hate me, Colette. Admit it."

She ducked, breaking free, and stepped into the doorway of the cabin. He matched her retreat with his advance.

"Keep retreating, Colette. If you fall back to the bed, I will spread your legs." He held her head in his hands and kissed her again. "Because you want me to do just that."

"Donato, don't do this to me."

"I dare you. Let me taste you, kiss you, and you will feel my hot breath on the very spot you hope to deny me. Go ahead, fall on that bed."

Colette collapsed against him, clutching his shoulders with her small hands. "I don't want you to be this person. First a pirate—"

"Whom you had to escape."

"Then a revolutionist."

"Whom you despise," he whispered. He knew she wanted compassion, but they were both straddling a very thin line. One misstep could render them enemies or lovers. He knew her passions, her needs, and that only he could fulfill them. "We are like gunpowder and flint, Colette, alone harmless, but together we ignite each other. Our passion is lethal and dangerous for both of us. If that is not true, then fall on that bed and I will prove otherwise."

He continued to walk her backward until her knees locked with the bed. She sank to the silk and wool coverlet he had put on board for her and lowered herself to the bed. He pulled his weight over her. She wrapped her arms around his shoulders and caressed the back of his neck. He kissed her with more determination than ever, to convince her of the hopelessness for either of them to think they could exist, live a life, without each other. For they could not.

Her lips parted under his; her breath mingled with the rapid pace of his breathing, hot and full of desire. She parted her legs under him and dug her fingers into his back as if to hold him in place. Her desire for him only fired up the flame he tried to put out, ignore, deny himself.

This wasn't for him, he tried to redirect his thinking. His whole purpose was to torture her with the passion he knew she had.

He pulled her gown up and slid his hands to the inside

of her legs and continued upward until he spread her legs apart. He kissed her at the apex of her legs, that glorious juncture that gave him so much pleasure. Holding her hips in his hands, he slid his tongue inside her, gliding back and forth, savoring the taste of her, as sweet as he remembered.

Colette groaned, moving her head from side to side as he teased her passion to respond. She opened for him, her heat rivaling his. He grew hard, throbbing with wanting to drive himself into her, claiming what he knew to be his— seven days left.

It was not the time.

He ran his hands along her inner thighs as he disengaged and pushed to his feet. She remained silent but watched him with those deep green eyes.

"*Buenos noches*, Colette."

He turned to leave, not wanting to consider staying and finishing what they had started.

"Because it is not day thirty-five?" Colette asked, her voice low and breathless. "Why? Why thirty-five?"

"Thirty-five months, a day for every month you were with me."

"I wounded you deeply, Donato."

"You didn't wound me, Colette." He turned and faced her. "You destroyed me."

Donato slammed the door behind him, funneling through the hanging hammocks to the liquor cabinet in the map room. He poured himself a glass of stiff, well-aged whiskey, needing to wash the taste of her out of his mouth, his mind, for his body still lingered in her bed, between her legs.

His plan had been to make her suffer with want of him

until she begged for release, but in the end it was only he who suffered every night in want. He had been a fool to think he could manage the close quarters with Colette and still come out the victor.

He headed for the stairs, and as expected, two men had waited, then followed him to the main deck. The men exchanged glances but they never said a word, for they were his men, loyal to him. In spite of the freedom cause for which they fought, he was still their lord and master. Donato was their superior simply by his birthright.

A revolutionist, she had called him. And he was exactly that.

He had fought too many wars, too many enemies, in the name of the monarchy and nobility. He had watched men, like those on his ship, bleed and die for their country in which they had little rights. Donato believed a man should forge his own future, governed by laws, not monarchs.

America had proven men could take charge of their own destiny. Born poor, die rich. It was possible in America; could it not be anywhere else in the world? Like Spain?

He loved his country, but loved his freedom more. And it was the freedom of his countrymen, the ones who fought and died on the battlefields, that he sought to protect.

Colette called him a revolutionist. What had her father been but an American revolutionist to free his country from the monarchy of England?

The Spanish constitution would succeed, Donato was confident. He contributed gold, and plenty of it. Every cent he had stolen from the French corsairs had gone right back to Spain. But this time, arriving in Spain, he'd have to put his politics aside. He had a wife and son to protect.

She had looked at him with complete horror tonight when she'd learned what he was, but that would be nothing when she learned the truth about the night she had been abducted.

He glanced around the main deck looking for a sailor known for his musical talents. Seeing him lounging near a cannon for the night, Donato walked over to him. He started to get up when he saw Donato approach. Donato motioned for him to stay sitting, but he needed to stop his mind from spinning so quickly. "Pablo, play me some music."

"*Si, Su Excelencia*, of the mother country?"

"No, Cuban. I believe our own flavor of music to be superior to Spain."

"*Si, Su Excelencia*."

Donato stood at the bow, which was cutting deep through the water. A light spray shed over his face with each dip in the waves. The night was quiet. The moon reflected off the rippling seawater and brilliant stars sparkled overhead to assist in his navigation. By his calculations, if he had gained at all on Rayna's ship, he'd know in the next few days.

If not…

It was a ruse, no doubt. Just how much did the crown of Spain know? Was he a man marked for death? Would he die a revolutionist? The king had put many to death who disagreed with his politics. The high finances of Rayna's voyage proved they wanted him back. But he didn't know why. With his son held hostage, Donato had no choice but to fall into their well-set trap.

Chapter Fourteen

Colette had tossed about her bed for most of the night and rose at dawn, exhausted but unable to sleep any longer. Her leg had burned with every turn she made, and no position was pain-free. She was washed and dressed before the sun had risen. Much seemed unsettled today. More so than yesterday, she needed to feel fit to face Donato.

She had made him sound the horrible man last night when she had learned of his politics. When in truth, her own father had been a revolutionist for America and had fought in the war against Britain. That was how he and her mother had met, in France, when he traveled to Paris with Benjamin Franklin during the war.

Colette loved her father and had tremendous respect for him and never would have thought him evil for revolting against tyranny. But it hadn't been like that in France, at least from her point of view, as a five-year-old child. Her fears from so long ago had haunted her entire life and now threatened to destroy perhaps the only love she'd ever had.

The seas were calm in the dawn's light, and she knew Donato was most likely at the helm. She hoped to engage him in a conversation that did not include a touch, a kiss, any hint of passion, for they were, as Donato said, dangerous for each other. Donato usually took a midmorning break to eat and check his navigations. She thought to join him this morning and create a new partnership that might get them through this without testing their passion but instead, celebrating their mutual love for their child.

She had made arrangements with Donato's cook to ensure they would have privacy while he ate in the stateroom. The cook made Colette promise not to bring a pistol, which she did…reluctantly.

She glanced at the clock and it was already half past eleven; Donato should arrive shortly. Fried bread and fruit paste with a choice of coffee and juice were already on the table. Captains ate well, she mused, after having choked down dry biscuits every morning since they had left the island.

The hatch opened, and she heard Donato come down the stairs into the stateroom.

"Colette." He wasn't at all surprised. "My cook tells me you wanted to dine in private this morning."

"So much for secrecy."

He smiled, then motioned to the table that had the food set out. "Join me. I know I will be fascinated by what you have to say."

"You mock me."

"No, only intrigued by your attempt to, ah…woo me into something." He had taken a chair without waiting for her. "I apologize for my manners, but my time is limited. Join me."

Colette lowered herself into the chair opposite him. She wet her lips in preparation to speak. "Donato."

"Are you not going to eat?" He waved toward the door, and the cook came out and started to fill both plates.

"*Oui,* I will join you, but I direct our discussion, for I called this meeting."

"Meeting?" he repeated but amended when she narrowed her eyes at him. "Of course."

The cook filled their plates with a salted meat stew and a bowl of pudding. For most of the journey, the food had been tolerable and rations small, but this morning, the cook had prepared a delicious meal. A menu that could have only been authorized by Donato.

He refused the coffee and drank wine, raising his glass in a toast to her before taking a sip. She reciprocated, waiting to begin what she had decided would be the best course of action.

"And what do we toast, Donato?"

A bright smiled eased out across his tinted skin. "You and me."

"As a team?" Pushing him into the discussion she wanted.

The smile disappeared but a mischievous sparkle reflected in his eyes. "As lovers."

Her mouth opened slightly as she drew a sharp breath, angry not over his words, but for the image that sprang into her mind, a very pleasant image. But having spent the entire night alone in bed after Donato had stormed out of the room, she had to do something to change the communication between them.

They both wanted Enio back, that was a given. But the

attraction between them could be toxic, and after he had proved her inability to resist him, would there be a cure?

Donato noted her silence before taking another drink. "Day six."

"I would like to talk of this, Donato."

He had just taken a mouthful of bread lathered with fruit paste and nodded that he understood. "A deal was made."

"I think we should acknowledge our differences and have an understanding of who we are and that our future is not the question on this voyage, but that of our son."

"But that is incorrect, Colette."

His comment left her surprised, for she did not expect it. "It is not incorrect."

"You have attached yourself to me closer than my shadow, and it is not about us?"

"No, it is for the sake of Enio."

"*Si.*"

He dropped his attention to his plate, seemingly unconcerned about the conversation at all. Her attempt to negotiate a treaty of some sorts had been lost the moment the cook had betrayed her and informed Donato of the special breakfast. She pushed her food around her plate for a second, then decided to eat, offering nothing more in conversation except polite table talk. She had abandoned her plan to reason with him, until he spoke on the subject.

"Colette, what is it you need to say?"

She jumped in, not wanting to lose the opportunity. "To acknowledge we are different people."

"And go our separate ways when we get Enio back?"

"*Oui.*"

"But he will live with me. Where, Colette, will you be?"

She swallowed hard, feeling her plan unravel. "We will face that decision when we have Enio back."

"That decision has been made, Colette. I respected the boy's need for his mother and kept my distance for more than a year, but now I will have my son with me."

"Then we are at an impasse."

"Only if you wish to live elsewhere."

Her heart paused through a missed beat. He had never said he wanted her back. In fact, to her brother he had made the point of saying that he didn't. But the inference was there. Would he say it? Would he say he wanted her back? She held her breath for what seemed an eternity, and he said nothing more as if he read her mind and was determined to continue this slow, agonizing, torturous game of lovers and enemies.

She tossed her napkin on the table and pushed out of her chair. "I will not live without my son."

She started for the cabin, making what she thought would be a dramatic exit until her leg gave out. She grabbed for the table, pulling dishes down atop her. Donato was on his feet in an instant and caught her before she hit the deck. He swept her up in his arms and started for the cabin. "I will be fine. I *am* fine," she protested.

"*Si, cariño*, you are." Donato carried her into the small cabin and deposited her on the bed. He then sat down on the edge of the bed near her feet and started to unlace her boot.

Colette silenced her protests, for he would not heed them, and deep down she longed for one of his massages that always washed away the pain.

He pulled off the boot and tossed it to the floor. His hands felt warm against the cool skin of her ankle. His fingers worked the muscles around each small bone, then her calf.

"And we are to ignore this?" he whispered.

She inhaled, knowing what he meant because she felt it, too. His hands worked the long muscles of her leg, massaging, rubbing the pain away.

She sighed, feeling the ache ebb, as always happened with his touch. She closed her eyes, allowing her body to relax under his ministrations. His hand slid upward and caressed the back of her knee. She fought her reaction, not wanting to desire his touch, yet luxuriating in every movement of his hand.

"Donato," she whispered.

"And this, are we to ignore this?" His other hand swept up her other leg, circled to her core, then back again. With each circle, he'd brush across her hub of desire with a light touch of his fingers. Her breath caught in her throat.

He rose from the edge of the bed and lowered his body over hers, his weight heavy, crushing, and welcome. His hair, loose and wavy, framed his face and fell forward to sweep across her cheek. He touched her lips with his, just a light touch, a tease.

She inhaled the scent of him, the pure male musk that wafted around their joined bodies. What a fool she had been to think she could in any way separate herself from this man. She had loved him on the island and had pined for him while in New Orleans, and now craved him on this dangerous journey. The reality was, she had failed to return to her old life in spite of her attempts. She had been reunited with her family, but her heart had remained with Donato on the island, waiting for this moment.

"But Donato," she said breathlessly, unable to draw

enough air to harden her voice, "you won't let me mend your heart. You are afraid I will hurt you again."

"Perhaps, *tesoro mío*." He ran his tongue along her lower lip.

"You call me your treasure, yet have made it clear you wish not to have me back."

He kissed and nipped at the hollow of her throat. She could barely breathe, never wanting this to end.

"I have made nothing more clear, but are we to ignore this, Colette?"

"I cannot think, you confuse me."

"I touch, you respond, why are you confused?"

"About how you feel about me. I am no more than a pawn for vengeance for taking Enio...and your heart."

He brushed her lips again with his, lingering long enough for her to taste the wine on his breath. "I have my vengeance every time I touch you and you respond."

"Then you will grow weary of it, and what happens when your game ends?"

He laughed. "I am most weary, but not of you. I would never grow weary of you."

"Do you speak of reconciliation?"

"Do I? What of you? We have been here before, Colette, you in my world. What about when we return, when Jordan comes again. For he surely will. Who will you be then? The dutiful sister who has spent her life nurturing others, working in hospitals, orphanages, and charities, but never giving to herself? Or the woman who wears beautiful gowns, a sparkling *peineta* in her hair, diamond baubles in her ears, and surrenders her body to the music and...me. I have to know, who is the real Colette? Because I love one but not the other."

She allowed her arms to wrap around his shoulders and arched toward him, wanting every touch, every kiss to radiate to her soul. "And of you? Who do I get, the pirate or Your Excellency?"

He laughed softly, nuzzling deep into her neck. "Hopefully neither."

"You want me." Colette tilted her head to kiss him, allowing her desire to surface as her fingers played with the muscles of his shoulders that moved with his arms. "Say it."

He chuckled, knowing her game. "For you, *cariño*, I will say it. I want you."

Release raced her heart so fast, she nearly gasped. "I am so sorry I took Enio from you."

"I know that." Donato brushed her lips with his until the kiss became complete. Colette tightened her hold on him, splaying her fingers through his thick black hair. Parting her lips for his kiss, a surge of energy whooshed through her body as if to say, here is where you belong. She spread her legs for him to comfortably sink in between them, her heart matching the beat of his.

He kissed her lightly again and pushed from the bed. "As much as I would like to stay in this bed fit only for one, I have to get back on deck."

A cool breeze wafted over her body, and she felt naked with Donato no longer there. She pushed herself to sit off the side of the bed and glanced up at him.

"For the delicious meal, *merci*."

"*No las merezco*."

Colette smiled from his Spanish response. "What language will Enio speak?"

"Spanish." He leaned down and tenderly kissed her forehead.

"I think not."

He sighed. "Ah, the battles yet to come."

"He will speak both, and English."

"A scholar. Is this what you wished to discuss?"

She nodded. "Not the outcome I expected, but I am pleased."

"We get Enio and return as a family, regardless of what Jordan wants?"

"Jordan will understand more than you think. Are we held to the thirty-five days?"

He chuckled. "*Si*, it is to continue our lives at the right time. One day for every month."

"Then you have added wrong. It is not thirty-five months, but thirty-three."

"Thirty-three?" he said more to himself than her, but she could see he was thinking about it.

"I was missing for thirty-five months, but the first two were with the men who took my ship, the *Loirie*. See, I am remembering things."

The expression of his face shifted to bleed out the natural tint of his skin.

"Donato?"

"Sail up! Sail up!" came a call from the main deck.

• • •

How in the hell had he miscalculated that? Why, when he finally had a consensus with Colette, did she have to figure that out? When he had learned of her plans for his morning meal, he decided, after last night, he had to put an end to their dance. With his plans to torment her hidden passions, he had become the tortured soul. His thirty-five days was to symbolize the reunification of their marriage and a continuation, but she was right. He had miscalculated in what she knew and didn't know.

She didn't know that it was he who had captained the ship that had taken the *Loirie*, the ship she and Jordan had been on as passengers. But in his efforts to keep Spain out of the fray, he had hired an American ship, *Lady Tempest*, to disguise the action as high seas robbery. Things had gone wrong. He had partnered with the wrong American ship, and though he had completed his mission, it had been grossly botched by the gluttony and greed of the American pirates.

She had no memory after her abduction, but at the end of two months, she'd been on the auction block in Port au Prince as a captive. Colette and Jordan had been unintended collateral. Though in his mind it had been a justified act of war, considering that the Spanish spy sent to root out the revolutionists had been on that ship and had to be stopped before countless lives were lost. Would Colette find it in her heart to forgive him? Having finally forged a tenuous alliance with the woman he loved more than his own life, what would happen when she learned the truth about her abduction? She was beginning to remember.

Donato took the stairs to the main deck. Amazingly, Colette was right behind him. Donato reached the bow and picked up a pair of binoculars. Just on the horizon, off the port bow, were the sails of a frigate ship with a royal flag.

Rayna.

Ramón stood to one side of him, Colette to the other.

"Is it?" she asked.

"*Si,* Rayna's ship."

"A royal ship," Ramón pointed out.

"Speed?"

"Nine knots, *Capitán.*"

"How fast do you think she's at, Ramón?"

"We will gain on her. She can't go much faster than five to six knots."

Colette looked over at the two men. "Then what?"

Before he could answer, Rayna's ship started to turn. "She's coming about."

Colette clasped her hand to Donato's arm. "Will she give him back?"

"Don't count on it. Clear for action!" Donato issued orders for the men to ready themselves for battle. A flurry of activity fell over the deck as men raced to predetermined stations. The guns were run out, loaded, and ready. "Colette, go below."

"Not on your life. That ship has my son."

"And you are a nurse. Set up supplies with our surgeon in the wardroom."

"When a shot is fired, I will do so."

He didn't bother to argue the point. He knew the futility of it, and if reversed, he'd do the same as she. "Then hang on. Stay at the helm—it's the most protected spot on the main deck."

Rayna's ship plowed the waters toward them, larboard bow. Donato tried to see her through the binoculars, but either he couldn't or she wasn't on the main deck. His men waited, braced for either a fight or a collision.

Suddenly the frigate turned starboard and fired. Though she had thirty-two guns on each side, she fired off one. It hit the water a hundred feet or so larboard beam. The water ricocheted into the sky and sprayed over the ship.

"What was that?" Colette asked.

"A warning shot, not to follow too close."

"*Capitán*," the crow's nest called out. "She sails protected!"

Protected?

Donato lifted his binoculars. As Rayna's ship slowed, other ships appeared on the horizon.

It was a trap.

The other ships had kept out of sight until Donato was close enough. The cannon fire was a signal to move in. She had an *almiranta* in her lead and a *capitana* that fell into the rear. Rayna's ship picked up speed, and the heavily armed escort dropped back to box in *El Rescate*.

"We are now prisoners," Colette whispered.

Donato nodded. "We are."

He raised his hand and shouted for the square riggings to be furled to slow down their speed. "We've been instructed to follow."

"To Spain?" Colette failed to hide the alarm from her voice. "Can we not get away and come back?"

"The results would be the same. She is heavily protected."

"Then we are to follow to Spain?"

"Apparently."

Their speed slowed with the riggings changed. The helm set to follow in the wake of the large frigate. For now, it was his only choice, but he had to think of something or Enio and Colette might be trapped in Spain forever, or worse, banished to France, and his head would roll.

He had no idea how much the Spanish Crown knew, or what Rayna knew.

"How long before we reach Spain?" Colette moved over

to stand next to him.

"A month or so."

"Following her like this?"

"Until I think of something, that is what we'll do. Besides, I feel better having my son's abductors in sight. Whether equipped or not, I cannot fight my way out of this. Enio is on that ship." Donato ordered the crew to stand down.

"You fought my brother."

"I surrendered to your brother, because he had you and Enio on his ship."

Colette's eyes widened with shock. "You've known all along we would go to Spain and did not tell me."

"Would that have changed your mind, Colette? Would you have stayed on the island and waited?"

She looked away for a moment, then back at him. "No, I would have come."

"Then it does not matter, does it? For I was not sure until this moment."

"If they want you, why not take you in New Orleans, instead of this elaborate plan?"

"I have no answers."

"Then we will learn together." She stepped forward to stand next to him at the helm, wrapping her hand around the crook of his arm. For the longest time, they stood together silently following in the wake of the ship that carried their son, imprisoned by the armed ships that sailed starboard and larboard.

"I long to see him, Donato, so much so, my chest aches." Colette broke the silence.

"I know," was all he could muster, for he felt the same pain stabbing at his heart.

She looked up at him. "Will you tell me now? Who you are? In English?"

He drew a deep breath, bracing for the discussion he should have had with her long ago. But memories of home were always bad ones, and rarely did he talk about it to anyone. Now seemed appropriate, for she was with him in this, and he needed something to clear his mind to once again think.

"I will start with my title. I am Donato de la Roche y Borbón, Marquis de Andalusia, Heir Grandes de España. I am His Excellency. My father is a Duke of Andalusia, Grandes de España, his address, His Very Excellency, and he bows to no king. The men sailing with me refer to me as *Capitán de Navío*, a ship of the line captain, but we are not in the Spanish navy, so it is just a title. My mother, María, died a few years ago, and my only sibling is one sister, whom you've already had the displeasure of meeting."

"You left Spain, why?"

"I was tired of fighting. I fought in the Peninsular Wars, as did these men who sail with us today. I was born in Madrid, but moved to Cádiz, the home of revolutionary ideas. I have met kings, queens, and emperors of Spain, France, and Prussia. I have seen power change hands, backstabbing, conniving, jostling for political position. But the men who died for them had no power, only blood to spill on the battlefields, fighting the interminable French. They even invaded Madrid."

"I remember the Madrid invasion. That was the year I was married in France."

"Our countries are still at war with each other, but war and revolution against Napoleon's occupation led to the Spanish Constitution of 1812."

"Which you support, even as a noble?"

"My status is higher than that of a noble. I do not have to bow before a king, but I have to remove my hat. My father does not. I have lived with these men who fought and died. I am no better than they, but I have privilege, where they do not. No man should be given such privilege simply because of his birth."

"You sound like my father. You should be American."

If not such a dire moment, he would have found humor in the comparison, though very true it was. "It is that cause, the defeat of the absolutist for which I fight…as a revolutionist. I want freedom for the mother country and for her colonies."

"You are an enemy to the Crown of Spain," she said more as a statement than question, but he answered her anyway.

"*Sí.*"

"From your distance, you fund the revolutionists who wish to overthrow the king."

"*Sí.*"

"Then what does this mean, to you, to me, to Enio, going to Spain? Do they know who you are? Are you under arrest?"

"Because of my rank, I can be arrested only if specifically ordered by the king. By the looks of this fleet, I have been summoned. Some of those privileges were annulled under Bonaparte, but—" He pulled her in close to him. "Whatever happens, I will do all in my power to keep you and Enio safe and get you back home. I promise you that. I have contingent plans."

Colette wiped her eyes, then snuggled against him, wrapping her arms around his middle, seemingly unaware of the other men on the ship or what was proper. He let her do it because it simply felt good in what appeared to be his darkest hour.

He had no contingent plan to get his wife and son out of Spain, should he be sentenced.

He drew a deep breath to clear his mind and returned her hug.

He must get them to safety.

Chapter Fifteen

"Toma, hermosa. Te hará bien."

Colette bolted upright in the little bed of the captain's bedchamber. She was breathing hard, covered in perspiration, and her ankle burned.

It was the dream. That damn dream.

She pushed her legs over the edge of the bed to collect herself, unable to shake the odd feeling that came with the dream. She was sure it was Donato's voice, but everything else seemed blurry. Except this time there was something different. This time she heard other voices, as if they stood over her, or around a bed with her on it. She rubbed her temples trying to erase it, not understanding why it came back to her night after night.

She glanced out of the window, and even in the soft dawn light, Donato's clipper followed behind the large Spanish frigate, as if connected by a towline. Perhaps they were, though the line was not of rope but of a little boy. It has been days since his sister's ship had been sighted. One day after the next, they had sailed in her wake, escorted by heavily armed ships on both sides.

Colette wiped tears from her eyes, missing him so much, and knowing Donato was in as much pain, if not more, for he blamed himself for the situation.

Day thirty-five had come and gone. Things had changed.

She pulled on a gauze morning dress, then exited the small bedchamber by a door that opened to the run. Across from that door was a small room called the wardroom. There Donato did most of his thinking and planning. A light shone under the door. Colette opened it.

Donato sat leaning forward with his elbows on his knees and hands supporting his head. He looked up when she entered, and brushed his hair off his face.

"What can I do for you, Colette?"

She sank into the chair across from him and took his hand in hers. "You are worried."

"*Si*." He nodded and ran his free hand through his long thick hair. "I will think of something. Why are you awake?"

She shook her head. "I had that dream again. The one where I hear your voice but it has no meaning. I don't know why but I think it has something to do with my abduction. I try to remember something, but it does not come."

"Don't force it, it will come." He ran his hand down the side of her face. "Colette, if something were to happen to me, know how much I care for you, and Enio."

Her eyes watered up, and she swallowed the emotion that swirled to the surface. "I know. We'll get out of this."

"I confess, my sister did ask me to come home. I received two letters from her, but all she said was that my father needed me, and that meant nothing."

"Your father means nothing?"

He stood up as if he couldn't contain his own energy. "It is complicated, Colette. You should get more sleep. It is early."

"I cannot sleep. I only toss and turn, or repeat that dream. Besides, morning is here."

"And it is time."

"Time?" It was only then she noted his change of attire from sailor to gentleman. Instead of sleeping, he had spent the time altering his appearance.

Dressed in nearly all black velvet, his coat had some designs embedded into the fabric, and both collar and lapels were velvet as well. Instead of breeches, he wore long tan-colored pants, a new style for men, and leather slippers versus boots. Ruffles neatly folded around his wrists. His neck cloth, which he adjusted as he stood, hung pleated and close to his body.

Obviously, he had a plan in mind, but in spite of his immaculate dress, he armed himself with pistol and dirk in his waistband, hidden beneath the coat.

"What are you about?"

"I want to talk to my sister on the main deck." He opened the door but turned back to Colette. "I will wait if you wish to come up."

"Try going without me."

Donato smiled. "I'd be damned."

It took her only minutes to finish dressing, throwing on a heavy wool shawl over her shoulders and donning lace-up leather boots. Donato waited as promised. She followed him to the main deck to stand atop the helm. He had binoculars in his hands and canvassed the frigate ahead of them. He then turned and motioned to one of the sailors manning a gun.

"¡*Fuego!*"

A large cannon belched out an iron ball followed with smoke and fire. It landed a hundred feet larboard bow. Satisfied he had their attention, he called out. "Signaler, send up the message for a parley."

Two men scrambled with flags, tied them off, then raised them on a halyard. Colette watched the small triangle flags flutter in the wind, each a different color and pattern, wondering about the code they must hold. "Are they looking?"

Donato nodded and replied, "They are reading my message." Though it was only a few minutes, it felt like hours before Rayna's ship responded. Soon a halyard went up with a slew of flags. The signaler read them. "She says you wish to meet why, *Capitán*?"

"Tell her I will no longer follow unless I know the purpose. Tell her I will listen."

Again more fidgeting with the flags, and the line was raised. This time Rayna's ship was faster to respond. "She says, she will come to your ship."

"Tell her to bring our son," Colette shouted to the signaler. Who stared back at her, then looked at Donato for confirmation.

He nodded and shrugged. "Ask her."

More flags, more time.

"She has responded, *Cap—*"

Donato raised his hands to silence the signaler. "I know what that means. No."

Colette's heart sank but beneath her disappointment she was livid, seething, anxious to meet Rayna de la Roche and wrap her hands around her skinny noble neck.

"They launch a longboat," came another call from the lookout.

Donato ordered the sails adjusted to reduce their speed.

Colette watched as the other ship dropped down the small boat. Without the binoculars, she could see activity but nothing more. Donato kept scanning the ship until he stopped and swung the binoculars back the other direction. She heard a slight intake of air and looked up at him. "What do you see?"

He looked down at her, handing her the glasses. "Look, right across from the main mast, near where they launched the longboat. Enio."

Colette's blood rushed her chest, hammering her heart, as the sheer thought of seeing him nearly brought her to her knees. Hands trembling, she tried to focus through the glasses. Finally, she could see their main deck, and there as Donato said, across from the main mast, stood a woman holding Enio.

"Oh my Lord," she whispered, fighting the mist in her eyes that threatened to steal her vision. He was held straddling the woman's hip and watching the smaller boat. His shiny dark hair fluttered in the ocean breeze, and every once in a while, his hand would go up and rub his face as if he was tired. "He is tired, perhaps not sleeping."

"But alive and well."

The woman turned and disappeared into the ship, and her little boy was gone.

"Oh…she is gone." Colette's breath disappeared with him. Trying to draw enough air to speak, she handed the binoculars back to Donato. "I cannot bear this."

"You can, because you have to. You've held up well, Colette."

Donato again raised the binoculars, and this time, she knew he was watching his sister board the longboat.

"What makes her think we won't take her hostage?"

"Why do you think she had Enio shown on the main deck?"

"She thinks to be clever. Is she?"

"She is." Donato lowered the binoculars. "It does not matter. She has our son. Colette, let me handle this, *os lo ruego*."

"Just stand by and—"

"*Si*, just stand by."

Colette forced her mouth shut, clamping down on every word that demanded to be heard. It was no use. In reality, she knew only Donato could handle the situation. But sister or not, that woman made Colette's blood boil, and it took all of her strength to keep it at a simmer.

The longboat started toward them, slowly making headway over the rolling sea. Closer they came. The chair was swung over the side in preparation of her boarding. The closer they got, the more the waves slapped against the hull.

There was some commotion as men were sent over the side to await the arrival of Donato's sister. Soon the chair was hoisted and with it, a woman was lifted over the bulwarks and onto the main deck.

Colette noted the striking red satin dress she wore and the smart satin slippers on her feet. In her thick black hair that hung the length of her back, she wore a sparkling *peineta* covered with a black lace mantilla. She was a remarkably beautiful woman, with wavy ebony hair and dark eyes trimmed in long heavy lashes. Her skin was very light, compared to Donato's, and contrasted sharply with the raven hair that shimmered over her shoulders.

Colette held her breath as the woman stepped clear of the chair. She looked around the deck with the air of royalty, surveying her subjects as if a queen had arrived. After her grandiose review of the ship, she faced Colette and Donato. She held her chin high, and her long ruby earrings caught the early morning light, sparkling to the rhythm of the seawater.

Two other men had accompanied Rayna, but only she approached.

Before Colette stood the sister of her husband and the abductor of her son.

Rayna de la Roche.

. . .

Donato gave a slight bow. "Rayna."

"Your Excellency." She gave a return nod of her head. "What took you so long? We waited."

So she had, and he had suspected as much. "Storm."

Colette took a step forward. Donato knew she wanted to be a part of this, but they were on such a thin layer of civility, it would take little to break off negotiations, if that was what Rayna intended. He had to see what cards Rayna held before slowly playing his.

He motioned toward Colette. "My wife, Colette, the boy's mother."

"Ah…" Rayna tilted her head to peer down at Colette. "The French—"

"Is my son all right?" Colette asked through very thin lips as Donato held her arm tight to prevent her attack.

"*Si*, we take very good care of him, senora." Rayna looked

around again and whispered to Donato, "Can we talk in private?"

"We can. Follow me." Donato led her down the main deck to the rear hatch and opened it. She halted, looking at the hole in the deck.

"You expect me to crawl down a ladder through a hatch?"

"Do you wish to speak in private?"

"I do."

"Then I expect you to crawl down that ladder." Donato went down first and waited to assist his sister. Colette followed after her with lips blanched white from keeping them closed. Her breathing was rapid, and he could see the pulsation in the hollow of her throat that hammered out war drums. He expected she might defy him and try to come to this private meeting, and was more than relieved when she suggested she'd wait in the stateroom. But that brought on a snicker from Rayna.

"A stateroom?" She took in all the hammocks hanging along the wall. "This is a small ship, *mi hermano*. I am confused. After hearing the tales of how you've terrorized the gulf waters with your piracy, I would think you'd have a mighty ship that would make even a frigate quiver. What is this, could you not find something smaller?"

Donato refused to take the bait and gently moved the party through the stateroom into the map room. It was small and private. To his relief, Colette didn't follow, though her expression was not to be trifled with. He nodded his appreciation at her statesmanship when he closed the door behind his sister.

Donato motioned to the chair opposite the small desk, and he sat on the other side. There was a moment of silence as they stared at each other, but Rayna didn't wait long to start.

"Father is in a difficult position. You must help him."

But Donato wasn't moved by her entreaty. He had questions of his own. "Why did you take my son?"

Rayna leaned back in the chair, adjusting her mantilla. "Leverage."

"How did you know about him?"

"I know you thought to be secret, but you robbed the *Loirie*. It was clever to use the *Lady Tempest* as a cover. But you were found out. If the king were to know who robbed his ship, he would suspect you a revolutionary."

"How did you know about my son?"

"There is much talk in the sewers of…what…New Orleans. Talk about a strange pair of medallions that lead to a treasure of gold and how a man was trying to buy a woman with one. You had the woman with you, and the man was murdered in Port-au-Prince. Is this bringing anything back to you? That woman, the child's mother, was on the ship you robbed."

Donato attempted to remain impassive, but he knew he flinched when she said the truth, and Rayna had not missed it. "Ah, she does not know that it was you who put her on the auction block in Port-au-Prince?"

She waited for him to respond, but his mind had left the ship and was standing in Port-au-Prince watching as they auctioned off Colette. He fought to keep his expression steady. With his silence, she continued, "We learned you had this woman with you and she returned to New Orleans with the little boy. One look at him, and, *mi hermano*, he is yours."

Responding to his continual silence, she added. "It was not hard to find him."

"What made you think that I would care, if the child was

living in America?"

"I knew you were watching that boy and waiting to take him at the right time. Am I wrong? I suspected with the dawn arrival, you had arrived to do just that, so I had to act."

"So, Rayna, what do I have to do to get my son back?"

She sat forward on the edge of the seat and leaned on the small desk. "You must help Father."

"How?"

"King Ferdinand is ruled by the camarilla, composed of priests and nobles."

"Including Father."

"*Si*, but the king has become paranoid and suspects revolutionaries at every turn. He wants you back. There are rumors that you might be a *comuneros.*"

"How would he hear this of me?"

"The captain general of Cuba suspects you as a revolutionist, but the king respects Father and is not quick to believe the general."

"King Ferdinand nullified the constitution and he didn't expect an argument?"

"Not from the ruling class, which you are, may I remind you." Rayna readjusted her position with a slight wiggle on the chair. "The king has purged the noble class. Anyone in disagreement has been put to death. Now because of you, Father is in a precarious position."

"I don't care about Father's position. What do I have to do to get my son back?"

"Return to Spain. Convince the king that you are not a *comuneros.*"

"I have to save Father to get my son back."

"*Si.*" Rayna leaned back in the chair, looking more

frustrated than victorious. A look he recognized, having seen it many times in the past. While growing up, their father had always been busy with politics, leaving Donato in charge of the estate. Rayna had to take orders from him, and more than once he had seen that same expression.

"And if the king does not believe me? I will lose my head, and what happens to my son?"

"It will take little to convince him. He wants to make an appointment of you."

"For what?"

"I do not know exactly, but Father suspects it will be to assist in the intentions of the Holy Alliance and the king to make Cuba a base of operations against the provinces of Spanish America that have revolted. He feels you know the islands, the people, a perfect candidate, if the king believes you're loyal to the Crown."

"How do you gain from this, Rayna? I cannot believe it is only Father's welfare that sent you across the ocean."

"Donato, you are a fool. If Father is stripped of his title, his life, so goes his fortune. I will not be reduced to a peasant by him or you. I will protect what is mine and the riches and luxury in which I live. If you do not accept this appointment, you will destroy us all. And that, *mi hermano*, is where your son comes in."

"You would harm a little boy?"

"No, I would not, but send him away I would. You and his mother would never see him again. Leverage."

"So King Ferdinand financed this flotilla."

"That is not of concern, except to say he is most anxious to speak with you, but a little wary, as well. But you will convince him otherwise, I am sure." When he didn't answer,

Rayna seemed to interpret his silence as capitulation. "This is the plan. We will continue to Cádiz. Before we enter port, we will transfer you to our ship."

"The boy's mother will not be left behind."

Rayna rolled her eyes. "She is French."

"Father aligned himself with the French when convenient."

"I know you blame Father for many things, but he did what he must to keep us safe, you and me. Without him doing that, we'd be dead. Which is why Spain is not a safe place for a French woman, especially in Cádiz. The peasants have killed many for nothing more than being French."

Donato had managed to keep his temper controlled through the entire discussion, but worked hard to subdue it now. Without half trying, his voice hardened, and his eyes narrowed on his sister. "Into this chaos, you have brought my son."

She straightened her posture and drew a deep breath. For the first time since she arrived, he saw a crack in her armor. "Politics, Your Excellency."

"Backstabbing and betrayal. Let's get it right. Change of plan. I will sail my own ship into port. This would be so much easier for you if I were a willing participant, correct?"

"*Si*, Donato—Your Excellency."

"Then to make that happen, you must do something for me. A measure of good faith."

"Which is?"

"Let Colette visit her child."

Rayna's face paled a little, making him wonder who was really making the decisions. If the king financed the voyage, others were involved. She shook her head. "Not possible."

"Then I will be most disagreeable and put you at risk. I will implicate you in all my follies. We will face the executioner's ax together."

"You speak foolishly." She glanced away from him, then back. "I will see what I can arrange and send my answer in the morning."

"Agreed. Do you not concern yourself with retribution from me?"

"Your Excellency, there is nothing you can do to me. At least at the moment."

"You have betrayed me, Rayna. Do not make a second mistake by underestimating me."

"Do you mean as you have underestimated me? You refused to communicate."

"We've communicated enough for today." Donato rose to his feet. "You have me, Rayna, but only if Colette sees her son. I will go to Spain and pretend to be the loyal candidate for the sake of my son and Colette. If I succeed, I will gain in power. Be careful, Rayna. I will retaliate. You will know you have betrayed me."

"I am so impressed, *hermano*." She pushed to her feet, attempting to stand nose to nose with him despite her petite height. "Then an actor you must be. If you fail, you will face the executioner's ax, and you'll be too dead to retaliate. The French woman will never see her son again."

Chapter Sixteen

"I want you, Donato. Our days have passed."

Colette glanced up and watched his expression, which told her little, but his arms were still around her. Finally, he breathed a slow, quiet breath that fluttered along the side of her cheek.

He had relayed the conversation with his sister and what Rayna wanted of him but after that had remained unusually quiet. His silence worried her, knowing he was from a world she did not completely understand. She knew continuing on to Spain was their only option. She'd go whether she understood what was happening or not, because of her son. But as a French woman, she wanted to enter her husband's country as one, a unified front. As dangerous as this would be, she needed to know how Donato felt, not in his words, but in his heart. He had said he wanted her, but without a mended heart, how secure was their alliance? Did he forgive her for taking Enio? Or were broken emotions hovering just beneath his facade to coalesce into betrayal or revenge? With a man like Donato, there was only one way to know: his touch. Lovemaking was a universal language and the language her body wanted to speak.

Donato ran his curled fingers along the side of her face, then lowered his lips to hers. He briefly touched her mouth before he spoke. "How decadent we've become, Colette. It is just past ten in the morning. I have a ship to sail."

"I have a man to love." Oh, how easily that came out, surprising even herself. She played with the hair at the back of his neck, threading her fingers in and around the shiny ebony tresses that waved to his shoulders. "What sailing needs to be done when in the wake of your sister's ship?"

Colette rose to her tiptoes and returned his kiss with her own, trying to steal the breath from his lungs into hers.

She needed his strength.

She needed to claim Donato as hers.

She needed to believe in them, together.

Perhaps he was right. Separate from each other, they were gunpowder and flint. Together they were explosive, but with a commitment to each other, they were a power that no mortal could deny. They were resolute, invincible, an unconquerable force that would save their son and themselves.

Donato allowed the kiss, rewrapping her in his arms and taking charge. It was a kiss meant to awaken every eager muscle in her body, to align his passion with hers, and she luxuriated in the heat of his touch. His hands migrated down her body, sliding and journeying over every curve, as if she were virgin terrain never trespassed by man. But he had been there before, exploring, lovingly touching her body as if she were more than a beautiful piece of art. Would now feel the same after so much had happened between them?

"You make this too easy, Colette—makes me wonder what plan you have."

"No plan. I believe we must be together to enter your country and get our son out."

He tensed, his movement halted, and she immediately regretted her words. She had made a mistake, knowing her attempt to solidify an alliance sounded more like a proposition than about two people whose love for each other would fortify them through the future challenges.

He stepped away, and the cool air skimmed over her body with a chill. "So you offer to give yourself to me, to buy my allegiance?"

"No, that is not what I meant."

But the hardened darkness of his eyes showed that reasoning would not be easy.

"You think you must sell yourself to me to ensure I will protect you in Spain?"

She had started to retreat until he made that accusation, bringing forward a rush of memories of an auction block, a dingy tavern, the rancid smell of ale and pork, and men bidding on her. She blinked from the images. "You did buy me, Donato. I was sold to you."

She wasn't sure why that suddenly became an important distinction or why it would have to be said now, but out her mouth it came.

A hint of a reaction flitted through his eyes. He widened his distance from her.

"I bought you to get you out of a dangerous situation, not to make you my slave. Was that what it was to you? Is that why you left when your brother came with his dramatic rescue?"

"No, that is not what I meant, but I need to know, Donato, that you are with me and together we will get Enio home."

"Because you don't trust me or because I own you?"

He lifted her in his arms and tossed her on the bed. Before she could catch her breath, he was on top of her. He pulled her arms up over her head and straddled her body. "Is this what I did? Take you against your will?"

"No, that is not true."

"Did you hate it, Colette? Every intimate minute with me, every time I touched you?"

"No, no, Donato, that is not what I meant."

"Did you accept this only because I owned you?" He leaned down and kissed her, but it lacked the gentleness of before and became demanding, and though it hurt her lips, her heart started to hammer with his closeness. She couldn't help inhaling the scent of him with the mint soap he used to bathe in the wee hours of the morning, while she slept, or feel the recently shaved skin of his face.

"No," she whispered.

"And this?" Holding her arms over her head, he sucked the lobe of her ear before settling into the hollow of her throat. There, he dropped light kisses along each collarbone and ran his hand over her breasts. Her body started to move without her consent, rolling with a heat she couldn't deny. She sucked in air, trying to grasp why he was angry and why she so craved his touch.

"And this?" He tore open the bodice of her gown and chemise and exposed her breasts. Her nipples pulled tight in anticipation. He rolled his tongue over their pointed nubs; his hot breath soaked her breasts like butter on a hot roll.

"No." She arched her back toward him, unable to feel as much of him as she wanted. "I found pleasure when with you."

He heard her and freed her arms, allowing them to drift down and over his shoulders. She turned her fingers into the rippling muscles of his back and ran them along his shoulder blades, as she anointed each collarbone of his with a kiss. The burn of his skin now against her bare breasts sent a spark that flitted down to her belly and spread outward in search of release.

"And this? Colette, can you deny this?" His voice had softened to barely a whisper as he reached down and pulled up the hem of her cotton dress. The flames from his touch swirled up around her body, then dived into that unprotected spot that tried to keep her passion in check.

"I cannot deny, nor do I wish to." Her hands fell along his arms, feeling the muscles glide with his movement. His full weight was atop her now, but she wanted him closer, inside her.

He pushed off the bed and pulled her to her feet. He pulled her gown over her head and tossed it aside, then the remaining undergarments until she stood naked before him.

Donato stopped as if seeing her for the first time. With his finger, he traced along her throat, the contours of her breasts, and across her stomach. "Did you hate my touch?"

"Never," she whispered.

He lowered himself to his knees and splayed his large hands on each buttock. She nearly liquefied from anticipation. He pulled her hips into him and kissed her core of desire. The heat soaked through to that very defenseless vulnerable spot that craved him and only him.

She put her hands on his shoulders for support, her knees having dissolved the moment his lips touched her body, feeling the work of his tongue penetrate inside. "I cannot deny."

"I grew up in a world of manipulation and betrayal. Do not speak of new alliances where one already exists." He rose to his feet, kicked off his shoes, then pulled off his pants and stood before her as a man of blood and flesh, muscle, and strength. The father of her son and…God's blessing… the love of her life. "If making love to you will give you that assurance, I will not deny you, for I can no longer deny myself."

He lifted her into his arms and gently placed her atop the bed. He leaned over her and brushed her forehead with his lips. Colette threw her arms up and around his shoulders, pulling him over her. "Now—take me now."

"Such demands, *cariño*." Donato smiled, spreading her legs with his. "Maybe you should buy me?"

"I will." Colette closed her eyes, waiting for him to enter her. "My husband is rich."

"I heard he is a pirate. I hope not a jealous one."

"No." Colette looked directly into his eyes. "He is secure in knowing that I love him."

She thought she saw a slight mist hit his eyes, but he lowered his head so quickly to kiss her throat, she wasn't sure. She reached down and wrapped her fingers around his swollen shaft and guided him inside her.

Slowly, he started to move.

She raised her hips to move with him. A swirling heat burned inside her until it plunged to her depths and ricocheted outward, banging against her hips, her thighs. He stiffened as he projected his life force into her body, the same life that had given them Enio. She held tight. Her fingers dug into his shoulders until they both lay still and silent.

For a moment or two, he kept his head buried in her hair, then started to move. He slipped out of her and rolled to his side. Colette had to move her body over to accommodate him in the small bed. She laid her head on his shoulder and stroked his chest, then ran circles over his heart.

"Tell me, Donato, have I mended this wound?"

He kept his eyes closed, but nodded. "I believe you have, *cariño*."

"I am happy for both of us."

"We will be in Spain in a few weeks."

"And I will be at your side."

"So we have established our alliance."

"With our hearts," she added.

A smile worked over his face. "At this point, I don't know who owns who, so we must stay together, do you not agree?"

Colette allowed a small chuckle at his logic. "Together we stand."

He nodded, then drew a deep breath. The muscles across his chest pulled against the strain. After a quick kiss to her head, he pushed himself to his feet.

Colette remained on the bed, drifting between ecstasy and sleep. As he washed up in the small basin of water, she watched, admiring the strong, broad shoulders, narrow waist and tight buttocks topping off his powerful legs, the soft tint of his skin, when suddenly a cold wave of memories invaded her sense of security.

She glanced over at Donato, fighting a feeling of something familiar but evasive, of something standing in the shadows of her mind, afraid to come out.

"Donato? Why were you in Port-au-Prince the night I was auctioned? It is a place of French corsairs, very dangerous for a Spaniard, *non*? Why were you there?"

"I have to get on deck."

. . .

Rayna de la Roche stood atop the forecastle, looking down at them as Colette and Donato boarded. The ship was massive, with gilding of gold and scrolls of silver covering ornate carvings. As Donato had explained, the ship had three stories of living space, four masts, forty-six cannons over two gundecks giving her broadside advantage, and at least three hundred men.

When the boarding was complete, Rayna took the stairs down and approached them.

She bowed to her brother. "Your Excellency."

Donato placed Colette's valise in plain sight. "This woman is the mother of Enio, and will care for him the remainder of our voyage."

Rayna's mouth tightened, and Colette heard a deep sigh. "Agreed."

Colette nearly collapsed from relief and joy, but managed to keep her body straight and upright. She would be with Enio. She glanced up at Donato and whispered, "I cannot thank you enough. *Merci.*"

Rayna gave Colette a long once-over. Compared to Rayna's style of dress, flamboyant colors, and radiant beauty, Colette knew she looked more the employed nurse for a child than a nobleman's wife.

"He is a good boy, senora." Rayna motioned for her to

follow.

They walked the length of the main deck and then took a winding stairway down a level. The run had several rooms; each one looked more glorious than the first.

Colette had never seen a ship like this, a city on water. Her body started to settle, knowing that with this kind of wealth, Enio had most likely received adequate care. She could hear the babbles of a baby wafting through the run. Her heart started to pound mercilessly against her chest, so much so she thought her ribs would give way. As they neared his room, she heard the child laugh and a woman's voice talking to him in Spanish.

Rayna halted and faced Colette. "The child has been well cared for."

Was Colette to thank her for that, for taking care of a little boy she had no right to have, for terrorizing the child's parents and leading them across the ocean on a perilous journey? Was she to thank her for that? Colette's fingers folded into fists and it took all of her strength not to swing, but she understood the tenuous situation and that the fragile relationship could change at a moment's notice. She wanted Rayna to disappear, but brought her temper under the simmer mark and barely uttered the word, "*Merci.*"

Rayna stepped aside and motioned for Colette to enter the room.

There he was, little Enio. His dark hair neatly formed around his head, his dark eyes enchanting as a child's can be. In his little hands, he held a small wooden ship. When he saw Colette, he dropped it and ran to her. "*Maman! Maman!*"

Colette burst into tears as she fell to her knees to hug her little boy, who wrapped his pudgy arms around her neck and held on so tight she thought she'd never breathe again. "Oh my *bébé*. Oh my little *bébé*. Mama miss you so much, n'est-ce pas?"

Rayna whirled away and left the room. Donato came forward and knelt on the floor next to Colette and his son. When Colette glanced over at him, his eyes had watered up. "Enio, here's your papa."

Donato smiled, running his hand over the boy's head. "*Tu padre*, Enio, I am your *padre*."

The nurse who had been caring for Enio had stood but kept her head bowed. "Your Excellency."

Donato acknowledged her, then nodded toward the door. "*Puedes retirarte*."

The woman again bowed and left the room, closing the door behind her.

Colette felt nearly giddy, vacillating between tears of happiness and joyous laughter. He looked well, but his little arms clung so tightly around her neck she knew he was aware of a separation. "*Mère* is here. We will not part again, my darling little one."

Colette glanced over to Donato wanting him to confirm, but he said nothing. He seemed nearly mesmerized by the small boy in her arms. Her tears of happiness disappeared. She reached out to Donato, with her palm to his cheek. "Can you ever forgive me for taking him away from you?"

An apologetic smile flashed and disappeared. "Do not dwell on that. I can and I do. We are here with him together now."

Donato stroked the little boy's head, then pulled him into his arms. Enio seemed to instinctively know Donato was his father, for he settled in and seemed to enjoy the feel of strong arms holding him. Donato kissed the top of his head. "He is a handsome little man, Colette."

For what seemed like hours, they held their son together, huddled on the floor of the cabin. Donato made the first move to leave. Colette felt her heart seize and her throat went dry. "Donato, they bow to you, call you Your Excellency, do they not have to obey you?"

He shook his head. "They are on a mission for the Crown. We are all subject to the Crown."

"Even Rayna?" Colette didn't know why she asked, but wanted to know how much of this was actually the idea of his sister, or was she too a pawn?

"*Si*, even Rayna." Donato kissed Enio on the forehead, hugged him dearly before rising to his feet. Colette stood as well. Her hip burned from sitting for so long, and she stumbled. Donato reached out and steadied her. That touch stirred everything to the surface.

"Donato," she whispered. "Tell me we will prevail."

"It is a promise I cannot make. I will accept God's will." He then winked at her. "I'll make some suggestions to the Almighty. Stay with your prayers and keep me in your heart."

"I know you explained, but I want you to stay."

"I surrender too much power if I do. I must be on my own ship." He leaned down to kiss her, but suddenly pulled her into his arms and crushed her against his chest. "I will do all that is in my power. I love you."

After saying the words she had so longed to hear, he left the room without looking back.

• • •

The days dragged with the burning sun, no wind, no Enio, and no Colette.

Every day, he awoke and missed both of them until he thought his body would physically break. He stood atop the helm and watched the mesmerizing wake of the large frigate that carried his son and wife. It had been four weeks since he had left her on his sister's ship, but to know Colette was there with Enio made all the angst worthwhile. Within the hour they would dock in Cádiz, Spain, the journey over.

For the past few weeks, Colette would appear at the bulwarks with Enio and wave toward Donato's ship. But it didn't alleviate the cool nights alone in the bedchamber, not being able to be with her or them. They were in danger, yet innocent of any wrongdoing. Donato was the guilty party, and he prayed again they wouldn't pay for his crimes.

Sooner or later, he'd have to tell her the truth about the night she had been abducted, for it seemed a secret destined to surface. Once she knew, maybe then the dreams that haunted her would cease and allow her peace in her life. But would she cease loving him, as well?

Before he had left Rayna's ship, he had learned both his father and King Ferdinand were in Cádiz, saving Donato a long journey to the Palacio Real de Madrid, the king's palace.

Rayna was intense. He could see the strain wearing on her, though Rayna would never admit it. She seemed to have no fear of the king or of losing her head, but seemed to think her actions noble to save their father's legacy. With the king's popularity plummeting, he had focused on saving the Spanish colonies. But they were already in revolt against the mother country, and there was no hope of Spain ever regaining control, Cuban military base or not.

As they sailed into port, he noted the San Sebastián Castle with the old large cannons that had once controlled the south sea lanes into the bay and La Caleta beach. High limestone walls, parapets, and drawbridges mingled with the many towers built along the water's edge for merchants to see what ships were arriving.

Cruising into port, Rayna's ship anchored closest. The two sister ships sailed past her and anchored to her starboard. *El Rescate* anchored larboard.

Donato raised his binoculars, watching her ship. Being back in Spain made him feel as if he had stepped back in time. He had expected a heavy weight to fall over his person from seeing his home again, but the only thoughts that plagued his mind were of Colette and Enio, their safety, and getting back to the island. He had set up emergency protocols should a fast escape be necessary. Over the next few hours, his little clipper, *El Rescate*, would be ready to sail.

His father's holdings were quite vast in the Roche, near Cádiz. His personal wealth rivaled that of the king's treasury. Today, Donato would again return home and, according to Rayna, have an audience with the king the following day.

He drew a sharp breath, pulling in courage and clearing his head. The next few days would determine his future. Could he fool the king or not? Did the Crown already know about him? There was no line he would not cross. He would lie, cheat, be deceitful, even kill, if that meant he'd get his son and wife out of Spain.

Rayna's ship disembarked first. As he watched the activity he noted that neither Colette nor a special little boy crossed the planked walk. Once the de-boarding process ended,

Donato knew Colette and Enio were no longer onboard.

He dropped the binoculars from his eyes and walked down to the American, the first man he had posted on watch, having posted men from every angle. "Which ship are they in?"

"The one farthest starboard."

"You are certain."

The American nodded, then glanced at Donato. "How did you know they would change ships?"

"Because it's what I would do if I were Rayna. Watch that ship at all times. Be prepared for anything. Get a message to my wife that I know where she is, and that is the safest place for her and Enio. It will be easier to take them with us when we leave. Provision the ship and keep her lying to. Be ready."

Ramón had packed Donato's personal items and met him at the end of the gangplank. "The men are ready whenever you say the word."

"Colette and Enio are in the farthest ship starboard," Donato whispered as they walked along the dock toward the waiting landaus. "If I were Rayna, I'd not leave my collateral behind, but it is best for us."

People milled around the docks loading and unloading ships. Some recognized Donato and bowed as he walked by, others only knew he was nobility by his dress and bowed, anyway. With the king in town, no one would chance anything that might appear revolutionary.

Donato caught up with Rayna. Walking beside her, he asked, "When do I see my wife and son again?"

"After you see the king. If the meeting does not go as we'd all like, it would be most dangerous for the little boy on Spanish soil. I will have them taken to France. I owe you that much."

Donato grabbed her elbow and spun her around. "You owe me a hell of a lot more, and I will collect, dear sister, I will."

"You have to live through tomorrow before you are any threat to me. Come, Father awaits, to welcome the return of his long-lost son."

There were four carriages lined up for the entourage. Guards rode in the first and last. Rayna boarded the second with her maids, and Donato and Ramón were in the third. The train of horses started through the village and into the countryside. Not far from town, and they were already on his father's property.

The high sierras offered excellent grazing lands for growing herds of cattle, with the best pastures reserved for his father's horses. The economy was healthy and growing. They passed his father's olive groves and numerous orchards of oranges, lemons, and limes. Though the sun dropped a veil of warmth on the entourage, and the smell of the ocean waters hung in the air, it seemed to be an unusually cool spring day.

They entered the Roche.

As they traveled along, Donato could only think about his son and Colette left behind. It was safest for them on the water. If things did not go as hoped with King Ferdinand tomorrow, they had a chance to escape, and that was the only thought that kept him going.

They pulled through the massive iron gates bookended by finials of cast stone, and traveled up the cobblestoned drive. Nothing had changed. If anything, the house looked worn, and the grounds needed more care. Everything looked older than he remembered.

The estate comprised more than twenty thousand acres

with stables, a carriage house, servants' quarters, and a seventy-two-room manor house, requiring a staff of at least thirty-five to run. The house was made of smooth stucco and red barrel tiles over the multiple sloping roofs at varying degrees.

The horse-drawn conveyances pulled through the inner courtyard surrounded on three sides by a wall. One by one they came to a halt under the carriage port. Two footmen were waiting and opened each door.

Rayna was the first to disembark. She glanced back at Donato before turning, her dress swirling about her, and entered the house. By the time Donato approached, Rayna had said her proper acknowledgment to their father and stepped aside for her brother.

After giving Rayna a kiss on her cheek, his father turned and faced his son. Donato swallowed hard, suddenly feeling twenty years younger in the wake of his father's stern expression. But he wasn't the tower of a man Donato remembered. His skin had aged. His hair more silver than black, and shadows collected beneath eyes that looked dull and tired.

"Donato, *hijo mio*," he said, though his lips were stiff and his face unyielding.

"Your Most Excellency." Donato bowed.

His father took stock of Donato's looks, his dress, seemed to measure him from head to foot. Donato had taken the time to dress appropriately and look the noble even if his heart was not in the same place. "I trust you are well, son. Journey safe?"

"*Si*, Your Most Excellency."

"He came as soon as he received word of his being

needed here, Father." Rayna interjected as if trying to diffuse the older man's reprimand, but Donato didn't need or want her help, for he didn't see anger in Father's face; he saw something much more disarming…love.

"You must be tired." His father came forward and dropped a hand to Donato's shoulder as if this meeting was under the most pleasant circumstances. "Come, come inside. You are home."

"*Gracias,* Your Most Excellency."

They stepped through the wrought iron door, adorned with helmets and breastplates overhead, and entered the vestibule.

"Allow me to have refreshments made for you. I've had rooms made ready for your return," his father was saying as they walked through the vestibule into the great hall.

Sun streamed in through the large stained glass windows of the great hall, which rivaled that of a castle. Surrounded by his father's land, the manor house was considered a castle, minus a moat. The large arching windows reached to the ceiling and lined a cloister that led to a flying staircase to the master portion of the house.

Donato remembered, as a child, being enamored with that flying staircase leading to the master's hall, which was on two floors, with the quarters consisting of bedrooms, sleeping porch, sitting room, and two baths. The third floor of the master's hall had a secretary's alcove.

The great hall had changed little. The coral-colored floor was trimmed in black polished tile and much of the furnishings were old, having been with the estate for several generations. The same tapestries from his childhood hung on the rib-vaulted walls.

A large twenty-foot table stood in the center of the room with two large candelabras on each end, and an iron chandelier hung overhead. Large rugs tried to warm the room during winter, but the sheer immensity of it made that nearly impossible. He could fit his ship in this room alone.

"I have arranged for you to stay in the west tower." His father broke into Donato's thoughts. "It is perfect. It has three bedrooms, a sleeping porch, a room converted to a playroom, and a room for the nurse."

Donato didn't miss the reference to a playroom and nurse, but said nothing.

"Rest well tonight, son. Tomorrow we speak with our cousin, King Ferdinand—" His father looked around confused. "Where is the little boy I've heard tell of?"

Rayna cleared her throat, stealing a glance at Donato. "On the ship, Father."

Donato caught something in that look of his sister's that said leaving her collateral behind had not been by accident but by design. In that split second, Donato knew her to be more friend than foe.

"But this is nonsense! I have made arrangements for your family." His father continued, "Bring him to me! I must see him."

Donato glanced over at Ramón.

Opportunity lost.

$\cdots$

Colette had no idea what to expect as she and her son were ushered in the landau toward the Roche estate. She greatly appreciated receiving Donato's message that he knew they had changed ships. They had been forced to dress like sailors when they moved to the second ship. Colette had feared they would be sent to France. She had had little contact with Donato's sister the entire time they had journeyed together to Spain. Rayna had never joined her for dinner, checked on her, or asked about the accommodations. It was like a mirage. On occasion, Colette had caught sight of her from a distance.

Much like her brother, Rayna had the silky raven hair that waved down her back and dark swarthy eyes. Unlike her brother, she was aloof and distant. It was hard for Colette to discern whether she was a pawn or perpetrator.

Enio found this travel exciting, pointing out all the sights along the way, having no idea they were in danger. Her heart broke with every excited word he blurted out. He liked the horses, the water, the ship, the pretty colors of the drapery in the landau. She kept herself calm and admired the many new sights that amused him, wondering how long it would be before she'd see Donato.

Leaving the sights of Cádiz behind them, they continued down a long forested road. Her mind started to work against her, fearing this was some kind of death march and that perhaps Donato knew nothing of it. Maybe he thought she was still safe on the ship, and would learn later they had been whisked off to France, or worse…

They had offered to let Enio ride up front, but Colette declined, stating she and the child would not be separated.

Was Donato all right? Who did these men work for?

She kept herself strong, smiling down at Enio every time his arm pointed at something new, but oftentimes she closed her eyes and silently prayed that Donato knew where she was and would soon join them.

After what seemed like hours of travel, the small entourage turned down another long, narrow cobblestoned road. Colette leaned her head out the window to see a castle appear on the horizon. A beautiful manor, or small castle, of white stucco trimmed in stone of warm gold and fire red. The windows were made of bronze-framed blue-stained glass. The entire manor had been softened with a cloak of ivy that hung from the windows and red tiles of the roof.

Her heart started to pound with both relief and excitement. Was it possible this would work out? That Donato was inside those stone walls, waiting?

They rolled up to the front entrance. Enio scrambled off her lap, ready to disembark. She held his hand and instructed him to wait. Her luggage, as it was only a valise, was unloaded, giving her hope.

The door to the cab opened and a footman took Enio out and set him on his feet, then turned to assist her. When Colette stepped free of the carriage, she was astonished at the immensity of the estate. It was beautiful. She stood within the enclosed patio of pebbled stone, much like the hacienda, but this was huge. It was surrounded on three sides with stucco walls, and every corner had a blue-and-green tiled fountain.

She lifted Enio into her arms and started for the stairs. In the corner of the portico, she noted a man standing. She recognized him from Donato's ship, and when her gaze met his, he very slightly nodded to acknowledge her. Her breath escaped her body as she relaxed just a little. Seeing him relieved her sense of isolation and eased her fears.

The large iron doors of the castle were opened for her, and a servant bowed as Colette walked by with Enio in her arms. She hesitated in the great hall, unsure of where to go next. Another servant brought in her valise and left it at her feet. Feeling, and most likely looking, the lost orphan on the king's door, she waited.

Men's low speaking voices echoed through the hall where she stood. They were speaking Spanish, and though she knew some Spanish, she could not follow the conversation. Enio was mesmerized by the height and size of the hall itself. He stared up at the chandeliers overhead and smiled.

"I will take the baby." A woman appeared from a side door with her arms outstretched to accept Enio.

Colette tightened her hold on Enio. "He stays with me."

The woman seemed surprised by the rebuke and bowed. "*Si*, Her Excellency."

The woman backed out of the hall and into the room where she had appeared. Colette remained standing in the hall until she heard the sound of clapping hands.

Colette turned toward the sound.

"A woman of contradictions, senora?" Rayna walked toward her. "You stole the child from his father and now you are his protector?"

"And you stole him from both his mother and father." Colette leveled her eyes on Donato's sister. "Do be careful, Rayna, for I am protective of my little one."

"You address me as Your Lady Excellency." Rayna's eyes flashed, but she quickly erased her expression. "I see you're passionate as well. That's what they say about the French, is it not?"

"I am a mother before I am French...Lady Excellency." Colette allowed a slight bow of her head, hoping to have diffused the situation. "If you please, will you inform Donato that I am here?"

"You do not direct me. His Excellency"—she made point of his title—"is speaking with Father."

Colette fought any reaction, but the relief of knowing Donato was there nearly washed her to the floor. "And his title is…?"

"His Most Excellency Lord."

"Will you tell Donato that I am here?"

Rayna stared at her.

"Will you tell His Excellency that I am here?"

Still no movement by Rayna except the slight curl of her lip and a way she had of looking down her nose. She motioned toward that strange side room and called out in Spanish. The same woman who had offered to take Enio again appeared.

"Assist the marchioness to her room. Dinner will be served at seven. You will see His Excellency then and, ah… dinner is formal dress."

Rayna turned to leave. The hem of her red satin dress swirled across the marble floor. Her long raven hair had been pulled back and coiled behind her left ear. From those ears hung sparkling jewels of rubies and gold. The chandeliers of the overhead lights played off the sparkles that lined every ruffle of her gown. Her steps revealed hand-embroidered slippers with a matching shimmer under the soft lights.

The servant motioned for them to take a winding staircase upward into a tower. She said something in Spanish. Colette smiled as if she understood, but hesitated, wanting Donato to know she had arrived. To be so close, yet so far. She took a step toward the area that she thought echoed of male voices, but hesitated when she heard Rayna's voice, as the woman had not yet left the room.

"His Excellency is in conference, Marchioness. I'm sure you have much to do to prepare for dinner." Rayna gave her dress a once-over. *Zut.* Colette certainly looked, as she had feared, the orphan on the king's doorstep. "And the boy, he will be taken care of for dinner. Allow, please."

Colette debated whether or not to stand her ground but decided since she was the foreigner here and knew that Donato felt the juggler learning a new balancing act, she had to tread with caution. Longing to scream to Donato that she had arrived, she kept her calm by simply giving Rayna a slight nod of her head. *"Merci."*

Colette quietly followed the servant up the stairs.

Colette did her best with what she had, and her maid, Lelia, proved to be far more helpful than Colette had expected and squealed with delight when Colette pulled out the yellow satin dress she had worn to board her husband's ship. *Orphan indeed.* Lelia brushed Colette's yellow dress clean, managing to remove most of the wrinkles. After a luxurious bath that Colette never wanted to vacate, her maid helped her dress and fix her hair in the proper Spanish chignon.

Atop her head, the servant added the sparkling *peineta* and white lace mantilla. Though Colette never thought to radiate like Rayna, tonight changed that. She had asked where Donato's room was and was pleased to learn it was attached to hers. Colette insisted Enio have a bed in her room. He played on the floor with a large assortment of miniatures he had been given, unconcerned about where he was or why.

Lelia left the room but returned shortly with a velvet box in her hand. She set it on the dressing armoire and motioned for Colette to sit before the mirror. Colette did as asked, curious about the velvet box.

"A gift from the marquis to you, Lady Excellency."

Colette watched with interest as Lelia opened the box to expose an exquisite set of earrings and necklace. It was beautiful, nothing like she had ever seen in her life. Even her mother, a French aristocrat, had never worn anything like it. But the titles confused her.

"Is this a gift from my husband?"

"*Si,* Lady Excellency, *si,* the marquis, most beautiful?"

"Do you know what they are? What stones are these, for I have never seen such beautiful gems?" Colette tilted the box back and forth, watching the gems transform from green to red, then back again.

"They are Tourmaline, Lady Excellency, Rubellite, meaning undying devotion."

Colette fingered the gems. What a beautiful gift. She smiled as the necklace was draped around her neck and hung just above the cleavage between her breasts. With each earring, she felt herself shifting from orphan to a princess. "I feel the princess in this."

The servant's expression changed. "Oh, no, Lady Excellency, you are not. You are the wife of a marquis."

Colette smothered a smile; of course, she had not meant literally a princess. "So when do I see my husband?"

"He will be at dinner."

Colette pushed away from the dressing table and stood up. "*C'est bon,* I'm ready to go."

After ensuring the care Enio would receive while she

attended the formal dinner, Colette made her pilgrimage to the dining hall, following her escort down the winding stairs of the tower and along a beautiful vaulted cloister with colored glass, illuminated by the setting sun.

From there, she descended another flight of stairs made of white stone and through double doors of walnut linenfold that opened to the dining hall. Men's voices filled the air, but halted the moment she was announced and escorted into the room.

There were three men in the room. She suspected she might have broken protocol in some way, as Rayna was not yet in attendance, but damn them all, she wanted to see her husband.

The dining room was huge, with frescoed walls and coffered ceiling. There were iron sconces glowing between the hanging tapestries. The table was long, maybe eighteen to twenty feet, and made from one solid plank. The chairs were leather and studded along the upper half, the seats covered in crimson velvet.

Donato stood to the far end of the hall. He set his glass down and started toward her. She had always thought of Donato as handsome, but in his royal attire his looks were devastating. She ran a quick tongue over her upper lip, taking in the mere sight of him.

He wore a Spanish short jacket of black velvet embroidered in gold that hugged his broad shoulders with style. Underneath the jacket, he wore a long-sleeved ruffled shirt, with the ruffles hanging over his well-jeweled hands. The gold waistcoat beneath the jacket was finished off with a red satin sash, tied neatly to his right hip and hanging to midthigh. He wore no cravat, his shirt opened to expose his well-tanned neck. As he walked toward her, she noted the sheen of the Hessian boots that reached over his knees.

His wavy black hair hung to his shoulders, combed neatly. Atop his head, he wore a crown of gold with four gold crosses all lavishly covered with emeralds, rubies, and pearls. He looked the king himself, more regal than an emperor. He nearly took her breath away, and when he reached his hand out to her, she fought not to faint and humiliate them both.

"Your Lady Excellency." He bowed before her. "Donato de la Roche y Borbón, Marquis de Andalusia, at your service."

"*Merci,*" was all she could muster and it was a whisper, at that.

"May I present to His Most Excellent Lord, my wife, Marchioness Colette." Donato smiled, took her hand in his, and led her to the center of the hall. She knew the moment she saw the older man that he was Donato's father by the familiar build, handsome features, and dark hair laced with silver. Donato continued with his introduction, "My father, Carlos de la Roche y Borbón, Marquis de Andalusia, Grandes de España."

Colette lowered herself into a curtsy. "I am most honored, Your Most Excellent Lord."

His father came up to her and with a hand to her chin, raised her to face him. "You are French?"

"I am."

"I thought that to be an error, for you are far too beautiful to be French." He smiled as he glanced over to Donato. "I will see the boy later."

Donato nodded in agreement, and with that His Most Excellent Lord turned his attention to the door as Rayna appeared.

"Do you have more rank than her?" Colette whispered to Donato, who responded with a smile and nod. "I thank you for the jewelry."

"*Fue un placer*," he whispered in her ear. "You look most beautiful, *cariño*."

Colette appreciated his thoughtfulness regarding her dress, but the burning question that nagged with every thought, every nicety expressed, every show of royal respect, was *what was the situation?*

Rayna, wearing a dress of a striking blue satin with ruffles of sparkling black lace, glided into the room as if her feet didn't touch the marble tile. Her hair, parted in the middle and pulled severely off the face, had been braided and rounded into a bun behind her right ear. Tendrils of curls hung before her ears, framed by a pearled *peineta* and a black lace mantilla. She wore blue sapphires and diamonds that reflected the vivid blue of her gown. And though a beauty, she couldn't hide her surprise at Colette's dress and jewels, making Colette's evening perfect.

The other man in attendance had been introduced as a special ambassador of Donato's father. Donato's number one man showed up, Ramón, well dressed for dinner, and was shown into the dining room.

The food was delicious and with only small talk about the weather and how the voyage was, nothing of significance was broached. Colette had the feeling that perhaps his father didn't know Donato had been forced on this journey or that their son had been held hostage. For he acted the warm, loving father, welcoming his son home after a long absence.

She couldn't help her eye from wandering over her husband. Her entire concept of who Donato was had changed so drastically over the past few months that she struggled to assimilate her thoughts. The man sitting across from her, a known pirate of the gulf waters, was the son of a royal noble on his own mission of rebellion. But she wasn't really thinking about the situation they were in, or of what revolution he partook.

But of him.

How kind a man he was, and how, when in her darkest hour, it was he who had rescued her. Taking her away from the awful men who had taken her ship, and though she had had no memory of who she was, he had kept her safe, helped her get well, and created a life for her. A beautiful life that she had so carelessly shunned when Jordan arrived.

She shook her head, trying to untangle her thoughts.

He caught the slight movement of her head with a raised eyebrow that asked *what are you thinking?*

Thinking?

She couldn't stop taking in his looks, sip by sip, as if an elixir, and she was addicted. His crown sparkled every time he moved his head. His hair more neatly combed then she'd ever seen, collected the overhead lighting, creating ribbons of blue tint that accented the dark color.

The soft black velvet of his jacket had draped itself over the rugged, broad shoulders she had navigated many times in the past. The candlelight reflected in his dark eyes, the same dark eyes she had allowed herself to sink into. A thin layer of perspiration formed along his forehead and along his upper lip. The same lips that coaxed her passion to the surface, the flint that ignited the gunpowder.

He was incredibly handsome with olive-tinted skin, smooth and swarthy, that covered his square face and highlighted the deep lines that had formed around his eyes and mouth that spoke of hard living. He was rugged, rough, weathered like the ships he sailed, and she loved every bit of him. Her gaze roved freely as she remained distant from the conversations.

He picked up his glass of wine and drank from it. His fingers wrapped around the silver stem as he lifted it to his mouth. She watched, knowing the feel of those fingers on her body, the massages, the loving gentle touch, all from those fingers wrapped around that glass.

When she glanced back to his face, she found he was watching her. Perhaps it was the long separation after having made love, but her thoughts were no further than the bedchamber upstairs.

He smiled at her as he forked another piece of dinner.

He knew what she was thinking, every single thought.

She wanted to simply luxuriate in his looks and the good food, but the conversation turned to her. His father asked her several questions about their son, which she answered to the best of her ability, oftentimes bringing laughter and smiles to the others at the table, except Rayna. But speaking of Enio made it easy to entertain, for the little boy was the absolute light of her life. She noticed the approving glances from his father, who expressed a loving interest in her stories and those of his grandson.

When the meal ended and they all retired to the hall, Enio was introduced. Colette had reservations, considering she was French and therefore so was Donato's son, but his father reacted far differently than she anticipated. His eyes grew misty as he took Enio into his arms. He held him for the remainder of the evening. Up and down from his arms, Enio would come and go.

Colette couldn't help but like Donato's father. He reminded

her of her own father and what he had missed, never knowing his grandson, and the place a grandfather plays in a young boy's life.

Others in the house had come to the vestibule to see the little boy, marvel over him, and asked for one story after another of his little life. Colette ignited a howl of laughter by comparing the little boy to Donato. Several times, she even caught Donato laughing freely, without restraint. The evening was filled with laughter and joy. She only prayed the feelings of good will would carry through Donato's meeting with the king.

Finally, Donato picked up his son and asked to be excused, for they were exhausted from the long journey. Before anyone could protest, she, Donato, and Enio were going up the stairs as a family. She could hardly wait to close the door behind them.

. . .

Donato waited, sitting on the outside balcony, taking in the sounds and sights of once again being home while Colette settled the baby for the night.

As far as he could see in any direction belonged to his father, and so would it belong to Donato someday, if he so wanted. Rayna would not inherit much of it, for she was a woman and could not carry on the title.

Donato's childhood room was in the east wing of the manor. His father had traveled often, especially to Madrid, to see King Charles IV, forcing Donato to be the man of the manor. A heavy load for a boy of eight years, but that was the decision his father had made. Because of it, Donato had learned to be self-reliant and strong, and it was only through wearing such armor that he could protect himself from the constant dangers of his father's world.

Donato's mother had been a weak woman, having surrendered control to her husband because she loved him. Donato had resented her weakness and her need to have his father love her. Marriage was never something he thought he would want, but Colette had inspired more in him than he ever thought possible. Love. So much so that when Colette had become with child, he eagerly married her, wanting nothing more than to love the mother of his child. Something his father had never done.

"Enio is asleep." Colette broke into Donato's thoughts, leaning out the door before she returned to her bedroom.

He returned a smile, pleased that they were together, as they had been on the island, when trouble had seemed an ocean away. Now he stood in the thick of things with no map to determine whether or not he'd make it through the treacherous royal maze.

He glanced through the window. Colette started to undress. He felt his breath catch somewhere in his chest, knowing the curves and soft places beneath that gown. The oil lamp stood on the table to the other side of her, illuminating her movements like that of the spirited bird who had nearly flown off the horse with Donato.

She was stunning. Her hair, freed from the *peineta*, dangled down her back and over her shoulders, shrouding her in a golden, glistening mantle. She had told him that she thought to be plain next to Rayna. He expected that of Colette, for she had no idea how beautiful she was, both inside and out. And tonight she had proved to be Rayna's equal, if not superior in many ways. By the time the night had ended, the entire House of Roche staff had been eating out of her hands.

Over her head, Colette pulled off the chemise and petticoat, leaving her in a thin shift. She hesitated a moment, glancing toward the balcony as if aware he was watching her. She pulled on a nightdress and adjusted her hair, tied off the waist of the gown, and came out onto the balcony.

"It is chilly, *non?*" Colette sat down next to him. Without waiting for an answer, she placed a hand over his. "You are troubled."

He looked at her. "*Si.*"

"Enio is asleep." She said it so easily, as if their world revolved around their son and the only worry at the moment was whether or not he slept.

He flashed her a quick smile, knowing her ruse. Admiring the woman of iron who sat with him, supporting him. "I know you have questions, Colette. Ask and I will try to explain. That is the least I can do, for you have earned it."

"I don't know where to begin. My family was wealthy in France, but nothing like this. This is the life of a king, n'est-ce pas?"

He glanced sideways at her. "Your family managed to bury a treasure with secret maps."

She laughed a little at his comment, and though she pretended it was nonsense, they both knew such a treasure existed.

"All right." She resettled herself on the settee. "Why did you leave here? It seems quite pretty. Your family seems nice, I think, though I still don't know Rayna."

"Yes, you do. You're being kind. Typical Colette."

"But your father seems nice."

"Nice," he repeated, finding the word odd in reference to his father. Rayna was of no consequence and, in her defense, had suffered through much of what he had growing up, but nice?

"I mean," Colette continued, "what made that final decision, to leave forever?"

Donato drew a deep breath, sensing a long conversation, something he never enjoyed.

"My mother died. She meant much to me and Rayna. When she died, she told me to follow my heart. She knew I was not a man to follow in my father's footsteps, and she knew what the war had done to me. She released me of responsibility here. I took the advantage, for I didn't love my father. I hated him and blamed him for her death. I believe she died of a broken heart, for he was so busy being a man of power, he had become bitter and cold."

"Did your father know why you left?"

"I think so. I don't know if he understands completely how I felt after the war. I think he chose to tell himself that I had an adventurous soul and needed to spread my wings."

"How did her death affect Rayna?"

"I don't know about Rayna. She seemed to close up, if that makes sense. She and I were close before mother died, but not afterward. I think she felt deserted by me. Perhaps I did let her down." He had not thought about how his leaving might have affected Rayna until now. He had left without consulting her or confiding in her. A mistake, in retrospect.

"Are you the oldest?"

He laughed. "I don't think Rayna would appreciate you not being able to guess, but *si*, I am the oldest by five years. There were other children, but none survived past infancy."

"But if not the adventure, what did you want?"

"Freedom to be my own man. The days of kings and queens with absolute authority are over. My father has spent most of his life catering and kneeling to men who are no more qualified to run a country than he."

"How did you get involved in a revolution thousands of miles away?"

"I live near Cuba. I know what goes on. Spain had adopted a constitution, perhaps not the best, but it was a start. King Ferdinand had promised to back it, but he did not. He believes he has absolute power over all lawmaking and men's lives."

"And your father agrees?"

"He's an absolutist. I am not."

"Does he know this?"

"Not entirely."

"Does Rayna?"

"She does, but it is in her best interest to keep it quiet. She would gain nothing by exposing me and possibly lose the entire estate if I were—" He stopped himself short of saying executed. "Not here."

"Then what is your plan?"

"Tomorrow I hope to play the part of a loyal subject and be honored to serve. If I were alone, it would be different, but I have no choice, I risk too much."

Colette slid forward and ran her hand down the side of his face. "You risk me and Enio and that is why you must humble yourself, bow to the wishes of this king."

"*Si*, but I do it with love, Colette. I cannot put my politics above my wife and child. My father did and it cost him dearly, for he hasn't a shred of honesty left. I never will."

"How did they find you? Why didn't they just request

you to come back?"

"They did. I ignored them, never thinking they, or Rayna, would go to such extremes."

"How did they know where you were?"

"I bought the island from Cuba with the money I earned from my short-lived shipping line—that was mine until the French buzzards destroyed it. That purchase would not have happened had it not been for my rank as a noble and father's power in the government."

"I see." Colette looked down, taking in the information. "Donato, you never told me why you were in Port-au-Prince the night I was auctioned off."

"No, I did not." He wanted to tell her everything, about her ship, and why he had taken it. But to tell her that when in a foreign country, in danger, with the only man she trusted, would be cruel, leaving her lost, alone, and frightened. He couldn't answer all her questions, for he had to preserve her faith in him long enough for them to be on their way back home.

Her green eyes, trimmed in long thick lashes, watched him. The corsage of her gown hugged her bosom and allowed a glimpse of the round full figure he so longed to caress, to lose himself within the warmth of her body and forget the problems that weighed heavily on his shoulders.

"That is not of import, and I wish to stop with questions for the night." He leaned over and kissed her on the mouth. Her lips partly open while thinking, tasting sweet and tender. "You know I watched you undress."

"I know."

"You undressed for me."

She nodded, her hair falling around her face. He

smoothed the tresses back over her shoulder. "I remember so much about your body, the curves, the soft areas, the special touches, such passion in a beautiful woman."

"I remember," she whispered, her head falling back, exposing her throat to him.

He leaned down and kissed that small heart-throbbing area. "*Si*, like this."

"I remember."

He pushed off his chair, lifted her in his arms, and placed her back on her feet inside the privacy of her bedchamber. He untied the dressing gown and dropped it around her arms, holding her in place. He kissed her throat, sliding along the silky skin to the tiny pulsation in the hollow of her throat. The gown slipped from his fingers to pool around the floor at her feet.

"And I remember the sweet taste of you," he whispered before lowering himself to his knees.

Underneath her shift, he parted her legs and ran his hands upward along her thighs until his fingers reached that sacred, coveted treasure at the juncture of her legs. He slipped his fingers inside her and stirred, enjoying how she moistened for him. He ran his tongue over her desire. She responded with a hitch of her hips. Straddling her legs around him, he lifted them to rest on his shoulders as he moved her to the bed.

Her nails dug into the flesh of his back with each sweep of his tongue, the pain oddly comforting. He cupped her bottom and pulled her into him, settling inside her. She ran her hands through his hair, removing his crown and placing it atop her own head. He kissed her again, deep inside her, pulsating with a need to take her.

Her fingers started to circle around and around on his shoulders, across the blades of his back until she gasped and arched for the sky. She held herself stiff for a moment before relaxing and exhaling as if satisfied.

He smiled.

She was.

He raised up off the bed to undress as fast as he could. Having removed the velvet jacket before, she tore through the waistcoat and shirt. She fumbled, pulling his shirt off over his head.

"It is you who undress for me now."

"For you, anything. If I must, I must."

She giggled as he lowered his weight over her and kissed her throat, running his hands up and over the bounty of beautiful breasts, round and full. He wanted to rip free the shift but knew she had only one with her. So he allowed her to unwrap herself, not enjoying the delay. He took his crown from her head and tossed it aside. It hit the marble floor with the loud *crack* of metal against stone.

He raised up to take in the beauty beneath him.

Her breasts rose with each breath and teased his chest, her nipples dark and ripe for kissing. Her slim waist and rounded hips blushed with color, and her beautiful slender arms wrapped around him in expectation, making him throb that much harder. "Are you ready for me, Colette?"

She wove her fingers into his hair and wrapped her legs around his middle. "Always."

Chapter Seventeen

He hadn't slept all night, even after the hours of lovemaking that took them well past midnight. Though neither gave their fears voice, the idea of this perhaps being their last night together weighed heavily in the air. Colette had fallen asleep curled up next to him with her head on his shoulder. But a wink of rest, he did not get.

His mind kept running over and over the challenges his audience with the king might hold. He dreaded the day but had no choice. He had been summoned, and he had to appear. He was a subject of Spain, a man of honor.

Enio awoke in the wee morning hours, fussing slightly with a stuffy nose and what seemed like a bad dream. Donato pulled him into his arms and soothed his tears before the child could awaken Colette. Caring for his son was a moment of retreat, a moment of doing nothing but loving the boy. To feel his small body relax in Donato's arms and trustingly fall back asleep brought Donato's heart to his throat. He so loved his son and his son's mother, a gift to his child that his father had never given him.

He had instructed Ramón on what to do if the meeting with King Ferdinand did not go well, and Ramón had seen to the task of having the ship lying to and provisioned. His men had been positioned along the route, each a job to perform should the need arise. If an escape were necessary, it was risky but set. He could do no better than that.

Donato washed and dressed before the sun rose. Colette was still asleep, as well as Enio. Donato kissed her lightly on her cheek and stole a little kiss off the boy's head. He stared at his son for a moment, wanting to always remember his little face, little smile, and cute laughter, and the pudgy arms he had wrapped around his neck last night. For after today, he had no guarantee of ever seeing them again.

He pushed through the door into the hall and took the winding stone stairway to the main floor, hoping to get a cup of tea before facing the king of Spain. To his surprise, his father sat waiting in the dining room, a cup of tea in hand.

"Your Most Excellency." Donato entered the room.

"I will go with you today."

"That is not necessary."

"It is important I be there to support you."

That made Donato most uncomfortable. As a member of the camarilla, did his father know something? After a quick cup of tea and a biscuit, Donato rose from his chair. "Then let us be on our way."

They traveled in four ornate barouches. In the first rode armed guards of la Roche; the second, Donato and his father; the third, Ramón and a private secretary of his father's; and the fourth, more armed guards.

Soon the carriages passed under the gatehouse into the inner ward of the castle, surrounded by a curtain wall on all sides. It was a small castle, used infrequently by the king but kept in readiness should he travel to Cádiz.

They all disembarked, but only Ramón and his father's secretary were allowed into the great hall. Guards had to wait outside. Donato and his father walked through the great hall and started down the long galley toward the lord's hall when his father reached out and stopped Donato, motioning for the others to wait at a distance.

"I am concerned," his father whispered. "I must ask that you don't be foolish."

The comment surprised Donato. "Foolish?"

"I know who you are, Donato." Not waiting for a response, he continued, "Sometimes as men of family, we must do things we don't want to."

Donato felt his world cave in around him, but that should not have been a surprise. He and his father had always been in opposition. Fears realized, Donato struggled to keep his voice below a whisper. "Things we don't want to, such as turn me over to the Crown? Is that what this is? Who financed the journey for Rayna? Are you being paid handsomely for my capture?"

His father's expression changed only slightly, but for a man who had lived behind a facade his entire life, that was an unusual show of emotion. For a second, Donato caught the sight of moisture reflecting in his father's dark eyes before the man turned away and collected himself.

"As I said, son, do not be foolish. I've spent many years answering to the whim of kings, whether Spanish or French, and have survived with my family and fortune intact. The king wanted to send the flotilla to bring you back, but I convinced him to allow me. I didn't want the king's men snooping around that area looking for you because of what they might find out. Your actions would put me at risk, Rayna, and my entire household. Yes, I financed the journey, at great cost, but it was to protect you and all associated with the House of Roche. You had to come back. You are a subject of the Crown, as am I."

Donato felt the blood leave his face and pool around his heart, which seemed to pump beyond what his body needed. A cool sweat broke out over his forehead. He wiped it dry with the back of his hand. The condition of the House of Roche, it looked deteriorated and neglected; now he knew why. "You spent your fortune on protecting me?"

"I have seen how you look at your wife, your son. Would you not do what you must to protect them?"

Donato nodded, feeling off-balance with this discovery about his father. "I would."

"Then spend this reprieve wisely, for the king is suspicious of you. Your young family will be in danger if he thinks you are not the man whom I have presented. I will not be able to protect them or you."

Donato's mind reeled, unaccustomed to the political dance of keeping one's life, but his father had done it for his entire adulthood. Donato nodded that he understood, though at the moment it was all he could muster. Having hated his father for years, this newfound alliance made Donato uncertain of everything.

His father started to walk again, but it was Donato who stopped him with a hand to his arm. "Why? I have to know why, if answering to the whims of kings, why not leave as I did?"

"I chose another way. We are not that much different, son. Sometimes the best place to be if one wants change is in the ruler's pocket. Come." His father motioned to the spiral staircase that would take them to the lord's hall. "Let us die together or walk away as free men. It is upon you I place my life, as does your family."

The weight on Donato's shoulders grew a hundred times. "I will succeed, Father."

His father's expression changed the moment he heard Donato address him as such. It was a slip of the tongue, a mistake that he could not undo. He only hoped he made no such mistake with the king. He swallowed hard and motioned for the two of them to continue.

Donato and his father entered the lord's hall, but waited to be announced.

King Ferdinand was sitting on the dais in a large ornate chair with his back to the wall, facing the entry. A long red carpet reached from him to the door, trimmed in gold cording to keep the traffic in place. There was no one else present, and for that Donato was grateful.

To one side of the wall was a large cast stone fireplace with andirons and a hand-wrought iron fire screen. Carved into the mantel was the profile of a knight in armor with shield and sword in hand, surrounded by a family crest.

The king had dark hair, short and combed forward in the Napoleon style. He was wearing a black velvet mantle encrusted with gold embroidering and jewels, reminding Donato of the ostentatious wealth of the monarch. He might have included his father in that assumption of the wealthy until learning he had spent his fortune to protect his only son.

The king wasn't a tall man, but had an imposing figure. He had dark eyes, and his nose was round and large. He wore black velvet breeches and white stockings. Donato thought he looked more French than Spanish.

King Ferdinand's expression brightened the moment Donato came forward. "Ah, approach, *primo mio*."

Being called his cousin was a good start. They were both from the House of Borbón. Donato walked forward, and though not required to bow before the king, he thought it might help show his loyalty. He held his hat in hand. His father kept his hat on, for his rank allowed him to do so. "I am humbled, Your Majesty, that you would request my presence."

"Rise, rise, let me look at you. I've heard much about you. Tell me, Donato, do you like living near Cuba on that island I granted you?"

That was a gentle reminder that the island had become possible because of the Spanish Crown and his father's rank. The transaction was an investment in Donato as a loyal subject.

"I appreciate the king's generosity."

"And what do you hear, living so close to Cuba? Is there talk of revolution against the mother country of Spain?"

And the trap closed.

• • •

"This appointment, *Virrey de Nueva España*, is an honor, son," his father said the moment the carriages were free of the castle yard.

"I did what was asked of me, Your Most Excellency. Now I ask, what would you have done if I refused to return?"

"I left it up to Rayna to ensure that would not happen."

"If she had failed?" Donato knew he was pushing the issue, but he had to know the answer to one question. Before he released the resentment he had held for years over his father, he had to know the truth. "What were her orders?"

"None," his father answered. "For I would not put your sister in such a place."

Then it all fit together in Donato's mind. The chain of events leading up to his arrival in Spain all fell together into a master plan.

"The American, a sailor, who approached me in New Orleans and helped hide my men. He works for you, doesn't he?"

His father sighed and looked away from Donato. "It is politics, son."

"Dead or alive, I was coming back to Spain. The American, was he to kill me?"

"It would be better to honor your death as a nobleman than watch your execution as a traitor."

For a moment, Donato had felt his heart soften slightly toward his father, only to harden again, confirming his belief that his father put politics above family.

Conversation halted and the air tensed as they both remained silent for the rest of the trip.

The carriages rode through the large iron gates of the Roche estate. Donato stepped down as soon as the brakeman had locked the brake. His father disembarked and disappeared behind the door of the great hall.

Donato hesitated, hearing a horseman ride up the drive.

From the distance, the man's blond hair was obvious. It was the American, pushing the mount he rode at a fast gallop. As he approached, he swung down before the horse came to a halt.

"What is it?" Ramón met him first.

The American pushed back the mammoth cap he wore over his head. "Being American, I don't know how this royalty thing works, but an American ship sailed into port last night. It was the *Lady Tempest*."

An icy chill raced the length of Donato's body. The *Lady Tempest* was the ship he had used to take Colette's ship. He had convinced the captain, Edgar Bennett, to take the *Loirie* for the reward of gold. In taking the ship, the king's spy had been disposed, keeping Donato's involvement with the revolutionaries secret.

Unable to quell his anger over learning this man was a spy sent by his father, Donato glanced around to see if anyone was about. Seeing no one, he grabbed the American by the shoulders and pushed him against the outside of the barouche and had a knife to his throat before he could protest. Ramón, though surprised, covered the other side to ensure no one could see.

"I know who you are," Donato whispered in his ear, piercing his throat with the sharp point of the weapon. "Now let me inform you of your situation. You work for me now, not my father. Do you understand? Or do I have you thrown in the king's tower? I am a marquis. I have been appointed viceroy of New Spain. You don't know how these titles work? It's enough to have you killed without so much as a question. I have not decided what to do with you, but right now, who do you work for?"

"The viceroy of New Spain."

Donato had to give him credit, for the American never lost his composure, nor showed fear, but listened and listened well.

"I understand, Your Excellency."

Donato released him and as he did, he noticed a crooked cross attached to a chain around the American's neck. It seemed familiar, but he couldn't remember where he had seen that. There was something about the American he liked, maybe his efficiency, his calm under fire, his loyalty to his father; regardless, Donato considered him a valuable asset. He hoped he wouldn't regret that conclusion.

Unsure of how much his American sailor knew, Donato asked again, "What of the *Lady Tempest*?"

"I was suspicious of them, for they asked questions about you. I followed a couple of men and shared a tankard of rum last night. I learned their midshipman is on his way to see the king."

"Why would he receive audience with the king?"

"He says he's on a mission of vengeance. He's the brother of Edgar Bennett. He claims to have evidence about you. They saw your sister's ship in New Orleans, told her the story of taking another ship called the *Loirie*, she rejected their premise, but that gave them the idea of going to Spain. He's here to give testimony to the king about the revolutionaries, about who killed the king's spy. He bragged on his ship that he would take down the mighty pirate of the gulf waters, Donato de la Roche. I'm telling you this per your father's instructions. I am to keep you safe. It is the deal made for what I want."

"Protect me. For what you want?" Laying the cards out,

Donato wanted no misunderstandings, but right now, he didn't care what the American wanted. "Unless I showed my revolutionary colors, then you were to kill me, or try at least?"

The American's face did alter a bit with that statement. "No, Your Excellency, I received no such orders."

Donato glanced toward the door of the great hall. Apparently, there was much he needed to understand about his father.

Ramón's face was ashen. "Let us leave, *Capitán*, leave today."

The American looked surprised. "You are a man of power, as you just said. Can you not arrest them?"

"And raise suspicions? No. This has to be done quietly."

"Give me orders, Your Excellency."

Donato glanced around him, taking in the grounds of the Roche estate.

He had never wanted this for himself and cared little about his title, but his power to create change had been handed to him by the very man he had hoped to change. Working from the pocket of the king was the place he could do the most good.

As viceroy over New Spain, he would have the ear of the king and perhaps open his mind to the changing world around him. There was too much at stake to allow a common thief from the *Lady Tempest* to derail what would mean salvation to thousands of Spanish colonists.

He turned to the American. "Work with Ramón. The men on my ship are experienced soldiers. Warn Edgar's delusional brother and the others to provision and set sail."

"And if they do not?"

"Ensure Bennett never sees the king."

Chapter Eighteen

Colette had waited by the window of the large bedchamber overlooking the Roche estate for most of the morning, terrified of what the meeting between a king and his not-so-loyal subject would bring. Packed and ready to go at any moment, all she could do was wait until shortly after noon when her husband's royal entourage rumbled up the long drive.

Soon, she heard his footfalls ride each step toward their adjoined room. After what seemed an eternity, the knob turned and he stepped inside.

She never anticipated being so relieved to see anyone as she was to see Donato. He stood tall, handsome, and proud. His dress was impressive, if not exquisite.

He wore the clothing of a royal. A deep blue velvet jacket, decorated with gold embroidering and gold epaulets on his shoulders. He wore a cravat and ruffled shirt in white, a matching sash, white breeches, and glistening black Hessians. Rings were on all fingers, and a small gold hoop hung in his ear. His thick coal-black hair, neatly combed, hung to his shoulders.

Though his dress caught her attention, it was his eyes on which she focused. He glanced around the room and caught sight of her valise packed and ready to leave. Enio was dressed for travel, as was she.

She slowly stood to meet him.

His dark eyes, trimmed in heavy black lashes that normally hid much of him, carried a new light, one she had not seen before. In them, she saw victory.

She drew a deep breath, waiting for him to confirm.

He casually removed the cravat around his neck and folded it before setting it on the table. He turned to face her. "I have been named viceroy of New Spain."

"Oh my Lord." Her hand went to her mouth, for her words were little more than a gasp. "Then you did it, you fooled him. Did he not suspect?"

"A little, but he has little option. I am safe…for now."

"Then we need not flee Spain now, but leave soon?"

"*Si, cariño.*"

She would never grow tired of hearing him say that. She had been in prayer during the early dawn hours after Donato had left for the castle. She had prayed for his safe return and for the right to choose a new life for herself. She had reconciled that she had indeed fulfilled her promise to God and that today was the first day of her new direction.

She had prayed for him and that her new life would be with Donato and not as a fugitive from the king of Spain. Surprisingly, she held no fear, for she knew with all of Donato's planning she and Enio would escape the country should the need arise. Donato had seen to their safety, as he said he would on the island when the British attacked, and as he had when on Jordan's ship. "I couldn't be happier. We will go back…to the island…home…as a family."

He looked at her as if he could not believe her words. "I am much pleased to hear you say that, but I cannot rush this. I must have permission of the king to depart."

He ambled over to the window. As he stood looking out over his father's vast estate, dressed in clothes fit for a king, she saw a new Donato. But his new appointment worried her. Would he forever travel from colony to colony, then back to Spain? Would he no longer have the same life he once offered her and Enio on the island? Had she lost Donato as quickly as she had won him back? Was this God's plan, for her never to have him?

Defeated, she walked over and put their son's blocks aside, handing Enio a book to look at. He didn't much like it, and his frown brought his father over.

"Leave the child with his play, Colette."

"I do not wish to hear the blocks anymore."

Enio began to cry, betraying her further. Her body started to tremble, and water filled her eyes. She looked away from Donato, not wanting him to witness her faltering belief in them.

"Colette." He reached over to still her busy hands. "Do not stop the boy."

She looked down through her tear-soaked eyes to see his broad hand atop hers, feeling the warmth of his soothing touch before he turned his attention to Enio.

"You play, *hijo mio*." Donato stacked the blocks into the wooden cart, then called for a servant to take the boy and his blocks to his own room.

"Colette…what is it?"

"I fear to have lost you…again."

He reached out and wrapped his hand in her hair. Pulling her up to his chest, he forced her to look up as he towered over her. "That will not happen."

He dropped his lips to hers. It was a kiss of sheer emotion and passion. He convinced her, because as always with Donato, his lovemaking was a language all its own.

With his kiss, he rolled her into his arms. It was a kiss meant to speak, meant to feel, meant to settle whatever burned between them. But as a French aristocrat in the arms of a Spanish royal, she felt lost, alone, wanting to believe the magic in that kiss.

She inhaled the scent of him, the minty taste of his mouth, the soap residue on his hair, and felt the smooth skin of his neatly shaved face. The width of his shoulders dwarfed her body, and if allowed, she'd sink into them for refuge and safety. But those shoulders were draped in royal velvet and trimmed in royal gold, and emanated the aromatic scent of rich wine, enjoyed recently and wholly.

As if he sensed her doubt, he lifted her from her feet and carried her to the bed. There, as the night before, when she thought he might die and they'd never see each other again, his body draped hers, never allowing a break in the kiss that demanded her attention, demanded she listen to him, demanded she accept her own feelings and give her body permission to respond. She tried to hold her breath, stop the fluttering of her heart, the aching that pounded deep inside her belly, between her legs, a wanting fire she could not douse.

He broke the kiss, suddenly, nearly brutally, as if he

had said enough on the subject and it was now closed. He unbuttoned the front of her dress, unlacing layers to find her breasts and kiss her flesh, until her nipples rose to his mouth and he nuzzled them between his lips.

She felt a shift in her body, abandoning all reason. She wanted him in any dress, with any title. She started to work on the jacket, unhooking each gold button as she did. His arms easily slid out of the velvet like a valiant soldier shedding his armor. Underneath, he wore the simplicity of a ruffled shirt, vulnerable and pliable. The turtle without his shell, he was a man of flesh and blood. A wanting man, who wanted her.

He continued his exploration down the curve of her breasts to her exposed ribs. She slid her legs apart, adjusting for his body to fit inside hers, aching for penetration, to feel his hardened strength meld with hers. He lowered himself between her legs and lifted her knees around his shoulders. She closed her eyes. Penetration would not be for a while, for he'd allow her to luxuriate in the sheer pleasure of his tongue inside her, moving, teasing, and forcing her body to beg for release.

Finally, he moved upward and slid inside her, slowly at first, then faster and faster until she thought they'd leave the comfort of the bed and land elsewhere. The movement against her body brought on wave after wave of spasms that left her breathless and exhausted. His body stiffened for release, then relaxed atop her.

She wrapped her arms around his shoulders and kissed the side of his face. She gained courage from the lovemaking. "Donato...I feel I might lose you to a world to which I do not belong."

"Never, Colette. You and Enio are my world and will

always be first in my life."

. . .

The House of Roche was in a state of excitement over the new title afforded to the young marquis of Andulsia. Donato had spent most of the early-morning hours going over the plans to present to the king, get his funding, and leave Spain. He understood Colette's concerns when she felt he had put politics above her and Enio. Having lived through the errors of his father, he'd never do that to her or his son.

But leaving Spain was not as easily accomplished as Colette, or perhaps, he, had led her to believe. Leaving as the viceroy of New Spain necessitated royal approval. He doubted he'd be allowed to leave on the same ship, much less without additional men and guns.

It was the additional men that worried him. His present crew were revolutionaries. The added crew were still loyal to the king. He wasn't thrilled to mix them on a long journey. One faction represented the king; the others wanted him dead.

He wrote out his request to leave Spain, and the missive had been sent by courier less than an hour ago. Donato expected a response by midnight. He assumed it would be in his favor, for the king was more aware of what and whom he needed, and insisting Donato remain in Spain served no purpose.

Donato entered the dining hall to find his father was already there, drinking his morning tea. There was a temptation to retreat, but having seen his father in a different light and uncomfortable with the evolving emotions, Donato continued into the room.

"*Buenos días*, Donato," his father said, motioning for him to join his table.

Donato angled his way across the room and slid into a chair opposite from him. A servant arrived instantly at his side.

"Just tea and toast."

The servant bowed and left the hall.

He waited in silence, like the ride in the carriage when coming back from the king's audience. The only sound was that of his father's occasional sip of tea. "Are you glad that you left Spain?"

The candidness of the question surprised Donato. "I enjoy where I live, but have fought hard to keep what is mine. As it is everywhere."

His father nodded, then took another sip. "I am proud for you to take the appointment you were so named."

"*Gracias*." Donato waited as the servant placed a cup and teapot in front of him, then a plate of toast and jam. Not used to receiving any type of praise from his father, Donato wasn't quite sure how to react. So he didn't.

"I know you blame me for your mother's death," his father said so suddenly that Donato, midsip, had to catch himself.

"I never said that."

"You left the day of her burial."

"She had suffered with melancholy for years. It was not unexpected. She had lost her will to live."

"But you blame me."

Again Donato had to calm his insides, which churned with every word his father said. The pain of the past that had adhered to his insides stirred to life. He fought the bile that formed in his throat, tasting bitter in spite of the tea. He noted that his hand shook slightly as he tried to calmly spread jam on the toast.

He took a moment, thinking, remembering the past with painful beats of his heart against his chest. He swallowed hard, but the feeling that had been unleashed swarmed to the surface. His father waited for an answer. Donato put down the remainder of the toast and met his gaze.

"That is true." There was no reason to avoid the conversation any longer. "The night she died, she was alone, save for me and Rayna."

"I was in Madrid."

"You had much warning."

"I was needed where I was." His father waved his hands as if to indicate Donato would not understand. "That was my decision at the time. You and Rayna did not agree, but I did what was necessary for—"

"For who, Father? For who?"

"The House of Roche."

Donato dismissed the claim that it was done for the family. He would never leave Colette if she was as ill as his mother had been the last few months of her life.

But he wasn't his father. Nor would he ever be.

"It does not matter, now," he told his father. "Mother is gone and you have your title."

The color of his father's face turned slightly darker, and Donato knew he had wounded him with the comment. Perhaps he had said it out of pity or because if he continued to talk of it, those dark waters churning deep in his gut would explode.

"I was a man who tried my best for my family. To believe

or not is your choice. I cannot say more." His father leaned forward on his elbows. "As I am old and tired, you are young and idealistic. Use me to your advantage, son. Communicate often and I will keep you informed as to the temperature here in Spain. The camarilla, remember it is church and state."

"Who are you protecting, me or you?"

His father smiled and sipped his tea. "Just politics."

"Like the American who never received such orders to kill me."

Again his father smiled, but this time more broadly. "The American, he is a good man to keep close by. I trust him, as you should. You will stay in communication. Perhaps I can help you see your desired changes."

"That will put you at risk, Your Most Excellency."

"A risk I am willing to take."

It was Donato who smiled this time, though slightly forced as he was uncomfortable with any alliance that involved his father. "I will appreciate your expertise, Your Most Excellency."

His father nodded his approval, then set his cup on the table. "I would like to know your wife and my grandson more. She has the entire household abuzz about her sweet smile, her beauty, her kindness to the servants. I must know this woman who has not only stolen your heart but that of a house full of Spaniards. A French woman at that."

Donato smiled, knowing the intoxicating effect Colette had on people. Perhaps her many years working as a healer has made her open to others. Regardless, he found her to be an asset to his standing. "And what is it you'd like to do, to advance your knowledge of my wife and son?"

"I'd like to take them for a ride today. Just her, the boy,

and me. In that way, the only conversation will be ours and not influenced by the past…or you."

"Will Rayna accompany you?"

"No, this is an excursion for Colette and me. I'd like to take a ride to show her Cádiz. Maybe I can make her fall in love with Spain, though she is French. But considering the years of the French occupation, they must love it better than France."

Donato hid the smile that dared approach his lips, but he liked his father's attempt at humor. "You will not pressure her in any way?"

"To do what?"

"Stay here."

"Son, it is a mere request to get to know the woman and the child who have captured your heart. Even a blind man can see how much you love them."

Donato nearly choked on the words, because they were never more true. The very woman he had sworn would never have his heart now held it in her hands.

He picked up his tea and drained the cup, though it helped little to wash away the uncertainty, the vulnerability he felt at the realization that Colette was his world and had been from the moment he met her.

"I give my consent, if Colette is in agreement."

"Excellent. Excellent." His father seemed to smile, something Donato had no memory of ever seeing.

His father took notice. "You honor an aging man, my son."

"Then I have a request in return."

His father's eyebrows lifted slightly. "And that is?"

"Rayna."

...

Colette accepted the hand of the footman as she was assisted into the landau to sit beside Donato's father, a grandee. She hadn't liked the idea, not for fear of him, but she hated to be separated from Donato even for a short afternoon and wanted to be sure she said nothing that would endanger any of them.

Enio squealed with delight at seeing a dog racing alongside the large black horses. The grandee laughed and pulled the boy forward to see in front. He was delighted and sat happily in his grandfather's lap watching out the window.

"He is a good boy, Colette?"

"*Oui*, very much," she answered. If only small talk, she might be capable of making it through this, but anything more detailed, such as what Donato had been involved in, she could not risk opening her mouth; not that she knew details, but she did know the truth.

The grandee continued to stroke Enio's head as the boy settled in for the ride. "Do you love him, like he does you?"

"I'm his mother; but of course, with all my heart."

"It is not your son that I ask about, but the boy's father, my son. I see it in the way he looks at you, looks after you, he is a man who is very lucky to love the mother of his child as much as he does you."

The shock of the grandee's words hurled her mind in a different direction, back to the Roche estate, last night's lovemaking, this morning's lovemaking, to the island, Donato's rescue of her from the men who had taken her ship. The beautiful little boy they created, not out of lust, but love.

She smiled and knew with certainty the matter of her heart. "Your Most Excellency, of course I love Donato."

His father nodded but gave her a quick side glance, as if she had revealed more than she would have liked, and she hoped the afternoon would progress without any more uncomfortable moments.

The grandee continued his tour, telling her the history of each area they rode through and what his hopes were for his country. The peasants supported King Ferdinand, he explained, for they supported the church and the church supported the king.

"It is good, *non?* That the people support the king."

"Not according to my son. You have lived near Cuba. Have you heard talk of revolution?"

And there it was.

But she was not unprepared for his attempt to garner information.

"Revolution? What a horrid thought, Your Most Excellency, for I as a woman do not speak of politics. That is a man's position, *oui*?"

He chuckled as if he hadn't been duped by her evasive answer, but she suspected he'd let it rest. She liked his laugh; it reminded her of Donato.

Their expedition took them down through the city of Cádiz. Soon they were riding at a slow trot along the water's edge where tall ships, six to eight deep, anchored in the harbor. She could see *El Rescate* through the window, but gave it little notice, not wanting to draw attention to it. She was pleased to see it was still manned and some of the sails in readiness. Standing near the water's edge was the American who had sailed with Donato.

The landau came to a halt on the wharf.

"Would you care to stroll along here, Colette? It is breathtaking, the beauty of the sea."

She accepted the hand of the footman as she stepped down. The grandee held Enio in his arms as they strolled the docks, putting more wear on her leg than she would have liked. But he walked slowly, allowing her to keep up with his pace. Donato's father pointed out the commerce, the frigates, the extensive trade that came and went through these docks from around the world. He spoke of the vision that many had for the port and how over the next few years it would become one of the most important ports in the world.

Colette enjoyed his recitation of the Spain he knew and the Spain he hoped to build. His voice was pleasant, his English articulate, his French even better, and when talking of his homeland, his face and voice became animated.

Patrons along the docks would stop their work and pay respect to the grandee, for he was a powerful figure in Cádiz, as well as Spain.

It was a beautiful spring day. The breeze off the water, scented with salt, sprinkled across her face at times. Enio was taken with the large ships and activity. The grandee asked about France, her life there, her family. Talking about her brothers made her heart ache for home, reminding her how much she missed them.

He was selling her on Spain, that she knew, but she didn't understand, for Donato would have to leave Spain to perform his new duties.

"Colette." He stopped with a hand to her arm.

She turned and faced him. "Your Most Excellency?"

"You could live here, with us, while Donato fulfills his

duties in the new colonies. It could be dangerous there, and here you would be safe." He ran his hand over the little boy's hair, pushing it off his forehead. "I so love this little boy."

"I think he knows it, Your Most Excellency." Colette smiled, appreciating the love he seemed to have for their son.

"You will think about what I said, will you not?"

"I will give it much thought, Your Most Excellency." Though she already knew her answer, the offer was endearing, and she wanted to treat it with the respect in which it was intended.

"*Gracias,* my son asked me not to pressure you, but I cannot resist wanting you and Enio to stay with me. Do not be offended, *por favor.*"

"I am not offended, but honored by your offer." Colette laughed about a grandee apologizing for doing something wrong. "Enio steals hearts."

"He has mine. He is the son of my son."

Colette continued to walk beside the grandee along the docks until something caught her eye. As they walked and the grandee talked on about Spain, she couldn't keep her eye from wandering over to a tall ship just leaving port.

She halted, staring at the ship as it eased along the docks toward the sea, silently parting the waters.

"Colette, are you all right?"

She couldn't answer as her eyes slowly traveled up the mast to see the flag.

Lady Tempest.

Frozen, her throat turned dry. A shearing pain, like fire-tipped blades of ice, cut down the length of her leg. She couldn't answer the grandee. She didn't know why, but her heart hammered at her temples as her body turned cold as death. Everything before her became wavy and fell out of focus, everything except that ship.

She reached for the grandee, trying to steady herself, but the terror that raced through her body made her muscles turn to mush. Her leg started to cave under her.

"*Lady Tempest*," she whispered. Her teeth rattled. Her skin turned to gooseflesh. Her knees caved and with that, she fell into a growling pit of flashing long arms, cannon fire, smoke. A dark pit with no air to breathe. That wild animal of the forest had returned and locked her within its teeth; she was carried off in a large churning cloud of memories.

Chapter Nineteen

Donato sank to the side of the bed and took Colette's hand in his. Her body felt stiff, and fever had seared a film of perspiration across her forehead. Her face felt hot to the touch, and her hands were cold as ice. Her color had blanched to nearly white, and her breathing, sounding raspy and wet, was slow and labored. "How is she?"

"Your Excellency." A physician, who had examined Colette, bowed before responding. "She has not come around."

It was the shock of seeing that damn ship.

"Has she said anything more?"

The physician again shook his head. "She does not speak. Her heart is very weak."

The physician rose and picked up another blanket and covered her body. She had started to shake. Her lips were dusky. Yet she felt so hot, he thought her blood must be in a roil.

Donato ran his hands through his hair, unable to dismiss

the fact that he had known that ship was there. He had never thought of it when his father mentioned the tour day.

Did she remember anything, everything?

For a man who thought he had outsmarted them all, Donato had fallen into a trap so tight, he had no idea how to wiggle free.

"Leave us," he instructed the physician.

"*Si, Su Excelencia,* I will be just outside the door for your summons."

"*Gracias.*"

Donato sat in the silence of the room after the physician closed the door. The sound of the door latching echoed into the bedchamber with the sound of death. After all his struggles, he was losing the most important thing in his world, Colette.

He lifted her hand into his, splayed her delicate fingers across his palm. They were pale and cool to the touch. He had seen death like this when his mother died. As if the body decided to shut down and the will was no longer there.

The physician had said her heart was weak, but there was nothing weak about Colette. She was the nurturer, the one taking care of others, a strong, vibrant woman, but seeing that ship had nearly destroyed her. Did she remember?

"Colette?" He leaned down and whispered into her ear, praying for a sign of recognition, but there was none. She was somewhere without him, somewhere alone. He took her hand to his mouth and kissed her fingers. Unlike his father, he was here with her now and would not leave her side until she was well again, for he refused to think she might die.

He could hear voices in the hall. His father speaking with the physician, puzzled over what had happened, going over and over the details. His father sounded confused over her reaction to seeing a ship named *Lady Tempest*. He had apologized a hundred times for bringing her back in such a state.

The only guilty party was Donato. The only one who knew and understood Colette's shock was the man who was supposed to love and protect her.

He pushed off the bed and walked over to the window, unable to bear the fruits of his labor. For he was the mystery the House of Roche wanted to solve.

There was a knock on the door before it opened slightly. He saw the ruffle of a green dress before the door swung open. Rayna stood there holding little Enio in her arms.

"Forgive my interruption, Your Excellency, but the child wants to see his mother."

Donato didn't respond, fighting the heated feelings of betrayal at the sight of his sister. She felt the venom in his gaze and turned away for a second. "I beg you, the boy."

Donato was able to pull his glare off her and refocus on Enio.

He took the boy from her arms. Enio was so small, like a miniature man, whose world had crashed in around him and he didn't know or understand what had happened. Donato kissed the top of his head and held the small body close to his chest, to his beating heart. The child he and Colette had created out of love. A mist blurred his eyes, adding to his dark mood. He turned away from Rayna and walked back to the bed.

Enio saw his mother and tried to get down. "*Maman maman!*"

"Hush, child." Donato leaned down and placed Enio on his feet. He held him in his arms and talked in his ear. "*Tu madre* is sleeping."

"Sleeping?"

"*Si*, Enio, I will have you come back when she is awake."

The small boy shook his head that he would not go. Donato pulled him onto his lap and hugged him to his chest. "Then you wait with me."

Rayna had remained in the room, standing a distance and a half from the bed. "Donato, I know you have not forgiven me—"

"No, Rayna, I have not."

"She saw the *Lady Tempest.*"

"I know that."

"With all of your power, why did you not destroy that pirate ship and the crew?"

"I was being merciful."

"No, you were trying to protect yourself. You didn't want to raise suspicion, bring attention on to you, but you only succeeded in giving them freedom. You had the power to have that ship destroyed, and you should have."

"It appears so. It is done. Leave us now."

She stood for a moment, then turned and left the room. He said nothing more to her, for what was there to say?

Enio reached over and patted Colette's hand with his. He slid off Donato's lap and stood next to the bed holding his mother's hand. Though Enio now understood who Donato was, his world was his mother.

Donato cradled his head in his hands, feeling the tension pounding at his temples, cursing his sister, his father, the damned king of Spain, but most of all, himself.

Another knock at the door broke into Donato's thoughts. His father stepped through the door, holding a missive in his hand. His face was pale, and the strain of what had happened to Colette shadowed every wrinkle in his aging skin. Donato never realized until this very moment how old his father had become. He no longer looked bigger than life but like an aging royal, hurting like a mere mortal.

"You have received an answer from the king. You have permission to leave Spain when you so wish."

• • •

Voices floated into her mind. Colette tried to hear, but everything sounded muffled and far away. Her body ached everywhere, and when she tried to move she heard her own stifled groan.

"Colette?" A man's voice, but he sounded so distant.

She thought she answered, but her lips did not move. Trying to arouse her body, she drew a sharp breath, but felt underwater and cold.

"Colette?"

The man's voice seemed to float through her mind, washing through her memories. Moisture filled her eyes and she choked on a sob.

"Colette?"

A strong hand took hers and stroked her fingers. A soothing, heated touch that seemed familiar, but she knew not why. She tried to speak, but her lips would not move. Images flitted about in her mind. She remembered being with the grandee on a ride through the countryside, but nothing more. Her temples pounded, and the front of her forehead ached.

She pushed her arm outward and tried to move her aching body until strong hands shifted her and placed something soft behind her back. She thought she could feel his presence, but wasn't sure. Pictures of things swirled about in her mind, and she found herself seeing Jordan and Loul, Jordan's darling daughter, Maisie, and his wife, Aurélie with their new son. Suddenly she was lost in time, hiding in the closet, frightened and alone until Jordan held her in his arms.

"Jordan," she whispered.

The hands that helped make her comfortable stopped.

"No, Colette, it is Donato."

"*Maman* awake!"

"Hush, *hombrecito*, she is trying to wake. Let us not scare her."

The words were clearer now; she could make out every one and…a child. There was a child's voice. Her heart started to pound, pushing a flush of energy through her limbs until she felt the pulsation at her fingertips and a smile on her lips, knowing the sweet little face that went with it. Slowly, her eyes fluttered open.

She focused her eyes with a couple of blinks, feeling groggy and lethargic.

Donato sat on the edge of the bed, and in his straddled legs stood Enio.

"Colette, how do you feel?"

"My two men. My two favorite men."

Donato smiled in response. His mouth stretched across his wide face and hitched up to his high cheekbones. Tiny droplets of tears laced the beautiful thick lashes of his eyes.

She reached up with her hand and stroked the side of his face, stubby and unkempt. "I make you cry. I do not mean to."

He took her hand in his and kissed her fingers. "You can

do no wrong, *mi vida*, no wrong. It is I who does not deserve you."

"I do not know what happened. We are in Spain?"

"*Si,* but we will leave the moment you are up to the travel. I have arrangements made to take you home."

"And you with me?"

"*Si.*"

Now her eyes filled with tears of joy. "Oh, *merci,* Donato, I am most anxious to go home."

Enio was pushing his way in between the two of them. He crawled up on the bed and gave Colette a kiss.

"Oh, a most beautiful welcome, Enio."

Someone knocked on the door.

"*Adelante,*" Donato answered.

A servant pushed through the door holding a large tray of preparations, but halted the moment she saw Colette awake. Colette smiled, knowing her surprise.

"Oh, Marchioness is awake! Oh praise God!"

Within minutes the entire House of Roche was in a uproar, echoing throughout the house that she was awake. Donato frowned from the intrusion. He arranged the tray next to the bed.

"This will wake up the house," he complained as he started to arrange her bedding around her. "Will you try to eat something?"

"Tea, only tea, I will try."

He poured a cup of tea and placed his hand to the back of her shoulders to help her rise.

"*Tomad, hermosa. Os hará bien.*"

"Here, beautiful, good for you," she repeated his words in English. "I have heard you say something similar to me once before. When were you taking care of me like this?"

Donato offered her a sip of tea, then placed the cup on the tray next to her. "Colette, there is a confession I must make."

She noted the seriousness of his expression, and for some reason, she wanted no confession right now, only his gentle touch and care, to luxuriate in the attention of the man who had her heart. "I am tired, Donato, can I not rest more?"

"Of course."

"And more tea perhaps."

He smiled. "Perhaps."

He had just raised the cup to her lips when a large entourage of people burst into the room.

The grandee reached her bed first. "Ah, my beautiful Colette. How do you feel?"

Colette was surprised by the excitement she had created, for she remembered nothing of what had happened that had left her in such a deep sleep. She laughed with the excitement she saw on all the faces staring down at her, surrounding the bed. "*Merci*, to all of you. I will be fine, much exhausted, but I'm awake."

Everyone laughed, heads moving as they all glanced about the group.

"Do you remember what happened?" the grandee asked.

"I do not, only a ride, *non*?"

"We were on the docks and you said—"

"Father—Your Most Excellency, all of you." Donato stood up and motioned toward the door. "She will receive visitors later. Allow my wife time to recover."

"*Perdón, perdón,* we have lost our manners in the excitement." The grandee ushered the others to the door. Many wished her well, others bowed, and others were beaming with smiles. It was a strange sight for Colette, unaware she had won so many hearts.

Donato had someone take Enio for a meal, leaving her alone with her husband.

"I think you have kind people in your world, too, n'est-ce pas?"

"They care for you, Colette."

"And Enio."

"Enio wins hearts with just a smile."

She laughed, how true. "His father's."

Donato smiled with her comment. She reached up and ran the tips of her fingers along the seam of his mouth. "One I do not see often."

His smile faded, and he drew in a deep breath. Something was troubling him, but her head pounded and she desperately needed to get out of the bed. It would have to wait.

"Will you help me get up and dress?"

He cocked his head to the side and raised an eyebrow. "Now why would I want to help you get dressed?"

"For shame. Aren't you a knight or something, to help damsels in distress?"

"Well, *cariño*, I am no knight, and you are no damsel in distress."

"Then pray tell, what am I?"

"Desirable. Beautiful. My wife."

"So you're the man I give myself to." She lifted her arms for him to join her.

"I am the only man you give yourself to." He slid his body over hers, the weight sinking her into the soft bedclothes around her. He brushed his lips across hers, reminding her of what it felt like to be alive and with a man who could stir her passion to the surface with merely a touch.

He raised up and looked at her. "You are smiling, Colette. You wake up from days-long illness happy?"

"I was lost, Donato, in a tomb that I thought I'd never escape. I made a pact with myself that if I were to break away from the darkness that held me prisoner, I would tell you that I loved you. That I wouldn't protect myself from hurt, because it meant to protect myself from living. And I awoke, and here you are and my son. I could not wish for more. The two loves of my life."

Donato didn't move, his body still atop hers. But moisture in his eyes reflected the morning sun that filtered through the curtains of the window. "There is much about me you don't know."

"I know enough to know that I love you and that you love me. What else could there be?"

Chapter Twenty

With much fanfare, they finally pulled out of the port of Cádiz. The entire town showed up for the send-off of the viceroy of New Spain. Most likely they had to, since the king was in the area. Cádiz was an area steaming with revolt. Donato didn't care how or why the send-off, he was just relieved they were on their way home.

He assumed home meant his island, but he did understand Colette would need contact with her family, and perhaps another home on the coast of America would be an option since he'd have to travel more. Either way, they had made it through the crisis, and united together as a family, they were leaving.

Before they left port, there was one more package Donato had delivered and kept in the hull. It wasn't long before everyone knew what had been smuggled aboard. When asked about it, he'd just smile.

The sky was blue with few clouds and the waters calm as

the sails picked up the wind and took them out of the coastal waters of Spain and into the open sea.

Donato didn't mind leaving the cramped clipper behind when he found himself captaining a new schooner for his return journey, a ship that was heavily armed and took the concern out of their safety.

Going across the ocean left any ship in danger of becoming prey, but sailing with ten thirty-two pounders along each side gave him a broadside weight of three hundred and twenty pounds, with two long guns as bow chasers. He felt well-armed. He sailed with his men only and did not take any additional personnel except an emissary of his father's. But there was one change he did make: his ship now flew the royal flag of Spain.

Colette had recovered rapidly when she learned their return journey rested on her health. She had been up within three days of regaining consciousness. Adding Enio to the mix made ship life more interesting with an element of humor stirred into each day.

The men on the ship loved the little boy, and he would often race around the main deck and shout out orders as if he were his father, in spite of the fact that no one could understand him. Though they were revolutionaries, the loyal crew would laugh and try to do as he said.

"Yes, Your Excellency," they'd say, claiming Enio was a marquis-in-training.

"I never thought I would be so happy to be back on a ship." Colette joined Donato on the bridge of the forecastle. "I don't mean to be disrespectful. I liked your father, and, well, I liked your father."

Donato chuckled at her attempt to be gracious. "I

understand."

Colette glanced up at him. "You can't keep her there for the entire journey."

"I can for a while. Rayna needs a little lesson in humility, don't you think? She took my son, Colette. I warned her I would retaliate."

"But the hull?"

"I know." Donato pushed the keel ever so slightly, keeping on course. "But this was an adventure I could have missed without a tear."

"But it brought us together."

"It did." He glanced down at Colette. "I will allow her to roam the ship after dinner."

"And then your plans?"

"I have special plans for her, after I make her fret a little."

"And your father knew you were taking her?"

"He did, but not the reason. He thought it would be an education for her. And it will be."

"Donato, you promised me we would not go to South America."

"No, I promised we would not move there. I will send missives and emissaries most of the time, but I will have to be seen there. The idea of Spain recovering the colonies is lost. Things will change rapidly, and when I go back to Spain, I will say I gave it my most gallant effort but was unable to turn the tide of freedom."

"And then what will happen?"

"I'll be rewarded with monies and land for my valiant endeavors."

She smiled, wrapping her fingers around the crook of his arm. "I pray you are right. Not for the money, but for your safety."

"I am right. What do you think the old viceroy did? I hope to manage a relationship between the colonies and Spain. I will do my best for a harmonious break. That is the most I can do."

"Donato?" She angled her body to face him. "Why is it that you never married?"

"I didn't want to. I had seen a loveless marriage and wanted no part of it. Another level of control I didn't want, nor did Rayna. She says she won't marry, much to my father's displeasure."

"You are both very much alike, both rebels at heart."

"We are cut from the same cloth. You never asked why I accepted the appointment."

"I expected you to tell me. If I must ask, then I do."

"It was something that my father said, about being part of the solution rather than the problem. He said his years of service for the Crown has been to effect change he believed in. Whether we agree on the politics or not, it was the idea of having the ear of the king and to present information that is truthful and direct. I think I can have more influence by doing this than if I were to remain a revolutionist on the outside. My position gives me power that I otherwise would not have."

"It puts you in a place of danger, Donato, but I am glad you and your father were able to reconcile your differences."

"It will be somewhat dangerous, but life is, or we are not living." He hadn't thought of their working together as a reconciliation, but in truth it was. Donato's persona as a revolutionist had evolved into a man with the power to create change. That wouldn't have happened had it not been for his father. "My father said he would direct me with his expertise of how the majesty thinks and will keep me informed of how things are being perceived in Spain. I am grateful for his insight."

"You never asked about my husband."

"I know why you married him. He was in need of you, and he died." Donato hesitated. "Is there something I should know?"

"You never asked me if I loved him."

"It did not matter to me. He is not a part of your life now. Whether you loved him or not. Did you?"

"I did not. I now know that. I never knew what it felt like to love a man until you."

He drew a tight breath, hoping she'd not take notice. What was her capacity for forgiveness, for once she learned the truth, her love might die with it? He didn't regret taking the *Loirie,* but he regretted whom he had partnered with and the chaos that had followed. But he had done right for Colette, then and now. *Would she agree?* "That is quite a testimonial, Colette. Would you love me unconditionally, no matter what was in my past?"

Colette squinted up at him, the sun streaking through her honey-colored hair that fluttered unhindered in the wind. She was wearing the Tourmaline necklace and earrings he had sent her the first night in Spain. A necklace worn often by his mother, the gems had never sparkled on her like they did on Colette. Would she forgive him? "What is it that you allude to that I don't understand about you? I think it time you tell me."

"It will be difficult to tell you—"

"Sail! Sail! Starboard quarter!"

Donato picked up his binoculars and scanned the horizon. A large schooner broke the waterline with a box hauling course set to intersect his ship. Atop the main mast flew the flag of the *Lady Tempest*. The moment she was spotted, another flag ran up her mast. A black one.

Ramón appeared on the bridge. "They cannot know who we are, or they would not think to attack."

Donato raked their deck with his binoculars, bow to stern. They had their guns run out, and from what he could figure, they were clearing decks, and he hadn't missed the flash or two of swords and grappling hooks.

"I think they know exactly who we are." Donato lowered his binoculars and called out to the deck. "Clear for action!"

Men scampered about the deck. Casks of powder were opened and ladled into flannel cartridges, then loaded into leather cylinders. The ship's surgeon assembled his tools in the wardroom, covering the tables with sailcloth. Sand was strewn about the deck for traction. Men climbed to the fighting tops of the masts with long arms in hand. Within minutes, all the guns were loaded and run out to firing position.

Then it was quiet.

All waited for orders; they floated atop the rolling waves as the pirate ship sailed toward them. Anticipating battle at sea took a toll on a man's nerves. There were dangers of being swept out to sea through a porthole. The cannons were huge, heavy, and lethal, and when fired they recoiled, often injuring or burning the men who fired them off. The biggest fear for all men on a fighting ship was the incoming cannons. When a solid iron ball weighing thirty-two pounds plowed into a ship, it could shatter the planking and framing, sending off slivers the size of a man's finger to the size of a long gun, and then there was the danger of fire.

From what Donato could see, the *Lady Tempest* had at least fourteen eighteen-pound cannons, a lesser broadside weight, but she had more than ten long guns.

Colette had her hand wrapped around Donato's lower arm, her grip tight. But as the *Lady Tempest* came closer and into view, the grip on his arm grew less and less. Donato glanced at her, knowing recognition of that ship was working through her memory until suddenly she gasped, "That is the ship. The ship…"

Her words fell silent as she slowly looked up at him. Her skin had paled to nearly white and her eyes were wide with disbelief. In that instant, Donato knew she remembered it all. "Colette—"

"No!" She turned away from him. "Enio!"

She raced off the helm, scooped the little boy up in her arms, then disappeared below deck.

He had to let her go, for the situation was urgent. He shouted for another sailor. "Get my sister out of the hull and take her to the wardroom."

"She's coming at six knots!"

That was a hell of a speed. *Lady Tempest* had chosen her sight well, for she had the weather gauge to her advantage, cutting through the water at a deadly speed.

She fired.

The ball just missed the stern bulwarks.

With those long guns, he'd be at a disadvantage no matter his approach, so he chose speed. He could take that ship, but not with the precious cargo he carried. He ordered the helm to get her up quickly within range of his cannons.

Ramón showed up at the helm. "Our plan?"

"We can't engage. We have two women and a child on board. I think to wear her, see if we can't force her to throw away powder and shot on us. Wait until in range. After the first shot, we start tacking, an unpredictable chase. In the meantime, be ready with the cannons. We will take one broadside shot before we turn out. That will be our only opportunity."

Rayna had been right. He so regretted not ordering the ship destroyed the moment they had sailed into Cádiz. It had been a risk he wasn't willing to take with the king in close proximity, for it would have raised suspicion. But now he paid the price. Out on the open sea, there was no one but him and that damned ship that had now begun to haunt him more than the cannon shot from her gunwales.

"Helm up! Hard to starboard!"

The helmsman did as ordered and the schooner pulled to the right, picking up the wind with cracked sails. The wind sent them barreling through the waves, just missing the collision.

The *Lady Tempest* had rounded again when suddenly a cannon shot came from another direction, just missing her.

Donato picked up his binoculars and focused on the new ship that had entered the fray.

It was a small sloop, but well-armed. It masts flew no identifying flags.

The *Lady Tempest* broke form and cracked her sails, her speed taking her out of range of either ship. He swung his binoculars back to the mysterious ship that had just helped him out of a tight bind. He couldn't believe his eyes. On the forecastle, returning a victory wave, stood Colette's brothers.

Jordan and Loul.

Donato lowered the binoculars. "Never thought I'd be glad to see them. Send out a message, we wish them to board."

. . .

Donato knocked on the door of the cabin and turned the knob, knowing Colette would most likely deny him entrance. To his relief, the door opened. She was sitting in the chair facing the large stern window. The daylight played into the room, creating a halo around her body. She didn't turn around when he came into the room, nor acknowledge his presence.

He swallowed hard, hating to have this discussion, but knew it was the only way for their marriage to truly heal. "I had asked if you could love me in spite of my past, and you said you could."

"You didn't tell me the past was me."

"No, I did not." He worked his way around to see her face, stained with tears. "I tried many times, but it…it just didn't come out."

She covered her face, with each sob. "You are a man of complete mystery, Donato, or should I say falsehoods and fraud."

"No, I am not at all complex."

Enio was on the bed and sat there quietly as if he knew something was terribly wrong. He reminded Donato of when he was young and had heard the harsh words between his parents. He would not do that to his son.

"I explain."

"No." She wiped her nose on her sleeve, her tears hardly

in check, and her shoulders shook every few seconds. Enio pushed off the bed and ran to his mother.

"*Maman*, no cry." He patted her knee as he stood next to her.

"Enio, wait on the bed, *por favor*." Donato lifted him and returned him to his perch.

Colette straightened her shoulders as if to do battle, a battle he could not fight, nor had a prayer of winning. He sat on the ledge of the stern window. "Colette, you must allow me to explain. Even a condemned man has his say in court."

She bent over and buried her face in her hands. "I cannot forgive you."

Donato glanced over at Enio, who had little tears rolling down his face. Donato went over and picked up his son. Hugging him close to his chest, Donato whispered, "Do not cry, *mi hombrecito,* all is well."

Enio put his arms around Donato's neck and held so tight, he had to pull away a little to breathe. Unable to leave him there, Donato returned to the stern window with Enio in his arms, stealing a glance to see how close Colette's brothers were to boarding. Once Jordan boarded, Colette would again choose to leave and return to be the dutiful sister. Though he had no choice but to turn her over to him while he went after the *Lady Tempest*, he didn't want that shift to be permanent.

"I will explain. If you listen or not is a choice only you can make."

She didn't respond, so he moved forward, for time was short. He had to give her to her brothers so he could fight this battle. That meant once again handing over all he loved and cherished to Jordan Kincaid.

"I left Spain when my mother died, hating my father for how he had treated her. I had a belly full of death and fighting in the war with France. I wanted something more for myself. I came to America and opened a shipping line. But the French pirates took everything I had. I could not protect all my ships and lost much of my net worth. The men who came with me were common soldiers turned sailors. We talked often of the monarch and the future of Spain. When we started to trade from the island, we were told we could trade with no other country but Spain. The United States was demanding hemp for naval cordage. Though illegal to trade with the United States, I was making a fortune, but without the Crown, the island would not be what it is."

She looked away from him. "That I know."

He was encouraged. "What you don't know is that living close to Cuba fed into our desire to create change in Spain. Ferdinand had promised to uphold the constitution, but instead he abolished it. He wanted absolute rule over Spain and New Spain. My father backed him. I did not. We needed money, so we decided to take back what had been stolen. I created the pirate facade and we stole from the French corsairs."

She wiped her eyes, refusing to look at him. "And how does that justify taking a civilian ship from France?"

"Because it wasn't just a civilian ship. The king is a puppet for Napoleon. When worried about the revolt among the Spanish colonies, the king sent a man, a spy, with more than a hundred thousand in gold, to buy information. His mission was to purge the islands of the insurgents, as he called us, and mark us for death. That meant a bloodbath. They thought hiding him on a French ship to America would ensure his arrival and secrecy. You and your brother were on a ship that was on a military mission for the king of Spain."

"And?" She turned and faced him. He tried not to show how relieved he was that she at least acknowledged him.

"I had concerns that if I took the ship, there would be panic in America about Spain. You know how frightened Americans are of the Spanish."

She nodded.

"I also needed to keep my involvement secret. So I drafted the *Lady Tempest*, an American ship, rather than a French corsair. The captain walked a thin line between legitimate work and not so, and I told the crew there would be a reward if they were to take the *Loirie*. I wanted the Spaniard on board taken alive. We had plans for him, to be sent back to Spain, to his king, with a message that even the Crown is not loyal."

He hesitated, wanting to ensure she was listening. Sitting in silence for what seemed an eternity, she turned to him. "The man you speak of was killed."

"I know, but that was not the plan. The crew and captain of the *Lady Tempest* were greedy. Having sailed with men of integrity, I was not prepared for men who were not. Chaos broke out on the ship. The king's spy was killed, your brother was thrown overboard, and you were injured. I was pistol-wounded in the process." He pointed to the wound she had asked about so long ago. "It was an act of war, not meant to hurt innocents but to save many lives."

Donato stroked his son's head, for the boy would never see his father mistreat his mother in any way. He walked the child back to the bed and laid him down. "Let your *madre* and me speak."

"Why was I sold in Port-au-Prince?"

"You were injured, your leg broken. We set your leg and the plan was to get you home. I was under the impression that had happened until I learned of the auction."

"And that was why you, a Spaniard, were in Port-au-Prince?"

"*Si,* I went to get you. They told me you had no memory of who you were, so they decided to sell you, rather than try to find your family. That's what I deserved for dealing with thieves. I bought you and took you to the island. I had no other option."

"But you refused to sell me to my father."

"I didn't know he was your father. He told no one."

"I thought you had rescued me from those horrible men, and you were one of them."

"No, I was not. I had hired them to do a job and they did it poorly."

Donato could hear the activity off the main deck. Jordan would board in minutes. Time was running out. If Colette didn't forgive him by the time her brother arrived, Donato knew he'd lose her forever.

"Why did you try to kill my brother in that ambush arranged in the bayous?"

"I did not try to kill him. I tried to prevent it. I warned Jordan about the meeting, but he came anyway. I knew Bennett was dangerous. Turned out your brother was equally dangerous and killed him. I took the contraband and gave you the crystal. I knew it was a message from your brother. I knew he'd find you, and I wanted to begin to prepare you for seeing your family. I didn't know he'd do it in the way he did."

Donato glanced over to Enio and gave him a reassuring smile. Enio flashed a quick smile back. Donato loved that boy with all his heart, but his hope of keeping him diminished with each moment of silence.

He leaned down and cupped Colette's face in his hands. She didn't retract from his touch, but she continued to look down. "Can you find it in your heart to forgive me?"

"I do not know."

There were voices and footfalls on the stairs, and within seconds Jordan entered the captain's room. "Colette!"

She whirled around to see him and nearly shrieked from shock. She raced up to him and threw her arms around his neck. "Where did you come from?"

"A ship." He laughed.

"Oh, and Loul." Colette pulled him into the hug. "I cannot say how happy I am to see you."

Loul nodded to Donato, but Jordan refused even a glance until after the reunion with Colette. "Wasn't that the *Lady Tempest* we chased off for you?"

"I was handling her." Donato didn't miss the sharp side of his remark.

"That's the same ship that took the one Colette and I were on, the *Loirie*. I'd like to sink her. Do we give pursuit?" Jordan offered.

Colette glanced over at Donato, and he knew what she was thinking. Jordan didn't know the connection. In the background Rayna was standing, with an interest in the proceedings.

"No, I'll give pursuit. This is personal. You will take Colette, Enio, and my sister to safety."

"And who will take you to safety?" Jordan laughed. "Never mind, I don't care. I will take my sister and yours, my nephew, and we will depart."

"I will stay, Donato, and fight with you." Loul stepped forward.

"No, Loul, I'd prefer you get them to safety."

Though Jordan looked a little confused at Loul's offer, he took Colette by the arm and started to escort her out of the bedchamber. Enio screamed and pushed off the bed. But instead of running to Colette, he ran to his father. Donato swept the boy up in his arms and kissed his head. "You go with your *madre* so that you are safe."

Donato nodded his head for all to take the stairs to the main deck. After the entourage assembled above deck, Donato handed the boy to Colette. Another man brought up her valise and Rayna's large trunk.

Loul was the first to board the tender. Rayna hesitated and gave her brother a hug.

"Be careful, brother. I will miss a sparring partner, should you perish."

"You have touched my heart, Rayna." He couldn't erase the sarcasm in his voice.

"I'm sure I did." Though the words were meant in jest, her sudden hug around his shoulders was not. Her display of affection surprised him, but then again, it was Rayna.

As Jordan guided her chair over the side and to the tender, Colette stood next to Donato. She turned to face him, her face ashen. For the time their eyes met, nothing else existed, only the two of them and the love they couldn't deny. Would she reject him or forgive him?

She said nothing, but turned and met Jordan to position her in the chair. As she was lifted over the side holding Enio, the small boy cried out. "¡Padre! ¡Padre!"

Donato turned away and stepped to the helm, unable to bear the separation again. He waited until Jordan's ship cracked its sails and rounded about, heading toward America.

"Bring her about!"

He raised his binoculars and caught sight of a sail, putting all else in his mind aside.

He had a damned ship to sink.

Chapter Twenty-One

The waves made her sick to her stomach, or perhaps it was leaving Donato behind that twisted her insides. Enio had slept most of the first day on Jordan's ship. He cried himself to sleep the night they left his father, waking up often and asking for his *padre*. Colette's heart broke with every whimper.

On deck, Colette heard her brothers speculating as to whether Donato would sink the *Lady Tempest*. She had no doubt that he would. Donato was a master at sailing and had an even greater reason to sink the pirates than either of them. Jordan commented about how good it would be to be back home, knowing that she was safe once again.

Colette heard the words, meaning that she'd be back where she belonged. But where was that? Jordan had rescued her once before, but had she been happy? If she looked back on the year spent with her family, had it offered the fulfillment she had so craved? Though she loved them dearly, in reality, it had not. Something was missing from the lives of her and her son.

She looked down at her plain dress and felt the knot of her hair tied back. She wore the beautiful necklace given to her by the marquis beneath her dress, and on her fingers she wore rings for the first time in her life, with the Tourmaline earrings.

When Rayna had opened her trunk this morning, Colette had been in awe of the beautiful gowns. Rayna pulled one out for Colette to try on, and it was gorgeous, but already feeling the wayward servant being returned to duty, she couldn't wear dresses like that.

Yet watching Rayna repack the dress, Colette's spirit didn't capitulate so quickly. After a moment's debate, she took the blue gown and tried it on. The jewelry from her husband made it dazzling. Jordan might wish to return her home, to where he thought she belonged, but that life no longer fit. Colette was far from the same woman who had left on a journey to Spain months ago. Would she make the same decision she had when she'd been rescued the first time?

But her sense of defiance, rebirth, and salvation sank as quickly as it had risen in her heart. Donato had lied to her. Her abduction had shattered her family; her brothers had sacrificed so much to find her and her father…her father had been killed in Port-au-Prince trying to buy her back, trying to reunite his family.

Her family had been torn apart because she and Jordan had been on the wrong ship at the wrong time. It mattered not how she thought to have changed, for that night would never end for her. To learn it was Donato who had instigated the attack nearly robbed her of her sanity.

She peeled off the dress, any memory of Donato, and tossed it aside and pulled off every ring and tossed it into Rayna's trunk. The Tourmaline necklace fell to the floor. She kicked it away from her.

Atop the ship, she could hear her brothers talking, laughing, as if all was well, for they felt victory was finally theirs. They were together again as a family. How could she ever tell them the man she loved, the man she had married, had a child with, was the very man who had torn their family apart?

She couldn't confess, and wouldn't, but the deception would be more than she could manage, and forgiving Donato would need more than an apology, perhaps more than a lifetime.

After changing back into her plain dress, Colette threw on a shawl and took the stairs to the main deck. Her brothers were on the forecastle.

"Can you not sleep?" Jordan asked.

"No, I cannot."

"Loul is angry with me, says we should have stayed to help him."

Colette shook her head, understanding how Donato was with his loved ones, his family and their protection utmost in his mind. "He wanted his family safe. He would not have allowed it. That is the only reason he turned us over to you."

"We could have sailed with him, stayed out of range but been there in case he needed us." Jordan offered.

"I should have stayed on his ship," Loul persisted.

"Donato will need no assistance." Colette wasn't surprised at Loul's show of loyalty, for the men had developed a level of respect through the early part of their journey. *Never could they know of Donato's involvement in the grounding of the* Loirie. *Never.* "You have me and Enio—wasn't that your mission?"

She didn't miss the shift of glances between her brothers.

"We wanted you and Enio safe. That has been accomplished."

"How long before we are home?"

"If you mean New Orleans, by nightfall."

Loul put his arm around Colette's shoulder. "But if you mean—"

"Sail! Sail!"

Jordan picked up his binoculars. "Well, I'll be damned. It's Donato's ship, still sailing under a royal flag. How clever or...is that real?"

Colette nodded. "It is most real."

"How so?"

"The king of Spain is his cousin. He has been appointed the viceroy of New Spain."

"A titled man." Jordan chuckled, watching Donato approach. "I'll be damned, that son of a bitch."

Having heard the excitement, Rayna came up to the main deck and joined the siblings atop the forecastle.

"He made fast time." She looked at Colette. "Hurry, we must be ready to board."

That wasn't Colette's first thought. Instead, she looked at her brothers and felt the pain of her abduction and the lost years of no memory. She now remembered it all, every detail from the attack: Jordan going overboard, and her running down the deck until she had stumbled and broken her leg. There had been a third ship that night, Donato's, and it was his ship she had been pulled aboard.

She thought of her father, his pain over losing his daughter just like she had felt when Enio was taken. Images of Donato's father enjoying his grandson raced through her mind. Her father would never know his grandson. It was too much to accept without serious consideration of her family.

No. Boarding Donato's ship was not an assumed response to his return.

"I will be below." Colette turned and retreated to the bowels of her brother's ship.

"Colette?" Jordan tried for an explanation, but she had none to offer except the truth, and that would hurt him more than she could imagine.

"Take me home, Jordan." Colette took the planked stairs to the captain's cabin and closed the door behind her. She watched from the stern window, having heard Loul calling out to Donato.

"Tell us, Donato, did you leave the *Lady Tempest* on the floor of the ocean?" Loul yelled over the bulwarks.

"In time she will be. I left her badly wounded. You might see a couple polly boats pushing about."

Hearing her husband's voice nearly brought Colette to her knees, relieved he was alive and that he had prevailed. She had told him she'd be able to forgive him for anything, love him for eternity, having never thought for one moment that he was the man who had changed and destroyed her life and that of her family forever.

Rayna was in the chair waiting to be lifted overboard when Donato's tender arrived. He was not in it, having stayed on board.

"Don't forget my trunk." Rayna said as she disappeared over the side.

Next load was her trunk. The tender waited.

"Where is Colette?" Colette heard Donato call over the bulwarks.

There was no answer until a knock on the door. "Colette?"

Jordan opened the door, then hesitated, taking in the items of her personal belongings strewn about the floor. "He waits."

Colette turned away, unable to sort through her feelings. Donato was the man who had made it all happen, taking three years out of her life and her brothers' lives, and indirectly had caused her father's death. It was too soon to forget, to forgive. Unable to free herself from the past, she could not take a step toward their future.

"Take me home, Jordan."

Jordan spun on his heels, and she heard him climb the stairs to the upper deck. "No other passengers."

Soon the air billowed up the canvas and they were moving through the water toward the shores of Louisiana and away from Donato.

Colette curled up in the bed with Enio in her arms. He had fallen asleep, but she was awake, watching the wavering shadows on the ceiling from the moonlit waters of the sea. They'd be in New Orleans in a short time.

The idea of being home finally and forever should have made her feel relieved, maybe even relaxed, but none of those came to her mind or body. Instead, she felt empty, so much so she thought nothing would ever fill the wound that had opened up inside her.

It was close to eleven in the evening when they docked in New Orleans, using the tender to reach dry land. Jordan had a carriage and horses waiting at a nearby stable. Soon loaded, they were on their way back to his house in the Faubourg Sainte Marie.

A warm welcome awaited her with hugs from her

stepmother and Aurélie. Maisie fussed over Enio, which normally made him laugh, but tonight he was a solemn little boy.

Hattie filled glasses with her special rum that made them pucker up with each taste, rambling on about how the sisters from the Ursuline convent had been out to see if Colette had returned and how they'd prayed for her safety.

The hospital was anxious for Colette to return to work as soon as she was able. Many of the soldiers at the hospital missed her caring hands and soft voice. The orphans missed their lessons in reading, writing, and arithmetic. Hattie assured her there was so much for her to do, she'd not think about any of this unpleasantness with her son's father.

Colette wasn't interested in that now. Exhausted, she made a polite good-night and took Enio upstairs to bed, praying the child would not again ask about his father.

She was just about to slip out of her dress when someone knocked on her door. Colette opened it. "Aurélie, I was just going to bed."

"I help you, *oui*?" Colette opened the door farther for Aurélie's entry. "Is the little *bébé* asleep?"

Colette nodded that he was. "He doesn't seem so little anymore. He misses his papa."

"Colette." Aurélie started working on Colette's buttons. "I do not wish to pry."

But knowing Aurélie's psychic mind, Colette suspected Aurélie had some insight.

"What did you read about me, Aurélie?"

"That you are with an unhappy heart. Your heart is sad and lonely and you think only of the man on the island. The man whose life you saved from your brother's saber."

"It is so." Colette found that so easy to say, to admit, but to live it?

"Then why do you come to us and not to him?"

Colette looked away for a moment, unsure of what she should share. How easy it would be to allow her sense of obligation to God and her charities, as her family believed, rob her of the life she craved. That alone would be a falsehood as she stood before God. She had paid for the life of her parents, working endlessly, tirelessly, for others. But if Jordan learned Donato had taken their ship, he'd never forgive him, and it would only serve to further their division. She opted not to share. "He has done some bad things."

"So has your brother. I once told him he was a man of passion, some of it good and some of it not so good. But he is more good than not. Donato is much the same, *non*?"

"My brothers sacrificed so much of their own lives to save me. How can I deny that and return to where they thought to rescue me? *Non. Non.* It is too late. It is better this way. He is hundreds of miles away, back on the island."

"But he will not stay there without his son." Aurélie brushed Colette's hair back and braided it. "I think you wish to understand too much when it comes to matters of the heart and underestimate your brother's compassion."

Colette stepped out of the dress pooled around her feet. She opened her wardrobe and sighed when she noted the boring dresses hanging within. But life wasn't dresses and jewelry alone, it was the underlying beauty of what they expressed, a love for life, a passion she had with Donato. She pulled on a tired old nightgown. "I wish to sleep, Aurélie, but I thank you for your kind thoughts."

Only minutes after Aurélie left, there was another knock

on her door. As Colette suspected she would, Aurélie had reported to Jordan.

"Jordan, what is it? I am tired and as I told Aurélie I was just going to bed." Colette opened her bedroom door to allow her brother entrance.

Jordan stepped inside and took a chair near the window and motioned for her to sit atop her bed. "Jordan, I am tired."

"So am I, Colette. Why didn't you go with him today?"

Her chest swelled with emotion much too dangerous to allow an escape route. "I am tired and have been through a lot—"

"Colette," he interrupted. "I don't want to be rude, but you are not the only one in life who has had bad experiences. It has been nearly four years since the abduction. Do you not think it is time to allow it to go away, find a life?"

"Find a life?" She couldn't stop the tears. "I have a life, with Donato, my son."

"Then why are you here?"

"You ask me that? Why? You sound as if you are disappointed I did not go with him."

"Loul educated me about the two of you. He believes you are in love with each other."

"As much as you hate him, you want me to go with him?"

"It's not about me, it's about you and your son, and God forbid, that Spaniard. I admit he's a little more palatable as royalty."

"But it *is* about you, Jordan." She pushed to her feet. The tears flooded her cheeks. She angrily wiped them away but to no avail, for the dam had been broken by her brother's prying. "I remember that night. I remember everything. There was a third ship, a third ship."

She collapsed on the bed; Jordan rushed to her side. He sat on the bed next to her, wrapping her within his arms. "What do you remember?"

"Everything, from the attack to when I was pulled onto the third ship." The rising memories tore through her muscles with spasms and twists that hurt, yet felt cathartic. The fire-tipped icy blades had returned, and the pain in her leg seared through her skin. Her lungs nearly collapsed; she strained for air. "I thought to have found myself. I have served the Lord and others long enough. I have paid my debt for our parents. I deserve my own life."

"Of course, Colette…but you have one."

Jordan pulled a handkerchief from the pocket of his vest and handed it to her. "Here."

She wiped her nose and dabbed at her eyes. "No, I don't. It is not real."

"Donato did not want you back? Could he not forgive you?"

That question jolted her out of her tears. She stared at her brother. "Oh my Lord, yes, he forgave me for taking his son."

"I speak as a father and husband, what crimes are greater than what you had done, that you can't forgive him?"

Colette pushed off the bed and stared out the window, seeing only darkness and stars in a cloudless night, as if the entire world awaited her answer. "I cannot tell you."

"Why?"

"I cannot tell you because his crimes were against us, our family."

Jordan stood up and came behind her. Taking her arm with his hand, he turned her to face him. "Then I think you better tell me."

Her eyes were so swollen from crying, she could not see her brother clearly. "I don't want you to hate him any more than you already do."

"That's not possible." Jordan chuckled. With his thumb, he wiped her tears from her eyes. "Tell me what he's done that you cannot forgive."

Colette was falling into a dark tunnel where no one could help her, suddenly feeling so alone, so frightened. Donato's Colette bled through to the floor. The fire-tipped icy blades melted to pool around her. No longer was she this woman of strength who had sailed across the ocean for her son, but a terrified woman aboard a ship on fire.

"Colette?" Jordan gave her a gentle shake.

"There was a third ship that night, the most horrific night of my life."

"Wasn't my best night, either." He directed her to sit down on the bed, and he sank down next to her, wrapping her in his arms, keeping her safe, like always. "But we survived to go on living."

She closed her eyes, afraid to say it, to confess. "The third ship…was Donato's."

The relief of saying it nearly melted her body like a candle on a hot day.

"There," she whispered. Though her vision was impaired with eyes swollen from tears, she could see enough to realize he didn't look shocked. She managed to stifle her gasps. "You are not surprised, shocked?"

"I already knew that. So does Loul. Rayna confirmed it. I might not know all the reasons why he'd partner with those skunks, but from the ashes, the phoenix rises. I have

Aurélie, children, a safe home. None of that would have happened had it not been for that chain of events that threw us together. I would not give up what I have now to change the past. You wouldn't have Enio, or this man you love. I'm flattered you think so highly of me, Colette, but I lived as a pirate for three years. I fought a war. I'm not proud of everything I've done. I'd like to be judged on who I am now, not the past. Did he make a mistake, yes, but no one knows it more than he. But I have to admire a man who sails five thousand miles to save his son."

"On a clipper," she clarified, to ensure he really appreciated what Donato had done.

"On a clipper," Jordan conceded. "And don't worry about me. I still have my revenge. He married into a French family. His son is half French."

Her eyes filled with tears, for she loved her brothers so much. "But Jordan…you mean the world to me."

He put his hands on each of her shoulders. "So can I forgive him? Is that the question that is tearing you apart?"

"If you can't—"

"I don't have to. Your choice is not between him or me. I love you, and that will never change. You will never lose me, Colette. I am your brother."

"But what am I to do?"

"About?"

"Donato, I love him, his son loves his father, we have a life—"

"*Hmmm…*" Jordan pushed off the bed, then leaned down and gently kissed her forehead. "I think you just answered your own question. You must live your own life, as I do mine, but I will always be here for you, whatever you decide. Good night, sweet sister."

. . .

The darkness of the night lifted slightly in the wee early hours. The moon still hovered over the gulf and cast a sparkling glow over the rolling waves. Water smoke had churned up from the sea and hovered around the top of the main mast. Soft sprays of droplets sprinkled the deck as the flying jib dived into the sends. The sails were unfurled to their fullest. The square riggings to the top of the main and fore mast were billowed, stretched by the wind.

Donato stepped onto the helm, allowing the misty night to keep him awake and wash the worries off his face. He had left the island, where Rayna was most likely asleep by now in one of the guest rooms he had prepared for her. She seemed to like the hacienda, not that it mattered; that wasn't her final destination, though she didn't know it yet. There would be plenty of time for surprises. As soon as he had settled Rayna and provisioned the ship, he was back on board and headed for Louisiana.

The men asked no questions, and there were no grumblings about leaving port again. They knew where they were going and why.

He had promised Colette his son would always be with him, and that was a promise he would keep, but that wasn't what drove him tonight and kept his heart pumping with a rhythmic cadence of a ceremonial dance.

He was going to get his son and…his wife.

He could think of nothing else through his battle with the *Lady Tempest*.

Soon he'd reach the soil of the United States. Being the newly appointed viceroy of New Spain, the officials of America would not touch him for fear of offending Spain. He sailed under the royal flag. His ship would not be seized, and his men would not be thrown into the Calaboose.

But if none of that were true, he'd still be in New Orleans tonight. If there were a price on his head and an order to shoot on sight, he'd be in New Orleans tonight. Nothing would keep him away from Colette.

As it was the last time he sailed into New Orleans, in the early-morning hours, the streets were relatively quiet. The only activity was near the Hôtel de la Marine off Rue de la Levée.

His men had been instructed to stay with the ship and to allow no one to board. Ramón rowed the tender ashore and would wait for Donato's return.

Donato threw the rope over the pier as they slid into the post. He hopped off and tied the tender. "I don't know how long this will take."

"You should not go alone, Your Excellency. Her brother is home."

"No." He motioned for Ramón to wait on the dock. "Return to the ship and wait until you see me before returning. I don't know how long I'll be."

Ramón nodded that he understood and settled back into the tender to wait.

Donato made his way down the levee and crossed the canal to the American side. The only sounds in this part of the city were those calling out the hour. It was now three in the morning. The water smoke that filtered through the sails of the tall ship had worked onto shore and hovered over the city streets in a shroud of salty mist. Vision was good for only a few feet, and everything felt wet.

He licked the salt off his lips, feeling more drenched here than on the ship. The street lamps fluttered in the fog and created large glowing balls of movement and shadows. The heels of his boots struck the stone walk with purpose.

Nothing would stop him tonight.

He hoped Jordan didn't get in his way. It would only end badly for one of them. Preferably Jordan. But either would only further divide Colette's sense of loyalty.

Nearing the corner where Jordan's house stood, Donato pulled out his flintlock and approached the house. It was a large, imposing house with white and green shutters. It had seven massive plastered brick columns holding up the front gallery and three doors on the first and second floor, interwoven with windows. The ground level was covered with louvers. The upper doors were open to the early fall night air. The yard was neatly manicured with beds of flowering plants, giving him a sense of where he was in the dark.

He stepped off the paved path to walk on the ground. Being near the river, he knew the soil would be wet and quiet. He remembered the layout of the house from the first time he'd been here.

The large brick columns easily bore his weight as he climbed to the upper gallery. Enio's room was just off the sleeping porch, and if he remembered correctly, Colette's to the right of that. He slipped over the balustrade and landed sure-footed on the veranda without making a sound. In the corner of the room, there was a loggia that allowed for a quiet place to sneak in.

His plan was simple. Wake Colette...well, he'd start

there, but this was the only way to see her and speak to her without the armor of her brothers.

As quiet as the air around him, he slipped in through the open window. But that easy open window made him suspicious. He wasn't alone. To his surprise a dip match was struck. A woman's hand lit the lamp and turned up the gas, illuminating the room.

Having landed on bent knees, he straightened and faced Colette.

The light fluttered over her face, allowing a brief look at her expression, hard and lean. She had a pistol in her hand.

"Like a thief in the night," she whispered. "Viceroy or not, some things never change."

"A talent, senora. Ah, this pistol, did I never take that away?" he returned in the same low whisper.

"Apparently you aren't so clever, for you did not. Now you must disarm yourself." She motioned with a wave of her hand. Beneath the large hooded robe she wore, he caught sight of the earrings he had given her in Spain.

"I am at your mercy, *cariño*." He pulled his pistol and dirk from his belt and placed them on the floor, trying not to wake her sleeping brother. He raised his hands in surrender. "Be gentle, I bruise easily."

She said nothing, but started to circle around him, one step at a time. Over her body, she wore a long robe that had a large hood draped over her head and shoulders. A heavy robe meant for…travel? A dainty yellow satin slipper appeared then disappeared under the flowing hem of the robe, only to reappear with another slow, steady step. The hood covered her hair, but wavy tendrils hung down across her shoulders to curl around her breasts, and when she peeked up at him, only a shadow of her face would show. He caught sight of her smooth, silky skin; those lips that formed a perfect square were slightly pursed, and though he could not see her eyes, a speck of light reflected from each beneath the hood.

Friend or foe, he had yet to know. But if she didn't speak soon, he'd take that damned little pistol out of her hand and have his way with her, regardless of dear Jordan down the hall.

Suddenly she stopped circling and faced him. Pistol still in her hand, but he noted the relaxed position of her trigger finger. "So…Donato de la Roche y Borbón, Marquis de Andalusia, Virrey de Nueva España…what in the hell took you so long?"

His lips turned up slightly in the corners as he fought a smile, not wanting to assume too much, too quickly, but he heard a hint of his Colette in her voice.

"Am I late, senora?"

Suddenly, she closed the distance between them and grabbed the lapel of his overcoat. He noticed she no longer limped, her steps smooth and even.

"Damn right you are," she whispered a moment before she raised on tiptoe and closed her lips over his.

Donato wrapped his arms around her and fell into the kiss with passion that only she could give him. Her body folded into his with a heated sweep of familiarity. His hand roamed over her delicate terrain knowing each curve and dip of her small frame by memory. The soft curve of her breasts, the narrow turn of her waist, the small pulsating point of heat at the base of her throat. He had been there before, and never again would he risk letting go.

"*Mi vida*," he whispered. "Do I have my Colette back?"

She pulled away from him and looked up with her beautiful green eyes, shadowed by the long lashes that surrounded them. Her lips moved into a smile as she pushed the cape from her shoulders, letting it drop about her feet, exposing her body to him. Underneath, she wore the sparkling yellow dress that curved low over her bosom, and the Tourmaline necklace she had worn in Spain. Her long honey-colored hair draped over her shoulders, wild with curl. "I think to enjoy being the wife of…the most infamous pirate of the gulf."

"*Mi vida*, my life." He pulled her into his hungry arms. "I beg you, my dearest Colette, might I tell Jordan?"

Epilogue

The night had cooled with the falling sunlight. Rayna walked into the inner patio of the hacienda, pulling a wrap around her shoulders to ward off a slight chill. With Colette back on the island, her brother's disposition had greatly improved, but she waited night after night for his retaliation, for she was sure he had a plan. Tonight, he had summoned her to his office.

She returned from the patio and walked through the *sala de recepcion*, a beautiful sitting room, through the *salon de baile,* an exquisite ballroom, until reaching the *despacho del gobernador* where a small light flickered.

Donato was there, seated at his mahogany desk, surrounded by leather-bound books and mahogany shelving. There was a fireplace to the back of the room, a few logs ablaze, and over the mantel hung a small replica of the family arms that had been engraved in stone over the hearth at home, in Spain.

He looked up when she walked into the room. "I hope I

have not kept you up too late."

"You do not, nor have you, but I wish to end the suspense."

"So you have grown tired of my company." He leaned back and smiled, running his fingers over a glass of whiskey next to him on the desk.

"Perhaps." She shrugged with disinterest, running a finger over the leather books, noting their pristine condition. Typical of Donato, he spared no expense, and she sometimes envied the lavish attention he poured on his wife and son. Could there be a man like that for her? Not so. There wasn't a man alive who would satisfy whatever burned deep inside her.

She had had her share of lovers and found life easier to dismiss them once she'd grown bored. Because whether Donato knew it or not, to be in love made him vulnerable. Colette had far more power over him than even he'd admit. A risk Rayna swore she'd never take. Having seen her mother's descent into a death spiral of heartache, she'd never surrender her personal power to any man.

"Am I to tour the new colonies with you? Is that your revenge? Or will you keep me locked up on this island until I am old and gray?"

He stretched out the length of his legs under the desk and slouched against the chair. "You have misjudged me, sister. I am no longer a man of vengeance."

"You are talking to me, Donato."

He ignored her comment, or at least the underlying meaning. "Tell me, Rayna, what is it you would like, more than anything?"

"You test me, brother. I tell you and you take it away. Is that the revenge?"

He chuckled and stood up. "Have a drink with me."

She sat down opposite his desk and waited as he poured her a glass of wine from the wine table. He had his back to her, and she had to admit, she was proud of him. Whether he cherished his new position or not, she was proud of him. She admired him taking a stand for principle, and surprisingly, she believed his commitment to his beliefs had won their father over the moment Donato returned home. Not that she'd ever tell him that. She was a woman of iron, prided herself on her strength, her ability to move about in a man's world. She was always in charge of herself and her surroundings. She glanced out the window of the office, seeing a skyline of mountains, and suddenly found herself very homesick and missing her father.

Donato placed the drink on the desk for her. She picked it up and took a sip. The wine was sweet, redolent, and scented her nose with each sip. "I want to go back to Spain."

"I will arrange a polly boat for you to paddle."

"Unkind. When I return, it will be with style."

"You challenged me, Rayna. You declared your cleverness as superior to mine."

"I did, for I am."

"Finish your wine, sister, then I reveal my plan."

She could drink like a man. Swallowing the last of the wine, she placed the glass on his desk. "I await your wisdom."

"Then this is the challenge you've waited to hear." He stood and leaned against the desk, looking down at her. "Listen very carefully, Rayna, for this is your only chance to hear it. That drink will have you sound asleep in a few minutes."

Rayna glanced down at the empty glass, now tasting the bitterness of tincture on her lips, knowing he had drugged her.

"You wish to go back to Spain. You will need money to do that." He handed her a leather-bound packet. "Inside that pouch you will find a treasure map. Find the treasure and you are a wealthy woman. If you do not, I will enjoy your return to my lovely island."

Rayna fought a smile. She loved her brother, and this was why. He shared her sense of adventure, both having spent their lives fighting the constraints of their noble upbringing. She unlashed the leather case and pulled out a small diagram that looked like a coat of arms or something similar. "What is this?"

Donato took the paper and held it up to the light. "Each side has a drawing. When viewed together they form a map; when apart, meaningless."

Knowing she was short on time to ask him questions, she dug out the rest. It was a large drawing of the two smaller maps with notations made all around. "And this?"

"A larger picture, but with thoughts, speculations noted."

"Is this real?"

"I believe it is."

"You're handing me a treasure map?"

Donato smiled. "You fancy yourself a clever woman. Find that treasure and you'll never again be subject to me or father for your livelihood. You'll be a free, wealthy woman."

She could already imagine how much fanfare her return to Spain would rouse if she was wealthy enough to hire the ship she wanted. Her lids started to feel heavy but she wanted more, her appetite for adventure stirred. "What is in this for you? If these are real?"

"They are real. They belong to Colette's brother, Jordan. He'd like to find his treasure, and I'd like him not to. He's the one who made the notations in French, but he made a mistake in his calculations. I will not tell you what it is, but I am confident you will figure it out."

"If I refuse to do this?"

"No harm done. You wake up tomorrow morning on this island...day after day...until I decide to take you back to Spain. Do you refuse?"

"Jordan's calculations are wrong?"

Donato nodded, seemingly pleased she was following him. "Correct, senorita."

"Then where is this treasure?"

"Study my notations, written in Spanish, and you will figure it out. You will have to find this on your own. I cannot be involved."

"You are wicked, dear brother, so wicked."

He smiled, pleased with his offer. "As are you. It must be in our blood. I give you ninety days to find the treasure. If you do not, you will have lost your way back to Spain."

"Why ninety days?"

"Because in about ninety days, Jordan will realize that all maps and references to his medallions have been taken."

"You know where this treasure is?"

"I have a valid idea."

"Does Jordan?"

"No, not yet."

She knew she could not fight the drug much longer. Refusing the challenge was not an option, because he wanted her to take this mission. A refusal would disappoint him, but she knew she'd wake up somewhere else tomorrow. The drug had wormed through her body, and she could barely keep her head from dropping to the desk. "You will send this with me?"

"*Si.*"

"And Nadia, she will come, too. I must have a personal maid."

"I'd have it no other way." Her brother leaned down close to her ear and whispered, "Say the word *mesteños*. Say it."

Her eyes fluttered shut; she was barely able to move her lips. "*Mesteños.* What does it mean?"

"It means mustang, the wild horse of Mexico, untamed, free spirit. Like you, Rayna, wild and beautiful."

"I learn this why?"

"It is your secret word if you are in need of me. Spend it wisely, for I come only once and the mission is over."

"*Mesteños.*" Rayna closed her eyes, unable to stop the inevitable.

Before she spilled out of the chair, Donato pulled her into his arms and set her upon a settee.

"Ramón! She is ready to board. Bring Nadia."

The men worked in silence, carrying Donato's discreet package from the house, down the walk, and to the ship without waking a soul at the hacienda. The sails were cracked and anchor rolled in. The package was placed in the captain's bedchamber, which would remain a private room.

Donato unwrapped the package and put his sleeping sister atop the bed. Her trunk was brought on board and personal items laid out. After Nadia changed Rayna into a disguise, the maid was removed from the ship.

Only his most trusted men would he send on the journey with Rayna. Ramón, not approving of the mission, had planned to stay awake all night and guard her room.

"Isn't Nadia coming with her? She has no maid?" he asked.

Patting Ramón on the back, Donato grinned, already enjoying Rayna's surprise. "Allow me some revenge, *por favor*."

Donato climbed back to the main deck and glanced around in the chilling darkness. "Where are you?"

The American stepped from the shadows. "I am here, Your Excellency."

"Did you stay well hidden on our journey? Did my sister see you?"

"I remained out of sight, as you ordered. She did not."

Donato placed a bag of gold in his hand. "Take good care of her, keep her out of trouble, and keep me informed of her activities. You must keep her safe, and that will be a challenge, for she is headstrong and clever. Her code word for me is *mesteños*. You are to notify me immediately. Understand?"

The man took the gold and bowed. "Yes, Your Excellency."

Donato stepped ashore and watched as his ship carrying his sister silently stretched away from shore. Yes, he was no longer a man of vengeance, and proud of that, but that didn't hinder his anticipation of snatching that treasure right out from under Jordan's nose. He had faith in Rayna that she'd do it. The lights of his sister's ship faded into the dark sky. But he almost pitied America, for they had no idea the storm that was about to come ashore in the form of…

Rayna de la Roche.

About the Author

Award-winning author Meg Hennessy lives with her husband amid rolling hills of Hartford, Wisconsin. Besides writing, spoiling her first grandson, and pampering her much-loved horse, she enjoys backyard birding and admits to being a gardening addict. As a history lover, Meg likes to create high-energy characters against historically rich backdrops, offering her readers a vivid peek into the lives and loves of yesteryear.